I0666062

Madness and Wonder

Book one of the Wonder series

R. R. Surbier

Copyright©2015 by R.R. Surbier

All rights reserved. No part of this book may be
reproduced or transmitted in any form or by any means,
electronic or mechanical, including photocopying,
recording, or by any information storage and retrieval
system, without the written permission of the author,
except where permitted by law.

www.facetsofwonder.com

ISBN:

978-0-9964643-0-7

For Kyber Bree Keefe

To my best friend: When we are old and misbehaving in a retirement home, I know you will still be encouraging me to follow my dreams, get out of my comfort zone, and enjoy life. Plus, you told me that you expected a dedication for Madness and Wonder... how could I disappoint a force of nature like Kyber?

ଔ

The clock struck 13, and the velvety night breeze blew through the mad tea party, subtly changing each thing it touched. Over was the time of children's teatimes, the night was a time for more grown up endeavors. The large table set itself for the night's revelries, clearing the spilt cups of tea and plates with biscuit crumbs. In their places sat a new teapot drifting an intoxicating steam into the air and small bowls filled with rich creamy delights.

The March Hare woke to the scent of roses and climbed out from under the garden hedge. She languidly stretched and with a ripple in reality she stepped from a fluffy auburn rabbit into a different kind of bunny with bare skin and feminine curves. She shook out her long straight red hair, and it tickled her long silky ears and the bare skin of her back and hips deliciously, making her fluffy little tail twitch as it faded into her skin taking the form of a heavily lined tribal tattoo. The moonlight highlighted her erect nipples perched atop firm breasts. The soft light accentuated her curves in a way that naturally lead the eye to travel down her body, giving shadowy glimpses of creamy bare skin.

She spied her Hatter sleeping in his red, wing backed chair, and was filled with a hunger not for food. His exaggerated brown leather hat tipped down, casting shadows over his face. She examined what she could see of her Hatter and he too had been changed by the night breeze. The moonlight shone on him and his clothing fit a bit tighter over a more muscular and lean frame. His paisley tie, so loose it was almost undone like half the buttons of his shirt, exposing a smooth and muscular chest. His brown pinstriped pants were snug, and from the look of his lap he was likely having dreams of the night tea as it might soon proceed. His lips were full and flushed, looking soft and kissable. Tousled bits of dark brown hair curled from under the brim of his hat, and she just knew that the long fringe of dark lashes on his closed lids hid deep and penetrating eyes. The moonlight also highlighted a faint but rugged scar on his left cheek that tugged at some long forgotten memory.

The March Hare inhaled the heady steam coming from the tea pot, enjoying its intoxicating buzz and felt herself moisten with anticipation. She approached Hatter, crawling under the table she noticed the scent of roses mixing with his skin's warm enticing musk. With much stealth, she undid his pants and began to pleasure him.

His soft full lips parted to release a moan as his dreams took on a more tactile nature. The Hatter woke slowly, back arching and face tilting to catch the moonlight. He opened his eyes and almost came at the sight before him, but gained control to not waste this encounter he had so longed for. The March Hare enjoyed the Hatter's reaction to her oral play almost as much as he enjoyed her talent's. He filled with the need to feel her flesh beneath his hands again, but was frustrated that the table blocked all but her head.

In a swift motion, the Hatter pushed his chair back from the table and pulled the March Hare up between his legs. Easily lifting her onto his lap, and swinging her across his body to cradle her in his arms. Hatter inhaled deeply, drinking in the smell of his March Hare. He memorized every enticing curve until his deep brown eyes settled, looking into her warm green eyes filled with passion and desire. He could feel need rolling off of her like heat waves shimmering between their bodies. Happily giving in to her want, Hatter kissed his March hare deeply and let his hands explore the curves of her bare skin.

As they kissed, his fingertips traced over the spiky little tail tattoo at the small of her back. His hand traced along her spine to grasp the back of her neck, fingers tangling slightly in her hair as their lips tasted and explored. He pulled her into a tight embrace for a long deep kiss that quickened their pulses and deepen their lust. They paused, gasping, but not for lack of oxygen as much as for the overwhelming electricity between them. Hatter guided his hand from her neck, down her back, and then curved around her bottom to pull her tight against him. She leaned in for more kisses, making quiet eager noises and rubbing her body against him in response to his equally eager hands.

His hand slid between her legs, making her gasp into their kisses with the edge of an eager whimper. His fingers quickly found her most sensitive spot and she cried out arching her back as he wiggled his finger. She threw her head back with a moan, letting his other arm fully support her, as she gripped his muscular shoulders. Her breasts heaved with panting breaths, feeling building warmth between her thighs. His mouth watered with her ample bosom so close to his face. He exuberantly buried his face in her soft flesh, covering her with kisses and nibbles.

The Hare grabbed the Hatter with great shudders of pleasure, rubbing herself against his body so she could feel every inch of taut muscle that pressed urgently against her. She steadied herself, gripping his strong shoulder with one hand as she grabbed his leg with the other. She stroked her hand up to his thigh, nails scraping into the fabric just enough to send a thrill up his spine.

His mouth explored both breasts, kissing and licking in rhythm to her rocking hips. The Hare let out a cry of ecstasy. He felt her body tighten with the beginnings of orgasm, and as she screamed with pleasure and near release, he disengaged. With fluid movements the Hatter stood and placed her on an open expanse of table. He hungrily stalked her with his eyes as he planned to pounce like a wild animal and ravish her.

The Hare felt his intent, licking her lips as she too surveyed her lover. His clothes were rumpled in a sexy disheveled way, and his pants still enticingly open from their groping play. She quickly sat up, pulling the Hatter to her as she wrapped her legs around his waist. They embraced in another series of long passionate kisses, bodies pressed tightly and needfully against each other.

The Hatter continued to explore the bare skin of the March Hare with lips and hands, thinking of how he had waited so long, wanting so badly to be with this intoxicating woman. Hoping, now that she'd found him, to have limitless time to know her again and again.

The Hare had had enough of the Hatter's skin being denied to her, and pulled at his jacket while untucking his shirt. But, as is the way with Wonderland, the desire need only be expressed and the want was met with the Hatter's clothes ceasing to exist. The Hare filled with glee, feeling his taut skin against hers. She rubbed her cheek along his smooth bare shoulder and licked his salty neck before lightly nipping at his earlobe in her excitement. She could feel his pulse pounding against her lips as she kissed her way down his neck. He moaned softly as she ran a trail of kisses down his muscular chest. But before she could move to kiss lower, the Hatter grabbed her and pushed her back against the table.

With a mischievous grin, the Hatter leaned over her and kissed her hard before stepping back to pull his chair up to the table. Sitting between her legs, the Hatter looked hungrily at the woman laying before him. He reached under her bottom, grabbing her and pulling her to the edge of the table. He pressed a hand against her soft belly to cue her to be still, and the Hare relaxed with anticipation.

With a lick of his lips the Hatter reached for one of the bowls to their side. He dipped a finger into a warm brandy custard and licked it. The Hare caught the Hatter's hand, and took the sweet finger into her mouth with a dexterous tongue. She removed the traces of custard with one long sensual suck to the tip, eliciting a low rumble of pleasure. She began to sit, but before she could move he withdrew his hand and shook his head playfully waggling his finger in mock reproach. He dipped his finger back into the bowl of warm custard and offered the reclining Hare her own taste. Just as she took his finger into her mouth and began to suck off the sweet warm sauce, she felt the Hatter dribble a bit of the custard onto one of her inner thighs. A moan escaped her lips as he licked the warm creamy custard off her tender skin.

The Hare lay back on the table forgetting everything else but this electrifying sensation. The Hatter dribbled more custard across from one inner thigh to the other. The warm creamy liquid dripped slightly down her skin before the Hatter caught each drop expertly with his tongue, licking the custard away and getting tantalizingly close to what lay between her thighs. He licked clean both inner thighs, getting closer still, but not quite touching the place she so wanted him to lick.

The Hare shuttered with anticipation, starting to sit up and reach for him. But he was quicker than her and was in a moment above her, pressing her to the table with another passionate kiss; skin on skin the length of their writhing and mutually longing torsos. With a twinkle in his velvety brown eyes, he reached past her and grabbed a red silk scarf seemingly from nowhere.

The Hare smiled, she liked where this was going and it shone in her eyes. The Hatter grabbed the Hare's wrists and tied them together with the soft scarf. Then, taking the end of the scarf, tied it securely to a ring appearing anchored to the table a little above her head. The Hare knew that this turned her on partly because letting her lover tie her up like this was an expression of submission and trust. She knew this man deep down and trusted him completely; she felt something so much more than just the carnal for him, a bonding of their souls that made their lust richer and more decadent. It also offered her a total abandon, letting her lover pleasure her while she lay back and enjoyed. She trusted that he knew every way she would want to be pleasured, and that it was his only goal. It heightened her fervor and lust with each touch.

He kissed her tenderly on his way back down her body, leaving an electrifying trail of kisses and deliciously teasing licks. He traveled down the curve of her neck, tracing her collar bone, and followed the path between her breasts, lingering with full attention to her ample bosom. She lay back and fully enjoyed the feeling of his hands stroking her body and his lips tasting her skin.

The Hatter took another bowl with a dark chocolate sauce, and used it as sensual finger paint across her breasts. He offered her his chocolate coated fingers, and she happily sucked them clean as he removed his painting with a skilled tongue. By the time he was done licking the chocolate clean, the Hare was writhing against him. Soon he was again kissing down her body, spreading her legs with strong hands to untangle himself and pin her hips down as he selected another bowl. He dripped sweet creamy sauces on her skin to lick away as he journeyed. Again he teased her, kissing her hips and thighs while squeezing and caressing her ass. The Hare moaned with anticipation, wanting him to lick her in that most private of places more than anything. And then he did exactly what she longed for him to do. The Hare screamed out in ecstasy, almost coming with the first forceful wet glide. But it only got better from there. The Hatter settled comfortably into his chair, and took a lick of a mint sauce. He blew cool minty breath against her skin, then grabbing her by the hips, buried his face between her legs.

Passionately he used his tongue, the cooling mint intensifying every touch. The Hare screamed in rapture as she came hard and long. Every nerve screamed with joy as the Hare was engulfed in an orgasmic Aurora Borealis of colors and shapes.

The Hare had climaxed, but the Hatter was long from done himself. He stroked his organ as he watched her naked form shutter and tremble with the aftermath of orgasm. The Hare's body calmed and her breathing slowed as the orgasmic glow ebbed, but with endorphins still coursing through her the Hare was already heating up again watching the Hatter prime himself.

Her mouth watered looking at him and she licked her lips with anticipation. Hatter could sense her hunger and was eager to feel the return of her soft lips and curious tongue. He went around the table and untied the scarf from the loop that held her down, freeing her to take what she craved.
She rolled over prone and reached out to pull the Hatter closer. She playfully licked and explored him with bound hands. Hatter's breath quickened, and a deep moaning growl escaped his lips with the intensity of the sensation. He grabbed the edge of the table to steady himself as she pleasured him until he was again close to coming.

Pulling away from the Hare's expert mouth to keep from exploding, the Hatter grabbed the scarf and tied it down again. The March Hare bit her lip seductively looking at the Hatter with sparkling mischief in her gaze; she liked this game. Hatter's intensely hungry eyes and playful half-grin confirmed how much he was enjoying himself too. The Hare shivered with anticipation as he bent to kiss her deeply before maneuvering around the table and grabbing her by the hips to pull her towards him. The Hatter couldn't help but take a step back to enjoy the view. She lay across the table now with her rear at the edge. Her legs hanging down so that she could grab the thick green grass with her toes, giving her the leverage to slightly lift her supple bottom invitingly. She wiggled her tail tattoo, but it was her hips and the curve of her ass that made him grunt with appreciation and grab her with a fierce strength.

With a firm grip still on her hips, he playfully kissed her lower back, tickling her with his quick tongue, as he kissed a trail over her glutes to the backs of her thighs. The Hare gasped with pleasure when his tongue flicked lightly over more sensitive areas in his lips exploration. He used both hands to grab her tender inner thighs and spread her legs. He crouched down to pleasure her more with his tongue. The Hare vocalized and undulated in a rapturous joy ready to cum again, but just as she was about to climax he stopped.

He thrust his cock inside her and fucked her hard grabbing her hips for leverage to penetrate deep. They both screamed in primal gratification crashing into each other in faster and faster rhythm. And then when they were both just about to cum he pulled out and dropped down to lick her again, fast & hard until she was crying out to primal gods in worship of the maddeningly intense pleasure. When she started to cum again he sprang up and penetrated her, fucking her hard as they both writhed in perfect sync so he could feel her climax in a wet gush. He was on the edge of joining her in glorious orgasm, but stopped just short lunging inside her and stopping; stilling his body through a feat of will.

The Hatter was not done yet, he wanted this to last as long as possible and the Hare could feel his every intent like he was a piece of her. He reached over her and untied the silk from the ring, grabbing the scarf binding her while he thrust deep inside her a few more strokes, then released her from the soft bindings as he pulled out to switch position. The Hare happily rolled over, face to face, but just as the Hatter was about to reach a point of no return the Hare pushed the Hatter back and sprang from the table, grabbing him and pulling him down into the soft grass so that she could straddle and ride him. The Hatter looked surprised at first but was soon groping her breasts and grabbing her hips as she rode him and he thrust deeply up into her.

They made love at a fevered pitch in the soft thick grass. The March Hare hit her third orgasm, and with each one more intense than the last as she came, their climaxes were like simultaneous explosions.

They were both spent to exhaustion, neither able or willing to move. They lay in the grass in a loose boneless embrace, with a soft warm breeze cooling their sweat covered naked bodies and the moonlight highlighting all the right curves.

03

Rosie Cotton woke feeling more content and satisfied than she could ever remember. Her body still tingled with afterglow, and she snuggled deeper into her pillows before she realized that she was alone. As she let go of the pillow, that seemed to be her lover's broad chest only moments before, she felt sad that it was only just a dream. It had been years since she had a dream so vivid, and with such total recall. Rosie played the part of the March Hare, but not like the March Hare in the childhood story of Alice or the Disney cartoon. Her hair was more like a bunny from a gentleman's club than a furry forest creature. She couldn't stop thinking about the gorgeous hunk of man, she somehow knew so intimately, playing the Mad Hatter. She smiled and thought to herself that he was really much more lusty than mad.

Rosie kept feeling like this Hatter was someone she should know, he was so familiar. She wondered if maybe he was an actor from a movie or TV that she couldn't quite remember. Her real life was so tame that she was sure that she'd remember meeting a guy like the Hatter in her waking world... well mostly sure. He just seemed so real, and so vivid that she felt like there was something else she should be remembering.

Rosie realized that the last time she had a dream so vivid was when she was a teenager. Those impossible dreams were long forgotten, all she remembered now was they felt so real and that she didn't want to remember. All that drama, brushing with insanity that came with mental abuse and a manipulative boyfriend. The crazy things he made her want to believe we're all just a way to control her and push her into madness. She was so afraid of being seen as insane, she shoved her strange little bits of memory to a deep private place. It had taken a long time to recover from that relationship, and it struck Rosie as odd that the mysterious and tasty Hatter from her dream seemed somehow linked to that hazy youth and her brush with insanity.

That craziness was years ago, and she grew up. Now she was a quiet librarian at a small branch of the Chicago public library, and avoided manipulative bad boys. Part of her longed for something magical, but she knew life wasn't really like that. She both wanted and feared a more interesting life, with a little adventure and romance. She'd convinced herself long ago that those things were not for her, a librarian in her late twenties going on what felt like sixty. Books, books were nice safe outlets for her desires; Rosie read lots of books.

She worried that maybe she was once mad for believing impossible things. She tried to explain the memories away as an over-active imagination or events spurred on by an abusive and manipulative relationship that had twisted her reality. But there were good bits, bits that didn't jive with the abuse from her teen years, or bits that were from when she was so little the world was still full of possibility. But those early memories really could have been dreams like her parents believed. She just went over her imaginings so much back then that she must have embellished the memories into more. She tried not to think of those memories, tried to live in the reality the rest of the world occupied. But why was she thinking about them now?

Her intense dream the night before somehow had the feel of her younger memories. A dream that was so adult, why did it remind her of those childhood dreams too? 'Kinda creepy'.

Her childhood dreams were so innocent, with their village filled with all manner of Fey creatures so happy to see her. But mostly she remembered the indescribable woman she knew as her protector. An ageless pure woman of infinite power who watched over Rosie in her dreams, until she lost her innocence. Once her innocence was gone so too was Rosie's protector, maybe that was why her really not-so-innocent dream brought back memories of her childhood protector. Strange. But now that her memory started to linger on that dream again... She blushed just thinking about it.

She felt a bit ashamed that her subconscious turned a childhood story into something that would make good porn. So, she had been the March Hare. Rosie wasn't really surprised that her subconscious mind took her there. With a last name like Cotton, the cotton tail jokes were inevitable, and only a short trip from there to the playboy bunny jokes.

The tea party had not been about un-birthdays or changing places... unless she thought of sexual positions as places. Her mental image of the Hatter was making her really hot under the collar, such a lean and well muscled hunk of smooth skinned yum. She knew she'd seen him before, but she just couldn't place him. Her mind went to the dream again, trying to recall all the dirty details that kept her blushing so brightly. Moments of pure animal magnetism, mixed with screaming pleasures. It was vivid in her mind now, and a dream she really didn't want to forget. She decided to write it all down before she forgot it, so she would have it... for future perusing.

As she began to write, each detailed image and sensation came into crystal clear focus. She thought it strange, usually as she tried to remember a dream it slipped further away. Not since she was a teenager was she able to so fully recall, not since those weird dreams she had seemed to share with her friends. She knew it was madness now, but it all seemed so real at the time.

This dream wasn't part of a manipulation, no chance of it making her question her mind, she knew it was just a dream. A dream she was ready to immerse herself back into as she remembered rich details. She smiled to herself as she wrote and thought that sometimes writing can be a lot of fun.

When she was done Rosie read over the bit of literary porn she had just written, and though she was wide awake she could swear that, as she read, she felt brushing ghost touches. She physically felt the echo of her dream lover's hands on her flesh, replaying sensations as she read them, though she was lying in bed fully clothed. It was a sensation not wholly unfamiliar. When she was a teenager in that bad relationship she had fantasized about a truer lover; the memory was fuzzy but she remembered those fantasies seemed to take on this tactile nature too. She had long since dismissed those times as imagination embellished memory. But now, in the moment, again feeling the soft caresses like a breeze just brushing against the tiny hairs on her skin, she dared to long for it to be real.

Putting aside her notebook, she lay back and opened her senses to the ghostly touches that made her quiver. She knew that she was alone, but she felt a lover touching her in ways that filled her with desire. She didn't touch herself, but soon was building to an orgasm as intense as one from the dream. She reached to feel where the Hatter should be, but found only empty air in a moment of odd déjà vu. Her rational mind struggled to make sense of it all, but was soon overpowered by sheer sensation.

If she had slipped into madness, she thought to herself, madness was not so bad. With the release of her worry she reached climax without a single physical hand being laid on her. In the afterglow, she felt a soft kiss on her lips and drifted into a light sleep, where she found herself lying in the moonlight-saturated thick green grass of the tea party. She was again resting in the Hatter's strong arms. His hand lazily stroking her arm as she lay across his well-defined chest listening to his heart pounding. She smelled warm musk and roses, it was oddly familiar but she just couldn't place it. She looked up into his deep brown eyes, eyes full of hope, and she knew him in a way beyond dreams. There was something safe and comforting about him, like he was a part of her. 'Well, of course he is', she thought to herself 'he's my dream' and with that she drifted off in her dream lover's arms.

○੪

Hatter so enjoyed the feel of his March Hare. She had been so present, so playful, and so frisky when she came to him after so long a departure. He thought that he had lost her forever when she didn't come back to him after so many years. He loved that she came to him in his favorite world, and took a role so intoxicating.

When he woke to find her gone he felt that same keening loss he had felt when she had gone away twelve years ago. He made sure not to speak, remembering how that had jarred her away from him when they had first met. He couldn't understand what he had done wrong, after being separated so long why hadn't she stayed? He wondered if she didn't want him to make love to her? Was it too soon after so long apart? But she had been the one to return to him and had begun their wonderful play.

Closing his eyes he reached for her, but she was gone, no trail to follow. He feared that their encounter was a fluke, and that he had gotten to be with his Rose one last time and now would never again see her sweet face. Desperately, Hatter thought that perhaps he could entice her back by making things at the tea party as they were when she woke him with such pleasures; she had set them such a wonderful scene. With a minor exertion of force the table reset itself, the bowls refilled with creamy treats ready for finger painting. He hopefully waited, feeling for a glimmer of her; but the edibles didn't bring her back to him. Feeling more lonely than he had since he lost Rosie the last time, he sat in his wing backed chair and had a cup of tea trying to think of a way to find her again.

After some time and on his second cup of tea he felt the tiniest breath of his Hare's presence. He stood to look for her, hope leaping in his heart, but he could not see her. He went over to the thick green grass where they last touched and he found a trembling connection that became a little more tangible every moment. With a half smile, he lay in the grass tipped his hat over his eyes and closed them to better focus his will. He reached for her, and could feel her mind. She was with him, remembering their play. He reached out an astral hand to touch her and felt her body quicken. She was recounting their encounter for him, so Hatter reenacted it as best he could. He traveled to her cold world, and when he put his lips to her flesh he could feel her respond, but why did she not dream walk back to touch him too? Had she forgotten how? He thought, perhaps if he tried harder she would come, and in a short time she had come to orgasm instead of Wonderland. It was impossible for Hatter to fully manifest in her world, he was still insubstantial to her, but he had to continue to try if there was any chance to be with his love again.

He kissed her lips, feeling the faintest electrical current between them, and finally she came full bodied to his arms in Wonderland. He held her as she snuggled up against him, and lightly stroked her arm just to be sure she was physically there with him again. He breathed in her sweet scent; she smelled of jasmine and honeysuckle, just like she used to. Hatter felt pure contentment with Rosie in his arms, where he knew she belonged. When she looked into his eyes, he just knew that she was his again as he had always been hers. Of all those he had met over the years, none compared to her. None had been so close his equal in power and ability to shape the worlds. He could tell that she had forgotten much, but he knew her soul and knew her strength, she could remember and return to him now in a way they had not been able to share all those years ago.

He could feel her drifting off to sleep and knew she would be gone soon. With a moment of panic he tried to memorize her every inch in case she didn't come back to him. But now that she had found her way to him twice so close together he hoped he wouldn't have to wait so long to see her again.

℘2 Twelve Years Earlier:

"Rosie, I just can't do this. Locking me out of your dreams is selfish baby shit, and I'm no babysitter." Jack's voice was cold, a calculated cold.

"But I didn't, my mind and soul are open to you. I don't know why you couldn't get into my dreams. I love you, and you are welcome to any part of me. I want you to meet the people in the village, and Her." Rosie told Jack about her unique dream world, but try as she might she could only pull him into regular dreams.

As long as Rosie could remember, about half the time she slept she had the same dream. It wasn't a recurring dream as much as a second life that she could only remember in bits and pieces. When she went to sleep at night she woke in her dream world. It was a world that seemed just as real as Rosie's waking world, when she wasn't there, the world went on without her. She could remember the little old fashioned village full of friendly Fey that she knew well, all teaching her their ways and the ways of magic.

Of all the Fey, Rosie retained the most about her protector. She was strong and beautiful, with Eurasian features that would be at home in almost any culture. She was ageless, and noble, and kind. She had wisdom carried with her since the dawn of life on earth. She was part of nature, and the elements bent to her will. The wind carried her gracefully so that she could lounge in the sky or lay just above the ground as she helped the plants to grow. She wore no clothes, but didn't need them, the temperature around her was always so pleasant. Her long hair was like liquid mahogany that flowed around her like ribbons on her own personal wind currents so that anything private was always covered and the skin exposed was just a natural piece of her. Rosie knew that her protector had been with her for lifetimes. Knew that She had been teaching and training her for something, she just couldn't remember what she had learned in that dream world when she woke. She had a feeling that her Protector was training her for a noble and good cause, she felt that it might have something to do with helping others like her, but that was just waking speculation. Rosie remembered images and feelings and felt that it was a real place where life continued when she woke, She just wished she could remember specifics.

Rosie continued to try to convince Jack of her sincerity. "If you met Her maybe you could remember what it is she teaches me and what I'm being trained to do. I want you to see the world I live in when I sleep." Rosie pleaded, confused and hurt over Jack's anger.

"If you really wanted me in your dream world, I would have been there. You are so young and naive. You just aren't mature enough to have felt pain like I have. Without having lived pain, I don't think you can really feel love. And since you don't really love me, you can't fully open your mind. I opened my mind to you! You waltzed into my dreams and I let you have access to my soul. You are protecting something, and as long as you do you cannot love me." this ploy had worked well for him in the past, and he was betting it would work on her too. Just threaten to leave enough times to tear down their defenses, and then they would do whatever you wanted. It was a power rush, and torn down like that, they would believe anything or do anything. Whatever secret she held in that dream world of hers would be his in no time. Sophomores were such easy pickings. "It's over, Rosie, I just can't be with someone who hasn't experienced life."

Rosie sobbed, curled in a ball on the floor and tucked against a corner. "But I love you, I don't understand what I did wrong. Why are you breaking up with me?" Rosie's first love had not been a kind love. When he turned on the charm it was disarming, like standing in the warm sunshine. But when Jack's mood changed that warm sunshine sure did leave a bad sunburn. One minute it was fun and wonderful, but too many minutes were more like this one. Their relationship was on again off again, and each time Jack called it off it tore Rosie apart.

"This pathetic display is why seniors shouldn't date sophomores." he stood over her with a sneer of disgust. She felt the look and it barreled its way through her soul. She felt emotionally torn to shreds. "Grow up little Rosie." Jack finished with a scoff, before striding out of the room. 'leave her stew for a night, and then return tomorrow to give her a last chance' he thought as he left the crying girl 'she'll be so grateful that I'll be popping that cherry by tomorrow.' And if her pain tasted good now, what would it taste like after she fully bonded to him when he took her virginity. He smiled to himself at how well she was falling into line, the innocent were so easy to control. And once he could get her to do anything for him, he owned her. Once he really owned her he would not need to be gentle, the feasts he would have from her energy would give him enough power to draw a harem of magically gifted women to worship him.

Rosie was left alone and crying, feeling as only a hormone-ravaged teenage girl really can, when ripped down by her first love. She was so devastated that she felt physical pain in her heart. She felt like an exposed nerve, her pain flowing out like a psychic tidal wave.

ଓଃ

Hatter was sitting on a mushroom three times his size, practicing turning day into night and back again.

Wonderland was his favorite world, it was so mutable that all aspects could be manipulated with simple force of will. He was contemplating spending some time in the garden next, blooming the roses and reverting them back to buds, when Hatter felt a wash of pain flow over him. The emotional tide almost knocked him off the almost twenty foot mushroom. He grabbed the spongy surface and reeled at the rawness of the emotion that flooded past. Hatter felt his soul reach out with empathy to whoever was so hurt and alone. He felt almost compelled to find the source of this pain, wanting so badly to help heal it.

Hatter forgot his idle exercises and was at once traveling to the world this emotion came from. With pain so raw, following it to its source was as easy as feeling sympathy. Hatter found himself in a world he usually avoided, a world so devoid of magic that he could barely manifest as an invisible insubstantial being. It was a world that hurt just to be within its bounds, a world so concrete and set in its ways, that he couldn't even interact with objects. But he was drawn to help, in a place where he was less than a ghost.

Hatter saw a girl huddled in a corner, silently sobbing. She looked to be about his age, not much older than fifteen or sixteen, but so small and helpless crying there. Hatter sat on the floor beside her and put an arm protectively around her shoulders. Hatter expected that the girl would only get subconscious comfort from this gesture, but to Hatter's surprise she responded like he was solid. She rolled toward his touch and snuggled against him like a teddy bear. Hatter could see she'd cried herself to sleep moments before he touched her, and wondered if that's why she was able to touch him. He held her and the pain emanating from her quieted, letting her fall into a sound sleep. Hatter could feel how safe his presence made her feel as she nuzzled her head against his chest and sighed contentedly. She was a psychic projector in perfect balance to his psychic receiver. Hatter stayed with the girl, who was clearly talented enough to unconsciously feel him; especially in this harsh reality. He thought it amazing that she had any psychic ability living in a reality where he could previously affect nothing and thought any magic was impossible.

Thinking about how remarkable she must be to have such ability, Hatter looked at the girl through a different filter. He calmed his mind and focused to see what usually was unseen, he looked at the energies flowing in and around her. Some called this aura, others chi, but no matter what you called it this girl's energy was damaged. He could see several dark spots, like open wounds. The energy that should flow smoothly through and around her caught on the spots, the way rocks in a stream can create rapids. Hatter wondered if these wounds were a product of the harshness of this world, or if whatever emotional injury she just experienced caused this damage. He tried to help her energy smooth out, so the muddy turbulence would slow and make it easier for her to heal the dark spots. His energy seemed to help some, but also helped Hatter notice that this girl had external attachments to her energy. She was grounded to the earth of this world. He suspected that the attachment to the natural was part of how she could have enough magical ability to call him and to survive in this world without having her magic extinguished. The tether he didn't expect was a thread of magic slipping into the aether between worlds. Hatter suddenly understood why he was so drawn to this girl, and why he needed to protect her. She was connected to another world, and tho he couldn't see what world it was, his heart filled with hope that he had found another that consciously traveled the worlds like him.

He kept watch over her, holding her protectively in his arms, as he could not remember ever having done with another living soul. There was a comfort in it for him too, a contact that he didn't know he'd been longing for. Despite the injuries in her energy, the feeling of peace and safety emanating from her was almost drug-like. It surrounded him like a warm blanket or like the hug he could imagine getting back from the sleeping girl. There was such a sense of bliss that Hatter could not imagine ever letting this fragile wonderful thing go. He sat with her for hours, hardly noticing the pain of being in her world. He hadn't been aware enough of anything but the girl in his arms to take in his surroundings.

When he finally looked around, Hatter realized he was in the girl's bedroom. Though they sat in a corner, not three feet away was her bed. Hatter could feel an invisible blush warming his cheeks as he became aware of not only how close the girl's bed was, but how beautiful the sleeping girl in his arms was. Hatter had looked at her most intimate connections and had even used his own ability to try to help with her wounded aura. But looking at the invisible, he had missed sight and smell. Her emotions were not the only intoxicating things about this girl. She smelled to him a little like a garden in summertime. Inhaling deeply, he used his keen sense of smell to identify jasmine and honeysuckle as the strongest notes. Her hair was long and straight, looking like liquid copper. Her skin was fair and creamy with a sweet sprinkling of freckles. Her closed eyes were still a bit red and puffy from crying, but somehow that just enhanced her soft vulnerability and made her look more beautiful.

Her naturally deep pink lips parted ever so slightly as she took in a deep breath, and he couldn't help but imagine kissing those soft lips. That breath also made Hatter very aware of the rising and falling of her breast, and how she continued to brush lightly against him with every breath. Hatter felt like a dog for staring so blatantly, but he was so filled with desire for the girl that he couldn't take his eyes from her. Just past her shirt's neckline Hatter could see the edges of her white lace bra, with its little bow nestled sweetly between full breasts. Lust spread through him like an electric current charging a battery. He couldn't imagine how he hadn't noticed how attractive she was the moment he saw her, or how he had managed to hold her for so long and not feel this delicious want.

She moaned softly in her sleep and it sent a thrill through Hatter. Could she be feeling his lust? And as if in answer to his question she got even closer with a wiggling adjustment. He could feel her warm breath on his neck as he struggled to calm his racing heart. Her sweetly sleeping face was turned up now, bringing her soft lips so painfully close to his own. He couldn't help but tip his head down to steal a kiss, gently brushing his lips against hers. Her soft yielding lips returned his chaste kiss, and it ignited a fire within him. Fire that threatened to burn him up if he didn't pull her against him and kiss her deeply and passionately. She responded to the kiss, returning his passion and pulling herself to press so tightly against him he thought they might merge. This felt so right and so amazing to Hatter, every other desire he had ever felt was shadowed by this building need.

The lusty kiss woke the girl. She blinked the sleep away and brought her vision into focus, but saw no one. She sat up, reaching out to where she was sure someone had been, but found nothing but air.

Her hands passed through Hatter, when only a moment before she held him so solidly. To his dismay, Hatter could feel her confusion as she looked around blushing. Satisfied that she was alone, she took a deep but shaky breath, smoothing down her rumpled clothes. Hatter was first heartbroken that, awake, she couldn't part the veil to see or feel him, and then he was ashamed that he had taken liberties. He hadn't met her consciously, so she couldn't have consented to their kiss. Hatter knew he'd done wrong, and feeling deep guilt he fled her world.

ଔଓ

Rosie felt disoriented. Despite being so distraught that she cried herself to sleep, somehow the pain of her broken heart was lessened now. She had thought someone was here with her, but couldn't find evidence of anyone having been in her room. Only thing even slightly out of place was a faint scent, like spicy roses. She could still feel a lingering comfort of someone safe and warm. A comfort similar to the way she felt with her protector in her dream world, only not so platonic. There was a strong masculine feeling to this safety that really turned her on. Rosie wondered how she could be feeling this sexual heat when she had just been dumped. Was it a half remembered dream? She could swear that she had just been kissed, she could almost feel his lips on hers and his arms around her. 'What a strange dream' she thought to herself as she pulled off her clothes and climbed into bed for the night. She fell asleep thinking of her imagined kiss instead of the painful breakup; and though her rational brain knew that no one could have been here she felt a bit of guilt for so enjoying the dream kiss.

∽

3

The next day Jack found Rosie before school and he apologized for his mood the night before, explaining that he was under a lot of stress with graduation coming up and his parents riding him about his future. He said that he would make it up to her when they could have some time alone after school. Rosie could think of nothing else all day, she just couldn't be mad when he turned on the charm. He had her wrapped around his finger and she was happy there. So long as he said he loved her he could do no wrong.

They met at the burger shack to hang out with Jack's friends like they did most days after school. Before long Jack had pulled her away from the rest of the group and led Rosie to the overgrown shady spot in the back corner of the parking lot. It was almost a private little corner, you couldn't be seen clearly except by the couple parking spots right nearby. Rosie started to speak but was quieted by a finger on the lips and Jack standing very close. It was always so hard to think, when he stood that close.

"Shhh" he whispered, leaning closer "no words" and kissed her. It was a rough groping kiss full of lust. She was carried away by his ravenous energy, feeling weak as he took all she had to offer and then a little bit more. Jack left her breathless as he reached under her shirt and roughly wrestled her bra out of his way. He could feel a quick peak of pain from Rosie, and he fed deeper from that energy than her eager lust. His kisses were deep, feeling like he was trying to reach inside her and take the jewel of her soul. Pushing her up against the wooden fence he grabbed both of her wrists with one hand and pinned them above her head. He was in control, and wanted her to feel his dominance. Rosie yielded to the force of his body pressed against her, and that energy was tasty too. He ground his pelvis into her so she could feel his hardness, and bit at her neck savagely, wanting to mark his property physically like he had her soul. A whimper escaped her lips at the sharp little pain from his bite, but feeling the power and his glee at her utter possession she was somehow aroused. She loved him, and whatever was his desire became her desire. She wanted to be wanted, and Jack's want was strong. He became more aggressive with his groping, pulling her shirt out of his way. It left her exposed, only blocked by his body and the few branches camouflaging them. Reaching down he started to undo her pants, and a small panic flooded her. Sure making out outside was exciting, and kind of a turn on, but being caught half naked was not.

"Wait, not here." Rosie pleaded, trying to pull her hands free. But Jack was focused, and pinned her wrists harder to the fence behind them, causing pain to radiate down Rosie's arms. The firmer grip was the only indication that Jack was aware of Rosie's protests, he continued devouring her neck and had her pants unbuttoned and almost unzipped when a sound came from the back door of the burger shack.

The old man who owned their after-school hangout was taking out the trash. He cleared his throat, seeing the vague shapes of the teenagers in the back corner of the small lot. "You kids shouldn't be doing that over there," he said, projecting enough for them to clearly hear his voice. "It's not as private as you think, and if some cops come by, I'm sure your folks wouldn't appreciate the tickets for lewd public displays." The old man chuckled at the way the teenagers froze when he spoke, like they thought that would hide them. He went back inside, the screen door slamming shut behind him.

Rosie was ashamed to be caught like that, hoping with every frozen muscle in her body that the old guy hadn't been able to see anything clearly through the foliage; or if he had seen something, it wasn't their faces. She wasn't sure how she would live it down if next time she went to order food he gave her a knowing look. She silently prayed that all he could tell was that someone was making out but not who.

ℓ

Jack had frozen when they were interrupted, but did not show signs of embarrassment like Rosie, instead he looked annoyed. Jack roughly released Rosie, growling under his breath, he hated being interrupted when he was so close to gratification. Damn virgins always took too long to crack. Sure, it was the safest sex, no chance of catching an std, but it was so much work to get there. As he steamed, she was quickly covering herself up, this just wouldn't do; time to kick things up a notch. Jack smoothed his ruffled feathers and turned on the charm. He was tired of waiting; he had needs.

As Rosie was straightening herself out, Jack caught her by the arm and pulled her to him. "You know I'm not done with you yet." he said wrapping his free hand around the smallest part of her waist in a way that he knew always made her feel feminine and sexy. He leaned closer to whisper in a husky voice "I need to possess you, I will not be satisfied until I own you body and soul." Jack's intensity was seductive in a dangerous way that Rosie knew was destructive but could not resist. When he kissed her again she forgot the pain in her wrists and the shame of being caught for a moment until he started to slip the hand on her waist under her shirt.

"Stop, Jack." she said pulling his hand out from under her shirt "What if he comes back out, or someone else comes back here?" Jack let her take control of his hand, but only long enough to let her think she had a choice.

Jack took both her hands in his, gently this time, and raised them to his lips kissing them. "I need to feel you. We need to finish this tease you have been carrying me along with." he looked deep into her eyes and knew that he had her. "You know that I love you, it hurts not to be able to express that," he paused for effect and came in closer so that he could hear her breath catch with the heat between them "physically."

Rosie could not speak for a moment, the emotion between them so intense. "I love you too" she finally whispered just before he kissed her ferociously. He fed on her emotion, tasting the love and desire like seasoning in a spice cake. The more he fed, the more she gave, and the deeper his control of her got. When they came up for air, Rosie had made up her mind. "I'm ready to give myself to you," her pause was a hesitation of trying to get the word out "physically." She could feel her heat rising in a blush. "We could go to my house, my folks are both at work and if we go in quietly we could get upstairs without my grandma knowing we're there." Rosie's pulse increased with excitement and the feeling of taboo at sneaking Jack in to her bedroom without anyone knowing.

Just last night Jack had almost left her for good, but now she was about to give herself to him in a way she could never take back. Jack's smile made Rosie melt before giving her a few quick electrically charged kisses. "You go ahead, so you can be sure we will be uninterrupted and have our privacy. I'll wait a few minutes before I come meet you, so no one will suspect what we're going to go do... If we leave together now, how could everyone not feel our shared anticipation and know what we'll be doing." Jack's words made sense to Rosie, and she was off, walking home at a excited half run.

ೞ

Jack sauntered back to the picnic table where they hung out in front of the burger shack, today it was just the guys hanging out. Jack had a cocky smile on his face as he walked up, he picked up his drink and fries enjoying the minutes passing as he slowly finished his food. The group could tell from his body language and expression that he was up to something. As he finished he grabbed his backpack, and leaned in to speak to his friend Nick. In a stage whisper, clearly audible to all, he announced "Time to go finally pop that cherry." He laughed and high-fived a couple of the guys as he left on his conquest, to lewd suggestions of how to 'give it to her' from the peanut gallery.

ೞ

4

Rosie raced home and climbed up the back steps. She heard her grandma watching Jeopardy in her first floor apartment as she tried to get up the steps to their flat without making a sound, and was equally careful unlocking the back door and setting it in the unlocked position silently.

Inside, she tiptoed to her bedroom and began setting the perfect scene. She tidied up her room and set out a few candles before changing into a silky little short nightgown and expectantly posed on her bed waiting for Jack to arrive. She wanted this to be perfect, a girl's first was something she would never forget.

&

Jack arrived about fifteen minutes later, sneaking quietly in the back door that had been left open for him. He stood in her bedroom doorway and spied Rosie waiting for him on her bed, and it made him think of a package just waiting to be opened.

"Hi" Rosie said more quietly than she had intended. Now that Jack was here in her room, with no one else in the apartment, and knowing what was about to happen, Rosie felt a little scared and very nervous. She had been with Jack for two months, he was her first kiss, and her first love. She knew that making love was the natural next step in their relationship. Jack had been pressuring her for weeks to have sex, but there was always something in the back of her head that felt wrong. She tried to convince herself that she was just nervous about facing the unknown. She loved Jack and he was the man she expected to be with for the rest of her life, so why wait to express their love physically? 'It's just nerves', she thought to herself in a repeating mantra.

Jack said nothing as he walked into the room, grinning mischievously. Rosie felt as if she were completely naked the way he stood in front of her and looked her over. Rosie blushed and Jack's grin grew wider, obviously a response that turned him on. The frozen moment of appraisal passed, and Jack hastily kicked off his shoes as he undid his pants and stripped them off while climbing onto the bed. He came at Rosie like an animal in heat, knocking her back as he lustily kissed her. At first Rosie's muscles tightened in response to Jack's aggressive tackle, but as he kissed her and grabbed her body she could feel his need and her apprehension washed away with the excitement.

Jack grabbed the little silky nightie and practically ripped it stripping it off her. She felt exposed and momentarily wished she could cover up, but as Jack hastily pulled off his own shirt and dove back in to fondle her, the pleasure of the moment washed back over her. His hands were large and rough, his arms strong, and his chest had just enough hair to let you know he was a man not a boy. He was a very masculine specimen, and he was taking what he wanted.

He grabbed Rosie's panties and pulled them off in one swift motion that made her think of a magician pulling a tablecloth off a table without disturbing the setting. Rosie was now completely naked and very aware that the only clothing between them was Jacks socks and briefs. He kissed her again, crushing her against him with passionate grabbing and fondling. His skin was hot against hers and all the sensations made her feel giddy. He ground his body against her and kissed her like a ravenous man eating; he kissed her lips, bit at her neck, and suckled her nipples. It was rough and fast and exciting as he moved around her body, grabbing here and licking there, all the while rubbing his crotch against any part of her body it was nearest to at that moment. Jack guided Rosie's hand behind his briefs waistband, groaning with pleasure as she touched him.

It was not the first time she had touched his manhood while they were making out, but as he pulled off his underwear it was the first time she had really seen him fully exposed. She blushed at the sight, but had no more than a moment to react before he was pressed against her again. He thrust fingers roughly inside her, and it took all her will not to scream out in pain and pleasure at the same time. Jack looked at her open gasping mouth and his deviantly gleeful expression betrayed what was on his mind before he rolled to his back and pushed Rosie's head down.

Rosie knew what Jack wanted, and in theory how to do it, but looking at him exposed could not imagine how she would not choke. She tentatively licked and Jack reacted by arching toward her. Rosie could always feel the emotions Jack projected, but this was a feeling of such lusty anticipation that it almost overwhelmed her. He grabbed the back of Rosie's head tightly by the hair, then he forcefully filled her mouth. Jack groaned, tangling both of his hands into her hair, and holding her head in place, thrust into her mouth. She gagged, surprised at how big he felt and how deep he was penetrating. But as he held her firmly and began to thrust rhythmically, the gag reflex relaxed. He moaned, and as his pleasure took root in her she began to enjoy the sensation and participate more enthusiastically. "Oh yea," he moaned "oh fuck yeah, just like that." He began to speed up and she kept rhythm with him, feeling herself respond to his emanating lust. She felt his muscles tighten as every ounce of energy was focusing on his pleasure and then like an eruption, he came. The quick gush of fluid took Rosie by surprise and she tried to pull away, but Jack held her head firmly in place as his body arched with the release. She was surprised by the thick saltiness and the force with which it filled her mouth, almost choking her till she swallowed it down.

He released her head as he finished cumming, and she pulled back, a dribble of thick white fluid at the corner of her mouth and dripping from Jack. He exhaled deeply, a look of satisfaction on his face as he lay back looking completely relaxed. "I thought you said you hadn't done that before" he teased, "you are a natural." he murmured pulling her next to him in a firm embrace.

"I, uh, I " Rosie began to quietly stammer.

"Shhhh," Jack put a finger to her lip as he lay back to relax "don't spoil the moment. It was a compliment."

Rosie could feel herself blushing. He held her, naked bodies pressed together, for a few long moments in still silence and Rosie wondered if he was done. Perhaps this would not be all of their firsts, just a first of sharing a bed and oral sex. He looked down at her with satisfaction, but when she leaned up to kiss him he pulled back. Rosie felt a pang of devastation, what had she done wrong?

Seeing her hurt expression Jack let out a chuckle. "You might want to clean off your face and go rinse your mouth, I don't much want to taste my own jiz." he chuckled again at his own cleverness releasing her from his loose embrace. Rosie got up and, looking around, found her nightie rumpled on the floor. She put it on, feeling self conscious, before walking across the hall to the bathroom. Again Jack laughed "you know I've seen you naked now, why cover up?" Rosie heard him continue to chuckle at her a few more times as she looked in the mirror.

Her careful makeup was a bit smudged, and her hair disheveled. She wiped the liquid from her chin and gargled with some mouthwash before running a brush through her hair and touching up her smudged mascara and lipstick. Something inside her felt a bit hollow and off, she now felt she understood the phrase 'walk of shame'. She padded back into her bedroom and saw Jack lounging on her bed, still naked except for his socks, no longer hard. She was a little surprised at the size difference between him erect and soft.

He let out an appreciative growl watching her enter the room, and Rosie could feel his re-building sexual excitement. "That's more like it." he said with a husky undertone, "Why don't you take that back off and come join me for the main event?" Rosie could see him starting to grow before her eyes. She blushed at his suggestion approaching the bed cautiously. He sprang out at her like a striking snake and pulled her back into bed. Rosie let out a tiny startled nervous scream as he flung her down on the bed and pounced on top of her. "On second thought, it's a kinda' sexy little silky thing you have on there. I might enjoy this more with it on." as he spoke he rubbed himself against her, the silk sliding between them felt soft and liquid; a sensation that quickly aroused them both.

Jack dove into deep kisses and hungry groping,

And when Jack moved Rosie's hands where he wanted them she responded with needy grabs of her own. The soft silk slid between them almost like a lubricant. He slid a hand under the negligee and was not gentle with his fingers. He rubbed himself against her with the same rhythm his fingers pounded into her.

Despite his rough treatment of her she soaked in his lust and was aroused. A fact that Jack did not miss. "I can feel how much you want me" he growled as he nibbled and sucked at her ear lobe, "oh, and she gets wetter when I talk about it."

Rosie rocked against his rhythmically probing fingers, almost enjoying the little shivers of pain she felt when he thrust too hard. He had three fingers inside her, and it was a tight fit, but so many emotions and sensations were washing over her that it was all exquisite, even the pain. Jack rolled on top of her and pinned down both wrists above her head against the mattress. Their kisses were like fire, igniting with the friction of their writhing bodies. Jack held both her wrists in one hand eliciting the memory of him pinning her to the fence, they still ached but Rosie was too focused on them to notice more than a twinge.

Jack reached down with his free hand and spread Rosie's legs, making her gasp with the forcefulness of it all. He moved the silk nightie out of his way and pushed against her. After a couple fumbling adjustments and some amount of resistance Jack was in position. He pushed harder and Rosie felt as if she were going to be split in half, the pain was so intense she cried out, "Wait, please, not like this".

Jack snarled and covered her mouth as he continued to thrust against the barrier within her. "Shhh, you don't want granny to hear you and come upstairs to find what you're doing, do you?" his voice was harsh and cruel as he continued to pound against her. Rosie's brain was silently screaming in agony, wanting to scream 'no' and run away, but being pinned down she couldn't. What was worse than the physical pain was knowing she was being hurt intentionally by someone she loved. Rosie didn't make another sound, but silent tears rolled down her cheeks, as he continued to push painfully and roughly into her. Suddenly, the resistance broke and Jack let out a grunt of pleasure as a new wetness lubricated each thrust. He sped up his rhythm, and Rosie watched him from a detached place that felt far away. He finished with a grunt, and looked at Rosie's face for what seemed to be the first time since pinning her down. "Whoa, what a rush. I know you have something different in you, but that is one magic pussy." he panted.

Rosie was tear streaked and numb feeling, he'd stopped hurting her, but she did not feel better. It felt like it wasn't just her hymen that broke, but like something had broken in her soul. She imagined that her first time would have been magical and beautiful, but it had been painful and she was now filled with a strange despair. Like something had been stripped from her instead of given.

Jack climbed off of her and sat at the edge of the bed. "ugh, you got blood all over me. Do you have a towel to clean this up with or something?" His tone was cold and matter of fact, not the intimate sweet nothing's she had expected to hear after they made love for the first time. She looked down at herself and saw a smear of blood between her legs, and more staining the sheets below her, but it was like looking at someone else, her brain was just not fully connecting. "Well ... Ok, not answering, I guess I could use your sheets; they're pretty ruined any way." and he yanked the stained top sheet out from under her to use to wipe himself off. "I guess you'll have to tell your folks you had a period accident or something." he said tossing the sheet to her as he stood and grabbed his scattered clothes. As he got dressed, Jack spoke to Rosie with a slightly condescending tone. "You should be fine, I hear it always hurts girls the first time. Next time it will feel better, and before you know it you'll be begging me to fuck you again, and again, because it feels so good."

Rosie lay there, unable to speak or move. Everything felt so wrong. Time had no meaning. When her detached thoughts started to come back into focus a bit and she realized Jack had finished getting dressed and had sat at the edge of the bed looking bored and annoyed as he used her sheet to clean blood from under his fingernails. "Soooo," he stretched out the word with an exhale. "I should get going." he patted her on the knee absentmindedly "I told Nick and Frank I'd hang out with them tonight, and I better head home so I can catch a shower before I go out. I don't want to go out covered in your dried blood." he laughed at his own joke dropping the sheet to show Rosie that there were still traces of blood under his cuticles. "I tried to make it easier on you, loosening you up with my fingers first... But, no good deed and all" he shrugged. "and tho the conversation is just thrilling..." he leaned in and gave her a peck on the lips. "I gotta go. I'll see you at school tomorrow."

Rosie managed to form a familiar but quiet phrase as Jack picked up his backpack by the door "I love you Jack."

"Sure, kid, love you too." he raised an eyebrow looking back at her "You might want to clean yourself up before your folks get home, or they'll pretty much know you didn't just ruin your sheets with your period." and with that he turned and left.

ଓ

That was not how Rosie expected things to go. She was so shaken, and she wanted comfort and tenderness not to be left alone. She could not face the world, not yet. She curled into a ball and sobbed. What had he done to her? Maybe this was another of his strange tests, maybe Jack would come back laughing and full of love to tell her he was acting so cold for a reason. He would not leave her broken like this. As soon as she heard the back screen door slam she knew that Jack was really gone and she had just kinda traumatically lost her virginity, and was left alone to clean up... Rosie began to rock a little while huddled tightly in a ball crying.

She felt comfort, like the safest place in the universe had just settled on her bedroom. The feeling was so different from her current mental state, it shocked her into alertness. Someone was there with her, she could not perceive them with any of her classic senses, but she felt a presence. Rosie pulled the sheets over her, despite them being damp with her own blood. "Hello?" it was a tentative quiet hello, and Rosie was strangely glad that no one answered. As long as no one answered, she could argue with her rational mind that the abrupt mood shift was a defense mechanism triggered by her own brain not by an external force. Her brain was just playing tricks on her to snap her out of it, so she could function and move on. She repeated that thought over and over as she pulled herself together.

It was 4:30. She had a good hour before anyone came home. That was enough time to make things normal, then she just had to get through the evening and when she went to bed she could fall apart quietly without bothering anyone. By morning she would have processed, and could deal. Rosie had her plan.

CR

5

Hatter usually spent his days world-jumping. Some worlds could be returned to and had internally consistent natural laws, but fixed worlds like that were rare. Most worlds were fleeting and chaotic, only in existence briefly and then never to repeat. But all worlds existed within a tangle of connections to infinite other worlds. When they existed, they could act as points of travel to others and all were connected at the speed and distance of will and thought. Hatter was pretty sure the fleeting chaotic worlds were human and Fey-born dream worlds. To Hatter's amusement, a good chunk of the fleeting worlds were quite pornographic. Humans were subconsciously, as a whole, really into lots of kinky sex. Hatter didn't blame them, they probably couldn't express it in their waking world.

Being a master of world-jumping and reality manipulation in most worlds, Hatter was able to steer clear of the stuff that was scary, and enjoy the worlds that suited him. He had one immutable rule that he would not break, and that rule was enjoy the setting, enjoy the constructs of the worlds, but never take advantage of the dreamer. He felt it would be like sleeping with someone so intoxicated that they didn't know what was going on. Without them aware of Hatter being not just part of their dreams, they would not be restrained by their rational mind and might do things they would never do consciously. Hatter felt it would be like rape to do anything to a dreamer. Unfortunately this left Hatter lonely.

Occasionally he found somewhat lucid dreamers, and was able to make superficial friendships. But usually when he ran into those souls again, they had forgotten him with the waking from their last dream, or were flighty spirits that didn't carry much in the way of memories any more. He suspected the latter were what would eventually happen to him if his life remained the same.

The paths between worlds were unpredictable at best, once a stable world was found, it was hard to find that world again once he traveled away. He might be in a world that suddenly ceased to exist because the dreamer woke and took all paths from it as it disappeared.

There were few stable worlds he had been able to consistently return to when he got lost, and his favorite was Wonderland. He thought of the magical world as his home world. He knew its natural laws and was able to manipulate its reality better than any other world. It was a world full of constructs, those he created And those there long before him. Rarely did a real soul stumble into Wonderland. So he world-jumped to observe what the dreamers imagined.

Hatter could move through infinite realities, exploring some of the deepest strangest aspects of a strangers subconscious, but since his stolen kiss he felt restless and no world really held his attention. He had broken his own rule by kissing the girl. She felt like a kindred soul, someone who could lucidly dream and jump like him. How else could he feel her emotions so clearly, and how could she be aware of him in a world so cold and set away from magics. He beat himself up for breaking his rule, and for wanting to go back to her and break it again. She was a horse of a different color, as they said in one or two worlds. He could feel that she was special, and that was why his transgression was so bad.

Hatter had fled her the night before, but no matter what world he jumped to, nothing distracted him or made him forget what he had done. He knew that he had just stolen a kiss, but if he could do that, was it just time before he justified more involved non-consenting contact? Had he started down a slippery slope? He went to the distressed girl with noble intentions to ease her suffering, but in a weak moment took advantage... He had to somehow make it right. Part of him worried that he would never see her again, part that he would be drawn back to her and wouldn't be able to resist touching her again. He also worried she would need more than emotional support and he could do nothing to physically help her. But no matter how he looked at it, she was all he could think of.

After a day of jumping through worlds that only served as a backdrop for his thoughts of the girl, he returned home to Wonderland and his tea party. Perhaps meditation and a good cup of tea could clear his mind.

It was almost working when he felt a connection to the girl again. Last night she broadcast her heartbreak. This time he felt something different, something quite intimate, and that he felt something like a voyeur for picking up. There was something happening with the girl, and it was not with Hatter. He tried to tune out her emotions, but it was hard to ignore such sensual projections.

As he was working not to psychically eavesdrop something changed, the emotions turned to pain and fear. This, he would not tune out to protect her privacy. With the speed of thought he was with her, standing in the same room as the night before. Still ineffective and insubstantial, feeling the pain of her world, and unable to help or stop what he saw transpiring.

He saw the girl pinned by a large strong looking man. He was hurting her in the worst way possible. Hatter could see the girl not only being taken physically and brutally, but her soul being shredded and torn too. He now knew how the girl's aura had been damaged, the dark spots were damage from this monster. He could feel the evil radiate off the girl's attacker as easily as he could feel the man drinking down her life essence. Intimate acts often had an exchange of energy, but this was different. Hatter could feel this guy gorge himself on the girl's energy without giving a drop in return. He was a psychic vampire of the worst kind, raping her soul as he seemed to be doing the same to her body. Hatter tried with every bit of his being to grab the scumbag and pull him off of her, but his formless hands passed right through. Hatter swung at the man, tried to pick up things to throw at him, but no matter what Hatter did, he couldn't stop this man from hurting her. Hatter was forced to watch what he could only think of as a brutal rape. Hatter cried as he watched tears rolling down the girl's cheeks, and felt her physical agony as the scum forced himself into her. Watched as blood flowed between the girl's legs, and the vermin got off on it. Watched as the thread of magic stretching from her in this reality to another world snapped and was jerked away.

Hatter grabbed at the insubstantial thread that once belonged to the girl before it could disintegrate, just barely catching it before it was pulled from this reality. It was the one thing he had been able to effect in this magic-less world during her assault. Her physical pain had ended, but Hatter could tell that shock was setting in. Her attacker got off her, and Hatter had to look away from the blood that left her looking so battered. The bastard spoke, but Hatter couldn't hear him. The rage over what he had just been impotent to stop deafened him. The man got dressed and left, like he had done nothing wrong. Hatter even caught the sound of this evil creatures mocking laughter before he left. But finally he had gone, and left Hatter's poor sweet girl curled in a ball shaking.

He had to help her somehow. Had to let her know that she was not alone, that he was here for her. Making sure that he still had a firm grip on the broken strand of magic that once tethered her to another world, Hatter sat near the girl and projected comfort. Hatter tried to reattach the thread, but it recoiled from the girl, and he could feel that her spirit had been too damaged to hold it now.

He projected the safety he wished he could have given her. He wanted comfort her, but feared that she wouldn't be able to feel his presence. She did. Hatter's heart leapt as he saw her startle in reaction to his projection. She stopped shaking, and pulled herself together. Hatter could feel this extraordinary girl, taking his offered emotions and using them to settle herself. It made Hatter's heart swell that she was taking his help. Then she spoke to him, it was the sweetest 'hello' Hatter had ever heard. He said hello back, but she couldn't hear him. It was like her fear was keeping her from being able to connect with Hatter. It was then that he realized that she was scared of her own magical nature, and something in her fear suppressed her talents.

He knew that she had to have the ability to travel

the worlds, or she would not have had that energy tether Hatter still held in his hand. Maybe she didn't know she was traveling. Maybe he could find a way to get through to her and help her travel without fear of her talents. With luck, some day maybe they could travel the worlds together. Hatter could have conversations with her that she would remember, and maybe he could find in her a true friend and companion. There was such potential in this girl, but until she did accept her gifts, Hatter only had speculation.

Hatter stayed with her while she cleaned up the blood stained sheets, and straightened out the room so no one would know what happened. A few times he could see her falter, bits of her torn up soul darkening into new wounds in her aura. Hatter tried to help by using his own energy again to help her Chi flow around the dark patches. He put an insubstantial hand on her shoulder, and though he knew she could not feel it consciously, she borrowed the strength he lent just the same, and was able to continue on.

She took a shower to clean off, and Hatter respectfully stayed on the other side of the shower curtain; no matter how much he wanted to peek. Soon after that her parents came home, they called her Rosie and Hatter was thrilled to have a name for her.

Hatter vowed to himself that he would find a way to help Rosie and protect her in a more tangible way. Now that she wasn't alone, Hatter decided a good place to start would be to follow the thread severed by Rosie's violent attack. Perhaps he could find answers at the other end to what made Rosie so different, or better yet, perhaps he could find her help.

ॐ

6

Following Rosie's thread was much like the world-jumping Hatter was used to, but with a parachute or zip line to make sure he went to the right place. He could feel that the world at the other end was fixed, much like Wonderland, and existed outside of a single dreamer's mind. Entering the world took a force of will that he hadn't experienced before. It took time to push through and left Hatter with time to think. He realized that this was a protected world, a place of power that he wouldn't have been able to enter without the thread. Knowing it was such a special place brutally ripped from Rosie seemed even more tragic to Hatter. He hoped even more that there was someone here who could help him reattach the connection to Rosie.

As he pushed through, the world formed around him. The first thing he perceived was that it was a pleasantly warm summer day, the next was that there was no sun in the sky. Day without sun. Then he became aware of many cottages around him. Hatter found himself standing in the middle of what looked like a vaguely Germanic medieval village's town square. But there was something else odd about it, it was somehow out of scale. Either he was too big or the buildings were all a bit too small, he hadn't eaten or drunk anything that would change his scale like it would in Wonderland... So it must be the houses, not him. As he looked around and saw hiding villagers peeking out at him, he realized why the houses were small. The world's residents were all little people, not in the 'they have dwarfism' way, but in the 'these were all creatures of the Fey' way.

Reaching out cautiously with his senses, Hatter could feel so many true souls that it seemed impossible. These hiding Fey were not constructs of the world, they were real. Most worlds he traveled to had one, or at most a small number of true souls in it. The dominant soul was almost always a Fey-born or human dreamer, but here there must have been hundreds of Fey souls in one place. Fey were so rare that in his years of travels, he had only come across a few fleeting glimpses, himself, and had heard of less than a handful of other encounters. He started to understand the significance of this world. If it was a refuge for magic, of course it would be protected.

Hatter tried to make friendly eye contact with those he saw, but every time he saw anyone, they ducked out of sight. He could feel their fear of him. He wondered how often they got unexpected visitors, and when they did, how often they came with good intentions. His light British accent was usually an asset when he first met dreamers, usually perceiving him as sincere and non-threatening, he hoped it would be seen the same by Fey. "Hello" he called out, trying to keep his tone friendly. "I'm sorry if I've intruded where I wasn't invited, but I'm here to try to help a girl connected to this world. Her connection was ripped from her, and I hoped someone could help me fix it."

Hatter waited for a response. As he scanned for the hiding villagers, he touched nothing, kept his hands in view, and made sure all his moves we're small and slow. He didn't want to spook the Fey creatures. He knew from experience and anecdote that many Fey were prone to flight, so he waited quietly. After a time there was a sound of quiet chittering, and Hatter knew it was the villagers whispering amongst themselves. He hoped this was a good sign.

More time passed and the whispering dwindled to a tense silence. Hatter instinctively knew that patience was important here, so he slowly lowered himself to the ground and sat on the hard cobblestone street and waited.

⅌

Hatter heard the sound of a throat being cleared, and startled. He must have fallen asleep waiting, which was strange since the only world he had ever fallen asleep in before was Wonderland... At least as far as he could remember. He blinked his eyes, and a small old woman with pleasantly round features and large colorful butterfly wings stood a few feet in front of him.

"Well, I guess if you aren't going to leave, we will have to deal with you, boy." Her tone was not quite scolding, but not quite friendly either. She stood to about his sitting height, but had the large presence of someone in authority. "I suppose you'll have to come with me child, we can't have you sitting here disrupting the town all day." Hatter could not remember the last time anyone perceived him as a child, but he supposed to a long lived being like a Fey he was no more than a baby.

The woman had taken a few steps and sighed when Hatter had not followed. "Well, don't just sit there dumb. Come along." The Hatter scrabbled to his feet, stiff from sitting in the same position so long. Funny, he could sit motionless in most worlds without a problem. This world seemed to have consequences for actions, interesting. He stretched and followed the tiny woman impatiently tapping a foot until he caught up. "OK, out of the town with you and your disruptions." She lightly rose off the ground, butterfly wings barely moving, to look Hatter in the eyes; and with a sincere expression, hit him square between the eyes.

ᛤ

Next thing he knew, Hatter was waking up in what looked to be a furnished cave with a fireplace warmly burning at one end. It was dim here, but cozy. He would really have enjoyed the over-stuffed chairs, round rag rugs, and the dark wood furniture, if his head hadn't been killing him so badly. He was sitting in a big wing backed chair, not unlike his favorite one at the tea party in Wonderland, facing the fireplace with a steaming cup of something brown and creamy on a small side table next to him. A few feet away sat the little old woman on a puffy stool happily humming and doing what looked to be knitting. The yarn looked made up of the golden translucent material that had connected Rosie to this world. He looked at his own hands and saw that the thread he had been holding for hours, that had guided him here, was gone.

"You might want to drink the cocoa, dear, it will help with that headache." Her words pounded in his head like fire, what had she hit him with? He picked up the cup and almost took a sip before remembering about not eating or drinking in the realms of Fey or gods lest he be trapped there. He set the cup back down. The woman tisked at him, "oh, we have a wily one do we? Fine, don't drink, but don't complain about your head hurtin' either." she set down her faintly glowing knitting into a basket at her feet. "Now, child, are you mute or do you want to tell me what is so important that you had to break into a realm you don't belong in?"

Hatter started to speak, but his throat was dry and his voice came out as a squeak before he cleared it properly and tried again. "I'm sorry to have come uninvited -" his own voice was like a freight train running through his head and he had to pause and hold it a moment until the throbbing settled.

"Cocoa will fix that, child, but I have told you that already."

"Sorry, I ..." the Hatter tried to clear his head again. "I came to help Rosie. She has been hurt, and severed from here."

"We know. The poor sweet child has been slipping from us for months now." The old woman shook her head sadly. "alas, it is beyond our talents to help her when she walks willingly into the monster's trap. So sad, she had more potential than any we trained in hundreds of years."

"Wait, what?" Hatter was confused. He didn't understand what this woman was saying about monsters traps, and his pounding head didn't help his cognition.

"Dear boy, do you really rush in to help this little damsel without knowing her monsters?" Hatter blinked at the round little woman, still not understanding. "As soon as I am satisfied that you mean her and us all well, I will gladly explain what you want to know. It interests me that you could travel here, but seem not to know what that means." She shook her head as a disappointed mother might. "What can you offer, child, to ensure our trust?" The woman's kindly tone took on a hard edge and grated into Hatter's aching skull. "We are not so easy to fool, and if you mean no good, you will not be the first to try to trick us and fail."

"I truly don't know what to offer as proof of my sincerity." Hatter struggled to collect his thoughts through the pain and was tempted to drink the cocoa and see if it would really ease his throbbing skull. But he knew that drinking was a trap, and that this pain was a means to an end for the Fey. Perhaps it was harder to lie when you could not collect your thoughts...

"We wait, child, and our patience is not limitless."

"I can tell you how I found Rosie, and how I know she needs help."

The woman slipped again into soothing tones and encouraging smiles. "If I judge your story truthful, that will do nicely."

"Yesterday her anguish washed over me, coming from across worlds. I had to find the source of this pain, to see if I could help. When I got to her she was so fragile and in such need that my heart went out to her."

"And before this, you did not know our Rosie? How is this so?" she sounded skeptical.

"I swear. I never laid eyes on her before that moment. And I had never felt a pull like the pain that brought me to her."

The small woman stood stiffly, showing signs of her advanced years, and shuffled over to look Hatter in the eye. He flinched as she got millimeters from his face, expecting another blow to the head, but instead a look of comprehension crossed the woman's round little face. "You are ignorant of much, young pup. I can see that you travel the worlds, but that you were not taught to do so, you found your own ways. And as much as you have learned on your own, you have forgotten much more. It seems that you have much to learn, not just of Rosie, but of yourself too. I had assumed you another Fey-touched, playing in dreams, but I see you don't wake in the Prime Material, do you?" When her question only got a look of confusion she continued."Perhaps we should begin with introductions, tell me who you believe yourself to be."

"I don't understand." Hatter's head hurt and this woman wasn't making sense, but he reminded himself that she was his best hope to help Rosie so he collected his thoughts and tried to start over. "Hi, I'm Hatter. I travel the worlds to find adventures, but mostly live in Wonderland." The woman interrupted him with a bark of a laugh, but gestured him to continue. "I felt Rosie's pain, and found her in a magic-less world where I can only manifest insubstantially and cannot interact with the world, but for some reason I could connect with her." Hatter felt anger rise within him as he spoke. "She is being hurt by a cruel monster of a man and when I felt her being hurt again today there was nothing I could do to stop him. He ripped this thread from her as he defiled her, and I knew following it was my best chance to find help. Please help her, this place must have been connected to her for a reason." The woman smiled and Hatter realized that his head didn't hurt any more.

"Good, you have passed. You are here to help our sweet Rose, and you have no intent to hurt our people or realm. You may be a lost boy, but by finding Rosie, you may yet find yourself."

"Look, I am not going to pretend that I know what you're going on about, but can you help her or not?"

"Yes, and no. We can help you, and you can help her. But to help her you may lose her and yourself in the bargain. Is that a risk you are willing to take, little shape-changer?"

"If I can get her away from that monster, I will risk my very soul... Wait, what do you mean shape-changer?"

"I suppose now I will start at the beginning," she said moving back to her stool and picking back up her knitting as she settled herself. "and when I am at the end of my tale you will know what you need to know. I am Kiri, the keeper of truths, and this is the story you must know."

ℭℜ7 Kiri's tale:

"Long ago, before magic left the land, we traveled freely between all possible worlds; and those other worlds influenced the world of man, the Prime Material. When magic was bountiful so was the prosperity of those who ruled, because of alliances made between mankind and Fey kind. The Fey nobility mingled our blood with royal lines of humanity, and the worlds stayed open.

Then came the age of reason. It was a catastrophe to all magical beings. Humanity began to cherish power and wealth over mystery and wonder. Conquest became more important than alliances. It was then mankind learned a new truth that all but wiped out Fey creatures. It was the knowledge that magic works on belief. Without belief in it, magic could not survive outside of our realms. The Prime Material became a cold and forbidding place for magic and it lost its substance there. All the doors were closed to the Prime Material, but the disease of disbelief had spread too fast. Entire worlds were lost, their wonders gone forever. Those that survived hid to protect themselves.

It was harder for the Fey races stranded on the Prime Material. Most of them died without magic, or were sacrificed by man to squeeze out their last little bit of enchantment. Only a very few survived, those with human blood could withstand the rolling destruction of mans banality.

They hid in a new way, pretending to be men, and passing their heritage through generations until it was all but forgotten. In these bloodlines, the children still could do subtle magics, if they were secretly encouraged their magics could sometimes last into adult hood, but it became more rare as mankind invested itself in the concrete world.

It became rare for any magic to stay with a Fey-born beyond the age of five, when their wonder died so did their magic. Those few that held on longest lost their talents with sexual maturity, because magical belief is often wrapped in innocence. With the loss of innocence, the Prime Material jaded the Fey-born and tore their magics from them, leaving them hollow without them even knowing what they had lost. If we were lucky they would have children with strong enough Fey heritage to try to nurture the magic in them, and the cycle would begin again. In each generation, the blood thinned and the chances of finding a child with talent dwindled. Some lines became lost to us, like you my strong little pup. Others continued to give us the occasional strong talents to try to guide. Then with a singular conjunction, many generations in the making, two unaware Fey-born married to produce Rosie. A child with such strong Fey blood in her that she was able to call pixies to the Prime Material and play with them as a young child. Rosie had so much potential that we brought her here to train her magic when she dreamt, she was given a protector so she could someday be a protector too. As long as she could maintain her innocence, she would be protected. Rosie's protector taught her the ways between the worlds through dreams, now that all of the physical doors have been closed you can only travel the worlds as spirit leaving your bodies asleep." Kiri punctuated that last comment with a significant eye contact with Hatter. "Rosie was also taught the ways to feel other Fey-born souls and know what kind of Fey they came from on sight. It also seems that she has recently figured out how to call Fey-born when she is in distress, like when you felt her pain and were able to go to her.

Keeping Rosie in touch with her magic has been a fight against the influences of the Prime Material since she was very young and started telling people about her magic experiences. That was when the corruption first got hold.

When she was a scared child she called the pixies to her for comfort and they came, but when she told others about her magic little friends coming to sing to her, the grownups around her told her that faeries weren't real, and that they must be dreams. When she insisted the faeries were real, they told her that she couldn't tell the difference between reality and fantasy. She held on in her heart, wanting to believe so badly that the magic did not desert her, so she kept us secret. She knew, that when she came here she was not simply dreaming. She worked hard to retain what she could in her waking world, and her connection to Faerie stayed strong. Rosie's protector continued her training, but tho she remembered bits and pieces her skills here remained here because her belief in her waking self was just not strong enough."

Kiri sighed, looking very old and tired. "Her mistake was trusting the wrong person. He had Fey heritage, she could see that with her gift, and he told her he believed what she knew to be true, but what he wanted was to use the magic in Rosie to increase his own power.

He realized that if he manipulated Rosie just the right way he could feed off her magic. He tried to come here before, jealous of the magical dream world she spoke of, thinking he would take our magic and twist it too. We were able to keep him out, but it weakened her connection to us. He twisted her emotions until she would do anything to please him, and as he fed off her the corruption of disbelief grew. Her innocence ebbed and the magic that bound us weakened too. And then it seems you were there to see the final straw break her connection altogether. With the loss of her innocence, her last connection to her protector is gone. Her soul has been so contaminated that her protector cannot see her any more, protectors can only recognize the pure souls of their charges.

Hopefully, her magic did not die when she was severed from us. Unfortunately, as her soul was changed by that wrong person, a part of her magic has been twisted into a darkness, a monster of her own fears. Until today, Rosie's protector has kept the monster small and at bay, but now she is unprotected. It stalks her dreams, and grows stronger with every fear she feeds into it. It could kill her if she does not defeat it. She may be the only one who can defeat her fears, but that doesn't mean another of Fey heritage can't help to fortify her will." Kiri looked at Hatter significantly. "Especially one with an animal affinity..."

Things began to make some sense to Hatter. "So, what you're saying, is that Rosie and I both have Fey heritage? And my Fey heritage is something beastie? And that whatever I am can be used to help her?" Kiri nodded encouraging Hatter to continue. "She called, and fate sent me to help her because her protector can't anymore?"

Kiri nodded again, "Rosie called you. It is a wild talent she showed when she was small and called the pixies, it takes an amazing amount of powerful magic to project emotional need out from the Prime Material. Whether by luck or fate, you were the one that heard her when she was in need. Now that she has lost her childhood protector, you can be there for Rosie. If you can feel her needs, then she can feel you. The more you try to help her, the more you should be able to connect with her and give her strength. She may yet face her monsters and win, with your help."

"But how do I do it?" he pleaded "When she was being hurt, there was nothing I could do to stop it. When it was over, all I was able to do was send emotional support, she wasn't even aware of me when I tried to touch a shoulder." Hatter grabbed his head in frustration, and yelled in anger at his inability to help.

"She sees and feels, but denies herself and chalks her strange experiences up to imagination. If she knew you were there and could believe it all real, you could get through to her." Kiri's words were motherly. "I think you might be a key to restoring her belief. If you are there for her, and she can feel you maybe she will regain her belief enough to shake the corruption that plagues her. If she sees this person who uses her for his own needs as he really is, and breaks his control perhaps she will find a new way to preserve the magic beyond her loss of innocence. But she must be the one to see it on her own, if you try to force her she will only cling harder to this person who hurts her. You can be her strength, but only she can be her own sword. You must be there for her and patient; but tread lightly, and follow her lead."

"Can you teach me how to give her my strength?"

"I can't, but Rosie's protector can. I'll take you to her. But in the mean time," Kiri took her knitting and quickly did a few ending stitches to the golden glowing thing. She shook it out to reveal a scarf. "wear this, and it will both give you an extra bit of magic when you need it, and it will give you a way back here when you need to know more." She looped the scarf around Hatter's neck loosely, and it was instantly a perfect complement to his hat and jacket. Its glow soaked into Hatter and made him feel more confident that he could help Rosie, and that in the end they would be together. "Rosie's protector may not be able to recognize Rosie anymore, but with that bit of knitting she will be able to recognize you as worthy to train."

ભ

8

Rosie lay in bed, and tried to get back the feeling of comfort and safety that had been with her while she cleaned up from the traumatic events of the afternoon. She just couldn't do it. Maybe if she could talk to Jack he would make things better, but Jack's Mom already hated Rosie and calling in the middle of the night would not help that.

She was so torn, Rosie loved Jack more than anything and he said he loved her too, but he could be so insensitive and cruel. Her first time should have been beautiful, but it was ugly. She wished she could rewind the day and take a different path. She just felt so alone and battered. Her neck was a mess. It was mottled with hickeys that no amount of concealer could completely hide, and she spent the evening constantly making sure her hair and shirt collar were in the right places and that she used all available shadows to disguise her bruises. Things would be tougher to hide in the morning light. She was raised to believe that hickeys were trashy and nothing more than a way to mark a person as owned property. She did not want her parents to see her like that. Now that she was a woman, she thought she would be happy, but all she felt was shame and loss.

She kept going over the act in her head, trying to make sense of it. Maybe she had overreacted, Jack said that it always hurt girls the first time. Perhaps the romantic media view of first times was another myth, something idealized like the guys in romantic comedies that just weren't like real people. Maybe it was good to have it all over and done with, she could put it behind her and look forward to the next time... She was not ready for the next time. Jack had said that it would feel better next time, but that just brought back the memory of the pain this time. Eventually Rosie cried herself to sleep, feeling empty.

ଔ

Rosie found herself in a dark place where she couldn't see anything. It had a musty smell and she could hear water dripping. She heard a clicking, like the sound of metal hitting stone... Or the sound of some big predator's claws clicking on a stone floor as it prowled. Fear gripped Rosie. She listened, trying to figure out how close the sound was. It was close, so close she could now hear ominous breathing to go with the occasional click of claw on stone. She heard it sniff, and her heart leapt into her throat. There was a rattling, almost like a rattle snake's tail only wetter. And then she saw something. Two red glowing eyes focusing on her. She could sense muscles tensing for a pounce, and she was terrified; She ran.

Rosie ran blindly through the darkness, bumping into things painfully that she could not see. She knew the monster was right behind her, so she ran faster until her lungs stung and her muscles burned. But it kept up, always right on her heels. She could feel it's hot fetid breath on her neck, and the smell of rot twisted her stomach into nauseous knots. The more she ran, the more terrified she became, and the more her terror grabbed hold of her the bigger the monster in pursuit of her sounded. It was like it was growing as it chased her, and with each step it got closer. She felt the air whoosh against her skin as a claw almost made contact and she screamed, it echoed in this vast dark place.

Then suddenly she saw a point of light ahead, and ran for it. As her eyes focused she saw a door sized opening with the silhouette of a man reaching for her. She could not make out much, but could vaguely make out that the figure wore a hat and old fashioned clothing. He felt like a point of safety in this terror roller coaster. She ran harder, feeling that she may not make it to the light, but just as she felt the monster taking a surging jump at her she was caught in the man's arms.

In an instant she was transported from darkness into blinding light and knew the monster could not pass from the shadows. She heard its roar of primal frustration, and shrank into the protective embrace of her savior. She could hear his heart pounding in rhythm with hers and feel the warmth of his body. She could smell roses and a warm spicy musk, it was something she swore she smelled before but could not place it. She took a shuddering breath and relaxed into the feeling of safety. She started to look up into the face of the man that saved her, but instead her eyes opened and she was home in her own bed. What a horrible nightmare. If not for the man at the end, she didn't think she would be able to sleep for weeks.

അ

9

Rosie didn't get any more sleep that night, so the next morning she was raw and exhausted. Getting dressed she discovered more aches and bruises than the expected hickeys on her neck and the stiffness in her wrists. She had sore spots and bruises in places where she had run into things in the darkness in her dream. Rosie justified them by telling herself that she must have been thrashing in her sleep and run into her bed frame somehow.

Getting dressed was a little tricky, especially hiding her neck, the marks went up to near her earlobes. Between a long sleeved collared shirt, with the collar turned up, and concealer she thought she could get past her parents for the short period she saw them at breakfast. She just hoped no one asked why she was wearing a long sleeved shirt on such a nice spring day. Fortunately her parents said nothing about her attire, sometimes it was a good thing that they weren't fashionable and a bit oblivious.

ങ

At school it was a different story. As soon as Rosie hit her locker, her friend Chris saw her and stopped.

"Do I need to ask?" he said leaning on the locker next to hers and tapping her collar. When Rosie's only response was a blush he continued. "I'm guessing that a turtle neck or a scarf would be too obvious." When Rosie couldn't look him in the eye Chris realized there was more to it than a tacky little hickey "Hey, it's ok little sis. I'm here for you, what happened? I keep trying to tell you that Jack is no good for you, sweetie, what did he do this time?" Chris wrapped an arm around her and pulled her into a hug. Chris was one of her best friends, like the big brother she had never had, and always knew just what she needed.

Rosie cried softly into his shoulder while he stroked her hair and held her. "Things just got kinda rough yesterday, and I can't talk about it."

He pulled on her collar and saw the bruising that wasn't completely covered with concealer. "Ok, you don't want to talk, you don't have to. Just tell me one thing. Did he do anything against your will?"

Rosie looked up a little surprised "No. No, I was willing. It just... Got rough."

"Oh, sweetie. You have got to stop letting him treat you like a plaything. You are not a chew toy; emotionally," he gently touched her neck making Rosie flinch, "or physically."

"I know," Rosie sounded meek "but I love him. And he is good to me most of the time."

"You may want to revisit your definition of most." Chris said with a touch of disdain. "But I'm not here to judge and I can't have my sweet little Rose looking like a wilted flower." he took her by the hand and swinging her locker shut led her down the hall. "I think there might be something to help fix this mess a little better in the drama room."

୭

A period later Chris had finished his masterpiece. With a bit of help from theatrical makeup, and a borrowed top from the costume rack, Rosie was passable for normal.

Chris was a great friend to Rosie, and one of the only guy friends Jack was okay with her spending time around. He was mostly okay because Jack thought Chris was gay, and Rosie was not about to correct Jack. He was partially right, Chris did like men. Chris also liked women, and if there were any other consenting options Chris would probably be good with that too.

Chris was one of the first people that Rosie knew was like her, something a little extra beyond the plain-vanilla variety human. When she looked at Chris she saw a free spirited satyr running through the forests reveling in sensation, he was a creature that lived for pleasure and joy. In his dreams he danced and fucked, in reality he managed quite a bit of both as well. In joke, Rosie often called him 'her favorite little man whore', a title he wore proudly and promised to do his best to live up to. But to Rosie alone he was her sibling, she called him big brother and he did his best to be that to her. Everyone else was fair game to flirt with and more if they were interested. He had a no harm no foul policy, he was always honest about what he wanted and he wanted lots of flesh, but Rosie was his platonic love, and she never felt pressure to be anything more.

She treated him as a playful forest satyr, like Pan, and he treated her as the Sidhe noble he saw in her. It started out as a kind of game between them, but once she started to see Chris as having a soul with an extra bit that was when she started to see similar things in the other people she surrounded herself with.

Chris could tell when people were beyond the mundane on his own, but it took Rosie to see who they really were. Most people were strictly human, but they felt so flat and one dimensional without that extra bit, and were never people Rosie wanted to get to know better. The Fey-born Rosie saw mostly had mixed heritage like her, so sometimes she saw one Fey type as dominant then another at a later meeting. The hardest type of person for Rosie to see were the people that so suppressed their inner natures that they were hostile to anyone different. They would never admit that they were different, and that broke Rosie's heart. Those who suppressed their natures were often cruel bullies, and Rosie suspected that some of history's biggest villains were this kind of suppressed Fey-born.

Jack was on the borderline of this when Rosie

first met him a few months ago. But she saw such change within him as she got to know Jack. Instead of lashing out at what he had to hide he now sought others like him too, to make a community. He told Rosie that she was an important part of this because she could recognize those with strong Fey souls, and then he could bring them into their community. Tho she didn't admit it to Jack, Rosie would not tell him of other Fey-born without their permission first.

Rosie felt what was in a person's soul was private and belonged to them. She felt like she was dipping into a private place when she saw people's true natures, and Jack did not always use kind methods to show people who they were. Chris was one person who chose to keep his nature from Jack, it caused a bit of tension but nothing the friendship couldn't withstand. As it turned out, Jack thinking Chris was a mundane gay man made it so that she could spend time with Chris without inciting Jack's jealousy.

With another jibe about not being a chew toy, Chris and Rosie parted ways to go on to second period. Rosie stopped to get a tardy slip, so she wouldn't have to explain missing first period, but Chris had other options being a teacher's aide who didn't care if he showed first period. The rest of the school day went pretty uneventfully, since Rosie didn't share any classes with Jack.

◌

After school Rosie was a bit apprehensive about seeing Jack, she wasn't sure if she really wanted to see him after he left her alone and crying the day before. Unfortunately the burger shack was on the way home, and Jack and his buddies were at their usual picnic table outside. She steeled herself for a bad situation as she approached, but to her surprise Jack was in a good mood and casually slipped an arm around her waist without even taking a break in his conversation with Nick and Frank.

Nick didn't acknowledge Rosie, he usually didn't, but Frank nodded to her as she settled in. Frank was Jack's friend first, but was a good friend to Rosie too. He often distracted Jack when he was being particularly cruel, and Rosie appreciated that. Frank was the group's comic relief in a way; he was always doing physical stunts to entertain everyone. He was like a court jester, tumbling and cart-wheeling across lawns or jumping fences just because they were there. When Rosie watched him she could imagine him in a forest leaping between trees as a wood sprite. Nick on the other hand, just seemed empty. He was as human as they came, and a bit of a misogynist. Rosie was thankful for Frank's influence on Jack, but Nick brought out Jack's worst qualities. The three of them usually came as a set, so Rosie did her best to make friends with both of Jack's best friends.

Rosie felt a bit awkward that it all seemed so normal, no different than any other day hanging out after school. She was relieved that no one seemed to know, losing her virginity was something private and she wasn't proud of what they'd done.

She went into the Burger Shack to get a drink and some fries, but while she was waiting she saw the guys joking around outside and soon knew that Jack had not kept things to himself. Nick was pantomiming humping the picnic table, and slapping it around. Not so out of his norm till he jumped onto the table and pantomimed the other part of someone crying dramatically. While Jack was laughing at the whole skit Frank caught Rosie watching and looked ashamed. They definitely knew. Frank averted his gaze, and Rosie wanted to run away. Only problem with that was that their picnic table was just outside the door and she would have to go past them to get away. She couldn't watch Nick making fun of her, especially not with Jack laughing about it, and she couldn't run away without having to explain why. She turned back to the counter, and watched her order being made, trying not to cry.

The bell jingled as someone walked in the door. Rosie mentally pleaded that it would not be anyone she knew, but kept her eyes averted to keep the tears welling up from spilling down her cheeks. She heard a throat being cleared behind her and knew it was Frank.

"Hey." It was an apologetic sounding greeting. "I'm sorry about Nick, he has the sensitivity of a rhino."

"Yep." it was all Rosie could choke out. Seeing her order hit the counter, she grabbed it and walked to the opposite side of the small diners interior and grabbed a stool at the narrow counter lining the window. She still could not look at Frank, who stood behind her and seemed to be awkwardly waiting for her to say something.

After a pregnant pause, and about three slowly eaten fries, Frank tried again. "I know it really isn't my business, but are you ok? Jack said you cried, and that you were all curled in a ball when he left yesterday."

The tears tumbled down Rosie's cheeks. "I," her voice cracked slightly and she took a long breath to steady herself. She was about to try to speak again when Frank put a hand on her arm sympathetically and her little bit of composure shattered. Her body shook with the tears rolling down her face, and after checking to make sure Jack and Nick were still occupied outside, Frank pulled Rosie into a comforting hug.

Frank stroked her hair and made calming quiet shushing noises. "I'm so sorry. I knew what Jack was up to, I should have tried to talk him out of it. I knew you really weren't ready."

Her voice came out in a whisper "I'm ok, I knew what I was doing." Rosie wiped her eyes and took a deep steadying breath. Frank handed her a napkin and she ungracefully blew her nose. She turned to face Frank. "I thought I did anyway." she let out a quiet half-laugh at herself "I guess I should have done more research; or maybe judged Jack's mood better." she shrugged.

"Well, I guess what is done is done. No sense in living in the past, better to deal with your current lot and move on. Right?" Frank had a look of guarded optimism. "Today is a new day. Um, be a survivor, not a victim?"

Rosie smiled at Frank's rambling, and started to relax. He was right, no reason to dwell on things that can't be changed. "Yeah, moving on."

"Awesome, because I was running out of clichés. So, you coming back out?" Frank gestured with a head tilt in the direction of the picnic table outside. "Cause it's much harder for us to steal your fries from in here. And Nick is just going to continue to be an ass as long as you aren't out there to catch him at it."

Rosie grabbed her food and started to follow Frank out. He was such a carefree sprite that it was hard to be sad around him too long. "You know Nick will be an ass whether I'm outside or not, right?"

"Yeah, but at least he'll stop humping the table." Frank shrugged. Before Rosie opened the door, Frank stopped her with a hand on her arm. "Just don't let Jack see that what he did hurt you. He has a sadistic streak sometimes, and if he knows he did something that hurt you he's more likely to do it again."

Rosie knew that side of Jack all too well. She nodded, took a deep breath and bumping the door open with a hip, stepped outside.

When she got back to the table Jack made eye contact, and after a moment a look of annoyance settled on his face. He stepped close to Rosie and pushed her hair away from her neck, then roughly rubbed a thumb across the makeup camouflage. "What's this?" his nostrils flared and Rosie could feel anger building inside him.

"It's makeup." Rosie was caught off guard and a little confused.

"It's makeup" he mocked her. "I can tell its makeup, you idiot, what I want to know is why you went to such lengths to cover your marks!" Jack took a deep breath and a look of hurt mixed with his anger. "I mark you as mine, and you conceal it? Are you ashamed of me?"

Rosie was speechless and utterly thrown. After a few moments of wrapping her mind around the idea she stammered out "You, you, you marked me intentionally?"

Her response seemed to anger him further. "Everything I do, I do with intent," he spat the words at her as if it was something she should know. He grabbed her by the arm roughly, twisting it painfully as he pulled her in close. "You. Are. Mine. The sooner you realize that the better things will be for you. If I want to mark you to show others you belong to me, it should thrill you." the last four words he emphasized by over enunciating them with his face inches from hers.

He held her there, and Rosie was so terrified by this sudden mood swing that she could not move to free herself despite the fact that Jack continued to crush her arm in his grip. "I'm sorry" her voice came out as a whisper "I didn't know. I love you, I wouldn't ever do anything to anger you on purpose." Jack turned from her and flung Rosie away from himself with such force that she would have fallen if Frank hadn't been close enough to catch her and right her before Jack turned back.

Rosie could hear Nick mocking her in a sing song voice, as he usually did when she was apologizing to Jack, "Buh-buh-but I love you." Rosie was humiliated, but remembering Frank's advice she steeled herself and did not let the tears flow that were threatening. She glared at Nick, forcing her humiliation down, she couldn't give him the satisfaction of seeing her bothered.

"I'm so done with you today. Go home." Jack's words were like acid to Rosie.

"I said I was sorry. I love you Jack, I didn't know that you saw hickeys as a good thing." her voice was pleading, as much as she feared his anger she was heartbroken to be sent away.

"I. Said. Go." his tone was now more cruel than angry "When I forgive you, I will call you."

Rosie turned towards home and slowly walked away, hoping that his mood would again change and he would call her back. Instead she heard Nick continue to mock her and heard Jack laughing at Nick's joke.

ᘉ

10

Jack didn't call her that night, and she fell asleep crying. Her dreams were plagued again by nightmares of the monster in the darkness with glowing red eyes. As she ran from it in terror, Rosie could hear noises like sweaty skin rubbing against leather and ticking creaking sounds. Tho she couldn't see anything clearly she just knew it was the sounds of the monster growing appendages and getting bigger as it chased her. She could feel the push of air against her skin as it swiped at her with near misses. The muscles in her legs burned but she knew that the moment she stopped it would get her. She felt like she had been running for hours, tho logically she knew it couldn't be that long. Just as she felt she couldn't run any further Rosie was grabbed and pulled by a strong hand into a blinding light and shocked into full wakefulness. She found herself sitting upright in her bed, but instantly collapsed utterly spent and shaking. There was a lingering smell of roses, and her terror was quickly being replaced with exhaustion, but a safe feeling exhaustion.

Laying awake in her bed she felt her heart pounding from the nightmare. Her muscles and lungs seemed to think that she had actually been running, they shook and burned with the fatigue. This was the second time she had been saved from the monster in her dreams. Jack had managed to share a few dreams with her before, she thought that maybe it was him who had saved her. She so wanted Jack to be her knight in shining armor that she imagined it must be him, despite the feeling in the back of her mind that it wasn't.

As the thought occurred to her, she again smelled faint musk and roses. Inhaling deeply to get every bit of the scent, she felt the faintest touch on her arm. Rosie could see that nothing was there to brush against her, but she could definitely feel something. The touch was calming and soothing, it felt almost healing as her pains eased away to a relaxed calm. It was the same soothing she felt the night before.

She experimentally touched her own arm where she felt the sensation, and though there was nothing there her skin was warmer. She closed her eyes and imagined that she was placing her hand over another's hand, and with her eyes not contradicting her sense of touch the hand she imagined became more real; somehow taking on a three dimensional quality. She could feel that the hand was bigger than hers and masculine. Logic told her it was impossible to feel a hand under hers and that it should freak her out, but instead she felt curious. Her gut said that this was a safe hand, and she was ok trusting her gut this time. She squeezed and felt her fingers slip between his. Rosie felt him react to her touch, gently squeezing her fingers between his. Her breath caught in her throat, as she felt the muscles in his hand flex, his thumb gently stroking her in soothing little circles.

Carefully keeping her eyes closed, Rosie felt her way across his hand and up onto his arm. She felt a thrill surge through her with this impossible contact. In response to her touch a trembling breath brushed against her cheek with a feeling of hope she wasn't sure was her own. The arm felt so real down to the light texture of the hairs that prickled into goose bumps at her light touch. From the direction of his breath and the angle of his arm, Rosie realized that her visitor was sitting on the edge of her bed leaned over her enticingly close. She moved her hand directly in front of her and found the texture of fabric and the warmth of a body beneath it. His heart was pounding in time with hers. She was grateful but slightly disappointed that he was clothed. The hand on her arm moved to caress her cheek. Rosie found herself leaning in to his touch and sliding her hand up his firm chest, over a well muscled shoulder, to stop at the nape of his neck. She played her finger tips into short soft hair, realizing it was silkier and a little longer than Jacks buzz cut. Rosie also noticed the man's shoulders were as broad but straighter than Jack's. That moment she was sure this was no astral projection of Jack, but before she could really process that info she felt soft lips brush hers. There was something so right about the feel of his lips that all thoughts of Jack were washed away by the chemistry of this kiss and the magic of the moment.

Her whole body tingled with that gentile kiss. Then things lower tightened and moistened with anticipation as she felt him caress her shoulder just before the hand on her cheek slid behind her head and he pulled her up into a firmer kiss.

Trembling breath brushed her face as he leaned back from the kiss. He gently lowered her back on to her pillow. He released Rosie and his weight shifted like he was getting up. Rosie was suddenly terrified that this would be his last touch, and reached out for him, catching his arm. In immediate response she felt the bed move as he hopped on, laying next to her, and wrapping strong safe arms around her. She rolled into the embrace, pulled to the heat of his firm body. Rosie Snuggled in and inhaled his spicy warm rose scent, and there was something so intimate and seductive about the thought of taking something of him into her. He held her gently, almost reverently, but with every brush she could feel energy flow between them as a tangible want. They both took shaking breaths, reveling in the shared sensation of this contact. It was all moving so fast, but it felt so right and good that Rosie didn't even think to stop.

Rosie leaned in to meet his lips this time, and this kiss was sensual and full of longing. His mouth tasted sweet and minty, and as her lips parted his tongue played gently but firmly against her own. Rosie embraced him, and she could feel phantom weight as he rolled carefully above her. Rosie was filled with need and his gentle touch just wasn't enough now. She kissed him again, deeper this time, feeding on his velvety lips and probing tongue. Rosie's fingers kneaded against his back and shoulders, pressing their bodies together so tightly that she could feel his arousal. As his hands urgently began to explore her body he released her lips to nuzzle the side of her neck. He kissed her neck, lightly but playfully dragging his teeth against her flesh. The sensation made Rosie gasp, arching her back and wrapping a leg around him wantonly. She lifted his face to hers again, needing the taste of his lips. As he kissed her back urgently, she ran her hands across his muscular shoulders and reveled in their solid warmth. The press of his body against hers felt so firm and real that in the heat of their passion Rosie forgot to keep her eyes closed. She looked at the man she could feel, taste, and smell but saw nothing.

The shock of his visual absence suddenly broke the spell, leaving the air above her truly empty. She was left panting and alone, at first feeling sexually frustrated and teased, wanting back that intense connection. Then guilty, because she should not want to be with anyone that wasn't Jack. That thought lead to the conclusion that either her subconscious wanted to be with someone else so badly that it made her have one hell of a hallucination, or she had just cheated with a ghost. Neither option made Rosie feel comfortable with herself. Was she as untrue as Jack?

And with that her rational mind took over, convincing her that what just happened was so impossible it must have been a dream. A really, really hot dream, but one entirely from her imagination and not like the dreams she had occasionally shared with Jack or some of her more gifted friends. She was sure dream travel needed someone she knew well and was really connected to; not a mysterious dream lover she had never met but longed for so deeply. Someone so amazing had to be imagination.

附

11

Over the next few weeks Rosie slept less and less, most of her dreams being overtaken by the monster with red glowing eyes in the darkness. It seemed to get closer to getting her each time. Most of the time she was able to get out into the light where the monster could not follow, but once or twice she thought she would not make it and had been saved by the mysterious man. His touch almost made the terror of being hunted worth it. But that thought, as true as it was, increased her guilt over wanting him so badly. On the nights she had the nightmares and woke afraid, she could always feel his presence there to comfort her but rarely felt the invisible brush of his touch. She felt his touch in her dreams when he caught her hand, pulled her into the light, and into his arms the split second before she woke. But once she was awake he never filled her senses like that night. Once or twice she smelled the musk of his skin mixed with roses, or a light caress but just for a moment. She began to think of him like a sexy guardian angel. His presence was subtle enough that she could convince herself that he was a construct of her imagination, then she didn't need to feel like she was being unfaithful to Jack.

She also couldn't seem to get to the Fey village with her protector anymore. Once or twice she thought she had gotten through to her protector, but it was only a momentary glimpses and when Rosie tried to follow She would be gone. Rosie never found another person who had a dream world like hers, and now it seemed neither did she. At least she didn't feel completely devoid of protectors, in some ways her guardian angel was becoming more real than the fading memories of her dream world. She thought that she may not be able to touch him, but Rosie felt his presence every time she needed to. He was a secret intimacy she kept to herself; partly because she mostly believed him to be something she made up but also in case he was a real spirit of some kind. She didn't want Jack to find out about him, the one thing she had that Jack could not twist into a flaw was that Rosie was loyal and faithful. An attribute she suspected Jack did not have himself. Jack refused to label their relationship, giving him leeway to do whatever he wanted, but told her that the same did not apply to her. If she wanted to be with him he expected faithfulness.

ೞ

Jack forgave Rosie for slighting him by covering the marks the day after he dismissed her, and now expected sex on demand. Jack had told the truth when he told Rosie that sex wouldn't hurt after the first time. She wasn't sure if it was as amazing as she had expected, but then she knew the world wasn't ever as good as it was portrayed in romances. Jack really liked sex, and her desire to please him gave Rosie enjoyment. She wondered if she would enjoy sex as much as Jack if he gave as much as he demanded of her. Jack had settled into a pattern, he wanted to get blown and then fuck Rosie. He wasn't so much interested in touching and kissing, or oral sex for Rosie; just him. Rosie was usually just getting into it when Jack was done, often leaving her all revved up and frustrated. That paired with sleep deprivation and the inability to access her regular dream world of magical Fey left Rosie depressed.

ೞ

Jack seemed pleased when she told him that she hadn't been able to get to her dream world. He told Rosie that if he could not experience her secret world it was fine by him that she couldn't either. Jack was still running hot and cold in a way that kept Rosie off balance, and even admitted it was on purpose. He said he was tired of her being sweet and innocent and that he would break her of it. He said that if she was going to survive in this world, she would need to be tough. It was almost like the opposite side of the coin from the energy she felt protecting her.

When Jack was on a good run with Rosie she told him about the nightmares, and how she was sleeping less and less out of fear. He was sympathetic and ready to help her. Jack had a plan almost before Rosie finished telling him of the nightmare monster. He planned to put Rosie into a lucid dreaming state so he could guide her and have her lead the monster into a controlled dream environment where they could trap it and confront the monster. He said he would get her into the lucid dream state by putting her in a trance over the phone, being in high school neither of them could spend the night at the other's house so the phone would do.

What he didn't tell Rosie was that he planned to let her fight the monster alone and use her more open mind to access the magical world she once traveled to, but no longer could. He'd start off with her and slip away as soon as she was occupied. That Rosie could not access the world was fine by him, then she wouldn't try to stop him from draining its magic dry. He was sure he could access it with Rosie distracted battling her nightmare and that it was a world built with a power he could tap and use for himself.

ભ

It was midnight, a fitting time planned to confront Rosie's fears. She clutched the phone in her hand, waiting for it to ring. She intended to pick it up before anyone could register the sound and wake up. It was Jack's preferred way to contact Rosie, late at night and without parental oversight.

Rosie had made a little nest of pillows on the floor of her room where she could be put into a hypnotic state comfortably and prop the phone so that it would stay at her ear without her having to hold it. When Rosie and Jack were first dating and he was still wooing her they had spent many nights whispering sweet nothings to each other till they fell asleep. They hadn't fallen asleep on the phone together since before Jack took her virginity, but tonight she had set up her nest again. The only difference in her setup was the lit candle near her on the floor. She set the white candle just enough away from her that if she fell asleep she wasn't going to knock it over and close enough that she could focus on the flame to get into the trance state needed to lucidly dream and be able to respond to the voice guiding her.

The phone rang at a minute past midnight, and Rosie was waiting with her finger on the switch hook so that it was answered before the phone made more than a chirp. If her parents heard anything, they probably would have assumed that the smoke detector battery needed to be replaced or that something was left in the microwave over night and it was peeping a reminder.

"Hello," she answered in a hushed whisper.

"Rosie" Jack stated over the phone knowing it was her.

Hearing his voice sped her pulse and gave her a tiny thrill, just like it did most times when they spoke. "Hi, Jack."

"You just said hello, you don't need to follow it up with hi." Jack already sounded annoyed with Rosie, she worried it was a bad omen.

"Sorry." her reply was simple, because she knew anything else might tip the conversation badly.

"Are you ready? This will only work if you are completely comfortable and completely trust me."

"I am, and I do. I love you, of course I completely trust you." Rosie was still whispering, beside not wanting to wake her parents in the next room it felt more intimate and appropriate.

"Good." Abruptly, Jack went from annoyed to sounding sincere and almost like a therapist. His unpredictable moods were the only thing Rosie could predict. "We'll start then." He began speaking in lulling tones needed to sooth someone into a trance. "Focus on the flame. Watch it flickering and rippling and let your mind relax and think of nothing but the flame and the sound of my voice..."

ೞ

With the scarf made of Fey energy Kiri knit Hatter, he was able to come and go from Faerie at will. He was an eager student, learning and training with Rosie's former teachers. Hatter knew that if he wanted to be able to get through to Rosie and give her any real help, he had a lot to learn. With this goal in mind he wanted to learn all that Fey had to offer, and was impatient that they only let him learn so much at a time. If Hatter wasn't training, it was only because his sweet Rose had called him to her.

Rosie's protector taught him to manipulate realities beyond the tricks he had figured out on his own. He could manipulate so much more than he ever realized, and his own form was part of that. She also taught Hatter fine-tuning of his world-jumping skills. All the physical disciplines were Her specialty. She was an intimidating force, and more of the strong silent type, but a good teacher. Kiri taught him about the worlds histories, and what worlds were kinder to Fey-born or could be manipulated easier due to their consistent physical laws.

Hatter could now return to any stable world he had previously visited, any world but the one they called the Prime Material. He still could only visit the Prime Material, Rosie's world, when he followed her call. He learned the Prime Material was so magic dry that its rules excluded most kinds of reality manipulation, and soaked up magical energies from anything without a physical body to shelter it. That was why it hurt Hatter to visit the Prime Material, without a physical body to protect him he could only withstand it for short periods. Rosie made it easier, but even with her energy added to his he often had to use more energy than he had in reserve. Kiri said there were other ways to build up his energy reserve, but he hadn't gotten there yet and Kiri made no exceptions for teaching him more advanced things before he mastered the preceding lessons. Kiri also assured Hatter that as his abilities progressed, he would be able to stand the Prime Material longer, and would be able to enter it at his will not just Rosie's call. Hatter really didn't see any appeal to the Prime Material except that Rosie lived there, though that was reason enough for him. He wasn't sure why anyone would want to live in a place that sucked the magic from all things and resisted even the simplest alterations.

He learned that he was as rare a find as Rosie, and that their talent to travel the worlds made it possible for others to learn to do the same. It took strong Fey heritage to be able to travel worlds without training. That meant Hatter must have deep roots somewhere, too bad Hatter had little memory of his past. He really wasn't as interested in digging up the past as he was in preparing for the future he someday hoped to share with Rosie. The more he learned of himself and Rosie, the more he knew she was a true kindred spirit. Fey heritage had been so thinned out that only a few per generation had any shot at being able to use magic at all. That he and Rosie were both such strong magical talents and alive in the same generation was unheard of, and Kiri even confided in Hatter that she believed their match was fated.

They had been teaching him to understand how his ability to manipulate reality applied to his heritage. He learned that his dominant heritage was a shifter, with his natural talent maybe more than one kind of shifting Fey, and with the training he received he could change his body into almost any form he wished; in most worlds. Despite the fact that he could change into anything, Hatter had a natural affinity for wolves, making that shift much easier than any other. His ability to manipulate the worlds around him had grown with his shifting in all but the Prime Material.

Hatter learned about the magical reserve within Fey-born. If he knew that he was using up all his reserves in the Prime Material he would not have worked so hard to manifest to Rosie as solidly or for as long as he did. When she responded to him that night and together they were able to touch, and especially to kiss, it was a huge use of energy. The encounter had used so much energy because he hadn't yet learned how to control his magical reserves. So when she opened her eyes and didn't see him, the Prime Materials laws took effect and her disbelief burned up every ounce of magic that let them be together. He was flung from the Prime Material so forcefully by that magic vacuum that weeks later he still hadn't recovered enough to really touch Rosie. He could be with her only as a comforting presence, and it was not enough for him. Unless Rosie shared her magical energy with him, he just didn't have enough juice to effect her. Hatter craved Rosie's touch like a drug, but try as he might he could not feel her skin beneath his hands when he reached out to touch her. He trained hardest to change that.

The monster that hurt Rosie in the Prime Material frustrated and confused Hatter as much as it enraged him. She could decide to walk away from that abuse, but she didn't. Hatter could not affect things in Rosie's world, so he could not really help her with her Prime Material problems. It broke Hatters heart to see the cruel things Jack did to Rosie, and that Rosie took it with professions of love for the manipulative monster. Hatter suspected that it was Jack's Fey heritage that gave him such power over Rosie. Hatter planned to save Rosie from Jack when he was stronger, but for now he worked to help her with the more immediate danger.

The monster made of her own fears, that problem he could work to help her with now. Rosie's fears created the monster that chased her through the darkness, and her self-doubts built a barrier so that Hatter could not enter that private world. If only he could find a way to speak to Rosie and explain what he had learned, things would be different in many ways. Without being able to communicate with her, all he could manage so far was to open doors from her nightmare into brighter safer worlds. Whenever possible he opened doors she could find and get through, but a few times when she couldn't get out on her own he used what energy he had to reach in and pull her out. The shock of it had always snapped her back to the Prime Material, so even in her dreams Hatter could not communicate with Rosie. In the end Rosie was the only one that could defeat her own fears, and until she faced it he could not help directly. So Hatter bid his time, practicing what he learned and built up all the energy reserves he could for when Rosie would really need him.

ᘓ

Either Rosie was beginning to call Hatter to her more frequently, or Hatter was able to find her now with much less need on Rosie's part. Either way, Hatter was nearby to witness Rosie staring at the candle light so intently that night. He wasn't sure her going into an open trance state was such a good idea, but he couldn't yet argue his case with her. Her energy felt off to Hatter from the moment her breathing began to change. Her breathing became slow and measured, in through the nose and out through the mouth. She was listening to a soothing voice on the phone, responding every so often with quiet yes and no grunts. Hatter knew it was Jack on the other end, and he did not trust or like the man who caused Rosie to cry so often.

He went to Rosie and tried to hold her hand, but even with his new found iron focus he could barely feel the warmth of her skin. Hatter watched as Rosie's eyes fluttered shut, and at that moment Rosie's hand became solid in his. She took a deep breath, and a slight smile curled her lips almost absently. "I smell roses," she sighed.

"Roses, that's not what I expected. Is the

monsters cave near a garden?" Hatter could hear Jacks voice over the phone clearly in the quiet room.

"I'm not sure. I don't see anything but white just yet." At Rosie's almost whispered description, Hatter felt a prickling of energy dancing over Rosie.

Jack sighed over the phone, "You need to focus more. Picture a door. On the other side of the door is the place that your nightmare monster lives. You need to find it, and let it follow you to me so I can defeat it." Hatter really didn't like this plan.

Hatter could feel Rosie's pulse speed with the fear of the monster. "Ok, I've pictured the door. I'm putting my hand on the door knob." Rosie's breathing quickened, and Hatter could feel the muscles in her hand twitch as she interacted with the door knob in her vision.

"Good, open the door." Jack sounded confident, but Hatter was sure that he was leading Rosie into danger that Jack had no way to help with.

"Ok." Hatter could feel something shift within Rosie, almost like she was stepping from her body up through this door.

The candle flickered and began to burn very brightly with the flame leaping up by inches. A blue silk scarf was draped over the edge of Rosie's nearby dresser, and with the flame so much larger than it should have been, he worried that the scarf was close enough to catch on fire. Instinctively Hatter let go of Rosie reaching out to snuff the flame between hastily licked fingers. The flame pinched out before Hatter had time to doubt that he shouldn't have been able to do it. He realized that Rosie was practically leaking her magical energy reserves for him to be able to interact with matter.

He turned back to Rosie but she had astrally projected out of her body. A blue ribbon of energy flowed out from her body's core through the front of her chest. The energy was faint, like she didn't think to keep part of herself anchored in her body. There was something vaguely familiar to this scene for Hatter, but his concern for Rosie took precedence over a moment of *deja vu*. He took her hand and couldn't feel the warmth of her skin with her soul departed. He faintly heard Rosie whimper in fear, but the sound had not come from her body it seemed to travel down the weak blue ribbon of energy.

"What do you see?" Hatter heard Jack's eager voice over the phone, but didn't think Rosie was in a place to still hear him.

He carefully touched the blue ribbon of energy, and it almost disappeared. It was part of Rosie, but it was almost detached from her body. Hatter somehow knew that if this thread of energy let go, Rosie could become lost and unable to find her body again. He needed to do something to keep her connected and something to keep her safe from her fear monster, but he couldn't do both at once.

"I said, what do you see Rosie?" Jack's phone voice became more impatient, and Hatter wished he could hang up the phone to get rid of him. "Rosie! You need to hear my voice and tell me what you're seeing." Hatter hated the hold Jack had over Rosie, how could she not see his intentions were never for anyone's benefit but his own.

Hatter's rush of annoyance made the blue thread of energy he touched flicker like a candle's flame in a draft. He got hold of himself, and refocused on the energy ribbon. Tuning out Jack's voice and listening for Rosie, Hatter played his fingers delicately over the ribbon. He pulled a bit of the energy back to Rosie's body with a force of his will, and the thread took on a faintly golden shimmer with the addition of his energy. But it wasn't enough and he knew Rosie was disconnecting. Thinking quickly, he pulled the end thread from the scarf Kiri had given him in the Fey realm and used it to wrap around Rosie's slowly dissipating energy. Between the Fey thread and Hatter's energy, Rosie's thread began to stabilize. Hatter was beginning to feel Rosie at the other end, and she was terrified. He worked as quickly as he could with the delicate thread and wove a braid of the scarf's Fey energy strand, Rosie's tether, and his own energy. He worked the threads, knotting them almost like macrame into a sling woven around Rosie's body. As he made a final knot securing Rosie's astral safety line to her body, he felt a jarring pain and heard Rosie scream from far away. Her body gasped, like it had forgotten it needed air, and a faint whimper followed from Rosie's mouth but Hatter could feel the scream that the whimper was an echo of. Gathering Rosie's body up in his arms, like he was as solid as she, he could see blood seeping through her cotton night shirt from three long slashing cuts.

No sooner had he seen the blood than he was suddenly with Rosie in the darkness. She was collapsed face down on a hard packed dirt floor with the fear monster on top of her. It had an odd tail like appendage tipped with three claws, two digging down and one digging up. The claws were raked into her back where Hatter had seen her body bleeding in the Prime Material.

Hatter had been too late, and Rosie was hurt. He grabbed at the monster, but it was huge with dozens of chaotically placed limbs making getting a grip on it without hurting Rosie difficult. It clawed at Hatter to defend itself and momentarily forgot the semiconscious girl under it. One claw swiped across Hatters face, leaving a bloody gash on his cheek, while others pummeled into his body. It was hard to defend against so many clawed limbs coming at Hatter through the darkness. He swung fists into the blobby furry core of the monster, but it was barely fazed. Hatter caught movement in the darkness going towards Rosie's limp form. The monster had flung another appendage towards Rosie, this one was more tenticular with barbed hooks. Hatter dove to block the hit, taking it milliseconds before it would have ripped into Rosie's skull. By taking the hit and grabbing the tentacle, he had managed to knock the monster off Rosie and was able to get in between them. Hatter was hurt and bloody, but the monster seemed to be untouched. He lunged at it again trying to grapple it and get it further from Rosie, but Hatter knew he was losing. The monster was continuing to maul Hatter, breaking his body with little effort. Hatter just hoped he could get Rosie to safety before he took the mortal blow. No matter what happened to Hatter he felt it would be worth it if he could just save Rosie.

Cz

As she gained some consciousness, Rosie made a pained noise trying to back away from the monster. She seemed to be having trouble focusing, like she had taken a blow to the head. Her back burned with pain, and she couldn't see what was going on in the darkness, but she could hear the grunts of a struggle between her and the monster. She couldn't tell exactly what was happening, but at least she knew she had help.

"Get away Rosie! Run!" A male voice with an English accent yelled from the grapple. She tried to see who it was in the darkness, and made out a vague outline that registered in Rosie's muddled brain as the shape of her invisible guardian. Disoriented, she started to follow his directions, but she heard the monster land a blow against him with a meaty squelch that she knew was serious. In that moment the fear of losing him was so much more than the fear of the monster that she instinctively called a bit of Her wild magical energy. Reaching for her guardian angel, her hands burned with radiant light. As she touched him, her energy flowed into him and as she lost consciousness fully she saw her brave defender for that moment suspended in time.

He wore a well worn brimmed hat, that confirmed he was the same man she had seen in silhouette pulling her into the light. But in the light from her hands she could see more than she had in those moments before waking. He had dark thick hair and big brown eyes and blood flushed red lips that matched the soft kissable perfection she had felt against her skin before. She saw him, handsome beneath the bloody cuts and bruises, and she saw he was like her; so much more than just human. Not a phantom, ghost, or construct of her imagination, but a flesh and blood man. All this she saw in the fraction of a second before the light emanating from her hand reached him. And in the next fraction of a second, his shape flowed in golden energy from that of a man into a huge glowing spirit wolf. He emanated power and light so bright the monster was lost from view. The wolf pounced and with his movement light trailed behind him. As her vision faded, she could hear the wolf tearing into the monster with wet ripping sounds. Then everything faded to black, but Rosie knew this battle was won and her avenging guardian angel had saved her.

ᘓ

12

The battle was still bloody, but with Rosie's energy the monster was no longer invulnerable. Hatter's Rosie-augmented wolf form was huge and glowing, and as an additional bonus the light seemed to damage the monster whether or not his natural weapons connected. He tore into the monster with teeth and claws. Viscous fluid sprayed from its wounds and the bloody substance burned in the light. It struggled to wound the wolf, but the wolf was not as soft and squishy as the man had been and it was not as easy to hurt. The battle wore on and as the monster took damage, it inflicted damage too. But over time it's wounds were so great that the monster had to flee the glowing great wolf.

As soon as the monster fled Hatter rushed to Rosie, slipping into human form before he arrived at her side. She was unconscious and her back was bleeding, but her chest still rose and fell with shallow breath. Hatter was so grateful she was still alive that tears welled in his eyes spilling salty tears into the cuts and gashes on his face. He was a bloody mess, but he wouldn't stop to tend himself as long as Rosie still needed him. His shape shifting had partially healed his worst recent wounds, and Rosie's energy had healed the likely mortal wounds he received from the first blows before he was able to hurt the monster. As the adrenalin started to wear off, Hatter hurt and knew he was going to be in some real trouble as soon as he stopped moving.

He had to get Rosie out of here, in this nightmare world he couldn't risk Rosie's monster returning to finish the job. But in Rosie's home world, the Prime Material, he would be powerless to help Her. He couldn't take her to the Fey realm, he had sacrificed his scarf that granted him passage to bind her spirit to her body. Without the scarf he wasn't sure he could get through with his injuries, let alone carrying another wounded person. The safest option was to bring her to his home, Wonderland.

He checked Rosie to make sure lifting her wouldn't make her injuries worse, and picked up her limp body. Hatter held Rosie in his arms, cradling her head against his chest, and being careful not to put too much pressure on the vicious slashes in her back. Even light pressure brought soft pain moans and twitching muscles. After such a battle Hatter was exhausted, and between his own injuries and carefully carrying Rosie it was a challenge to open the path to Wonderland. His vision swam with exploding black spots as he moved them through the worlds, and he almost lost consciousness. But Hatter could not give up until he knew Rosie was safe.

As he stepped onto the familiar grass of his garden tea party, he fell to his knees unable to stand any longer. The jarring drop made Rosie moan, and her eyes fluttered open for a moment. Hatter clutched Rosie to his chest, kneeling in the thick grass, and despite his condition smiled when she looked up into his eyes.

"You're going to be alright, I've got you." He murmured in soft British tones as he looked caringly into her eyes.

"You saved me." Rosie breathed contentedly curling her body against his.

"You did some impressive work too Rosie, we would have never won without you." Hatter's arms were beginning to quake with the effort of holding Rosie, so he lowered her gently to the soft thick grass.

Hatter tried to stand, but his legs failed him and he swayed with the effort. Rosie's hand reached out to him weakly, but her contact steadied him. "Don't go. Please, stay with me."

"There is no place I would rather be." Hatter replied, sounding tired but happy. With effort, Rosie lifted her hand and gently pulled Hatter toward her.

He fell as much as lay down on the ground beside her, and felt blood trickle from open wounds. Still a little dazed, Rosie snuggled closer to her angel. Sliding an arm around him, she could feel the sticky wetness of blood soaking through his shirt and jacket. "You're badly wounded, and you got hurt saving me. You've done so much for me and I don't even know your name." The effort to speak in her weakened state showed as each word came out quieter than the last.

"Hatter," he replied sleepily, "You can call me Hatter."

"Like the mad one in the tea party?" She asked with a half smile.

Hatter smiled weakly but genuinely, "Maybe a little less mad than that one, but yes, like him."

"Hatter." She sighed his name like it was something intimate. "God that feels sexy, the shape of your name passing through my lips. Hatter." She took a slow breath, savoring his touch and the feel of him. "Sexy name, sexy accent, everything about you..." she trailed off looking deep into his eyes, "you are my guardian angel, my hero."

"Hero, huh?"

"Sexy hero." Rosie confirmed with a blush.

Hatter was losing consciousness, and he knew his injuries and blood loss was pulling him under. But with Rosie calling him a 'sexy hero', he felt he could die a happy man. He smiled weakly, as he felt himself slipping away.

Rosie felt him slipping too, and she knew she could not bear it if he died saving her life. "You said you'd stay. I feel like I've just found you, you can't leave me so soon." A tear streaked down Rosie's cheek. And with great effort Rosie pressed herself even closer to Hatter, curling one leg over his, and holding his face in both of her hands.

Hatter shifted his arm weakly to drape across her waist, and stared at her with such wonder. He had been alone so long, and was so grateful to have found Rosie even for just this brief moment. "I'll do my best." He promised, knowing that his best might not be enough.

"Good," Rosie whispered, their faces so close that their lips almost brushed against each other as she spoke. "because now that I've finally found you Hatter, I don't want to ever lose you." with that their lips met in a tender kiss, tears rolling down both their faces.

Hatter whispered in a husky breathy voice, making their closeness so much more intimate. "From," he brushed kisses on her lips with every pause "the first, moment, I ever, felt you, I have loved you."

Rosie stared into Hatter's deep brown eyes, drowning in the reflection of his soul. "I think I've loved you from the first time I felt your comfort, like our souls have always been connected." She tenderly kissed him again, keeping her eyes open to memorize every pore and she laughed weakly when she realized he was doing the same. They stared into each other's eyes, both feeling too weak to move but not wanting to be anywhere else. Rosie could feel Hatter's heart pounding sluggishly, getting slower and slower, and watched as the fire in his eyes seemed to flicker and dim as his eyes closed. His heart beat held long moments between them until she feared it had stopped. Rosie's heart keened, breaking.

"Hatter?" Panic pulled energy from deeper in her depleted reserves, she couldn't let him die like this. Rosie instinctively gathered every bit of stray energy that she could and kissed Hatter, hard, with everything she was and everything she could use to save him. A wind stirred around them, just like the one that constantly swirled around Rosie's childhood protector. Then a wash of healing light poured from Rosie into her Hatter, closing open wounds and healing bruises before she fell away from Wonderland.

◌

13

Back in the Prime Material Rosie's efforts had a cost, as the wounds in her back pulled further open and bled, her memory of their meeting leaked away. She struggled to hold on to the memory of Hatters face, but it slipped away from her in the gray place between worlds.

Rosie was snapped back to consciousness by both the pain in her back and the sound of Jack yelling in her ear. "Rosie! Answer me! What happened? It was not supposed to go like this. Rosie!"

"Calm down, Jack, I'm here." Rosie sounded bleary. "I'm ok, I got away."

"What is wrong with you! You screamed and then went quiet for like ten minutes!" Rosie could hear anger burning in his tone before he took a calming breath and switched jarringly to a very neutral tone. "You are not allowed to scare me like that. What happened to you?"

Rosie tried to piece things together, but was having trouble thinking around the pain in her back. "I don't know, it's all a little fuzzy. I remember going through the door into a dark place..." She started to sit up and her back twinged with the motion. "Ow."

Jack sounded annoyed "Ow, really. If something really hurts you don't say ow."

"I'm sorry Jack, I think I must have hit my back

on something, it really hurts."

"Then scream, saying ow is fake. If I have to I'll hurt you till you know real pain, till I break you of 'ow'." His tone was disgust, and Rosie was too tired to deal with Jack right now.

"Jack, it hurt so I said ow. I went into my nightmare, where you sent me, and was attacked by the monster in the dream." Rosie was pretty fed up with Jack's quirks and moods, and as her head cleared her back hurt more and there was something rubbing her wrong about Jack. Usually Jack's threats struck like a blow she felt she deserved, but at this moment she was in too much pain and felt such loss of something that she saw Jack's comments as nothing more than manipulation to keep power over her.

"Don't blame me, you were supposed to take me into your dream so I could help you." Jack was on the defensive, and it was a position he knew he should not be in with Rosie. He was sure something happened in her dream that was somehow weakening his control over her. Months of work to get her just where he could take whatever he wanted whenever he wanted and she was too close to ruining it. Putting her in a trance state to find out what was stalking her dreams was supposed to make him a hero and bind her close enough for him to feed off without even having to be together. He should be able to push her into doing anything he wanted, but instead she was pushing back.

A champion must have showed up to help her, it was the only thing he could think of that would give her an inch to pull free. He needed Rosie to see him as her protector, if she had any other option or she stood up for herself he would lose control of her and all her tasty little friends he was lining up to keep too. Jack needed a plan to leave him on the top of this food chain. He decided to gamble that she would not remember who helped her. "I went in after you to pull you out of there. Don't blame me that you went in alone, or for how long it took you to wake up. If I hadn't scared your little nightmare off, who knew what would have happened to you."

Something didn't seem right about Jack's claims, but she had a fuzzy memory of someone standing between her and the nightmare monster. Why was that memory already so hard to access? Wasn't lucid dreaming supposed to make it so you could remember more? Maybe he had come to help her. Rosie suddenly wondered why she had doubted him at all. He was her boyfriend and he loved her, of course he would come to help her. "...Was that you? I'm sorry, my memory is just so foggy. I remember someone standing between me and the monster now, of course it was you."

Jack thought to himself 'well that paid off' and decided to press it further. "I wanted to see if you could defeat it on your own, but I had to help you when I knew you needed it. Like the other times the monster almost got you, you know I've come to help you before, right?"

Rosie's cheeks flushed with embarrassment and shame, she had been thinking that the person who helped her in her dreams was the presence she had felt here in her room; hadn't she? Maybe what she felt here was really all in her imagination. "I'm, I'm sorry, I should have know that was you." She stammered "Why didn't you tell me it was you pulling me out of the nightmares?"

Jack was furious, he knew it wasn't him, and now he knew that there was someone else. She would pay for her infidelity. "I find it interesting that you didn't mention being helped before. Why was that, Rosie?"

"I don't know," Rosie was feeling nervous and was having trouble forming thoughts around the pain in her back, how did she explain spending intimate time with a possibly imaginary ghost-like presence that she thought was the one responsible for saving her. "It's hard to remember details from dreams once you wake up, especially after such a crazy recurring nightmare."

Seemed plausible, but she hated lying to Jack. The pain in her back flared again when she brushed against one of the pillows in her nest and she took in an involuntary hiss of breath. What had she done to her back? Rosie looked around her, but she couldn't find anything that she could have hurt herself on. Maybe she just strained the muscles worrying about the monster catching her.

As Rosie searched for what had made her back sore Jack commented. "See, that's a pain sound. Not 'ow'." There was a edge of venom to his tone that made Rosie pause in her search, wondering if Jack knew that she'd lied about why she didn't mention the help out of her nightmares. "Didn't I tell you to set things up so that you wouldn't hurt yourself?" The words conveyed concern, but not Jacks tone.

"I did. I set things up so that if I moved around I would be fine. I'm looking around and I can't see anything I could have hurt myself..." She searched for anything hard or sharp as she spoke, but instead noticed some dark damp spots on her pillow cases and blankets. A feeling of apprehension stole Rosie's words. She rubbed a finger in one of the wet spots and slowly turned her hand face up. From the first glimpse of red, she knew exactly what was on the bedding. "Oh my God." She whispered in shock.

"What's with all the drama?" Jack sounded tired and annoyed "Did you break whatever little girl toy you were laying on?"

Rosie stared at her hand in shock, "No," she whispered "it's blood."

Silence filled the air as the seconds ticked by, feeling like hours to Rosie. She sat frozen, staring at the blood, thinking it looked too bright in contrast to her pale skin. She knew that the blood must be from her back, and It struck her as all too surreal.

"What do you mean blood?" Jack sounded surprised and shaken. He couldn't understand where blood would have come from. "Do you mean your period started?"

"No" Rosie almost whispered the reply in a numb tone, still staring at the bright red of fresh blood smeared on her fingers.

"Then what did you cut yourself on woman?" Jack's outrage began to creep back into his tone. "Where's the blood from?"

"I, I think it's from my, my back." She stammered out harshly. "There is nothing anywhere near me that could have cut me, but I can feel the cool wetness of blood soaking through the back of my shirt and there's blood on the bedding where I was laying."

"But that's impossible. How are you bleeding if nothing cut you? There has to be something you cut yourself on."

"Nothing here." she said, fear creeping into her hoarse whisper. "But the nightmare monster, I remember something happening." A sudden visual memory flooded her mind's eye. She saw a weird nasty hand like claw at the end of some weird long spindly appendage slashing at her. The hand like thing, or was it more like a fleshy talon, had three jointed 'fingers' with long nasty sharp hooked claws. She saw it reaching at her through the darkness, grabbing for her. Rosie thought she would suffocate in the thick fear this image brought her. "I think it got to me, grabbed me by the back..." She trailed off because it was just too much to take in. She was hurt in the dream, and now she bled in the waking world. She was afraid, but knew she had to look and see if the marks on her back would match the monsters claws. Her rational mind screamed that there was no way she could bring injury out of a dream, there must be something here she hurt herself on.

As she tried to convince herself that there was a rational explanation another flash of memory hit her, like her subconscious fighting back against her denial. The three fingered claw swiping at her from behind in her peripheral vision as she ran. This had happened in her nightmares many times before, but this time the claw swiped close enough to see and then landed. Pain raked down her back as the claws latched into her flesh like a grappling hook pulling her off her feet. It all happened so fast, the flash of image was so real that she felt the claws hooked into her skin and being pulled backwards, flung to the hard ground, the air pushed from her lungs with the impact. She struggled to breathe just with the memory of the impact. Then she remembered the weight of the monster, the pain in her back as it used the claws in her to pull itself on top of her, a drip of cold slimy saliva hitting her cheek as she started to black out, then someone wrestling with the monster in flashes of muddled images. The memory was intense and overwhelming.

She came back to her senses with Jack again yelling in her ear. "Rosie! You will answer me! What is going on?" She tried to answer, but found it hard to breathe enough to get around her own fear. Was that the attack she just survived? "I said answer me bitch!" That snapped Rosie out of it.

"What?" her voice was faint, coming out almost as a squeak.

"Where did you go?" Jacks voice trembled with rage. "Why are you toying with me girl?"

"I'm sorry Jack, but something happened..."

Rosie heard a door slamming on the other end of the line, followed by yelling. She couldn't make out what was being said, but recognized the voice as Jack's mom. Rosie could hear Jacks placating tones as he responded to the yelling. The sound was a little muffled, like he had his hand over the receiver. "I'm sorry. I didn't mean to wake you. I'm getting off now." And the line clicked off.

Hanging up, Rosie felt abandoned and traumatized. She also felt weirdly emotionally numb, she knew that her back really hurt bad but it somehow wasn't getting through to her. She had bits and pieces of her nightmare back, but knew that there was more she just couldn't remember. She was missing something important, something she just couldn't put her finger on. The numbness was helping in a way, she would probably be freaking out right now if not for being in shock.

଍

Rosie collected herself and took stock of her situation. She needed to check her back and see how bad the damage was, and she needed to clean up the blood before morning. Rosie wasn't sure how to explain any of this to her parents. They were logical rational people that didn't believe in any kind of magic, they didn't even believe in religion; how could they believe in a monster that attacked through dreams. No, they definitely couldn't handle dream walking, seeing people's Fey natures, or that monsters were sometimes real. Best to handle all this without them. Which meant all evidence had to be cleaned up.

Rosie reached for one of the blood stained pillows and the pain in her back caught her off guard. 'Ok. Deal with the back first.' She thought to herself. With a little effort and a good amount of pain she managed to carefully and slowly make her way across the room to the mirror mounted on the back of her closet door. She gingerly pulled her hair to one side and tried to see her back in the mirror. Her night shirt was ruined, the back was soaked with blood already drying brown and crusty at the edges. She didn't think she could pull it over her head, but needed to take off the night shirt to tend to her back. Continuing to move slowly and cautiously she got the scissors from her desk and cut up the center of her shirt like they did in medical TV shows. She managed to peel off the night shirt with some difficulty, the blood was making the fabric stick to the wounds. It was tough, but she managed to get a look at her back in the mirror, and as much as she really wanted to explain the wound away it was clearly made by her nightmare monster. Two jagged down slashes with a gouge between them clearly going up. Blood was still welling from the scratches and smeared drying across her back. The blood made it hard to see how bad it really was, but it was clear that Rosie needed help to dress the wound.

She couldn't call Jack, he had trouble of his own to deal with besides the bus trip from his house at this time of night would take an hour at least. She started thinking about her friends, and quickly ruled out most of them because of travel time and chance of parents picking up the phone angry. Eventually she came to Janet. Janet was one of Rosie's best friends in grammar school, but they hadn't hung out much in years. That was true for a lot of Rosie's friends since she started to date Jack. There were a few reasons to think of Janet. One was because her folks were older and less likely to hear the phone ring. Another was because Janet's bedroom was just off the kitchen and the wall phone in there was almost in grabbing distance from her bed. Then there was the most important bit, Janet knew her way around a first aid kit. She was the youngest in a big family, and was always her mother's helper when injuries happened.

Getting Janet's number was tricky with Rosie's injury, but with a little patience she was able to get to the Rolodex in the kitchen and call. A sleepy voice picked up on the second ring "yeah?" Rosie was relieved that her gamble paid off and it was Janet's voice on the other end.

"Hi Janet, it's Rosie." She whispered, feeling very exposed standing half naked and bleeding in her kitchen. All Rosie needed was to have her parents wake up and find her like this.

"Rosie? What are you doing calling me at..." There was a fumbling sound on the other end as Janet found her watch "1am?" Janet was whispering too, her talking was less likely to wake her parents, but some of her siblings were old enough to be as much trouble as a parent.

"I'm sorry Janet, but I need help and I didn't

know who else I could call at this time of night."

"What about your parents?" Rosie could tell from Janet's tone of voice that she was suddenly wide awake and concerned.

"They aren't an option, they'd never believe what really happened. And I need help dressing a wound I can't."

Rosie was feeling increasingly self-conscious whispering in the kitchen, and was beginning to worry she would have to explain the whole situation when Janet quickly responded. "Your wound?"

"Yes." Rosie responded sheepishly.

"Are you home?"

"Yes."

"I'll be there in fifteen." She paused for a quick moment of thought "Do you need me to bring bandages?"

"It might be tricky to get stuff out of the bathroom without waking my parents." Rosie sounded apologetic.

"Ok, I'll be there in twenty with the first aid kit. Front door or back?"

"Back." Rosie said with some relief, then heard the phone click as Janet hung up. Rosie was thankful that Janet was such a true friend that she could not speak to her for years and still count on her like they were just as close as ever.

◌ঽ

14

Twenty minutes later Rosie was waiting at the foot of the back door steps, with a dish towel covering her chest, feeling a bit chilly. It was late enough spring that it was shorts weather during the day, but it was still nippy in the middle of the night. With much effort she had managed to get some pants on, but couldn't figure out any way to put a shirt or bra on without disturbing the wound. Getting down the steps was also a challenge, but she thought moonlight would be better than darkness to clean her back. Turning lights on would likely wake someone, and if cleaning the wound hurt, she was far enough away that any noises she made wouldn't wake anyone.

Rosie heard the side gate squeak before she saw Janet coming. She had her long blond hair in a disheveled ponytail and was wearing slightly rumpled hello kitty pajamas and gym shoes. She was carrying a backpack over one shoulder and Rosie could see Janet's bike tucked in a shadow in the gangway. Janet looked worried when she saw Rosie, and it made Rosie wonder if she looked worse than she realized.

"Oh, honey. What happened to you?" Janet sounded concerned as she guided Rosie out of the shadows to get a better look at her.

Rosie started to shrug as a reflex and pain stopped her mid-motion with a hissed intake of breath. "I'd say it was a long story, but it's more weird than long. Um, ok maybe it's long and a little unbelievable." Janet swept Her friend's hair around to the front and elicited a pained "ow" from Rosie. "Could I explain it after I'm patched up and have a shirt on?"

"Of course, sweetie. Now come sit down so I can clean you up." They sat in the small back yard on the old wooden bench that sat up against the red brick garage, and Janet pulled a first aid kit out of her backpack setting it up like a little triage station. Rosie had always loved Janet's kind but practical nature. She was confident about her abilities in a way that was comforting to Rosie, and she was glad that Janet wasn't asking questions just yet. Rosie really wasn't sure where to start or how to explain things in a way that didn't sound insane. She was grateful for the time to think.

Janet started with cleaning Rosie's back, explaining "Once your back's all cleaned up, I should be able to see how bad the damage is." She pulled cotton swabs and a brown generic looking plastic bottle out of the kit. She handed Rosie a bottle of pills, "It's ibuprofen for the pain," and then handed her a bottle of water. "Take a couple while I prep." Rosie took two generic white tablets while Janet soaked the cotton balls in hydrogen peroxide.

"Ok, back facing me." Rosie turned sideways on the bench a little stiffly, trying not to jostle the wounds. Janet started to blot at Rosie's back, gently wiping away the smeared blood, and sighed "I am sorry honey, but the waistband is a little soaked, looks like you've almost stopped bleeding but it's been dripping and you are probably going to have to trash these bottoms and undies when were done."

"I kinda figured that would be the case." And with that the conversation was over except for a few hissed intakes of breath as the peroxide bubbled and fizzed painfully cleaning her wounds.

∞

Some time, half a bottle of hydrogen peroxide, several butterfly bandages, and a roll of gauze tape later, Janet had Rosie all patched up. She was helping Rosie get a shirt on over her head when Janet broke the silence. "Ok. So now that you are all bandaged like a mummy, want to tell me how you got into a fight with Captain Hook at one in the morning."

Rosie resisted shrugging, "It was closer to midnight when it happened." It was a statement, but Rosie's voice crawled up a bit at the end almost like it was a question.

"That's what you really want to lead with." Janet commented dryly.

"It's the only believable part of the story."

"Rosie, we have been friends a long time. I've never known you to lie, so I will believe what you say; even if it sounds unbelievable."

"Well," she paused deciding how to start. "You know how we could visit each other's dreams sometimes when we used to hang out a lot?"

"Yup." Janet was wary of where this story was

going.

"And I've told you about the dream world I used to go to about half the time when I slept?"

"Used to? As in not anymore?"

Rosie started to nod, and could feel the butterfly bandages pulling so stopped abruptly, "Yeah, used to. Things have changed a lot recently. I haven't been able to," she took a deep breath "since I lost my virginity." Rosie blurted out the last bit quickly, not sure how her friend would react.

Janet's eyes widened in surprise, but she said nothing letting Rosie finish. "I also haven't been able to get there since I've either been imagining or, how do I say this-" she screwed up her courage and let out the confession. "So, either I'm crazy, and should be medicated, or I kinda have a spirit hanging around to comfort me..." She paused, blushing, "and he's a kinda sexually charged guy." Rosie couldn't make eye contact with her friend, "So, I'm thinking its kinda an innocence lost kind of 'can't find my way back' kinda thing." As Rosie said it she knew deep down somewhere that what she had just said was right.

"Ok, but where does your back getting mauled come in?" Janet's tone was curious, where Rosie expected disbelief. This encouraged Rosie, and she met Janet's eyes to finish.

"So, ever since I couldn't get to my protector, I've been having these nightmares. There's this monster, and I kind of remember him from before as being small and not so dangerous back when I was with, Her."

Janet knew from Rosie's stories of dream training with her protector, that the woman was 'beyond needing a name' so Rosie usually called her 'Her'. Janet liked the image Rosie painted of the ageless and beautiful woman with almost godlike power that trained Rosie for something she could never remember after she woke up.

"But since I haven't been able to get to Her, the

monster has gotten really, really, scary. It stays in the dark, but it's grown and has more appendages and claws and tentacles." Rosie shivered pulling up bits of images of a huge thing undulating in the shadows chasing her. "And it's been hunting me almost every time I fall asleep. I got away every time, sometimes with the help of ... Jack I guess," as she said it didn't feel right, but she continued. "I always got away, that is, until tonight."

"No, you're shitting me. Right?" Janet sounded more scared than skeptical.

"I wish."

"The monster in your nightmares did this to you in reality?"

"Yea. Jack talked me into trying to bring him along into my nightmare, to help me deal with my monster. And I remember him putting me under, over the phone..." Rosie paused again looking for the right words "Then the dream is kinda foggy, except for the monster getting me, and it had me by the back, and someone came to my rescue," again Rosie wondered why she didn't say Jack instead of someone. "Jack, I guess, and then waking up feeling like I lost something important and my back killing me." Rosie made full eye contact with Janet, eyes wide with the fear she'd been suppressing with shock. "I swear, I looked all over and there wasn't anything in my room that could have scratched me like that. The only explanation is that the monster really scratched me."

Janet nodded slowly, a look of dawning realization crossing her face. "Like elm street? For real." She said in a loud whisper, like if saying it louder would give the idea more power.

"I think so." Rosie replied apologetically. "I'm kinda afraid to go back to sleep."

"I would be too." Janet seemed to completely believe Rosie, and that took some weight off of Rosie's shoulders. "Those claw marks in your back are not something you'd get bumping into something in your sleep. I butterflied the cuts, but if you aren't careful they won't hold and you'll need stitches. Those are some serious wounds. And they are weird cause all three scratches are parallel but the middle one goes in the opposite direction from the others."

"It hooked me with a three fingered claw. Two going down and one gripping up like an opposable thumb." Rosie gestured with her thumb and two fingers in example pinching at the air.

"That fits the wounds alright." Janet confirmed.

"So, that's why I can't tell my folks. They wouldn't believe it at all, and I'm kinda scared they might commit me. They really don't believe in magic."

"You did the right thing, calling me. I'm glad you trusted me enough to let me in on this. You shouldn't have to face this thing alone. I'm thinking that maybe we make sure you aren't alone while dreaming for a while."

Rosie felt hopeful. "You offering to take a shift?"

"For you, sweetie, I'll be there to watch your back. So long as we can figure out how to jump into each other's dreams again. It has been a couple years."

"I've been practicing, I could pull you in if you're willing." Rosie started to think of other friends that might be willing to take a shift. Maybe she'd be able to sleep again after all.

"Ok." Janet sounded a bit scared. "Think the monster will come right back?"

"I think he's wounded. It's all really jumbled, but I remember someone fighting it after it attacked me." Rosie kept trying to say Jack, but it set wrong. Jack didn't seem hurt at all, but she was sure there was fighting and blood aside from hers. But the more she tried to remember the more elusive the memory.

Janet took a deep breath, obviously relieved. "Ok, then, chickie. You are all patched up for now. If we are careful, your folks won't be the wiser. But we both better get back to our own beds before the parents wake up and find us missing." Janet packed the first aid kit back up and shoved it into her back pack. "Give me half an hour to get home and back to sleep, then you go to bed and grab me. I'll make sure you get some rest. But, I need the dish on you not being a virgin and this hot ghost guy, soon." She raised her eyebrows a few times quickly in a suggestive manner, and that got a smile from both of them.

Rosie walked Janet to the gate. "You don't know what it means to me that you believe me." She went to give Janet a gentle hug, and touching her arm she could clearly see Janet's little bit of more than human. Rosie saw Janet as a spirit of home and hearth, like a gnome, a brownie, or a Hobbit from Lord of the Rings. Janet had rosy plumper cheeks, and was built stouter and shorter than she really was; and as soon as the image overlapped Janet's appearance, it was gone. It was how Rosie often saw her friends' heritages.

They hugged goodbye, careful not to disturb the bandages, and after Rosie watched Janet take off on her bike, she went back upstairs to hide the rest of the evidence. She hoped her parents didn't remember what p.j.s she wore to bed, 'cause she'd be getting up in the morning wearing something else.

The rest of the night went pretty well. Rosie got things cleaned up, and was off to sleep in about an hour. Once asleep she grabbed Janet with little effort, and Rosie was able to rest. Sleeping on her stomach.

ଓ

15

In the morning; or the morning for Rosie, she slept in till noon, Rosie checked her wounds in the mirror. They looked a little scary, but they had scabbed over nicely and were healing well after just one night. She wondered if maybe the wounds weren't as bad as she thought.

It being a Saturday, Rosie was able to spend a few hours tearing apart her room looking for anything that could make two scratches down and one up, but despite her thoroughness she found nothing.

Rosie tried to call Jack a couple times, but both times the line clicked and hung up. She wasn't sure if her phone was having technical difficulties or if he was hanging up on her. But Rosie figured after getting Jack in trouble with his mom last night, that maybe giving him some cooling-off time would be good.

That afternoon Rosie got together with Janet to fill her in on the intimate details. They met at Talley park, where they sat on a bench along one of the trails. It was far enough from the playground to be quiet and almost private except for the occasional dog walker or someone riding by on a bicycle. Perfect for a private conversation.

Settling in, Janet started. "So, how's the patient?"

Rosie smiled at her friend, "Thanks to you, I'm on the mend." She took Janet's hand looking really serious. "Truly, I don't know what I would have done if you hadn't picked up the phone and been willing to sneak out to help me last night. Not to mention, I don't think I would have been able to sleep for weeks after..." She trailed off for a moment, she couldn't seem to say the attack so settled for "that, without knowing someone was keeping an eye out for me. I think it's the first solid sleep I've gotten since the monster started chasing me. So, really, really, thank you."

Janet shrugged, "You would have done the same for me." Then changing topics slightly, "I brought along antibiotic ointment, and fresh bandages if you want me to take a look."

"Ya know, when I took a peek this morning the scratches didn't look nearly as bad as I thought they were last night."

Janet looked skeptical, pulled on the back of Rosie's collar and leaned over to peer down the back of her shirt. "Whoa, that is much better than last night.

Seriously, like freaky fast healing." She lifted up the back of Rosie's shirt to get a better look, to the surprise of a random jogger passing on the path. "I figured you'd need the gauze to protect the open wounds for at least a week, but you don't even need it after a night's sleep. Freaky." Janet poked at the scabs gently. "You're even able to wear a bra already. That's so weird."

Rosie, feeling very exposed holding down the front of her shirt with her back naked to the world, cleared her throat to get Janet's attention. "Oh, sorry." Janet smoothed down the back of Rosie's shirt a little awkwardly.

"Things are obviously not normal about any of this." Rosie said turning back to Janet. "I kinda feel like I've fallen down the rabbit hole lately."

Janet laughed, but sobered a bit when she realized that Rosie was serious. Trying to lighten the mood she commented. "Does it help any that you are more like the white rabbit than Alice."

"Cotton tail joke. Cute. Never heard that one before." She kept her tone dry, but couldn't help but smirk at Janet's sheepish smile. They laughed a bit together. "Your right, if I take things too seriously I'll go madder than the Hatter."

Something about Rosie's last statement caught her own attention. Was it something about the Wonderland reference? Something about the Mad Hatter? It felt like loss, like it was related to dreams she couldn't quite remember and couldn't quite let go of. Was it related to the dream world she seemed to be locked out of, or was it about last night?

"What's going on in that ginger head of yours? You suddenly looked real serious, did you remember something from last night?" Janet snapped Rosie out of her thoughts.

"I don't know, it's like there's something on the tip of my brain that I just can't quite access." Rosie shook her head trying to clear her thoughts. "It bothers me that I lose so much when I wake up. I feel like I'm always in the dark with my own life."

"Maybe there's a reason we forget our dreams. Maybe our minds are protecting us from what's over there or something. I mean, look at what happened to your back. How much worse do you think it was before you woke up."

"I don't know, I feel like something really good happened before I woke up. I got hurt bad, but there was something..."

"Like your invisible hunk of man?" Janet said suggestively, worried that Rosie would get sucked into a melancholy of loss.

"No, Jack said he was the one that came to save me..." As Rosie said it, it sat badly with her just like last night.

"Sounds like you are trying to convince yourself. What do you really remember from your nightmare last night?"

"Mostly flashes and images, I'm pretty sure I've even lost some since last night."

"Just walk through it with me, maybe it'll jog you're memory." Janet encouraged Rosie to continue.

"Jack wanted to do this at midnight, so I set up some soft blankets and pillows and lit a white candle to focus on. He called on time, and led me into a trance state."

"I don't think putting someone in a hypnotic state over the phone and sending them into a nightmare is a safe idea at all." Janet commented dryly.

Rosie shrugged, not disagreeing, and continued. "I focused on the flame," Rosie caught herself recalling a detail from when she woke up. "That's odd, I remember lighting the candle, and it was going when I went under, but it was out when I woke up a few minutes later. I'm sure I didn't blow it out, and there's no breezes that would have put it out. I wonder what put it out?"

"You wake up with your back all clawed up and

a candle going out is bothering you?"

Rosie shrugged again and continued on. "Well, you wanted me to go over the whole night." Janet gestured for Rosie to continue. "Ok, I remember Jack telling me to go through the door into my nightmare."

"Trance door, not physical door right?"

"Right. Construct in my mind, not a real door." She continued on with her story. "After the door is where everything gets fuzzy. I have images of a weird appendage reaching for me while I ran. And I remember the claws hooking into me, and incredible pain. I kinda remember thinking I was going to die. And then there was someone there fighting the monster to save me. When I woke Jack said it was him." Again it sat wrong with her.

"You obviously have reservations about that. Why?"

"I don't know, something just feels wrong. Maybe the shape was wrong of the man standing between me and he monster. But it was pitch dark, it couldn't be that." Rosie picked at her memory trying to put a finger on it, then it came to her. "Roses! I smelled roses!"

"And this is significant why?"

"It's the smell of my protector." Rosie's heart pounded jut at the thought of his scent.

"Her?" Janet prompted.

"No, him." Rosie blushed, feeling kinda tingly just invoking his idea.

"Sexy spirit guy?"

Rosie nodded, averting her eyes, her blush deepening.

"Not to change the subject, but what exactly has happened with your invisible friend?" Rosie blushed, but didn't offer Janet an answer. "Rosie, you are in a relationship. What is going on with this guy while you are with Jack?"

"I know. I feel awful. But I don't even know if

he's real. It could all be in my imagination." Rosie defended herself, but still couldn't make eye contact.

"But, what kind of 'comfort' did you get from mister 'sexually charged' that you know what he smells like?"

Rosie was blushing crimson by now. "I can smell him before I can feel him."

"Ooh, feel him huh? How much feeling are we talking about? You didn't lose your virginity with a ghost did you?"

"No, that was Jack." Rosie said with more than a little shame. "I'm in a relationship with Jack. I love him. We've been dating for months before I said yes. It wasn't perfect, but the first time usually is bad right? Painful?"

"It wasn't for me." Janet shrugged. "But I hear sometimes the first time isn't what you'd want it to be." She said consolingly. After an awkward moment Janet prompted Rosie. "So, you are with Jack. But it was painful so you took comfort in the arms of a possibly imaginary invisible man?"

"Yes." Rosie almost whispered her answer. "Makes me sound like a slut doesn't it?"

"I don't know about that. But so far, you've said that Jack hurt you during sex, and convinced you to put yourself in mortal danger that I had to come help you with. I'm wondering why you're with Jack, whether your mystery man is real or not."

"No, I love Jack. I want to spend the rest of my life with him. I'm just a little confused about the other guy. Jack is complicated, and has a lot of stuff going on. He has some unorthodox methods, but he loves me too, and means well. 'He's' just kind when Jack is cruel."

"If he loves you, why would he need to be cruel?"

"It's complicated, and I don't want to go into that. I love him, that's all that matters."

"If love is enough for you, why fool around with the other guy?"

Tears began to flow down Rosie's cheeks. She was so guilty about Jack, she loved him. But there was a deep connection with her guardian angel too. "Maybe because I don't know if he's real. He feels like everything I want when I want him; that can't be real, can it?"

"I can't say if he's real, but it seems like he is real in your mind if nothing else. If he isn't real outside yourself, and he makes you feel good, and is able to jump in to help you when you think you are about to die..." Janet shrugged. "I guess what I'm trying to say is, if he is a construct of your imagination there's no harm done and help gained. If he is real, you can choose between the two of them when you get evidence of that. No reason to beat yourself up over a boy you can't see. It's obvious he fills a need for you." Janet wrapped an arm around Rosie's shoulder. "I'm sorry, I was trying to get dish, not get you crying."

"I'm sorry too. I hate being all weepy." Rosie wiped her cheeks and sniffed her running nose. She laid her head on Janet's shoulder and sighed. "I think I have real feelings for both of them, but I wish I knew if my guardian angel was real. I just feel so guilty, and you are the only person I've told."

Janet looked down at Rosie and waggled her eyebrows "What exactly do you have to feel guilty over? I soo want details."

Rosie sat back up and smiled at Janet's attempt to change the mood. She made the effort to follow Janet's lead. "Oh my god, you don't even know. Every moment of contact with him is just so hot. He smells like spicy antique roses, and when he touches me it's like palpable desire."

"When he what? You can feel the incorporeal spirit guy touch you?"

"Yeah. When he first shows up its like tickling touches, just like electric currents with no substance behind them. But once when I closed my eyes, and focus on him he felt real."

"Like, real, real?" Janet prompted, totally engrossed in the idea.

"Oh, yeah. Really real. And my God can he kiss, it's just so beyond description." Rosie took a shuddering breath just thinking about him. "His lips are full and soft, his hair is thick and short but long enough to play with. And he is fit, 'cause I could feel his muscle tone when I touched him, and when he pressed against me..." She bit her lip thinking about how she would have easily gone too far if she hadn't opened her eyes and broke the spell.

"How much pressing are we talking here? Like kiss and a hug? Or a little heavy petting."

"Him on top of me kind of pressing, but fully clothed. Just thinking about him makes me want him like a drug." Saying that, Rosie felt a prickle along the skin of one arm, like fingertips trailing across her forearm and smelled musk and roses. Rosie inhaled deeply and put a hand over the place she felt his faint touch. No hand, but there was that warmth again that made her secure in his presence. His presence was faint, like he was struggling to be with her.

Janet's eyes widened, "What is that? My skin just broke out in goose bumps. You are generating some major psychic energy."

"He's here. It's faint, but he's here. I've never felt him anywhere outside of my bedroom."

Janet looked very seriously at Rosie "You just raised enough energy to pull a ghost to you, you have really gotten stronger than you ever were before. If he is a figment of your imagination, I get how you are able to make him feel real now; but if he is real and you are pulling him to you, and he was on the other side of the fight that wrecked your back last night..."

"Are you saying that me accidentally pulling him here could be hurting him when he needs to rest and heal?" The idea of causing further injury to her guardian angel pained Rosie. "I don't want him hurting because I accidentally called him." Rosie closed her eyes and whispered to him "I'm so sorry." Then she focused to actively shut down any power that might have pulled her angel to her. While she focused, Rosie felt a faint brush of his lips against hers and she almost lost her nerve and melted into the feel of his lips. But it was a parting kiss, and the smell of roses faded with the faint brush of his soft skin. His energy going was almost a physical pain, she wanted him so badly.

But before Rosie could call him back Janet placed a hand on her shoulder "Don't sweetie. If he needs to heal, and you make him spend energy getting to you, you could make things worse."

Rosie knew that Janet's logic was sound, and resisted the urge to have her angel with her. "Thanks, I just want him so bad. You're right, I won't risk calling him till he has a chance to heal too."

"Seems like you don't have any doubts that he was the one that came to your rescue last night. I guess that makes Jack a fibber for taking credit for helping you, and either ignorant or an ass for sending you into danger in the first place."

Rosie sighed and nodded. "I think you're right."

"So, was that all you remember from the nightmare?" Janet asked before Rosie started to wallow in being lied to.

"Pretty much. He saved me. I have some flashes of fighting with some truly awful damage sounds, he must have been wounded worse than me. But when I woke up, Jack was upset he didn't know where I was. He said he chased my monster away, but he wasn't hurt at all. He almost had me convinced that it was him who pulled me from my nightmares the times before when I almost didn't get away." Rosie smacked her forehead with realization, "And now Jack knows I have a male protector. No wonder he sounded so pissed after he took credit for saving me."

"Maybe you can convince him that the guy saving you is an aspect of you, since he might be." Rosie nodded, but was pretty sure that Janet thought Rosie's spirit was an entity of his own, not just a manifestation of Rosie's imagination. "Or maybe it's time to break up with the liar."

Rosie considered breaking up with Jack for a moment, but couldn't think of it longer than that. "I know he lied to me, but I still love him; and I don't toss that around lightly. I know he isn't perfect, but I love him." Rosie realized that before her first encounter with her angel, she wouldn't have even considered breaking up with Jack for a second. She wondered if her love for Jack wasn't as pure and true as she thought.

"Ok, not my life. Who you are or aren't with is up to you. No judgment. Maybe there is more to this Jack than I know, if you love him he must have great qualities. But don't tear yourself up over the sexy ghost, sounds like he's been working hard to protect you. And the way you react to him is cosmic, don't let that go unless you have to."

"Thanks for the advice, Janet." And Rosie meant it, another voice of encouragement over her guardian angel made her feel a little less guilty for wanting him so badly.

"The only question is, what are you going to do about your nightmare monster? You look really tired, and you need enough sleep to finish healing that back of yours."

"I wouldn't ask you to dream walk with me every night, but if you will some nights, maybe some of my other friends would too."

"Ok. I got your back again tonight, but not every night. I don't think I'm as rested the next day after going into your dreams."

"I'll find friends to rotate through, I promise I won't use you every night." They formally shook over the agreement, and said their goodbyes. Rosie needed to go home and figure out who else would and could act as guard for her dreams. Safety in numbers, the monster only chased Rosie when she was alone in the dark so long as she kept the lights on in her dream they should be fine.

ᘓ

16

When Rosie got home it was already dinner time, so she was preoccupied during the family meal thinking about who else to asking for help. She pulled off normal for her folks, and they were none the wiser about her injury. But they were a little skeptical when she skipped on TV to go 'read'. She didn't want to give away anything by being uneasy leaning back against the sofa.

Rosie tried to call Jack, it distressed Her to not hear from him for a full day, but again the phone picked up and hung up. If there had been any doubt before, Rosie was sure now that Jack was hanging up on purpose. With the last thing she heard from him being Jack getting in trouble, Rosie bet Jack blamed her for all the trouble he got in. That would probably be enough for the silent treatment, but Rosie knew Jack had figured out about the man saving her. Jack was really territorial when it came to other guys around Rosie. It wouldn't be the first time he accused Rosie of cheating, but it would be the first time that there was anything to it. Whether Rosie's guardian angel was a construct from her own mind or not, she lusted after him in a deep primal way; and Rosie shouldn't be thinking of anyone like that unless it was Jack. But her guilt wasn't helping anything, and she was tired after so many nights of disturbed sleep.

Rosie needed to sit down and figure out who she might be able to pull into her dreams that would be willing to help. Rosie had more practice dream walking than most, and not everyone was able or willing to share their subconscious mind.

Maybe it would be best to just go to sleep tonight and see who she could make contact with. She would start with Janet, since she was already in. The next person that made sense was Chris, he was like a brother to her so he'd totally be willing to take a watch, and Rosie was pretty sure she could pull him into her dreams. Rosie knew that Jack could come into her dreams, but she wasn't sure he wanted to talk to her much right now. She decided to save Jack for last.

Rosie wanted a couple more options so that no one got too tired out walking into Her dreams. She thought for a bit, which other friends would have enough extra to dream walk? There was Wendy, they had shared dreams a few times, but Rosie lost trust in Wendy. She was encouraging Rosie to break up with Jack while on several occasions Rosie found out Wendy was spending time alone with her boyfriend. Rosie hadn't spent much time on their friendship after that. Jack and Wendy said they were just hanging out as friends, but Rosie was a little skeptical. Never the less, Wendy had been a good friend for years before Jack came along and Rosie was sure Wendy would help if she asked. All Rosie needed to do was decide if their friendship was stronger than a boy.

Rosie thought of her other friends, and wasn't sure if there was anyone else that had enough extra to dream walk with any control. Then she thought of a friend that probably could easily enter Rosie's dreams. She hadn't known Frank for long, but he was a good person and she knew he had that something extra in him. If Rosie could make contact, she was sure Frank would be willing to help. Including herself and Jack it would give them three boys and three girls, if everyone was in it would be a well balanced group.

Something tugged at the back of her mind, a thought of her mysterious guardian angel in Jacks place. But she knew that was a wrong thought, it should be her serious boyfriend. She should want the man that she loved, enough to give her virginity to, to be the one she trusted most to protect her. She should have no reservations about Jack, and she usually didn't, why was she doubting him now? And why would she deep down prefer a man she wasn't even sure existed outside her own psyche. Rosie spent some time trying to convince herself to not doubt Jack. The more time she spent telling herself that she loved Jack, the more thoughts of her protector slipped behind her conscious intentions. He was always there when she needed him, and Jack was often the cause of her distresses; but Jack was real, and Rosie had made a commitment to him.

The situation plagued her mind so much that she had to find another topic to deal with or she'd drive herself mad... What was it about being mad, but not that mad... Mad as a Hatter...Rosie just couldn't place the thought. It must have been something half remembered from a dream.

In the last few hours before bed Rosie tried to take care of mundane things, like homework, but found that she just couldn't focus. Her thoughts wandered to the friends she would try to contact in her dreams and if just having a friend stand guard would keep her nightmare at bay, then if it worked how long would it work. Wondering what was going on with Jack, then thoughts of Jack brought on her guilt over her angel. Her heart was torn between Jack and her guardian angel, and it was very unsettling.

She knew she wouldn't be able to get anything productive done, so she got ready for bed early. She was afraid to go to sleep too early because she would be alone until she could make contact with another dreamer, and her friends had to be asleep before they could dream. Alone she felt like too much of a target, even sure that the monster was at least as hurt as she was, she didn't want to risk it taking a run at her because of opportunity. She tried to read again, with little success. Time ticked slowly by, and despite her fear Rosie's exhaustion was beginning to get the better of her.

Cβ

Rosie drifted off, and found herself in a hedge

maze. The hedges were at least half again Rosie's height, so she couldn't see over them. She walked along the path, sticking to the left whenever a turn came up. Rosie walked for a long time, following the path through turns and double backs, until she wondered if she was just walking in circles. She stopped for a rest and tried to peer through one of the bushes, but the foliage was so dense she couldn't see more than a few inches in. There was something in the hedge just past where she could easily see, and it looked like plastic tubing. Rosie reached in and pulled out a length of the clear tube, it seemed to have liquid in it. She pulled a little more and found a small plastic slide clamp followed by one of those drip things that get the air bubbles out of an I.V. line. Rosie tried to pull more of the tubing but found resistance.

She smelled roses and musk and dropped the tube to look for her angel. Rosie didn't see him, but the tube was gone now. She followed the maze further, thinking she might get a glimpse of her guilty secret, and found the center of the maze.

In the center was a well manicured lawn with a large stained glass window suspended impossibly in the middle. It had no supports, it just hung in mid air. The stained glass depicted a blue shield with three wheat sheaves and a yellow chevron in the middle. As Rosie continued to examine the window she realized it was lit from one side. It looked like sunlight was streaming through much brighter than it was in this garden maze.

She looked through a lighter glass pane and could make out a scene beyond, it didn't have the view this window should have had. She saw a large open meadow with softly rolling hills in the distance, some large old trees scattered around, and a few cows grazing on the light green grass. She was looking down on this idyllic vignette, like the window she was looking through should have been on a second floor somewhere.

Curiously walking to the other side of the

window, she looked through and saw a different scene. It was harder to make out this scene, because it was a dim room that looked to be lit only by the light through the stained glass window. Rosie looked through a few of the lighter panes and was able to make out that it was a bedroom with dark wood accents and a robust four poster bed with heavy tapestry curtains. A bedside table held a large bouquet of red and pink long stemmed roses. She also saw something out of place for this posh bedroom, an I.V. stand with an attached vitals monitor. She saw the little spiky line monitoring a heartbeat and numbers that she couldn't make out. The I.V. tube and some other monitoring cords snaked behind the closed bed curtains.

A sad masculine voice with a thick English accent, coming from behind her, startled Rosie. "Why did you send me away?" It tugged at the edge of a forgotten memory, she knew his voice. The sound was not just memory but dream, something velvety and foggy around the edges. She knew that there was a memory there that she just couldn't access, but she knew his voice. Rosie turned to see who was speaking, and saw a figure she couldn't quite make out, slumped in the shadows of the hedge. His face was obscured by a brown leather top hat. The hat matched the vague memories of the back lit figure who had saved Rosie from the nightmare monster, and Rosie just knew that it was the same man.

Rosie's heart leapt with joy and hope. "I wasn't trying to send you away. I was worried that you were hurt and didn't want you to be hurt worse using up energy to come to me."

"Really?" his tone was hopeful. He started to lift his face to Rosie but before she could see him, she was torn from her dream.

cs

Rosie awoke to the sound of her mother calling her. "Rosie, you have a phone call!"

Rosie wanted more than anything to go back to sleep and finish this dream. She tried to hold onto the curious dream shed just had, but felt it slipping. Had she seen her angels face? She'd heard his voice, and it made her think he was a part of her subconscious even more than before. It was too much of a coincidence that his accent happened to be the one that always made Rosie weak in the knees. And his hurt over being sent away, that was too perfect too; he reacted just the way Rosie would in the same circumstance, and the way she would want to be pined over. If he were real, he couldn't match her idea of the perfect guy so completely, but he did every time she encountered him. And what did the maze with the stained glass mean? It was a window out of place, she wondered what place it might belong to.

"Rosie did you hear me?" Her mother called again.

"Yes, I heard you. I'm coming." Rosie yelled back as she pulled the covers aside and got out of bed. Glancing at the clock she saw it was only 9:30pm.

Rosie walked out into the kitchen and picked up the phone on the wall by the back door. "I got it!" She called over her shoulder before putting the receiver to her face. Rosie heard the click of the phone being hung up from the front room before she spoke. "Hello?"

"Took you long enough to answer, I only have a few minutes before my mom gets back and I can't be on the phone when she gets back." It was Jack and he was annoyed with Rosie as usual.

Hearing Jack's voice did something to Rosie. A moment before she was sure that Jack had chosen to give her the silent treatment, but now it was obvious to her that it was his mother who was hanging up on her. "I'm sorry, I was laying down when you called. I haven't slept well since the nightmares started." She took a shaking breath, suddenly afraid to do anything to upset Jack.

"Fine. Come quicker next time I call." Jack sighed, and his tone changed. "I've been worried about you. When mom pulled me off the phone last night, I didn't get the chance to find out what happened to you. My mom's grounded me from the phone for a week and doesn't want me seeing you anymore."

Rosie felt sudden panic, and her voice came out almost as a squeak. "Are you breaking up with me?" Before the phone call Rosie had been debating why she was with Jack. But after hearing his voice, she felt a need to be with him that was overwhelming.

"Why do you always jump to conclusions?" His voice sounded stern, but Rosie could swear that there was a smile in his tone. "It just means that we need to be careful not to be caught. Don't call my house, I'll call you. And you can't come over here unless we know it will just be the two of us. School should be the same, except if you see my folks dropping me off or picking me up you don't come around till you are sure they are out of sight. We won't be able to see each other as often, but that will make it more special when we do see each other. And when we want to go out on the weekends or at night, I'll have Nick pick me up so that my mom thinks I'm out with the guys and I'll come see you instead."

All of Jack's plans seemed sound to Rosie, but in the back of her head she felt a bit like this plan was stilted in Jack's favor. He could see Rosie whenever he wanted, but she would always have to wait till he was in the mood to see her. If it was accept these new terms or be without Jack, then she picked Jack because when it came down to it Rosie loved him and it was better than losing him. "Ok. If that's what we need to do to get around your mom saying you can't see me, I guess it's what we'll do."

"So, what happened after my mom kicked me off the phone last night? Short version because mom will be back any minute, she just went to the corner for a gallon of milk." Rosie decided to slip out onto the back porch so that she could speak more freely without the chance of her folks over hearing. She stretched the phone cord through the door and pulled it shut over the cord.

Rosie kept her voice low, and told Jack what he wanted to know. "Well, I have some nasty gashes in my back from the dream monster. And I can't remember what exactly happened while I was in there, ya know how dreams are." She sighed and thought about telling Jack that she knew he wasn't the one who saved her, but decided to let it go, since her knight in shining armor probably wasn't anything more than a construct of her own mind. Rosie didn't want Jack thinking she was being untrue to him when what she was doing probably wasn't much different than imagination enhanced mental masturbation; all just her. "I got my friend Janet, I've told you about her before, to come over and patch me up. But I'm already healing pretty well."

"So, do your parents know what scratched you up?" Jack asked, seeming to be testing the ground for if Rosie ratted him out to her folks.

"Nope. Since Janet came to patch me up, they don't know anything about what happened. Besides, they wouldn't believe a nightmare scratched me in a dream and I have the wound in the real world. I think they would rather believe I lied than some nightmares can really hurt you."

"Did you have any more nightmares when you went to sleep?"

"No. But I think the monster got hurt, so it's less likely to attack unless there's an easy target. And I pulled Janet into my dream to keep watch, so no nightmares."

"Janet can dream walk too? I think it's time I got to know your friend Janet. It's always good to keep those of us with powers close to each other. Why didn't you just call Wendy? You've dream walked with her right?" Jack sounded genuinely interested, and Rosie was enjoying the conversation a lot because of it.

"Well, pulling anyone into my dreams or me going into theirs tends to be pretty tiring. It's not as bad as staying awake, but it's being alert all night -"

"Get to the point Rosie, you are rambling and wasting precious time. If I hear the garage door I'll have to hang up whether you are done or not." Jack's impatience was showing a bit.

"Sorry, Jack. The point I was making is, until I'm healed I need rest. And with the monster hurt, it won't stalk me as long as I'm not alone. But if I have the same person share my dreams every night to keep the monster at bay, they won't get enough rest."

"Any day now Cotton."

Rosie was starting to get a bit flustered by Jack's pressure, but continued. "Sorry. I was thinking that we could get a kind of team together, of people that can dream walk and stay with me while I sleep but not tire anyone out with too many nights too close together."

Jack was liking the idea of Rosie bringing him more talented people to give him their power and energy. He could have Rosie cultivate them, and then Jack could take what he wanted and they would chalk it up to being tired from being on watch. As long as no one Rosie picked was a threat to Jack's control over Rosie, it would work great. "Who were you thinking would make up this dream walking team of ours?"

"Well, Janet has already agreed to help some nights. And, of course, you would be part of the team."

"Of course." Jack's patience with Rosie was thinning, and he was tempted to hang up on her and tell her the next time he wanted to talk to her that his mom had come home, but decided to let Rosie finish so he could see if anyone she listed sounded tasty.

"And I had thought of asking Wendy, since we used to be close and had shared dreams not too long ago."

"Uh huh." Jack had been thinking about a way to

manipulate Rosie and Wendy into a three way. He was working on Wendy privately and it wouldn't be long until he had Wendy believing that Rosie was too suicidal to break up with so they'd have to keep their new relationship secret and he could get into Wendy's pants. The trick would be finding an angle to get them both to sleep with him at the same time. It would probably be better to keep the two women supervised so they didn't swap notes. Jack really liked the idea of two girls blowing him at once, then fucking each of them while the other one watched. Definitely images to save for later when he had some private time.

Jack realized Rosie hadn't stopped talking while he plotted his next sexual conquest, and tried to catch who she was talking about.

"... So I think if I approach it right I could teach them to share dreams and help out."

Rosie seemed to be talking about people other than Janet and Wendy, but Jack missed who. Sounded like Rosie was implying they hadn't dream walked before, Jack could use this. "I don't know if one person with you would be enough Rosie, maybe we should do watches of three at a time. You should pull one experienced person in with one of the new people. Who do you think would work well together?"

Rosie thought about pairings briefly. "Makes sense, safety in numbers right. So, how about we pair Chris with Janet, and Frank with Wendy? Frank and Wendy already know each other and are friends, and I bet Chris and Janet would work well together too."

"Were you thinking of anyone to pair with you and me?" Jack wanted to be sure there weren't any other people Rosie mentioned that he missed, or anyone else she knew and hadn't mentioned with Fey energy he could use. Jack was disappointed that the other two people Rosie was suggesting were off his menu, Jack was too hetero to feed off guys. But at least neither were threats to his feeding pool. Frank was loyal to Jack and wouldn't ever make a move on any girls Jack had tapped for himself, and Rosie's friend Chris was a fag so he wasn't much of a threat.

"I don't know if anyone else I know would be talented enough to dream walk with us. I could rotate people around, but I thought you would be powerful enough to keep the nightmare at bay without help." Rosie knew she was stroking Jack's ego a bit, but it was better than suggesting the only other person that could help may or may not be a part of her imagination that she had kissed.

"Good point. Besides, I bet a dream blow job would be almost as nice as a real one. And if we had an audience it'd be hard for you to do that for me without being all squeamish." That idea gave Jack some new currency to deposit in the spank bank, and he was ready to make that deposit now. Jack made sure to lower his voice and speak quickly to sell his performance. "I think I heard the garage door, you recruit the people we discussed tonight and I'll call you tomorrow to see how it went." and he hung up.

ॐ

18

Rosie looked at the kitchen clock as she came in and hung up the phone, it was still early for a Saturday. She hadn't been on the phone much more than ten minutes with Jack, making it not quite 9:45pm. Probably too late to call most of her friends' houses because of younger siblings' bedtimes, but still too early for anyone to be asleep. If she had been out, Rosie wouldn't be coming home for probably an hour or so, but her parents would likely protest if she wanted to go out now because it was too late to start an evening. Rosie felt restless and unsettled, she wanted to do something but was having trouble focusing because she was so tired.

Part of her really wanted to go back to sleep, and hope she could find her way back into the dream she was having. Rosie had almost seen her angel's face, and was intrigued by how the maze, and out of place window, related to him. She was sure there was a reason he was brooding in a shadow right by that stained glass window. She remembered that the window was a kind of knightly shield, and that matched with his English accent. Rosie went to her room and pulled out a sketch book and her colored pencils. Sitting down at her vanity, she drew the window to the best of her memory.

The background edges of the stained glass had been a milky white, so she left those areas the color of the paper. Most of the window had been taken up by a shield. It was dark blue with three golden yellow tied bundles of wheat, two at the top and one centered at the bottom. The three wheat sheaves were separated by an upside down v of the same golden yellow. There was a scrolling blue ribbon above the shield with writing she just couldn't remember, but was pretty sure was Latin or something similar based on other family crests shed seen before. Above that was a knights helmet and above that a small stag in the same golden yellow. Rosie was pleased with her final product, aside from the lettering it was pretty much what she remembered.

Rosie flipped to the next page in her sketch pad and started to draw out the room she saw through the window to the best of her memory. It didn't turn out quite as good, because the room was in so much shadow and she was trying to judge what colors would have been if she hadn't been looking through colored glass. Rosie worked to get the most detail that she could out of the bed with its heavy deep red drapes and carved dark wood bed frame, then she drew the big bouquet of red and pink roses with long dark green stems and leaves. Her memory of the I.V. and monitor was more vague but she tried to get the idea across with its white plastic case and the dark monitor with green readouts. When she was done with the bedroom sketch, she wasn't as satisfied, but it was as good as she could do without seeing the room better. She was sure she could do better if she saw the room again.

She flipped to a third page and tried her hand at the landscape she had seen looking through the stained glass on the opposite side from the bedroom. It turned out much nicer than the dark room. She got the meadow and the grazing cows, her cows weren't great but they were passable, and the trees and softly rolling hills in the background. When she was done it looked close enough to what she saw in her dream to help her remember the image.

Rosie finished up the third sketch and put her pad away. Looking at the clock, it was after 11:30pm. She had managed to focus on something long enough to get to a time when she might be able to find her friends in their dreams. She still felt unsettled, but was so exhausted that she needed to try to sleep.

She nestled back down between her blankets and lay in bed ready for sleep. But now that it was late enough she found fear of the monster keeping her awake. Rosie was exhausted, but she kept getting flashes of the gruesome three fingered clawed hand that had ripped into her back. She tried taking calming breaths but the fear rode her like she knew the nightmare monster was waiting for her just the other side of consciousness.

She had fallen asleep earlier without issue, what was different now? She just wanted so badly to be held and protected from the monster, why was it gripping her so badly now? The more she tried to relax and let the fear go, the tighter its grip felt. No matter how tired she was, sleep was not coming to her any time soon.

Rosie got back out of bed and grabbed her sketch book again. When she had a song stuck in her head sometimes hearing the song got it out. She thought the same might be true for the monsters clawed appendage. Rosie flipped past her other three drawings and started sketching the hooked claws. She used no color aside from the black pencil, and as she drew she put its odd three fingered hand in much more shadow than she usually drew with. When she was done, Rosie looked over her work and got a shiver. It was dead on. Exactly the image in her mind's eye. Rosie was often frustrated that her drawings didn't look enough like what she saw in her mind, but in this case part of her expected it to reach from the page and take a swipe at her. The image increased her anxiety instead of lessening it.

Rosie usually didn't draw much outside art class in school, and now she had done four in one evening. She flipped back to the stained glass image and tried to focus on it instead of her fear of the monster and how badly she wanted to burrow into a safe warm embrace. She wanted to be in Jack's arms... But why, he had never been protective of Rosie. She thought about the instinct and realized that it was her angel she really wanted, he was usually there to comfort her. Why was she substituting Jack in that role? As her boyfriend and the man she loved, Jack should be her safe place. Rosie's head began to hurt because it was in such conflict. Why were her emotions around Jack feeling so forced lately? And why did it feel like her nightmare monster was breathing down her neck

Her fear peaked and she hugged herself. Rosie made a dash for her bed, jumping the last foot because the irrational part of her mind expected the monster to grab at her ankles from under the bed. She wrapped herself in blankets and felt like she was fighting some mental trauma.

The smell of musk and roses settled over Rosie and her fear eased. She could feel the presence of her guardian angel nearby, and just knowing he was with her she was able to breathe easier. She felt her knotted muscles begin to relax with the brush of an invisible hand against her cheek. Her angel had such a safe calm presence that Rosie stopped thinking about the monster and instead lay back and took a few deep breaths. Inhaling the scent of her guardian, she was able to close her eyes and let her weary body sink into her bed. The way her covers were wrapped around her, it was easy to imagine she was snuggling into her angel's arms. As she drifted off, Rosie felt strong warm arms wrapped around her and the soft pressure of lips gently pressing to kiss the top of her head.

𝜙

Rosie inhaled her guardian angel's warm scent and opened her eyes. She knew instantly that she was in a dream, because she lay safe in his arms in an open meadow in the shade of a beautiful old oak tree. It was idyllic and peaceful, and there was no place Rosie would rather be. She snuggled against his warm chest and listened to his heart beat, feeling truly content. He had taken her away from her fear monster and brought her to this wonderful safe place with him. "Thank you." She breathed out the words, and felt him give her a little squeeze in response.

"How could I not come when you needed me?" He whispered, but there was a slight catch of pain in his smooth British accent and Rosie realized that he must still be very hurt, and he must have used too much energy to come get her.

Rosie wrapped her arms around her angel to hug him, but as her hands slid around him she felt him flinch. "You're still really hurt, aren't you?"

"Just a few scratches, I'll heal." His breathing seemed a bit labored, pointing to wounds much worse than a few scratches. "Thanks to you."

Rosie carefully touched the spot again that made her angel flinch, and saw blood seeping through his shirt. "Are your wounds opening back up?"

"For you, it's worth it." He said resting his cheek against the top of her head.

Rosie wasn't sure if she was really aroused by his selfless act and voice that could make a root canal sound sexy, or kind of mad that he risked himself again for her sake. "I love that you came to help me, but not if it hurt you." She propped herself up on one arm, and he let his arms drop to his sides. He was weak enough that he couldn't carry the weight of his arms for long. Rosie looked at the patches of fresh blood seeping through the fabric of his shirt. "Just look at you, this is all my fault." Rosie felt awful about his wounds, realizing that he must not have anyone to patch him up like she had.

Rosie quickly started to unbutton his shirt to see how bad it was, and he stopped her with a hand over hers. "As much as I would love for you to undress me," they both paused to ponder that image, "you need to understand," He used his free hand to tip her chin up so he could look her in the eyes. "Rosie, it's not your fault I'm hurt. I chose to fight the monster, but it is because of you I'm alive." He weakly dropped his hand from her chin, but Rosie was mesmerized by his eyes.

Rosie was stunned by his soulful brown eyes, so full of concern and love that it was overpowering. To just call them brown made them sound plain, but to Rosie his eyes were a warm rich mahogany with tiny flecks of copper that made his eyes sparkle in a very sexy bedroom way. His long dark eyelashes were the kind mascaras wished they could reproduce, and they were a perfect frame for his intense intimate gaze. From the silently passing moments as they looked into each other's eyes it was obvious that the feeling was mutual.

She breathed in his scent, and smelled not only roses but the almost salty musk of his skin. Rosie could feel his warmth, his heart pounding where her hand rested on his firm broad chest. He just felt so right there with her. It took her a long time to be able to see anything beyond those deep sensual eyes.

Eventually she started to take in the rest of his features, and his injuries. His lips were naturally full, but swollen where there was an angry cut on his lower lip trailing down to his chin. He had scratches and bruises all over his face and neck, and she was sure they continued all over the rest of his body where clothes hid the damage. He was wearing the leather top hat that she had seen in silhouette many times before as he pulled Rosie into the light and away from her nightmare. She couldn't help but wonder what head wounds it might be hiding. He was also wearing a button down paisley shirt mostly in dark reds, and dark brown pants, both of which would hide blood.

The worst of the damage to his face was a deep cut on his left cheek that was red and puffy and probably needed stitches. He was a mess, but at the same time she couldn't help but think how handsome he was, and how sexy it was knowing that he had gotten this hurt saving her.

Rosie wanted so badly to make it all better, so she leaned in and gently kissed the wound on his cheek. He flinched slightly from the pain at first, but was quick to wrap his arms around Rosie's waist and sigh contentedly. In that lingering moment of kissing his boo-boo she felt warmth grow between them, and a healing glow emanated from her lips with a gentile electrical tingle. Rosie pulled back, in surprise, to find the cut on his cheek had partially healed.

Before Rosie could express her surprise about what had just happened her angel was kissing her. The cut on his lower lip felt rough at first, and she tasted the light metallic flavor of blood, but his kiss was so urgent that she was swept into it. Knowing that she had just accidentally healed his cut cheek she tried to heal his lip the same way. The tingling glow came easily between them but didn't stop at his split lip. Rosie felt like she was caressing places deep inside her angel, healing him from the inside out. Her energy sought out his deep injuries, and knit together the tares that were seeping blood from his internal organs. Rosie was pretty sure she was knitting holes in his lungs, kidney, and intestines. She followed ugly jagged stabs from inside out, mending the tissue with strange ease. The sensation was both calm and careful, and thrilling at the same time. The healing work left Rosie panting with fatigue.

"What was that?" Rosie felt so weak that if he didn't have his arms around her she might have fallen over.

Her angel chuckled, and answered playfully "Your magic." The way he smiled at Rosie lit his whole face, but his smile dimmed a bit when he saw her confusion wasn't a joke. "It's how you saved my life last night, and how you healed me now." He kissed her quickly again, "Thank you."

He seemed energized and well now, but Rosie was so tired. "I can't remember a lot from last night. It's all kinda fuzzy. It's coming back in bits, but I don't know what I did to help. The only clear memory is you standing between the monster and me."

Her angel was able to enjoy his health only a moment before he realized Rosie's condition and sobered. "You gave me too much last night, the memory loss is probably the cost of what it took out of you. And now you've given me too much again." He swept her legs across him, lifting Rosie effortlessly into his lap, and she felt almost like a child cradled against him. "You need to take some energy back. I can heal on my own, you need the strength to heal yourself. When the monster comes back I need to know you won't be weakened and vulnerable because you used up your energy reserves healing me."

"I don't know how to take it back. I don't know how I did it in the first place." Rosie was feeling faint and knew her angel was right, she had given him too much and was feeling it.

Her guardian angel looked worried "I'm going to try to give you some energy back. But if you try to heal me again..." he paused looking heartbroken "if you do it instinctively, maybe I should stay away until I'm all healed."

Rosie felt like she couldn't breathe, thinking about weeks apart from the comfort of her guardian angel. Even if he was a possible construct of her mind, she didn't want to go back to how alone she felt before she met him. "I don't want to be without you so long. If I don't touch you, I won't accidentally heal you. Then you can still be around, right?"

He smiled warmly, understanding her reaction and feeling the same about being separated from her. "Okay. I promise, I'll be there if you need me." He looked at Rosie very seriously "But after this, barring emergencies, I won't touch you again until we are both completely healed."

"As long as I know you're close I'll be okay. But I will really miss this." She said, snuggling weakly against him.

"Are you ready?" He said, very seriously. Rosie nodded, and he kissed her gently before laying her carefully in the grass and kneeling over her. Her angel settled his right hand caressingly over her heart while he closed his eyes and focused his energy. Rosie felt a rush of warm prickling energy enter her body, and it was wonderful. She could feel her angels love in the energy too and it made her feel safe and secure. She put a hand over his, and it was almost too warm to touch. Rosie hadn't expected the energy he was pushing into her to have temperature, but it was a warm glow in more than color. She searched his face to see if it was difficult for him, and he seemed lost in his focus but like it was almost relaxing to give her energy. Rosie could feel his energy filtering broadly through her chest, slightly caressing her breasts as it passed, then tingling up and down her spine as little tendrils like electric sparks reached out to the three gouges delicately knitting the flesh back together. The sensation was intimate and arousing in a way that was unique to them.

As she watched him she saw his frame sag a little with the effort, and then saw some of his injuries reappear. "Stop." Rosie tried to pull her angels hand from her heart, but he continued to press his palm to her chest. "You're giving me too much now. Please, I don't want you hurt again." Pulling on his hand was not snapping him out of his trance like state, so she reached for his face with her right hand. She pleaded, with her hand against his cheek. "Please stop now, you're hurting yourself."

When he didn't respond she decided to give him back some healing energy, with his energy flowing into her she would try to balance it. She pushed her energy into him, and the moment she began his eyes snapped open. His eyes blazed with a golden light, looking startled. Rosie's touch completed a circuit, and now energy to flowed between them.

His gaze quickly searched Rosie's out, and softened into a look of wonder. "God, that's amazing." As they looked into each other's eyes, the feeling of the energy exchange slid smoothly into something more sexual. Their energy was so mingled that Rosie wasn't sure which of them was guiding the change. The sensation felt so good that Rosie blushed, bringing a very male grin to her angel's face.

His energy began to caress more than just lightly over her breasts. He slid over her, tingling around her bottom before tentatively touching her inner thighs. A small moan escaped Rosie's lips. Embarrassed, she pulled her hand from his face, breaking the flow between them. He caught her right hand with his left and kissed her palm, letting the energy surge back to complete their circuit.

As he kissed her palm she let her energy caress over his body too, and was amazed that she could feel him almost like she was using her hands. She traced her energy along his soft lips, around the angles of his jaw on each side, playfully through his hair, and down to the nape of his neck. Rosie moved slowly across his broad shoulders, rippling through his muscular biceps, only to come back to shoulders and linger there like she was giving an energy back rub. Rosie inched slowly down his back, feeling every muscle beneath taut, smooth skin.

Rosie's eyes closed to fully enjoy the sensation of touching and being touched with energy. So she was caught off guard when he was suddenly above her, kissing her lips instead of her palm. Rosie responded, wrapping her arms around him and hooking a leg across his back as he pressed against her. His hands were now both tangled in her hair as he kissed her passionately. The energy continued to flow between them crossing and mingling at every place their bodies met.

Rosie caught herself mentally before she caught herself physically, and pulled back before she got carried away. She was left panting, like she had forgotten to breathe; which was totally possible. Her angel still held her intimately, looking at her with the most amazing bedroom eyes.

Rosie whispered in a voice gone husky with desire. "If we don't stop now, I'm not sure I'll be able to stop myself later, you just feel so good."

"So, why stop?" He whispered back as he nibbled her earlobe, still pressing his body against Rosie.

She almost moaned, "You don't know how good that sounds."

He slowly licked Rosie's neck, and her breath came in shuddering gasps. "I think I can guess how good it sounds to you, because it sounds really brilliant to me."

Rosie sighed as a tangible expression of her conflicted emotions. "Yes, it does sound good, but don't we need to conserve our energy for healing? Maybe you're more of a tempting devil than a guardian angel."

"Me?" he patted his chest dramatically, but kept a playful puckish grin on his face "a tempting devil? I could play that role if it would turn you on." And he stole a kiss.

"If you wanted to play one of those roles, you have really been more of an angel for me than a devil, and angel wings could be pretty sexy." She sole the kiss this time, but lingered a moment longer.

"Well, I suppose if you'd rather me on the side of angels, I'll have to be good." He kissed Rosie again, lightly running his tongue between her lips to part them slightly before whispering intimately "Soon." And then kissed her deeply and thoroughly before rolling off Rosie and onto his feet. He extended her a hand, and lifted her easily to her feet when she took it.

Rosie's guardian angel was looking much better than before she touched his cheek, but not as healed as he was just before he started to give Rosie energy back. She was also feeling better than she had been before their exchange, but was pretty sure the wound on her back was not as healed as it had been after his tingling energy entered her.

"Self control is so much harder when I can see you." She lifted their entwined hands to her lips and kissed his before releasing it. "When you're with me, and I can't see you, can you see me? Or is it all 'feel' like you are for me?"

He wrapped a hand around her waist and pulled their bodies together. "I do love to feel you," he lingered on the word feel as he ran his other hand up over the curve of her bottom and settled it at her waist too, "but I can see you."

"If you weren't so damn hot and so damn sexy, it would be so much easier to resist your whiles." She said, punctuating her sentence with a kiss.

"Would you prefer it if I made myself homely and obnoxious?" He said playfully.

"I wouldn't want you to change a thing about yourself. You're perfect the way you are." Rosie's compliment awarded her with another of his knee wobbling grins. "It seems like you're everything I've ever wanted, how can you possibly be real?"

"I'm really not perfect, honest. I think we're just a perfect match. Because you're everything I've ever wanted too. I think the worlds work in mysterious ways and they must have a reason to put us together, I think we've always been meant to find each other." His words were sincere and confident, leaving no question or doubt.

"So, you think it's fate we found each other?" Rosie sounded unsure, fate was too fickle in her mind to give her such a gift.

"Most definitely." He kissed her again. "There must be a reason I was drawn to you so strongly, and want you so badly."

This time Rosie urgently kissed her angel. She was consumed by their shared desire. Feeling his want flood her doubled her arousal, and then fed back to him increasing his need. Their desire escalated in a wash of groping hands and greedy lips until they were again on the ground panting.

"I think we better stop, or we might cripple ourselves by using up all our reserves, and we will need to be strong and healthy to face the monster when it returns." Her Angel made sense, but it was almost physically painful not to tear his clothes off him and have her way with him.

"Mmmmmmm" he rumbled an appreciative sound and undulated against her, embracing Rosie in a way that did not match his restrained words of a moment ago. "Oh, I really like that image you just gave me. And it is killing me not to encourage that impulse," he kissed her with yearning before finishing "or to follow my desire to strip you too."

"You are sooo not making this any easier. I really didn't mean to project that thought, though it's something I really do want to do. I am so glad you want me as badly as I want you." They kissed lingeringly before disentangling from each other. "I am so close to the point of no return with you. If we don't stop now, we will definitely cripple our defenses, but it's just really hard." Rosie saw him glance down, and realized its double meaning and it made her face flush.

"Yes, it is, very, hard." He paused for emphasis. "But that is a problem we can look forward to remedying as soon as possible." He started to reach for Rosie but caught himself and stopped short with a sigh. "Possible may take a few weeks for us to heal." He stood back up, dusting off his pants and re-buttoning the couple buttons on his shirt that had come undone in their amorous gropings. He stretched his hand out to Rosie, "Shall we try this again? I promise to behave if you do."

"I won't promise to like behaving, but I promise to behave." Rosie said, taking his hand and letting him help her to her feet. They continued to hold hands standing beneath the large oak tree, but resisted getting closer. "I intended to travel to some of my friends' dreams tonight, and convince them to take watches with me." Something niggled at the back of Rosie's mind, was she forgetting something important? "I should probably go do that now."

"You don't know how relieved I am that you've friends that travel the worlds. It's a good idea, your nightmare monster won't take the risk of attacking while its hurt, unless it sees an easy meal. As long as there are more than one of you together, it probably won't risk trying for you. But if it tries, or you just want me near, I will only be a thought away." He raised her hand to his lips and brushed them against the back of her hand with the faintest energy caressing around her wrist and a little up her arm. He held her hand to his chest and Rosie felt his heart beating strong and healthy. He continued, with a husky desire filled voice. "When you want me with you, I feel it and come to your call."

"You are really, really not making this easy." Rosie said squeezing his hand with frustration.

"I'm sorry Rose. I won't try to delay you any further. You should go find your friends before they wake up for their day." They managed to exchange a chaste but lingering kiss goodbye followed by a long moment of their foreheads leaning together, before Rosie reluctantly let his hand go and turned to leave.

Rosie took a few steps and concentrated on going to Janet's dream. As she stepped out of her angels world, she heard him whisper in her mind 'I love you', and it warmed her soul.

ℭ𝔅

19

Rosie stepped from a day lit meadow with a tree, to a dark dense forest; and almost walked into a large limb of an evergreen. The wind whipped through the trees, like a storm was coming. Rosie heard disembodied screams coming from all around, and saw flashes of quickly moving smoke in the wind; one moment there and the next gone. She looked around, and saw Janet standing rigidly before a ghostly figure.

Janet extended her right hand, fingers stretched in a powerful gesture of stopping. "You will leave this place!" Janet yelled into the wind, "move into your right and proper place." The vague and transparent figure screamed at Janet in defiance, but she pushed at it with her will and it was flung away from her. Suddenly the wind and noise stopped, and the ghostly figures were gone.

"Hey, Janet." Rosie spoke into the silence, and Janet turned to face Rosie like she had been expecting her friends arrival. "cool dream. I just caught the end, but looked like you were kicking ass."

"Hi, and thank you. I was just clearing a little bad juju." She wiped her hands down her shirt and pants in a cleaning gesture. "I thought you were going to look for other people for watches tonight."

"I was. I will be. I just really wanted to talk to you first. I just had the most amazing dream with my not so ghostly guardian angel." Rosie tried not to blush with sensory images of what just passed between her and her angel. "And since you are the only one who knows about my new friend..."

"Ooh, dish." Janet came over to Rosie and sat on

a large fallen tree, like it was a bench in the park, and patted the mossy wood next to her.

Rosie sat next to Janet, and found herself a little unsure what to say about their energy sharing. "Well, I was feeling scared to go to sleep, and he came to comfort me and help me. Ya know, in an invisible spirit kind of way."

"But you just said not so ghostly, when does that come in?"

"I fell asleep feeling him with me, but woke up in my dream kinda in his arms."

"Nice." Janet said suggestively.

"I have to be more careful, tho, just thinking that I wanted him when I was scared called him to me. And he was injured much, much, worse than I was last night. So when he came to me in the park it was just like you thought, it hurt him. Reopened wounds, and set back his healing."

"So, manifesting in the waking world causes him damage?" Janet confirmed.

"Yeah, I'm pretty sure it does. The last thing I want to do is hurt him, Janet. But used so much energy to be even a whisper in our world, that it took away what he'd healed." Rosie took a deep breath feeling guilty for wanting him when he's hurt, and continued. "So, I woke up in his arms, and it was just so right." She sighed with the warm fuzzy memory of just being in her angels arms. "But he was injured, like bleeding open wounds injured, like internal bleeding injured. It was really bad. And I wanted to help him, and then I sort of did."

"What do you mean you sort of did?" Janet seriously prompted.

"I used my magic, and I healed him. Like serious magic, tingling from me through him. I could feel him bleeding inside, and I closed the wounds. It felt so good, too, healing his wounds. Kinda sexy, and mmh." Rosie made a groping gesture to go with her guttural sound. "But I gave him too much, and got all woozy. And then he gave me healing back, and I could feel his energy inside me..." She closed her eyes and sighed with the memory, before looking back at Janet's expecting face. "But he was giving too much back, and was hurting himself doing it. So I tried to give him some back, and it created this amazing flow of energy between us. Janet, it was sooo hot, it was like a whirl pool of energy and sensation." Rosie averted her gaze, blushing slightly thinking about what happened next. "And lips, and hands, and pressing bodies. I have never felt anything like it."

"So, you broke up with Jack before you went to bed then?" Janet asked with a note of skepticism.

Rosie's eyes widened. Suddenly she felt a crushing weight of guilt hit her almost like a physical blow. "Oh my god, how did I forget about Jack? I was so wrapped up in my maybe imaginary..." she was suddenly at a loss for words for how to describe her relationship with her angel. "I don't even know what to call him. I want to say lover but, we haven't gone that far yet. I can't say boyfriend, because I have one of those. And friend isn't nearly enough to encompass what I feel for him. But whatever he is, I was so intoxicated with him that I completely forgot about Jack. The man I love. How can I do this to him?" Rosie buried her face in her hands and screamed out her frustration with herself.

"Wow, that's some major mojo. If your connection to this spirit guy is so strong, maybe you shouldn't be with Jack."

"But what if he isn't even real? What if he is a defense mechanism I've constructed to fill my needs?"

"That you have such strong needs that aren't being filled by Jack, might say more about your relationship with him than whether or not your secret lover is real or not. What's mister naughty's name anyway?"

For the second time in this conversation, Rosie looked over to Janet, eyes wide in shock. "How was I there with him, talking to him, and totally making out with him and I didn't ask him his name. The thought didn't even cross my mind. So, what, I construct the perfect man out of a part of my soul, so that it defends me and cares for me, and has this amazing English accent, and a face and body that make me cream my pants just thinking about him, and I don't even give him a name." Rosie shook her head at herself.

"Let me ask a question, why do you seem so sure he's a construct and not another dream walker?"

"I don't know, he's just too exactly everything I want in a man. If he's too good to be true he probably isn't. Right?"

Janet shrugged. "So, if he's not real, why is he so wounded?"

"I'm thinking, if he's a construct my subconscious created, he has to be made from part of me right? And if he's fighting this nightmare monster that is real enough to wound me in the waking world, then he would take real wounds too, kinda injuring the part of me that he's made of. So, until I'm all healed, I'd guess that he wouldn't be healed yet either. Right?" Rosie did not sound confident in her possible explanation.

"Who are you trying to convince, Rosie? Me or you?" Janet asked, arms crossed for stern effect. "And why, for heaven's sake, if he isn't real, do you feel so guilty for indulging your imagination and filling your own needs? If he is a construct of your own making, being with him is like masturbating not cheating."

"The problem is, I just don't know. I want him to be real so badly, but I just can't imagine that the universe would make me the perfect guy. A perfect man that I can see in dreams but not in the waking world, it just seems too impossible be real. And I kinda don't want him to be real too, because if he is, I'm a big cheater. And I'm just not that girl. I'm a serial monogamist, I don't cheat. I can't stop thinking about him, but I love Jack too and I have made a commitment to him that I feel like I'm breaking with a man that I can't figure out if he's real or not."

"Too? You said you love Jack too. Does this mean you are also in love with the maybe real guy?"

"Yes. I am. I'm in love with someone, and I don't even know if he's real. How can I be in love with both of them?"

"I guess the heart wants what the heart wants," Janet shrugged "polygamists do it all the time."

"That doesn't help much, Janet. I don't want to be in a relationship with two men at once. If my guardian angel is real, it's not fair to either of them."

"But if he's not real, and you can't figure out if he's real, why torture yourself? Until you know either way, why not just enjoy your mystery groper?"

Rosie feigned indignation. "Janet! How crass!" They both giggled a bit, "mystery groper, you make it sound so dirty."

"Isn't it?" and they both giggled over Rosie's risqué behavior.

When they settled, and had taken a beat Rosie continued. "Ok, so I leave well enough for now, and deal with it if I find out my 'mystery groper' is real." They both let out a few short laughs. "But either way, the thing I came into your dream to tell you about is that I found out that I can do some kind of astral healing; at least with him. I wonder if it's something I can do for other people, or if it's something that can work in the waking world?"

"That could be a handy trick to have access to. Especially if you're convincing a bunch of us to help protect you from that monster of yours, and one of us gets hurt. I don't want to hurt myself to test it, but if someone else volunteers..." Janet shrugged, "You should really see if it's just a mystery groper thing, or a stand-alone talent."

"I totally get it. If I'm wrong, and can only heal myself and things I make." Rosie shrugged, "I wouldn't want anyone to get hurt, and then find out it's not something I can use with anyone other than my angel."

"If you're planning to get other dream walkers together, maybe one of them would be willing to test your theory."

"Can't hurt to ask, right?" Thinking about dream walkers brought Rosie's other topic to mind. "So, when I was talking to Jack about the idea of getting a group together, we decided that groups of three would be good. Ya know, safety in numbers, and the monster probably won't attack if it's hurt and doesn't see any easy prey. Right?"

"Sounds good to me. Who else are you planning to ask?"

"You know Chris, right? He's a friend from school, and he feels like someone who could dream walk. He has definitely got some Fey in him, and he's a pretty loyal friend. I was thinking he would be a good team with you."

"I think I met him once or twice, but I don't really know him. If you think he'd be a good choice, go for it, let's see if you can pull him into my dream."

"It's usually easier to step into someone else's dream, than pull them into yours the first time. I could go try to make contact."

"Is there any danger of your nightmare hijacking you, if you go on your own, before you find Chris?" Janet asked.

"I don't know. As long as I'm not sure, it would probably be good to stick together. If that's ok with you."

"Sure. Lead on, Mac Duff." Janet stood and gestured for Rosie to take the lead.

Rosie stood and turned to take the few steps that would cross them into another dream world, but paused and looked over her shoulder back to Janet. "I should warn you tho, Chris is kinda a player. Not in a misogynistic kind of way, more of a free love kinda way. He'll probably flirt with you, so you should be aware that he's kind of a slut; but not in a bad way."

"Noted. And sounds like fun." Janet grinned at Rosie, and nodded in gesture for her to get moving.

Rosie faced back into the vast dark forest and focused her will, concentrating on Chris and feeling for his sleeping soul. She grabbed Janet's hand blindly behind her, and they crossed into another world.

ભ

20

They stepped from lush forest into a hallway that looked like it belonged to a really posh hotel.

"Whoa, that was cool." Janet stopped as they arrived in the new dream and looked at Rosie with wide eyes. "I didn't realize other people's dreams would feel so different. Your dreams don't feel all that different from mine, but this dream feels, I don't know, polished. No, that's not the right word, it feels shinier. No, still not the right word, maybe silkier. No, I can't find the right word. Do you feel it?"

"Yeah, every dreamer feels a little different. And it's hard to explain how they're different, they just feel a little off from our realities. Even dream to dream there's variation. I've never been in Chris's dreams, but this feels kinda like him, so I know we're in the right place." Rosie started to feel like she was teaching a dream walking class, so she decided to tone down the lecturing. She couldn't say how she knew what she did about dream walking, it always just came to her. Rosie assumed it was how her dream training with the Fey came back, so she never doubted things that just came to her like this. "Not that I've been in that many people's dreams, but they've all had a slightly different feel, and the feel always kinda goes with the dreamer." She tried to wrap the expository lecture, and get back to what they were doing. "Any way, were here to find Chris, so he's likely in one of these rooms."

They looked down the hall and noticed one of the doors ajar. "How about that one." Janet suggested, striding towards the door.

"Hang on, having someone walk into your dream can be a little disorienting. When your subconscious is creating the back drop and the characters, then an outside influence arrives it can go bad if the dreamer feels threatened. We have to approach carefully. See what he is doing, and then pick the moment to say hi."

Janet stopped in her tracks. "Point taken. Quiet and stealthy to start. No barging into someone else's subconscious."

Rosie tip toed down the hall, followed by Janet, and approached the open door cautiously. Peeking into the room, Rosie could see that this was a fancy suite with a really big bed on a platform, and the bed was pretty full.

Rosie tried to avert her gaze, to give Chris his privacy, but the damage had been done. She had seen the whole scene, and it was crystal in her mind's eye, whether she wanted it there or not. Chris was having an orgy dream, and Rosie was pretty sure that there were at least ten people on the bed performing various acts on each other. The split looked to be roughly fifty-fifty male to female, and it seemed every mouth was kissing or pleasuring another person. Every cock was either being sucked or being thrust into an opening, and every pussy was either being licked or fucked. Each person was definitely attached to at least two other people, and one or two were attached to three. One of those was a woman being fucked, eaten out, and had a cock filling her mouth all at once; and she was looking like she was having a great time. Rosie didn't see Chris in the scrum, but a lot of faces were hidden in the wash of naked flesh.

Rosie looked at Janet, expecting her to be averting her gaze too, but Janet was watching like it was her favorite TV show's season cliffhanger. Rosie backed away from the door, and pulled Janet with her. "Hey, I was enjoying that." Janet whispered as Rosie started to pull her a little way down the hall.

"Is someone out there?" Chris's voice called from inside the room.

Sighing, Rosie stepped back into the doorway, and half looked over at the orgy. "Sorry, I really, really, didn't mean to disrupt your dream."

"Super awesome fun dream." Janet interjected quietly to Rosie following her into the doorway.

Rosie was able to make out Chris in the very middle of the bed now. He had been lying down with a large breasted blonde woman sitting on his face when Rosie first peeked in, but the woman had shifted to start playing with another of the beds occupants and Chris was now half sitting, propped on one elbow, looking at the pair in the doorway. No one else on the bed seemed to notice the new arrivals. Chris's lower half was still in use tho, as a zaftig brunette woman continued to suck his cock while herself being fucked doggy style. Rosie tried not to giggle awkwardly or to look too directly at Chris. She averted her gaze, looking at the paisley pattern on the rug, instead of the pile of flesh. Rosie was a little creeped out by seeing the man she thought of as a sibling being blown and surrounded by people happily fucking each other.

"Rosie, is that you?" Chris sounded a little confused, "Wow, I wasn't expecting you here. And is that your friend Janet? Did you want to come in and join us?" It was all so matter of fact, that Rosie was sure Chris was still inside his dreams logic.

"Hi Chris, yes its Rosie and Janet. And, Um, no thanks. We won't be joining, thanks for the invite tho. We'll just wait till you're done in there and talk to you after. We'll, be out in the hall." Rosie awkwardly blurted out words, trying to stop noticing all the various acts being performed to and all around Chris.

"I don't know, looks kinda like fun to me." Janet said quietly to Rosie, grinning broadly. "If we can't join, can we at least watch?" Rosie was pretty sure Janet was messing with Her, pretty sure.

"Ok," Chris responded to Rosie, "but I'll probably be a little while. I'm only about three quarters done with the people here. I haven't had sex with three of them yet." Rosie stood dumb, not sure how to respond to the matter of fact way Chris was talking about the orgy.

" 'S ok, we can wait. Take your time. We'll be in the hall." Janet piped up, and pulled Rosie from the room when she failed to answer.

Outside, Rosie looked a little shell shocked. This was not a way she had wanted to see Chris, and it really bothered her that the question of if his penis was that big in real life or if it was dream enhanced kept spinning around in her mind. She could not un-see the orgy, it was burned into her brain. She knew Chris, she should have expected that this would be a likely dream for him. Sex noises filtered from the room, and made both Rosie and Janet laugh at their own awkwardness.

"Chair?" Rosie offered, and when Janet nodded, Rosie pulled two nicely padded comfy chairs from thin air. They oddly fit in with the halls posh decor. Janet accepted the trick without surprise and they settled into the chairs to wait a bit. Rosie noticed Janet angling her chair a bit so she could see into the room, but adjusted it back when Rosie gave her a look. What seemed like quite a while later, good for Chris that he had that kind of stamina, the moans and screams settled.

A few minutes past and Chris came out of the hotel room with a towel wrapped around his waist. "Did you say you didn't want to 'disrupt my dream'? If you are part of my dream, how come you are aware it's a dream?"

"I'm glad you know it's a dream, most dreamers don't." Rosie began, "and we know it's a dream because we aren't constructs of your dream, we're here dream walking. We really are Rosie and Janet, and we came to ask for your help." Rosie tried to explain. She knew Chris's reaction would determine how capable of lucid dreaming he really was, and further if he could be brought into her dreams.

"So, let me get this straight. That whole orgy was my dream, but you two aren't part of it. You are really you, what, like astrally projecting into my dream?"

"Yeah, something like that." Rosie confirmed.

"Good, I am so relieved. I would need some serious therapy if I put my little sis into a sex dream." He turned to Janet, "You on the other hand, I would have loved to join." Chris winked at Janet, while she tried not to blush. "The fact that you didn't join in makes me believe you really are both here. That's kinda cool." He looked down at his towel. "I should probably go put some clothes on, huh."

Janet piped in, "It's your dream, just manifest some." Both Rosie and Janet watched Chris closely, to see if he had enough control of his dream to manipulate his environment.

"Right, why didn't I think of that. It's a dream." He said, not missing a beat. And suddenly was wearing a purple t-shirt and black jeans. Test passed. Chris was capable of lucid dreaming, and could at the least be lead into others dreams. "So, what's up? What help do you need?" He said looking between Rosie and Janet.

"I need a few friends to watch my back," Rosie said bluntly, "and you have just enough weird in you that I thought you'd be a perfect pick."

Chris looked around the hall, took a couple steps back towards the room then stopped shaking his head. He turned back to them, mumbling to himself, "Dream. Right." Then pulled a matching chair out of thin air, much like Rosie had, to sit down with them. "Whatever help you need, you know I'm in. But what is it you need help with?"

Rosie and Janet recapped the events leading up to and including the monster attack last night, leaving out the gruesome details or any reference to Rosie's angel, aside from 'someone' saving Rosie and wounding the monster. Rosie finished her story by showing Chris the scratches on her back, that were currently pretty close to looking healed.

"So, what you're saying is, you want me to spend a couple nights a week keeping watch in my dreams, with you two, to make sure a big nasty monster won't make another try at you until you can fight back." Chris recapped his role.

"Pretty much." Rosie confirmed and then asked. "You in?"

"I'd be in just for the company." He said making significant eye contact with Janet before turning back to Rosie. "But, it sounds like you really need help, and you know I would do anything to help you out Rosie. Count me in. Will you be teaching me to dream walk so I can really help?"

"Yes, brother of mine. We can teach you that. When we need you night after next, we'll come get you, and we can teach you what we know while we pass the time on watches." Rosie confirmed.

"And I'll be on watches with Janet?" When both Janet and Rosie nodded, Chris grinned seductively at Janet, "I really look forward to spending time with you, and getting to know you better."

"Biblically?" Janet asked playfully, nodding towards the hotel room.

"If that's what you want." Chris replied a little too husky and sexually for Rosie's comfort. "But I'd like to get to know you before I get to know you." And he winked at Janet.

"Ok, I get it," Rosie sighed "there will be much flirting between you two. Just don't forget when I'm in the room ok?" They all laughed and talked pleasantly for a while longer until all three of them were feeling tired. A sign that they should be waking soon. Chris promised to call Rosie the next day, to confirm that he remembered their meeting.

સ

The next day, Chris didn't call in the morning and Rosie was both worried that Chris had forgotten their shared dream, and a bit relieved that maybe she would never have to admit what she walked in on.

Instead of calling, Chris stopped by on his way to work. He worked mostly weekend nights as a ticket taker at a movie theater, and snuck Rosie in for more than one free movie since they started hanging out.

Chris played with Rosie a bit, saying he had a feeling he should stop by but wasn't sure why, before he confirmed that he was messing with her and remembered the dream. Now that he had confirmed recall of their dream, Rosie was expecting it to be a bit awkward. Considering what she had seen, Rosie felt awkward, but Chris really seemed ok with her and Janet dropping in on what Rosie thought was a really private dream. Often things that seem normal in a dream look very different by light of day, but that was not the case this time. Chris even suggested that they could drop by his dreams again some time, tho he wasn't sure he could guarantee that the entertainment would be as interesting next time.

Chris expressed excitement over learning how to dream walk. He also admitted he had stopped to talk in person so he could ask if Janet was available, and was thrilled to learn she was single. Knowing Chris's short attention span with most women, Rosie was a little concerned about him hitting on Janet. Chris promised Rosie not to do anything to pressure or hurt Janet, and that he would be clear about his intentions and lifestyle before anything happened. He also agreed to let Rosie smack him with a big stick if he broke his word in any way. Rosie was pretty sure her two friends would hit it off, she just wasn't sure where it would lead after that.

It was mid afternoon on Sunday when Chris took off for work, and Rosie considered if she should call Frank and Wendy to give them a heads up before walking into their dreams. Rosie did not want to accidentally walk into another private dream like she had with Chris.

She thought she'd call Frank first, because she was still a little uncomfortable dealing with Wendy. Rosie had hung out with Frank more times than she could count, but it had always been with Jack present, so it felt kinda weird calling him to broach such a crazy topic. Janet and Chris had accepted dream walking pretty easily, but she'd known them for years and had many conversations about how they were more than the standard kind of human beforehand. With Frank, she had seen the Fey heritage he held, and had commented on it, but all things out of the norm other than that were dominated by Jack. Rosie wasn't even sure if Frank was really a believer in any kind of paranormal or extra sensory anything. She always worried that people would think her mad if she spoke about Fey heritage or dream walking, so she usually waited until she was really sure the person wouldn't think she was crazy before broaching anything. That was why she had been planning to approach her friends in their dreams, it's much harder to disbelieve things happening in dreams. If they remembered the shared dream the next day it was good. If they didn't remember, Rosie knew not to bother because they didn't have enough control of their dreams to remember and were probably too closed minded to believe any kind of magic was possible.

If she called Frank and laid it all out to him, and he thought she was crazy, Rosie would feel humiliated. But if Rosie was right, and Frank had the potential to dream walk. if he could lucidly dream to change his dream environment, he would be perfect to stand watch. If she left it at Chris and Janet, they would get tired out too fast. Rosie needed more dream walkers. So the question was, which was more awkward, calling and being thought crazy or walking in on something private. In the end, she decided it would be worse for her friend to think she was crazy.

That left Wendy. When they had been close, they

had shared dreams a few times. Lately, things were strained. Rosie didn't like the way she saw Wendy look at Jack, or that they had spent time together and kept it a secret from Rosie. She hated that she'd lost trust in Wendy, they had been so close. But if nothing was going on, then why not tell her that they were spending time together? It just sat wrong with Rosie.

Rosie sat in her kitchen in front of the phone, staring at it like it might bite her. She knew she needed to pick up the phone to call Wendy, but she felt deep down that something was going on between Wendy and Jack and talking to Wendy might confirm it. Rosie decided that she just wouldn't bring up the topic. She would focus on solving the problem at hand, and leave possible infidelities alone. Especially since she wasn't so free from that mark now.

Taking a deep breath, she picked up the phone and punched in the familiar number before stepping out onto the porch and pulling the door shut over the cord. The phone rang and Rosie was about to lose her nerve and hang up when she heard Wendy's voice on the other end. "Hello."

"Hi Wendy, it's Rosie."

Wendy sounded both surprised and apprehensive, "Hi Rosie, what's up?"

Rosie let a long moment pass before she could will herself to speak. "I need to ask you a favor."

Wendy let out a breath, like she had been holding it waiting to see what Rosie wanted. Her voice sounded relieved, "Of course, I'm always willing to help a friend, what do you need?"

Rosie was suspicious of Wendy's reaction, but pushed her feeling down. "I need help with a dream walking problem." Rosie took a breath to shake the feeling in the pit of her stomach, she knew that Wendy was a good friend deep down, even if there were issues with her and Rosie's boyfriend. "I know we haven't talked in a while, but I wouldn't ask if it weren't serious."

"What's going on Rosie? What could be so serious about dreams?"

Rosie sighed, "This may sound kinda weird, but a nightmare's been chasing me for weeks and night before last it attacked me. It hit me pretty bad in the nightmare, slashing up my back, and when I woke up I still had the wound it gave me."

"Are you sure you didn't just hurt yourself while you were tossing and turning in your sleep, and it translated into the dream?"

"Absolutely positive. I checked everywhere, and nothing could have cut me like the nightmare monster did. Like I said, it'd been stalking me for weeks, but I always got away until two nights ago. And, I barely got away..." She left out the part where she was rescued by a man who was either fictional or was a man being wronged by Rosie, because she was in a supposedly monogamous relationship with Jack.

"You still there?" Wendy snapped Rosie out of her trip down guilty conscious lane.

"I'm here, sorry." Rosie thought fast, "I was just lost in bits of memory of the fight for my life." The words were true, even if she was leaving important bits out. "When I got away it was pretty badly injured too, and I'm hoping it will need time to heal, so I figure it will only take another try if I'm an easy target."

"Wow, Rosie you sound really shaken. If it was a fight for your life, how did you get away?" Wendy sounded genuinely concerned.

Rosie felt like scum, she couldn't tell Wendy the whole truth, because it would get back to Jack. And until Rosie knew if her angel was real or a really good defense mechanism, she didn't want anyone gossiping. She decided to go with an answer that was a safe truth. "Things sometimes get so muddled in dreams, and large chunks of the dream are just gone aside from flashes of images here and there. Jack says he saved me." The last five words stuck in her throat, she hated giving credit to the wrong man.

"But you're ok now?" Wendy prompted.

"Yes. I'm healing well. Janet came over to patch me up on Friday night when this all happened, you can ask her how bad it was, but now it's not much worse than healing scratches. Seems I have a knack for healing that kind of damage."

"Wow, that's a pretty handy talent to find out about. Sucks how you got there, but still something good came out of it."

With Wendy's comment that something good had come out of it, all Rosie could think of was her sexy angels face. Then the crush of guilt over it. How could she want to be with her angel so badly, while she was with Jack. She felt so selfish for wanting them both, but Jack was real and she was happy with him most of the time, besides her angel could be a manifestation. A manifestation of her desire for a man that wants her as badly as she wants him, a man who protects her from danger and puts her first. Manifestation or not her angel felt real, and had really saved her life, so even if he was a part of Rosie's mind Jack would have issues with him. Wendy could be trusted to help Rosie if she was in danger, she just didn't trust Wendy with a secret that would cause trouble between Rosie and Jack.

"Rosie, you still there?"

"Yeah, sorry. I was just thinking that you're right, I guess something good did come out of it. But the nightmare monster is pretty vicious, and I could use the company to deter it attacking until we figure out how to deal with it." Rosie recovered, getting the conversation back on track. "Would you take a watch a couple times a week? Sometimes three, until we figure out how to get rid of this monster. I know it's a lot to ask, but you're a natural at dream walking, and I just don't know enough of us with the talent to dream walk that I can afford not to ask every friend who can." Rosie realized she was rambling and that Wendy was waiting for her to stop.

"Boy, you are rattled. Are you serious about this?" Wendy sounded a little skeptical, like she thought Rosie had slipped a cog.

"If you want to get together, I can show you the scratches. Or you could call Janet and confirm with her. I really did wake up with injuries from a nightmare monster." Rosie took a deep breath, trying not to be defensive. "I barely got away from it alive. But before, it only chased me when I was alone and now that it's injured, I think it will leave me alone as long as I'm not alone."

"Sorry, I didn't mean to be so skeptical. I believe you, and of course I can hang out with you while you're sleeping. Count me in."

Rosie took a deep breath, "Thanks. I guess come on by my dream tonight. You think you can find me?"

"Haven't I always been able to find you in your dreams?" Wendy said confidently.

"Of course, silly of me to ask. I guess I'll see you tonight." Rosie thought for a second, "Jack and I were thinking teams of three a night, so Frank will probably be with us."

"I didn't know Frank was a dream walker." Wendy sounded surprised.

"Yeah, we don't know for sure. But I thought I'd pay him a visit to see if I'm right. I think he could be a good dream walker."

"Cool, I guess I'll see you tonight then."

"Hey, Wendy, what time you planning on going to bed tonight? I'll go to bed after that, so there's no down time when that thing might get any ideas."

"I usually go to sleep around midnight, but I could go to bed earlier if you want."

"No, that's good. Actually, I'll recruit Frank and then we'll come find you. That way you won't pop in and spook Frank as he's coming to terms with lucid dreaming."

"Ok, sounds like a plan. I'll go to sleep and wait

for you to show up."

"See you tonight then." Rosie said feeling a little awkward making plans with a friend she was so suspicious of.

"See you then Rosie. Bye."

"Bye." Rosie thought that the conversation went a little too easy, but accepted it at face value and hung up the phone.

ଓ

21

The rest of the day dragged while Rosie waited for the night to come. She got caught up on homework, cleaned her room, and watched TV to pass the day. She kept expecting Jack to call, but he didn't, and the longer Rosie waited the more she thought about her angel and the less she thought about her boyfriend. How was their relationship going to work if she couldn't call him on the phone or go anywhere where Jacks mom might see them together. It made Rosie feel more like the mistress and less like the girlfriend, an irony that wasn't lost on her considering her growing feelings for her guardian angel. Maybe a breakup with Jack was the only logical outcome to the whole situation. Rosie had no doubt that she loved Jack, but he was kinda cruel sometimes with his need to toughen her up, it was so different from the energy she felt from her mysterious guardian. When her angel was near she felt so safe and warm and cared for, even now when she knew he was keeping his distance she felt safer just knowing he would come if she needed him. With Jack, she felt alone even when they were in the same room sometimes. Jack only paid attention to Rosie when he wanted to, leaving her in the background most of the time. Rosie hadn't been bothered by Jack's behavior before her angel showed up, but she definitely felt neglected by him now. It made her think that she must have subconsciously created her angel to fill her need. He really did fill a hollow place inside Rosie. She longed for him, even knowing he may be a really convincing piece of make-believe.

Rosie thought of the energy circuit that completed when she'd touched her guardian, and wished she could touch him again. Rosie realized she was mentally reaching for him and caught herself. She reigned herself in trying to keep from calling her sexy angel, but it was already too late. She felt his familiar warm comforting presence, and smelled the scent of roses and musk that preceded him. Rosie's heart leapt with joy feeling her angel's insubstantial presence, while her rational mind chided herself because she knew he needed to heal and it took energy to be near her while they were awake. She closed her eyes, and felt her guardians presence, but there was a slightly different quality to his feel. Tho she could feel the safety and caring that came with her guardian it felt a little insubstantial, even for him.

Rosie focused, trying to understand what was different, and realized that he wasn't here in her waking world, but there seemed to be a psychic connection that had been opened between them despite the metaphysical distance. Knowing that he was at a safe distance, Rosie relaxed her guard and let his comfort wash over her like an intangible cuddle. She reached for him with her mind and soul, and could see his full and kissable lips curl into a warm smile with her mind's eye. A smile she couldn't help but mirror in her excitement to see him in a way she hadn't known she could. It seemed that Rosie's powers were developing with every encounter she had with her guardian angel lately.

Rosie thought that if she could remotely see his smile, maybe with a little more effort she could see more. She was sitting at her vanity in her bedroom, but decided to get more comfortable. She walked over to her bed and settled into her pile of pillows and stuffed animals. Rosie relaxed her body and focused on the work she wanted to do with her mind.

She closed her eyes again, trying to focus on her

angel's energy. She took a deep breath and could smell his scent. She focused harder and could feel his encouragement. A thrill ran through her that her guardian was aware and open to her experiment. The more she thought of him, the clearer she could feel his emotions. She felt love, patience, and the deep desire she always felt when he was near. She pictured his smile as she had glimpsed it a few moments ago, and saw it again but this time she saw him seductively bite his lower lip before his smile playfully returned. Something deeper than a thrill ran through Rosie, and her deeper want added enough extra energy to let Rosie see all of her sexy guardian angel and his surroundings.

He came into focus, and she could see him draped across a red wing backed chair. The chair was outside, on a neatly trimmed lawn in a lush and well manicured garden and was across from the head of a long table set with mismatched china for tea. It made Rosie think of the Mad Hatter's tea party in Alice in Wonderland, and that tugged at another memory that she just couldn't quite access. As she tried to remember what it was, the image started to fade; and Rosie was having none of that.

Using this new far seeing, Rosie focused on the man in the chair. He had one leg draped over the chair's arm, and an arm stretched behind him over the chair's tall back. His other hand rested in his lap, holding a mostly empty teacup. He fit the scene very well, wearing a dark brown leather top hat with slightly exaggerated proportions tipped low over his eyes. She could see his coy smile, sexy dimple on his right cheek, and the nearly healed rugged scar across the left. His drape across the chair was easily one of the sexiest displays Rosie had ever seen, but it was the smile more than his pose that gave away the fact that he knew he was being watched.

He wore scuffed black boots, and nicely snug jeans. He had a pair of loose leather belts crossing his trim waist to hang across his slender hips. He wore a vest in a deep chocolate suede embossed with an intricate paisley pattern buttoned to accentuate both the narrowness of his waist and the broadness of his chest. Beneath the vest was a burgundy silk shirt with the top two buttons open, showing just enough of his smooth chest to make Rosie's mouth water. He wore a long brown duster over the whole outfit that gave his appearance an almost western flare juxtaposed with the posh almost noble looking vest and shirt.

When Rosie saw her angel it stunned her for a few moments, he was just so tasty. As she played at being a voyeur, he finished his tea, slowly sipping the last couple mouthfuls in a way that made Rosie's lips ache for his.

She thought to herself, 'That's so not fair, when we can't touch until we're both all healed.' To her surprise her angel looked up directly at Rosie, or the perspective she was 'seeing' from. The look of surprise then guilt crossed his face, like he felt bad for teasing her. His whole demeanor changed from sex kitten to sincere as he sat up. The earnest expression made Rosie's heart pang even stronger with desire for him.

"I thought it was what you wanted. Was I wrong? If I was, I'm sorry." She heard his smooth British accent in her mind, surprising her enough to make her jump and unintentionally brake contact. His image was gone from her mind, but she wasn't likely to forget such a scrumptious tableau any time soon.

She reached out to her angel, trying to communicate without visuals. Rosie willed her thoughts into a tight broadcast just to her guardian angel. "I'm sorry, it was what I wanted. I just didn't know I could do that. See you while you aren't with me, I mean. Or even in the same world."

"Rose, you are a unique woman with nearly limitless potential. I don't think any new talent would surprise me, you are such a strong magic user that you can heal. Telepathy with someone you have a connection to is easy compared to that, and I'm almost positive remote viewing is like an advanced discipline of telepathy for you. I feel like there isn't much between the two of us that's impossible."

Rosie blushed at his compliments, but had to agree "There does seem to be something about us together that brings out something magical. You inspire me, and suddenly I have a new talent."

"You inspire me too. I've developed more talents since meeting you than in years of traveling the worlds. I can't wait till we're all healed up and can be together again. I crave your touch," he sighed with need, using obvious restraint "and your kisses," even telepathically Rosie could feel his breath tremble with longing.

Rosie sighed out her own frustration, "I crave you too, it was why I reached for you so recklessly. I want you with me so badly that it almost hurts to be without you. That can't be healthy, can it?"

He gave a quick chuckle, "If it's not healthy, I think we must both be terminally ill."

Rosie laughed too, "I guess it's not a bad way to go, if it's terminal." She sighed contentedly, feeling truly happy on their psychic phone call. She suspected that the reason she craved him so badly was because he was a part of her soul, but when he spoke he was so convincingly real. Rosie couldn't decide if she wished he was real or a wonderful insanity. "I wonder if my new talents only work with you, or if I could use them with other people."

"Why wouldn't they? I'd guess you might need a connection to the other person, but I don't think you'd have such brilliant gifts and only be able to share them with me. Don't you travel the worlds on your own? I might have pulled you to Wonderland last night, but you stepped into another world on your own, like you've done it many times before."

"You mean dream walking?"

"Yes. You can move through worlds like me,

world-jumping. I don't know, maybe what you do is more like astral projection, since you leave your body in the Prime Material."

"I hadn't thought of it that way. I don't think I've ever gone anywhere that weren't friends' dreams, is it the same thing as astral projection?" Rosie could see the similarity but wasn't quite convinced that they were the same thing.

"If it's not the same thing, I'd think it's likely a connected discipline. And if you can travel between friends dreams, I'm sure you could explore other worlds than those."

"I didn't know there were other worlds. I just thought of it like creating a shared dream. Wait, are you saying that the worlds are there after we wake up?"

"Some. Most worlds are chaotic and fleeting, but some are fixed. I spend most of my time in Wonderland, it's a sometimes chaotic and always a mutable world, but it's stable." He paused, like he was unsure if he should continue, "But, you know that there are worlds that exist beyond dreamers fleeting creations, don't you? The Prime Material is fixed, painfully so for me. But more than the prime, I know you used to go regularly to another of the stable worlds." Her angel sounded like he was treading lightly.

Rosie knew instantly he meant the dream world she used to travel to with her previous protector, and wondered how he could know about that world unless this was proof that he was really a part of her imagination like she suspected. "Yes, I guess you're right."

"Wait." he said with significant confusion in his tone. "You feel sad. I was expecting you might be upset about me knowing about something so private for you. Or I thought you might be curious how I knew of your training with Her. But I didn't expect sad."

Rosie could feel the caring emanate from her angel, and understood how he could feel her sadness.

For her, their advanced telepathic connection was one more reason to believe that he was a manifestation of herself.

"Why are you so sad? Is it because you can't get in? Or do you miss Her that much?" He guessed, "Or does it hurt that I've gone to the Faerie realm you are no longer able to enter? I'm sorry if I've hurt your feelings by bringing up a world that denies you entry."

Rosie felt herself pulling away from her angel, feeling silly for indulging in her fantasies so completely that she was beginning to think he was truly real. "The only one hurting my feelings is me. 'Cause, how would you know about that world when I've never told you about it unless it came from me."

"I don't understand, how have you hurt your own feelings? I know you never told me about that world, but I found it for you. To help-" He started to explain.

"What am I doing?" Rosie cut him off, "I'm spending time dreaming with you when I still have to recruit at least one more person, and I have to get watches going," Rosie took on a frustrated almost angry tone, "and then once all that's set I still need to figure out how to survive the monster before it comes after me again. I can't keep my friends on watch perpetually, and I can't spend my life running from it."

"So, let me help you. Please." Her angel sounded concerned and confused by Rosie's sudden mood shift.

She took a breath and tried to calm herself, what was the point of getting frustrated with a man probably of her own creation. Rosie continued in a calmer but sadder tone. "You were wonderful to pull me away all those times, and to protect me and save my life when I didn't get away, but I need to find a better solution. I need to stop playing with imaginary powers, and focus on stopping the nightmare that can really hurt me." With that Rosie willed their psychic connection closed, and opened her eyes.

Looking over at the clock she saw it was already

evening. Rosie gathered herself, and went to take a cold shower to get her mind off her sexy angel. She needed a clearer head before she went to sleep tonight.

◌

Hatter sat in his chair, stunned by Rosie's abrupt departure. He wondered what she meant by imaginary powers? He guessed maybe imaginary powers was an American slang for psychic abilities or telepathic talents because they worked through imagining a thing to manifest it. Rosie was clearly distressed, and if two new talents in the span of minutes was too overwhelming to deal with while she had the future threat of her nightmare monster looming over her, he would focus on helping her with the big problem too.

Hatter pondered what he could do to help. He had learned a lot from his training with in Faerie, but he hadn't gotten to anything that would protect Rosie from her monsters. Since he used Kiri's scarf to tie Rosie to her body he had no way through Faerie's protections, but they were the only people Hatter knew that might know how to help. Hatter was almost healed from the battle with the monster, thanks to Rosie and their healing effect on each other. So, scarf or not, he needed to get back into Faerie to help his love.

Hatter stood and took the step from Wonderland into the membrane between worlds. He pushed against the resistance that was the wards keeping people out of Faerie. He screamed as the pain increased, feeling like his flesh was searing. but he continued to force his way into the world, repeating to himself "For Rose." over and over like a mantra. He pushed through the blinding pain for what felt like hours until he felt his consciousness start to slip away. He knew deep down that getting into Faerie was his best chance to help Rosie, so he fought to stay conscious and keep pushing through the barrier. Feeling his mind sliding into darkness gave him the extra bit of adrenaline he needed to push even harder, and with that final thrust he broke through the barrier with a loud thunderclap.

Hatter fell from mid air, in the middle of the town square. He landed heroically on bent knee, head bowed, and panting from the pain. As the pain past he straightened his spine and lifted his face to take in his surroundings.

He saw the same scene as the first time he arrived at the end of Rosie's thread, all the neat little buildings perpetually stuck in an idyllic spring day. The world's occupants hid like they had before, but came out slowly as they recognized him. Hatter stood stiffly, stretching and shaking out a few kinks as he recovered from his entry. He was pretty sure the only reason he was standing was because the adrenalin hadn't warn off yet. He needed to rest and recover, probably for days based on how he felt, but first he needed to have a chat with Kiri.

"Sorry about the dramatic entry, but I had to use Kiri's scarf for an emergency, and now I need their help for the solution to the same emergency." Hatter spoke to the surprised looking crowd, as he dusted himself off and checked for any serious injury. Despite the extended pain he endured, he seemed to have taken no new wounds except for the exhaustion of such long trial.

"Always gotta make the big dramatic entry, don't you?" Hatter heard Kiri's voice from behind him. "Didn't I warn you that losing that scarf means you lose access to this realm?"

Hatter turned to Kiri with an innocent smile and a shrug. "Like I said, we had an emergency."

"Ah. When we didn't see you for a few days, I figured something happened." Kiri shaded her eyes and flew the short distance into the air to the spot Hatter had broken through the wards into Faerie, she smoothed a hand through the air like she was feeling something. "I didn't think anything could get through that barrier alive, but you are one stubborn, love struck, reckless boy, and you have proven me wrong for the second time." She sighed as she flew back to the ground. "Lucky you, you didn't break our protection, you just squeezed through it. Tho I guess we will have to make the barrier tougher yet for next time, if you get through an impenetrable barrier it's no longer impenetrable." She started walking along the path out of town, towards her home, when Hatter didn't immediately follow she called over her shoulder. "Well, come on child, you've created enough of a disturbance for one day. Come back to the cave, and we'll have a nice little chat."

Hatter walked after her, every muscle protesting being used as he caught up. "Again, sorry about breaking in. But it's really life or death."

"I would expect so. You really look like shit, child. That membrane you pushed through would have killed almost any other Fey-born soul. I'm glad you are so strong for our Rosie." They reached Kiri's cave on the outskirts of town, and she opened the door gesturing Hatter inside.

Once inside, he gratefully accepted a seat on a big comfy chair. He was pretty sure that if he had waited any longer he would have collapsed. The chair was a very welcome support, and he found it hard to stay conscious.

"With what you've been through, dear, you'll be needing some serious rest. Why don't you just close your eyes for a wink and well talk after you've rested."

That sounded like an excellent idea to Hatter. He tried to say so, but not much more came out of his mouth than unintelligible mumbling as he fell fast asleep.

༄

A moment after Rosie stepped into the shower she suddenly felt like her skin was almost on fire. She adjusted the cold water to be less extreme, but the sensation didn't get much better. She wondered if the water just started much too cold, and that she'd hurt herself without realizing how cold it was. Her whole body ached and felt really out of proportion to anything a cold shower would do, and made her wonder if she was feeling something having to do with her connection to her angel; and again she was struck with uncertainty about whether he was real or not.

She showered as she thought of the implications of the pain she was feeling. Because the more she experienced the sensation, the more it felt like the pain she was feeling was an echo of something outside herself. Rosie started to get angry with herself, she wasn't usually so indecisive. Why was it so easy to come up with arguments for both him being hallucinatory, and for him feeling so real. It was like her heart needed and wanted him so badly that her rational mind couldn't help but disbelieve him. After all, there was a reason for the saying, too good to be true. Also, using Occam's razor the simplest answer is usually right, and him being real would be very complicated. But, she felt him so viscerally, and he was just so amazing, and she wanted him so badly, how could he not be a real person?

She felt this pain was coming through their connection, was it also an illusion of her mind? And why would she feel that this was an echo of pain from her angel? Even if she knew he was real, why would he be in pain like this? It didn't feel like the nightmare monster taking swipes at him, it was too uniform. Rosie worried way too frequently about her own sanity lately.

Finishing her shower and getting into p.j.'s, Rosie tried to push her emotions aside. Rosie took a moment to put all sanity concerns out of her head, by refusing to feel any pain that wasn't hers, and to not pine for someone that may be fictitious.

She felt she needed to focus on one thing at a time, and the first thing was making sure she never dreamt alone until after she figured out how to get rid of the monster for good. Being that it was a Sunday and tomorrow was school, she figured Frank wouldn't go to bed too late. The alarm clock on her bedside table said it was a little after ten pm, so she figured it would be a safe bet Frank would be going to bed within the half hour and would be asleep by eleven. So she thought about ways to occupy the hour.

Her folks were in the living room watching TV, but it wasn't anything she was even remotely interested in. Her homework was done, and she was even ahead in some of the reading thanks to her trying to pass the time earlier in the day. She didn't even have any books in her queue that she thought she could focus on enough to make it worthwhile.

On top of not being able to think of anything else mundane to do, try as she might, she couldn't keep the image of her sexy guardian angel looking like a character from Alice in Wonderland out of her head. He'd said that where he lived was called Wonderland, was that why he dressed like the Hatter at the tea party? Rosie had liked the book when she was a kid, it was weird in her kind of way. The thing Rosie wondered was if he was made from her imagination, why would her subconscious place her perfect guy as a character from a kids story? He was definitely not the Hatter from the children's story, she could not imagine the children's Hatter looking nearly so tasty. But there was some fascination with the setting when she was a kid, so she guessed there must be something to it. She looked around her room and saw her sketch pad silting on her dresser. She wasn't sure she could do him justice, but she had been in a artsy place lately, and decided to try to sketch her imaginary guardian angel. Rosie sat at her vanity, picked up her pencil, and started to sketch.

Half an hour later, Rosie was getting frustrated. She had a pile of torn out crumpled failures and was crumpling another that was not quite what she wanted. She didn't expect to make a masterpiece, but hoped to capture something that didn't look so stiff. The image of her angel draped across the chair should have some of his animal grace, but all she got when she tried to draw him was flat and wrong.

She tried to shake out her muscles, thinking that maybe the tension she was holding in them was Part of the problem. She felt tired and sore all over, but couldn't think of anything rational that she'd done today to make her feel so out of sorts. She worried for her angel, and felt powerless to help him or even know what could be happening to him.

Rosie decided to try something a little different, and if it didn't work this time she'd give up and go to bed. She decided to think of one individual feature at a time, and focus on the image one detail at a time, starting with his scrumptious lips. As she imagined the softness of his lips and the eagerness he so often expressed when he used them, Rosie's pain eased. She got the feeling that his pain was done and he'd come through a trial successfully. Not sure where the thought came from or if she could trust it Rosie decided to ignore it for now.

Rosie turned her attention back to the drawing notebook in front of her. She thought of his lips again, and of his different expressions. Should she do his ecstatic smile, his teasing bit lower lip? She settled on her favorite look for him, and tried to draw his playfully mischievous smile, the one that made her squirm in such a wonderful way, and this time she captured something much closer to what she imagined. With that success she went for a harder bit, his dreamy brown eyes. She had to rework the shape a few times, but once she added his dark long lashes she would actually recognize them as her angel's eyes. Rosie flipped to the next clean page and found herself drawing his broad chest and strong shoulders. Her hands knew the feel of him, and tho she had never seen him bare-chested, it was somehow harder to draw such a deliciously masculine torso clothed. Rosie had felt his well defined pecs, but guessed at his hard little nipples. She had felt the way his shoulders were strong and well muscled, and as she drew them she tried to capture the way the shadows would fall across his collarbones and the muscles to give the suggestion of a powerful stags horns. She added his muscular arms and, filling to the bottom of the page, she added in his softly defined abs. The drawing came out very good by Rosie's standards, it was a good looking chest without the stiffness she had been having trouble with earlier. Rosie caught herself looking over her work and thinking she didn't really know how accurate it was but really wanted to find out. Then she felt really guilty for thinking such thoughts, and for wanting her mysterious dream man so deeply when she had a real boyfriend. She'd never been inspired to draw Jack, but then she had photos of Jack and that just wasn't possible with her ethereal guardian angel. Someday soon she would have to pick between a real man and a man she could only see in her dreams, and it worried her that the man she probably imagined was winning. Rosie had sworn loyalty and fidelity to Jack when she said she loved him, and even if it was just in her mind, she was breaking those promises to him. During a good time, Jack and Rosie had planned their lives together. After graduation he planned to join the military, and though Rosie didn't really want the life of a military wife she was willing to sacrifice to make Jack happy. But now, she wondered why she was making all the sacrifices. She had always done what Jack wanted, but if she went with him she would be giving up college and the academic world she really enjoyed. Perhaps she had created her angel to give herself the strength to leave Jack, knowing that she would not live up to her potential if she stayed with him.

Rosie looked over at the clock, and saw that it was well past eleven thirty. She put her sketch book away, taking one more lingering look at her drawings of her angel before tucking it under a few books. She poked her head out of her bedroom and found all the lights off and her folks in bed.

ᘒ

Rosie crawled into bed, and settled for the night. She pictured Frank as she fell asleep and found herself in what seemed to be a burnt out and ruined house. It was dark, and grimy. There seemed to be random crying and screaming from some non defined outside source. She looked around, but didn't see anyone to go with the disembodied wails. Rosie wondered if she was in Frank's dream, or a nightmare of her own where she needed to fear the monster.

Thinking quickly, Rosie manifested a flashlight, and shone it around the charred room. It didn't look any better with light to show the crumbling walls, and ruined furniture.

Rosie made her way carefully out of the room. Before she crossed any shadow, she checked to make sure she wouldn't have surprise company. The whole scene reminded Rosie of a movie style haunted house.

Stepping into the next room Rosie found herself in a front hall just as decrepit as the room she'd left. There was a narrow and dark hall to her left. To her right was the front door hanging broken on its hinges, looking like someone had used an axe to bust the door down, with a mostly collapsed front porch visible through the busted door. Directly in front of Rosie, was the remains of a staircase leading up to a second floor. Beyond the stairs was another room to mirror the one she'd just left, it looked to be a dining room once. But now was mostly charred burnt wood.

Not seeing anyone in this ruined shell of a house, Rosie cleared her throat to call out. But as she took a breath to yell, she heard a noise from the dark hall. She fought herself and whispered instead. "Hello?"

"Shhh," a voice whispered back, "they'll hear you and wake up."

Rosie thought that it sounded like Frank, and shone her flashlight towards the voice. She saw Frank in filthy and torn up T-shirt and jeans, cowering in a shallow corner made between the wall against the stairs and the doorway to the room beyond. He held a dirty ash smeared arm up to shade his face from the light. Rosie clicked off the flashlight. "Frank?" She whispered as quietly as she could as she carefully approached.

Frank looked up at her warily, and whispered almost inaudibly, "Rosie? What the hell are you doing here?"

"I came to find you, actually. Want to get out of here and come talk?" She offered him a hand and a friendly smile.

"But they're everywhere. There's no place we can go where they won't get us. I'm sorry you've ended up here, but they'll get you too now." He sounded certain, and defeated.

Rosie knew that they were in Frank's dream, and that she probably wouldn't be hurt by anything in his dream as long as she kept that in mind. She doubted that he had anything as real as her monster in his nightmare, but taking him out of the nightmare would be the safest thing to do. "Trust me, and we can step right into a safe place."

Frank gave Rosie a suspicious look, and she tried to reach him again. "You know me Frank. And you know I wouldn't lie to you. Just trust me. Take my hand and I'll get you out of here."

Frank cautiously took Rosie's hand, and stood looking around with wild fear clear in his eyes.

Rosie imagined a door in the wall next to them, and reached for its handle as it manifested. Frank rubbed his eyes looking at the door in disbelief. She opened it, imagining a blank room in a neutral dream beyond, and pulled Frank through.

Frank blinked his eyes in the well lit room as Rosie closed the door and vanished it. "Did I mention we're both dreaming?" Rosie said as Frank took in their new surroundings.

"We're what?" Frank said still in a whisper.

Rosie manifested two comfy dark blue chairs

with a casual hand gesture, using one she'd seen in a store recently as a template, and Frank jumped. "It's ok, I've moved us out of your nightmare into a neutral place. This is a whole new dream. No need to whisper now."

Frank soaked in what Rosie was saying, and his expression started to show his dawning realization. After a few long blinks his body language began to relax and he sat heavily in one of the chairs looking stunned.

"You ok?" Rosie asked tentatively, sitting in the opposite chair.

"Yeah, um, I'm good. This just became one of the weirdest dreams I've ever had." Frank's head seemed to clear a little more.

"It's about to get a little weirder." Rosie made eye contact with Frank, making sure he was tuned in before she continued. "Now that you know you're dreaming," Rosie waited a moment and he nodded about his awareness. "I can tell you that I'm not just part of your dream. I'm really me, not your dream of me. I entered your dream and removed you from it so we could have a chat."

Frank took more time to process this new information, and Rosie half expected to see steam coming from his ears. "So, I was having a nightmare." Frank began, watching for Rosie's encouraging nod. "Then you came into my nightmare, for real." She nodded again as he continued. "And ended my nightmare by pulling me from my dream into yours."

"Yep, sums things up pretty well." Rosie confirmed.

"But why?" Frank asked with some lingering confusion.

"To see if you could dream lucidly, and so I can ask for your help." Rosie still wasn't sure if this would work with Frank, but her instincts said yes and were rarely wrong about this kind of thing.

"So, am I lucidly dreaming now?" Frank asked, still confused.

"Yup. You're aware you're dreaming, by definition you are now having a lucid dream. The other bit I think of as lucid dreaming is manipulating your environment. Think you can?" He looked at Rosie, and it was clear he wasn't getting it, so she elaborated. "Like I did by creating the door to this dream, or the chairs we're currently sitting in."

"Ok." he said slowly, continuing to process it all. "I'm not sure if I can do that or not."

Rosie thought about how much easier Chris had taken the transition, or Janet, or Wendy the first time she dream walked to them. She knew Frank had Fey heritage, it was strong enough that she'd felt it from the first time Jack introduced them, but maybe his talents didn't rest in dream walking.

After a few minutes Rosie waved a hand in front of Franks face. "Did I break your mind there, Frank?"

Frank flinched, clearly snapping out of a long inner monologue. "No, it's just a bit to process. Makes me wonder about dreams I've had, if they were all entirely mine or if I've had people coming into my dreams before and I just didn't know it."

"It's possible, but probably not likely. Why?" Rosie settled into her chair, feeling the exhaustion of weeks without enough sleep.

"Well, there's this one person I've seen in my dreams a few times. I was beginning to wonder if there was a reason she keeps showing up, maybe if you are real she might be too."

"From what I understand, dream walking is a very rare talent." The thought of Rosie's angel came to mind and made her wonder how similar Franks situation was to hers. "Being able to control it without being taught is even rarer. It took me years to figure out how to get into someone's dream without it being some random subconscious thing. But anything's possible."

"That would be pretty awesome, if she's real I mean. I've met her in a few dreams over the last few years, but much more often in the last few months. She's," he paused, looking for the right words. "I don't know, it's like she's my soul mate or something."

This girl of Frank's sounded like way too close a correlation to her situation with her guardian angel. She wished she could confide in Frank, but he was Jack's best friend. He was not the person Rosie could admit she's also got a, maybe real or may be imagined, friend that she has a romantic relationship with. Instead she used the same logic she did with her angel to try to help Frank figure it out.

"Well, she could be another dream walker. But I feel like I should be devil's advocate for you, so you can figure out if she's real. Dream walking is rare and I've been doing it for years and I can really only walk into a dream I know is there. So, if you don't know her in the waking world, how did she happen to stumble into one of your dreams? It's possible she may be a construct of your subconscious wishes, it's what I would worry about in your situation. Maybe she feels like a soul mate because she came from your soul. And it's desire to connect with someone special that could have created her. I'm not saying she's definitely a dream construct or that she's a real person outside of your dreams. But I am saying that I would look really carefully for proof that she exists before I got my hopes up."

Frank stared at Rosie flatly, "Buzz kill much?" He lifted an eyebrow and laughed before continuing loosely. "I figure I'll just talk to her next time I see her in a dream, and find out if she's real. If she's a dream walker like you, I can give her my number and ask her to call me when she wakes up. If she calls I know she's real."

"It sounds so easy when you put it that way." Every time Rosie was with her angel he so occupied her attentions that she still didn't know his name, but knew he tasted like peppermint. Next time she talked to him, she would really try to find a way to figure out if he's real or not. It wasn't as easy as just asking him, she'd been way too intimate with him for it not to be impossibly awkward. She wondered how he would feel about her thinking he was a construct from her imagination if he was real. Or, if the opposite was true and he was a construct and didn't know it, would he cease to exist when confronted with his origin? Rosie didn't want to risk that, she didn't want to lose him, even if he was make believe.

"Hmmm, deep thought on this one. You have a dream friend you aren't sure about too, don't you?" Frank chided Rosie playfully.

"You're right. I've known them for a while, and I still haven't figured out if they're real." Rosie admitted before her brain caught up with her mouth.

"What's Jack think of your dream friend? Is he in the real or dream character camp?"

"Um..." Rosie's brain locked up, sure that she had just brought a whole bucket of trouble down on herself, and it showed in her expression.

"He doesn't know?" He said with a hissed intake of breath and a look of mock pain. "Oh, Rosie. You better hope that she's not real, Jack does not respond well to his girlfriends keeping stuff from him."

Two things caught Rosie's attention, the first was that Frank assumed her friend was a girl and she decided to leave that one alone. The second thing she noticed was that Frank used the word girlfriends. Rosie wondered if that meant girlfriends prior to her, or other people he was currently with in tandem to her. Something made her think he meant at the same time, but she was sure Frank wouldn't say if pressed for details. Besides, she thought, who was she to judge when she had clear feelings for two men; her feelings were real even if she doubted his existence beyond her own soul. If not for her own guilt, Rosie would have been much more suspicious of Frank's wording.

"I know. When I figure it out, I'll tell Jack."

Rosie sighed with frustration, "I guess it just bugs me that he feels it's ok to decide who I can be friends with. I know he says it's to protect me from people who would want to use me or hurt me, but it's been feeling pretty controlling lately. And I think I can judge the worthiness of people to be my friends myself, thank you very much."

"Wow, Rosie starts to grow a backbone. Good for you." He grinned in a way Rosie wasn't sure how to read. "Don't worry, I won't nark on your dream friend."

"Thanks. I appreciate that." Rosie said, feeling pretty unsure.

An awkward moment passed before Frank changed the energy of their talk. Frank ruffled his fingers through his hair, messing the short cut as much as he could, while taking a deep breath and letting out a noise half between a scream and a grunt. He stood shaking out his muscles before stretching his arms and shoulders in a macho display before taking a relaxed stance."Ok. So, how do I do a trick like pulling the chairs out of nowhere."

"I don't know how you'd do it, it's a little different for everyone. But when I manifest a change in a dream it's a force of will. You just imagine something and kinda push it into being."

"So just focus and do?"

"Yep." Rosie nodded, waiting to see what Frank would manifest.

"Ok. Here goes." Frank did a quick neck roll and shook out his arms again. He clasped his hands in front of him and closed his eyes. He looked like he was focusing very hard on something, but nothing happened as a couple minutes passed.

"Maybe your just trying too hard. Relax a little, and let whatever you are trying to manifest just be. What are you trying to manifest?"

Frank looked at Rosie with one eye, and exhaled heavily, like he had been holding his breath. "Maybe I am trying too hard." He closed his eyes again. "I was trying to make another chair appear with the girl I was talking about in it."

"Why not start with something a little smaller." Rosie said encouragingly, "Something you are more sure of. If you suspect she's real, you won't be able to manifest her even if she is a dream construct. Confident belief is key when you manifest anything."

"Ok, something smaller." Frank stood there a few moments longer. "Got any good first time suggestions?"

"Why don't you sit back down and relax." She motioned to the empty chair, "How about a warm damp towel to wipe the grunge off your face and hands?"

Frank sat back down, but didn't look like he was relaxed. "A towel, I should be able to do a towel."

"Just relax and believe you can do it." Rosie encouraged.

Frank put his hands palm up in front of him and looked at them, nothing happened. Rosie could feel Frank getting frustrated, so she pushed a bit of her belief towards Frank. A moment later, a thin white washcloth appeared in his hands.

A look of astonishment spread across his face staring at the bit of wet terry cloth. "Wow. That's pretty cool." He wiped his face and hands, "it's warm too! It feels like it's a real washcloth. And it looks just like I imagined it."

"Well, in the context of this dream, it is as real as anything else. Anything you can imagine is possible in dreams, because you create it all with your thoughts, but your subconscious is running the show so you don't know you're really in control. Manifesting is what happens when you steer things consciously instead of subconsciously." Rosie took a breath, and waited for Frank to finish using the cloth.

Frank looked up from the now dirty cloth and smiled at Rosie. "This lucid dreaming stuff is pretty sweet."

"Even sweeter if you remember it in the morning."

"You mean I may not remember this when I wake up?" Frank sounded alarmed.

"Think about it, how often do you really remember your dreams? You dream every night, you need to process everything you experience while awake, but most people only remember a small portion of their dreams. Dream walkers are a little different. We learn to dream lucidly, and to manipulate the fabric of the dreams we walk through, but the big test is can you start to remember more of your dreams? If you can remember some when you wake up, or can use what you've learned to learn more, then you're a dream walker." Rosie shrugged, thinking of the dream world she went to when she was a kid and how frustrating it was that she could remember so little of what her protector taught her. But that was different, she always got the feeling it was information she still had locked away somewhere, she just wasn't supposed to remember it yet. She could remember most of her lucid dreams elsewhere, except when it came to her new protector. But maybe, she thought, the problem with her angel and the faerie dream world were because they were both elaborate constructs of her own mind.

Rosie became aware of Frank's hand waving in front of her face. "Helllloooo, anybody in there?"

Rosie snapped out of her internal monologue. "Sorry. I guess I drifted off there." She took a focusing breath, "I haven't had a good night's sleep in weeks."

"Aren't you sleeping now?" Frank asked with some confusion.

"Yes, but you don't get very good rest while you're dream walking, your mind is as active as when you are awake, so it's only your body that gets rest." Rosie figured this was as good a time as any to explain why she came to see Frank. "Plus, until a couple nights ago, I wasn't getting much of any kind of sleep because I was being chased by a nightmare monster."

"What happened to manifestation? Couldn't you just change the monster?"

"No." Rosie looked smaller and more fragile suddenly. "I was just too scared. I knew it was a dream, but I couldn't change this nightmare. All I could do was run from it, and as it fed off my fear it grew and got scarier in this horrible loop. It's lives in the darkness, and can't tolerate light, but I just couldn't create light to banish it. It felt like I couldn't get out of the dark, and I couldn't get away from it. And at the last moment, when I was sure it was about to get me, I'd manage to find a way out; and then I'd be shocked awake."

"You ok Rosie?" Frank looked concerned.

Rosie took a deep breath and forced herself to sit straight in her chair. "Yes, I'm ok. That thing really terrifies me tho. I'm so glad I have a break from it."

Frank looked thoughtful for a moment, "Ah, so whatever happened a couple nights ago is why you have a break?"

Rosie grimaced, "Perceptive." She took another calming breath, "Yeah, Jack had a plan. He put me under and was going to join my dream and fight the monster. But it didn't go that way. The monster caught me. It clawed me up pretty good, and I'm sure I almost died." Rosie closed her eyes, trying to keep from crying. "I got away, but not without some of the damage following me into the waking world."

"What?" Frank sounded alarmed, "Are you sure?"

"Yes. I woke with three bleeding gashes in my back."

"Are you sure? I mean you could-"

Rosie cut Frank off. "No, there wasn't anything I could have cut myself on where I was sleeping. Don't you think I tore my room up trying to find any rational explanation? Knowing that a nightmare can kill me is knowledge I never wanted to be true."

Frank held up his hands in a submissive gesture. "Sorry. I know you'd look for a rational explanation, it's just so out of the bounds of what I ever thought was possible. But then here I am, having a chat with you in a dream and knowing you really are Rosie."

Rosie took a deep breath. "Sorry, I shouldn't have snapped, it's just the first question I've gotten every time I tell anyone about the wound."

"Can I see it?" Frank asked cautiously.

"I could show you now, but in a dream I could change how it looks so it won't be much proof." Rosie thought for a moment." How about you ask me at school tomorrow, and I'll show you then."

"Why would I need to ask you? Why wouldn't you just show me?"

"It'll be proof that you remember this dream."

"Right, right." Frank shook his head at himself. "I should have guessed that. This is just all kinda weird to me. It doesn't seem like we're in a dream, so it's strange to think that I might not remember this conversation when I wake up."

Rosie shrugged getting back her composure. "It's harder for some people to wrap their heads around than others, but my instinct says you'll get it."

"Ok, so I think I get lucid dreaming, and I'm not sure how you did it but I kinda get dream walking. But you said something about needing help, does that have to do with the monster that hurt you?"

"Yes. It does." For some reason it was harder for Rosie to ask Frank for help than it had been to ask any of her other friends, she supposed that it was because she thought of Frank as more Jacks friend than hers. "In the fight that hurt me, the monster was hurt too. So it'll be licking its wounds for a while, or at least that's what I'm hoping. I'm pretty sure it won't come after me again until its healed up, but if it finds me alone, I'm pretty sure it would go after easy pickings even hurt."

"And you want me to kick its ass to keep it from attacking?" Frank suggested.

"No! No, that's not what I'm asking at all. I don't want to put my friends in its path any more than necessary." Rosie was caught off guard by Frank's assumption. "I'm just asking you to take watches with me a few nights a week until I figure out how to deal with it in a more permanent way."

"But you'll have to deal with it in some permanent way eventually."

"Yes. But I want to find a way that I can face it without endangering my friends."

"Wouldn't it be our choices if we are willing to take the risk to help you?"

"Of course it's your choice, and it may come down to that. I hope not, but it might come down to a bunch of us having to take it on. I'm just looking for a better solution first."

"It's your monster." Frank said with a shrug. "If you want me playing baby sitter, I can do that. But if its hurt now, maybe now is the time to take it on. Once it's all better it will be tougher to beat."

"I know that." Rosie sounded a little defeated. "But right now we are easier to beat, and with more practice and some time to plan I think we'll have a better shot at getting through this without serious injury."

"Ok, sensei, I'm in. I'll watch your back, and you teach me to dream walk and manifest shit. Then when the time comes, we'll all kick its but together. By the way, who is we? Aside from you me and Jack. Is Nick part of this?"

"Nick is so not part of this. First, he hates me. And second, he just doesn't have..." Rosie struggled for a PC way to say he's human and pure humans aren't able to dream walk.

"Doesn't have what?" Frank asked with an eyebrow raised and a suspicious tone.

Rosie sighed. "I just don't think he would have

the talent to dream walk. I don't see it in him."

"Oh, so this is all about your Fey-blood thing? You don't see anything magical in him, so you dismiss him out of hand." Frank sounded annoyed. "How do you know, unless you try?"

"Because that's my strongest talent. I can look at a person and see what non human heritage a person has and can feel their magical potential." Rosie blurted defensively. "Frank, I'm not trying to offend your friend, I just don't feel anything from Nick. He's like a void. I'm sorry."

"But what if you're wrong?" He argued.

"I'm not. But if it'll make you feel better, we can take a trip to his dream to prove it." Rosie said with her hands up in a submissive gesture this time.

Frank was instantly calmed, "Sounds fair. I just don't think you should dismiss anyone out of hand just because he's an ass. If Jack and I tell him to defend you he will, no questions asked. It's hard to find loyalty and obedience like his, he'll make a good foot soldier some day."

"If you need to see, I'm willing to try." Rosie conceded and changed the subject slightly. "So, aside from you and Jack, my friends Chris and Janet are going to help, and so is Wendy."

A look of surprise crossed Frank's face at the mention of Wendy, but he was quick to catch his surprise and blank his expression. It made Rosie a bit suspicious, but she knew Frank wouldn't say anything against Jack, so decided not to try.

"So, six people against a monster that nearly killed you. I know Jack and I can fight, I suspect you aren't really the fighter type," he looked at Rosie and she nodded. "Wendy is strong, but not really the violent type either so I wouldn't tap her for a fight. How about your other friends?"

"I wouldn't consider Chris or Janet to be the kind of people I'd expect to get into a fight, but they are both really strong dream walkers and are resourceful. They are also both really loyal friends, and I think they would do whatever is necessary to help me." Rosie looked Frank in the eyes seriously. "I picked you guys because you can share a dream with me, fighting is something I hope to avoid."

"But if this monster almost killed you for real, don't you think we should be developing our fighting skills just in case?"

Rosie looked at Frank sheepishly, "You're right, it's better to be safe than sorry. I know you can fight, if I teach you dream walking would you train Chris, Janet, Wendy, and me? Assuming they're up for it too." When Frank nodded Rosie added, "I still only want to fight it as a last resort, but while I'm trying to find another solution it wouldn't hurt to train for a worst case scenario."

"Glad you can see reason." Frank said smiling before another thought crossed his mind. "What about your dream walking friend that you aren't sure is real. Why isn't she on your list?"

Rosie felt a twinge of guilt, not correcting Frank's 'she', but was not about to open that can of worms. "I think you know why that isn't a good idea. Jack wants to pick everyone I associate with, and he won't like me having a friend he hasn't heard of. It's just not the right time till I know more."

"One more set of hands could be the difference between winning and losing. If you want, I could train her when Jack isn't around. Maybe help figure out if she's real."

"I already know they can handle themselves in a fight. They were there to help me when the monster got me." Rosie was having trouble not using gender specific language. "They stood between me and it, and fought it to get me away."

"So no training necessary with her then." An awkward silence followed, and Rosie was sure Frank noticed her lack of 'him' or 'her', but he didn't say anything and Rosie wasn't about to bring it up.

Frank stood, "So, Nick?"

Rosie almost flinched after the long silent moments but managed to stand confidently instead, happy for the change of subject. "Ok, we'll try." Rosie stood and held her hand out to Frank, who took it without reservation.

Rosie closed her eyes, and focused on Nick. It was hard to feel for his dream, but with hard concentration she found him. Nick's mind felt greasy and slimy, and tho Rosie really didn't want to go there she took a deep breath and stepped forward. She stepped into Nick's mind pulling Frank behind her, her focus was so tight that she almost missed Frank's surprised gasp.

ଓ

23

She opened her eyes, looking back at Frank who was white as a sheet. "You ok?" She asked, and watched him nod slowly before she took in their surroundings. It was dark, humid, and hot. They could hear insects wings buzzing all around them, and something big sloshing through water. As their eyes adjusted to the darkness Rosie could see that they were in an old overgrown swamp standing on the tilted remains of a porch belonging to a house long rotted away. Nick was nowhere in sight, but Rosie could feel that something was close and it wasn't too friendly.

Frank was still staring at Rosie, but she knew that danger was close and Frank like this was a liability. "What Frank? Did I grow a third arm or something? 'Cause this dream is a little more pressing than I am."

"But, what you did was impossible. Making a door to walk through is one thing, you... I ... How?"

"Get it together, Frank. We just stepped from one dream into another. It's not a big deal." Rosie turned to follow the sound of a large splash, but didn't see what made it. A small seed of fear took root in Rosie's gut, she needed more light to see the danger she knew was coming. "Shade your eyes, I need more light to see what's out there." Rosie manifested a lantern, and the area around them came into stark relief. The dream was in black and white.

Frank made a pained sound, and Rosie spun expecting to see him being attacked; instead she found him rubbing his eyes. "What the fuck?"

"Sorry, I did warn you. There's something out there splashing around, and I need to see it." As Rosie spoke, a smell of something rotting hit her. She held up the lantern and searched through the moss strewn trees and across the murky water.

There was a gust of wind as something moved past behind Rosie so fast that she didn't even see a blur. "Did you see what that was?"

"I didn't see anything, I've still got spots from your lantern trick." Frank finished rubbing his eyes and took his first good look around. "Are we in a black and white movie or something?"

Rosie continued to scan the area around them as she absently answered. "Every dreamer has a different flavor to their dreams. Some people dream in technicolor, some people dream in black and white, some people dream entirely in sepia tones. Nick seems to be a black and white kinda guy, at least in this dream."

She heard another splash, then from the opposite direction she almost caught a blur of motion out of the corner of her eye, just as a large rock came flying at Frank from a third direction hitting him in the head.

Frank cried out in shock and surprise, putting a hand to his scalp where the rock hit, and coming away with blood. "Ow, what's throwing stuff at us?"

Rosie automatically envisioned a force shield of white light wrapping around her body protecting her from projectiles, and no sooner did she pull up the shield, something bounced off it landing beside her. "I don't know what's throwing stuff, but I need you to imagine an impenetrable force field protecting your body and manifest it. Quickly." Rosie didn't remember ever making a force field before, but she'd done it so easily that she knew it must have been something she'd done before; perhaps in training with her childhood protector. She looked down and saw that the object thrown at her was a ripped and muddied white lace parasol thrown like a javelin.

"Ok. Glowie field. Check." Frank closed his eyes and screwed his face up in a comical look of concentration. A field flickered a couple times before glowing to a steady light. "Do I have to keep concentrating to keep the field up?" He asked, keeping his eyes closed tight with concentration.

"Only if you believe you need to." Rosie said with a laugh. "Now, know that it will work and it will." Another object flew past them to fast to recognize and landed in the water with a loud splash.

Rosie looked around again for who or what could be randomly throwing objects at them, but saw no one. She looked but also knew that there may not be anyone throwing anything, flying objects might just be a feature of this dream. Another object flew at them, this time bouncing off the shoulder area of Franks shield.

"Nice trick, the whole light shield thing. I didn't even feel that thing hit me." Frank reached down to pick up the object, and retrieved what seemed at first glance to be a solid lump of mud. "What is this?"

Rosie took the messy thing from Frank, scraping some of the mud away. The first thing she felt was hair, and almost dropped it out of sheer gross factor before she realized it was a doll that had been covered in mud. "Looks like one of those fancy old fashioned porcelain dolls. It's filthy and a little crushed, but it's definitely a creepy old doll." She said putting the doll back down.

She caught more movement out of the corner of her eye, and this time caught something big and green and scaly disappearing below the water, leaving a trail of ripples as it swam towards them, before submerging without a trace. "Frank, did you just see that?"

"I hope not." He said scanning the water where the ripples ended. "'Cause that looked like something that could swallow us in one bite." Another object flew at them, bouncing harmlessly off the gut area of Rosie's shield, and clattered to the floor between them. Despite the mud, they could see it was a very dead and probably drowned rabbit. "Oh, fuck! That's so nasty!"

Rosie had had enough of this dream, she tried to ignore the smell of the not to fresh bunny, and projected in her loudest stage voice. "Nick! Show your ass! I am not liking being in this dream much, and the sooner you show yourself the quicker I can walk out of your head."

There was a rumbling beneath them as a pretty obvious response to Rosie's challenge. The wooden plank floor beneath their feet shattered upwards as the giant blur of green scaly something burst up from the floor taking swipes at Rosie and Frank with large clawed hands. They avoided the blows, but were knocked into the hole created by what looked like some kind of lizardy, toad-like swamp man.

Rosie had expected to fall into the murky swamp water, but laughed at herself for expecting things to follow any sense in a dream as they fell down a long dark gray concrete shaft. As they fell the wind whistled past them and Rosie hoped that Frank would hear her. "land softly!" She screamed. "Focus on slowing your fall and landing softly or you might break a bone falling out of bed."

"What!" Frank screamed back, but Rosie wasn't sure if he hadn't heard her or if he didn't understand the directions

Seeing the floor approaching, and no time to speak, Rosie grabbed Frank's arm and used her force of will to slow them both. "Land soft!" She yelled again just before they hit the ground, but Frank still hit the ground much harder than Rosie. Rosie landed on her feet a little heavier than she'd planned with Frank's added momentum. Frank hit the ground, landing palm first to keep his head from hitting. His arms took the weight of his landing, each making clear cracking pops.

Frank screamed in agony, rolling to his side clutching his arms to his chest. They had landed in a empty damp concrete room with a drain in the floor and a flickering fluorescent light. One padlocked gray wooden door was the only exit. It seemed that they were again in a black and white setting, with no sign of the technicolor green swamp monster. There was also now a concrete ceiling above them.

Rosie kneeled next to Frank, trying to calm his screams. "Frank, are you ok? can I help?"

"What do you fucking think!? My arms are fucking broken! I am not ok!" He lashed out verbally in his pain. "Fuuuuuuuucckkk!" He swore in a long screaming exclamation, and the volume echoed off the walls mocking his pain.

"Come on Frank, you can do this. Try to calm yourself, and take a deep slow breath. Please, let me take a look and see if I can help."

Frank tried to take a few slow breaths, but they were shaky and broken as he tried to breathe through the pain. He continued to clutch his arms against himself so that Rosie couldn't see exactly how bad it was. She touched his shoulder gently and he flinched. He looked up at Rosie, tears streaming down his cheeks making clean streaks on his still dirty face. He shuddered involuntarily as he moved his arms just enough for Rosie to get a look. "How? How could you help with this?" He spoke in a pained squeak.

Rosie looked at his forearms, and they were both bent at strange angles about halfway between his wrists and elbows. "Wow, that does look really messed up. But, like I said, I might be able to help."

"How?" Franks voice had settled, now sounding

tired and defeated more than anything else.

"After my monster attack, I found that I could speed healing in myself. I've never tried to heal someone else," Rosie thought of her angel, but she decided to count him as part of her not another person. "It's a new talent, so I don't know its limits, but I might be able to give you some healing." She looked Frank in his puffy red eyes, "can I try?"

"Ok." he said bracing himself. "Try."

Rosie helped Frank into a sitting position, careful not to touch his arms, and settled in next to him. She gently touched his left arm, and Frank cried out in pain. She tried to use her energy to knit Frank's bones back together, but getting her energy to flow into him was much harder than it had been with Rosie's guardian angel. She wondered if one reason she was having troubles was that the breaks were still unset, she also thought about how the healing between her and her angel was a passionate sexual thing and was not willing to take this test in that direction. "The good news is I might still be able to heal you, the bad news is I think I'll have to set the bones first."

"Well fuck. Of course you'll have to do that first." He sighed. "Give me something to bite down on, and go ahead."

"I hadn't thought of that, good idea." Rosie wondered if he'd done this before in the waking world, and realized that she really didn't know that much about Frank outside the context of Jack. "What do you want to bite down on?"

"I don't know. A thick piece of leather or a wooden broom stick or something."

Rosie pictured a six inch piece of nice thick pine dowel covered in leather, and manifested it. "This what you had in mind?" Rosie said offering Frank the object to bite down on.

"S and M much?" Frank commented under his breath.

"Did you say something?" Rosie asked perplexed by what she thought she'd heard Frank say.

"Nope, nothing important." He said gritting his teeth in agony. "that will work great, put it in my mouth and set the bones before I pass out from the pain."

Rosie nodded and placed the leather bit between Franks teeth. She took his left hand first, and got a little queasy looking at the arms bent so oddly. Gripping the arm just past his wrist, she braced his elbow and pulled hard. Frank screamed in agony as they heard his bone snapping back into place. At first Rosie was worried she'd done it wrong, she had never in her life set a bone, but seemed to do it like she'd done it before. Perhaps, Rosie thought, it was more of that forgotten childhood training kicking in. When she looked at the arm, it was again straight and the way it should look, aside from major bruising. She made eye contact With Frank, and he nodded approving her work. He motioned to his still unset arm and gave her a brave look that was, with the bit in his mouth, not quite as serious looking as it should have been. Rosie let go of his Left, and took hold of his right arm in the same manner. She pulled his right arm into alignment with a little more confidence this time, but Frank screamed with just as much pain as before.

"Ok, I think we have them set." Rosie looked at Frank's face, he was drenched in sweat from the pain and trauma. "Let me try healing again."

Frank spit out the bit, and it clattered to the floor where Rosie noticed his bite pattern crimping in the leather straight through to the wood. "I'm ready. I assume I don't need that anymore."

"You shouldn't. Assuming it works, this part shouldn't hurt at all." Rosie just hoped it wouldn't feel too good, the way it had with her angel, that would just be really awkward later.

She took his left hand with her right, vaguely recalling that the right hand is best for giving energy and the left for receiving. She wondered how often bits of knowledge would just pop into her mind like this, and how they had taught her in such a way that she forgot all her training until she needed the info.

Rosie emptied her mind of thoughts of her mysterious training, and focused on sending her energy into Frank. To her relief, the energy didn't take on any of the caressing sensuality it had with her protector. Instead it felt like a cool stream smoothing out the shattered bones, like leaves being swept downstream. She worked for some time with her eyes closed sitting motionless. As she used her energy to work through both arms, she felt the bones knitting back together and the soft tissue that had also been injured by the impact unkinking and smoothing out. While she was at it she healed the little nick on his head from the flying debris. Rosie tried to use Frank's own energy to fuel the bulk of the healing, absorbing his protective white light shield to fuel most of it, but she had to use some of her own energy. Rosie could feel some of her back wounds reopening just a little, but not too badly. When she was done, she was utterly exhausted and so was Frank, but his bones were knit strong and a bit of faint bruising was all that was left behind. All in all, Rosie was proud of the control she was able to exercise helping Frank without really messing herself up. She wondered if there was just a learning curve for healing that she hadn't gotten past yet when she tried to heal her angel, or if healing her angel was just different because she was really transferring energy between herself and herself.

Rosie settled on the cold floor with her knees up, noticing that the cold felt good against her back. "I think I need to just rest a little bit after that."

"No problem." he said, moving his hands and arms around to test his range of movement. "This is fucking amazing Rosie. My arms don't feel like they were broken at all." Frank had a note of wonder in his voice. "And the tingling I've had in my right pinky since I was a kid and broke my wrist is gone too, I think you fixed ten year old nerve damage. Will that be better still when I wake up?"

Rosie spoke with her eyes closed. "To be honest Frank, I have no clue. I can only heal where magic works, and not much works in the Prime Material. So, I wouldn't hold my breath." She did a tired half shrug.

"Dude, it's like I'm wasted but I'm buzzing." Frank laid down on his back, knees up like Rosie, and stretched his arms before lacing his fingers behind his head. "Thank you. I don't know if the breaks would have transferred to the waking world, but it's a risk I'm glad I didn't have to take." He looked over at Rosie, "Why don't I have my glowie field anymore? Did you use that to heal me? And why didn't it protect me from the fall?"

"To be honest, I don't know. Not consciously any way. I didn't know how to do the shield until I needed it. Same with knowing how to set a bone, makes me wonder where that would have come from? What was I doing that I had practice setting bones? Knowledge has just been coming to me recently. I'm pretty sure it's from the dream world I've gone to since I was a kid, well until recently. I was being trained, I just couldn't remember what they were training me for after waking up. So now I'm remembering exactly what I need to know when I need to know it, like She knew what I'd need. Ageless far seeing magical beings are kinda cool like that. I guess things are unfolding like they are supposed to, like fate or something."

"That's real?" frank sounded surprised, "Jack talked about your silly little girl dreams like they were a joke." He paused, with an 'oh crap' kind of expression. "I really shouldn't have said that. I'm sorry. Your dream training just let you do some pretty cool stuff for me."

Rosie shrugged with a smirk, "Aah, don't mention it."

Just then they heard claws clicking on concrete as something made its way towards the locked door. Rosie and Frank scrambled to their feet, remembering that they were still in Nick's dream with its dangers, and stood ready to deal with whatever came through the door. Rosie noticed that Frank had manifested a big threatening looking Bowie knife, and smiled at his quick learning. Rosie reinforced her shielding.

The door unlocked and swung open on its own. From the shadows beyond the door they heard a long hissing kind of growl. An inhuman voice came from the same shadow. "Looks like your fall didn't tenderize you enough for my tastes." it sounded disappointed. "Doesn't matter that much, meat is still meat, even if it's a little tough now and then. Besides I get to play with my food a little bit now, fun."

Frank clenched his jaw as he heard the voice, and responded like he wasn't taking it seriously. "I don't think we'd be tasty at all, were both all grubby and dirty, maybe you should let us go and wait for more palatable morsels."

The creature let out a deep booming laugh at Frank's suggestion, cutting it off suddenly and leaving an awkward beat before speaking. "Food doesn't get to make culinary suggestions, but it can run." The creature stepped into the room. It was a strange amalgam of a crocodile and a b-movie swamp creature. "I like it when their hearts really get pumping during a chase, your blood will be like a warm rich little burst in my mouth with your heart pumping nice and fast."

"Nick, that is really disgusting." He twitched with a queasy look on his face and tone of voice to match, Frank swallowed and continued in a calmer tone. "It's Frank, not any kind of morsel, you need to snap out of it and talk to me. This is your dream Nick, you are dreaming, not a monster. Please quit this Nick, we came to talk not be stalked by you."

"What?" the monster screeched, using inhuman vocal cords. "How could you know it was me?" As he spoke his form slipped into that of the Nick they knew in the waking world. "You know my secret identity, and now you both will have to die."

"You don't have to kill us Nick, we aren't part of your dream, we came to talk." Rosie said in soothing tones, like you would with a crazy person.

"Nick, it's Frank, we're buds. You don't need to kill us. We're here to talk, just like Rosie said." Frank tucked his knife into the back of his waistband and showed Nick his palms, in a passive calming gesture. The show of submission only seemed to excite Nick.

"You say you're my friend, so I'll be friendly and give you a five second start before I come after you, and kill you, and eat all the succulent meat off your roasting bones." He took in a breath and exhaled a jet of flame at them. Rosie had just enough time to step in front of Frank and strengthen her shield enough to protect them both from the blast.

"Hey! I thought we got a five second head start!" Frank yelled at Nick.

Nick inhaled after his fiery breath, and replied with an amused chuckle. "I lied." He exhaled again, covering them both in flames.

Rosie called over her shoulder to Frank. "Have you seen enough that we can be done? Nick is still entirely engaged in his dream, not lucid dreaming. His brain just isn't set up for it."

"Ok, yeah. I give. You're right. Let's go." He said putting a hand on Rosie's shoulder so he wouldn't be left behind, and followed her as she took a step and exited Nick's dream.

଼

Rosie was focusing on the flames not consuming them, and stepping safely out of Nick's dream, but forgot in the hustle of the moment, to envision where she was going. As she stepped forward she realized her error, but she was already stepping into an unknown world.

They stepped onto thick soft grass, and felt a warm fragrant summer breeze caress their skin. Looking around, Rosie saw that they were standing on the top of a hill looking out over a rolling countryside. The edges of her field of view was forest, but in front of her was a large ornate castle flying blue and gold pennants and banners. It stood atop the neighboring hill in front of her with sprawling formal gardens surrounding it and lawns that stretched from the front of the castle to the hill they stood on. She could make out an intricate and tall hedge maze to one side, and a large patio of black and white paving stones resembling a chess board next to a pond with a gazebo on the other side. Many large birds strutted through the open lawns closer to the castle, looking much like peacocks but in a rainbow of colors. Squinting to see detail Rosie also could see a few people stationed at entrances and gates around the castle. They were dressed like palace guards in helmets, light armor, and bright blue tabards with yellow chevrons. Seeing the scale of the guards made her realize just how big the castle was and that the birds wandering the lawn were more like the size of horses; she now spotted at least one wearing a saddle. This idealized countryside was mesmerizing and breathtaking to Rosie. It was the kind of palace Rosie imagined held extravagant costume balls, formal teas, and elegant garden parties. It was every little princesses dream castle, or at least the little princess still twinkling inside Rosie's imagination.

Frank jabbed Rosie in the side and she turned to see a giant mushroom towering just behind them, and suddenly she knew exactly what world they were in. Frank was staring slack jawed at something sitting under the shade of the tree sized mushroom. It was a sleeping man sized white rabbit covered in fluffy soft looking fur wearing a fancy red brocade vest with a big pocket watch poking out of its waist pocket, fancy gauntleted black leather gloves, and an elaborate but deadly looking sword strapped to its side. Beside it was one of the horse sized ruby red peacocks with a green dead scaly thing strung across the back of the saddle that looked like it might have been some kind of a small dragon.

Rosie caught Frank's eye and put her index finger to her lips, encouraging his silence. He nodded, but his eyes kept darting to the sleeping rabbit and the riding bird that was eying them suspiciously. She took a look over her shoulder searching the formal gardens for the tea party set up that she last saw her angel at, and found it tucked next to the maze, barely visible around the tall hedges. But it was there, she could see the top of his red wing backed chair and was sure it was the chair he had posed for her far seeing eyes. Looking around, she also found a hill beyond the mushroom that had a large tree surrounded by grass that she was sure was the tree they lay against just before she learned she could heal and be healed by her Angel.

Rosie opened her senses, feeling for the velvety safe feel of her angel, but he wasn't home. Frank lightly tapped her arm again, and when she looked over at him, he looked both confused and cautious. He pointed to his cheek, then to her, and shrugged. Rosie felt her cheek and it was wet with tears she hadn't realized she'd shed.

They both jumped as the bird let out a loud alarm call, it sounded to Rosie as if some kind of large brass horn was calling 'hey you' repeatedly. They swung their heads to look towards the bird, and saw that it's alarm call had woken the white rabbit who leapt to its feet sword seamlessly drawn with the motion. "Who are you?" It demanded.

Not knowing if the armed man bunny was friendly, Rosie thought it might be better to err on the side of caution. "Just a couple travelers passing through." She said, grabbing Frank's hand and shifting them out of Wonderland with a step. This time she remembered to have a destination in mind.

CB

Rosie stepped into Wendy's dream, with Frank in toe. She stumbled, feeling dizzy, and Frank caught her before she fell. She knew it was too much energy spent on travel, shielding, and healing while she was in an injured state. She mentally chided herself for overdoing it.

"Shit, you ok?" Frank asked with concern obvious in his expression and voice.

"I'll be fine. I just need to get some rest. I'm trying to do too much too close together." Rosie said, looking with slightly unfocused eyes for a good chair to sit in. Frank made sure Rosie was steady on her feet again before releasing his stabilizing grip on her arms.

"Classic Rosie, burning the candle at both ends." Frank and Rosie jumped at the new voice coming from across the room, it was Wendy.

They took in their surroundings, and found they were standing just inside the door of a classic fifties diner. The diner was empty except for Wendy sitting at a booth a few tables from Frank and Rosie. They walked over and joined her. Rosie slid into the booth relieved to sit down, but needing more rest than just sitting could give. "Hey Wendy, how's it goin'?"

"Good. I'm doing pretty good." Wendy responded to Rosie pleasantly, but gave Frank an unwelcoming squint with a twitch of her lip.

Frank slid in next to Rosie nodding a greeting to Wendy, trying to ignore her unfriendly reception. There seemed to be some silent tension between Frank and Wendy that niggled at Rosie's suspicions about Wendy and Jack, but Rosie wasn't about to rock the boat when her access to other dream walkers was so limited.

They sat quietly in Wendy's dream diner for a few awkward moments until Rosie broke the silence. "So, Wendy, constructed dream or something from your subconscious?"

"Constructed," Wendy said with a not entirely sincere smile "Since I knew you were coming, I figured a nice uncomplicated dream would be a good place to hang out."

"It's nice." Frank commented. "Much better than the nightmare I was having when Rosie came to get me, or Nick's monster fantasy dream."

Wendy looked mildly surprised, "Wait, I can accept that Frank is a dream walker, but is Nick a dream walker too? I thought he was just vanilla human."

"You sound surprised I'm a dream walker, didn't you think I could do it?" Frank said dryly to Wendy.

Rosie responded at the same time with a conversational tone. "No, Nick wasn't able to realize he was dreaming, but Frank wanted me to try to see if he could, so we did."

Wendy ignored Frank and spoke to Rosie. "How many dreams did you go through tonight? Especially pulling a newbie along with you. If you have the injuries you told me about on the phone, a bunch of skipping around is going to waste you."

"I just picked up Frank, took him to a neutral pocket, and checked out Nick before coming to meet you." Rosie grinned in a slightly impish way. "Just a normal night."

"You left out the part where you did some major dream remodeling on my broken arms." Frank piped in. "It was pretty impressive," he said, looking pointedly at Wendy. "I landed on my hands after a several story drop. Both my arms were royally fucked. But this one sets the bones like a field medic, and heals the breaks like it was nothing." He rolled up his sleeves and showed Wendy the faint bruises, "Barely a mark left after. Not to mention the whole fire proof protective shield she pulled out of thin air, it was really fuckin' cool."

"You said you had a talent for healing yourself, but I didn't realize that you could heal others too. And a protective shield? Is that new?" Wendy looked really interested.

"I'm just sayin', our sweet little Rosie is made of tougher stuff than I realized. She's not someone to be crossed." The last comment sounded really pointed at Wendy. "I mean with that monster after her and all."

Rosie didn't miss Frank's innuendo and decided

to ask him what it was about another time when Wendy wasn't with them. "Frank was my first non-me test subject." Rosie mentally added 'unless my guardian angel is a real man', but wasn't about to say that bit aloud. "I was a little surprised it worked so well."

"The dream healing is pretty cool, but what's the protective shield?" Wendy was persistent.

"Things were flying around like a poltergeist was playing, and I didn't want Frank or myself getting hurt by debris. I guess I just knew how to make a protective shield from will and white light. I think I'm accessing training from that dream world I used to go to, you know, the one with my nameless ageless protector."

Wendy had a look of delight over the news, "Well that's pretty huge isn't it? You're remembering the training that eluded you after you woke up. You used to be so frustrated that you knew you were being trained for something but just couldn't remember what." Her expression suddenly shifted to concern as all of Rosie's words sunk in, "did you say used to, as in you don't go there anymore?"

"I've been locked out since I lost my innocence." Rosie said blushing and unable to make eye contact with either person she sat with.

"What's that mean? Lost your-" Wendy's eyes widened "You mean you lost your V! With Jack?!" Wendy did not sound happy, but tried to cover it up with tones of concern. "When did you lose your cherry? Why would you have sex with all the problems you've been having?"

"Because I love him, and he's my boyfriend." The answer slipped out of Rosie's lips like a trained response, and left Rosie feeling a little odd. "Why would you think we were having problems? I didn't tell you we were having any issues." Rosie felt her defenses going up and suspicion bubbling to the surface.

Wendy was looking pretty defensive too, but forced her voice to come out like honey. "We have a lot of mutual friends, and I just heard that you were having trouble."

Rosie started to respond, but Frank subtly touched her elbow outside of Wendy's view to get her attention. She glared at Frank's intrusion, but read his cautiously warning expression and it snapped her out of her building anger. She understood wordlessly that it was a topic he wanted Rosie to drop, and that he was trying to protect her.

Frank gave them both an out. "Perhaps discussing your private stuff could happen without me around. It's like imagining my little sister in a porn, not something I want to think about."

"You're right Frank. No more sex talk in front of honorary siblings." Rosie said with a calming breath. "The topic was shields, we should talk about that."

"Yeah, I was thinking that if we're here to get Rosie's back, maybe we should train to beat this monster of hers." Frank started with a grin. "And I'm thinkin' the first step is we all learn how to make light shields. The next is we learn to fight, and I'm thinking I'd make a decent sensei for a group of dream walkers."

Wendy nodded "Sounds like a plan."

"Back up plan," Rosie interjected. "I'm hoping we find another way to get rid of the monster. It ripped me up horribly. I almost didn't get out alive. It's the most terrifying thing I could ever imagine. I don't want to put you guys or anyone else in its path. I don't want my friends getting hurt."

"Then why are we here?" Wendy stated flatly. "You want us around to discourage another attack, but what if it decides to attack when we're with you? I think Frank is right for once. We train to battle it and take it out permanently."

"It has only chased me alone, that's it's m.o. I don't think it will attack as long as we have numbers. Maybe I can find something that will convince it to leave us alone."

"Where? Where would you find something? I'm pretty sure the book store and the library don't have how to sections on getting rid of dream monsters." Wendy's words were blunt but true.

"I don't know. But I don't want anyone getting hurt if there's another option." Rosie sounded stubborn and a little hopeless.

"Then it's settled. While we're spending time dream walking, we train for the worst case and hope we don't need it." Frank was as stubborn as Rosie, and they all knew it. Rosie and Wendy nodded, and the topic was settled.

Wendy brought the conversation back to her interest. "Ok, so, how do we make energy shields? Is there a trick to it?"

ജ

24

The next day Rosie saw Frank at school, and he was quick to show her the bruises he carried on both arms from the dream breaks into the waking world. Frank also confirmed that the old nerve damage was gone too, proving Rosie's usefulness as a healer outside dreams. That the injuries showed up in the waking world spooked them all a little bit more than Rosie's injuries alone. Then, with Jack chaperoning, Rosie showed Frank the scratches on her back. It made Frank more adamant about training than in their dream conversation the night before.

Rosie spent the next few nights teaching her friends how to make an energy barrier. After that a few nights were spent teaching Chris and Frank to dream walk, a skill Chris excelled in but Frank just couldn't get a hold of, on his own. After a few unsuccessful tries Rosie and Wendy decided to just take turns picking him up from his own mind.

Once the mental basics were covered, Frank took over the training. He spent a few days on Wendy before rotating with Chris, then Janet, and finally Rosie.

Jack wasn't too happy to have his sex time taken up, so he skipped out on those nights. Jack made sure Rosie knew he was being denied, and that she'd be expected to make things up to him. Frank didn't train Jack, Jack made it clear that he already knew how to fight.

By the end of a month, they were all manifesting weapons and doing hand to hand combat like soldiers. Tho they only trained in their dreams, Rosie noticed her muscles felt it when she woke. She wasn't as toned in the waking world as her dream training would have brought in the Prime Material, but there definitely was a little transference.

The only nights that Rosie wasn't training was when it was just her and Jack. Much like any other time they were alone, it was filled with sex. Rosie was enjoying herself much more than her first time, just like Jack had said, but it wasn't really something she was begging for. She learned to enjoy Jack's cock in her mouth, but he never reciprocated, saying that he didn't like the taste of her. Jack was not a giving lover, but Rosie worked hard to please his desires. Not that she wasn't enjoying herself, she thought, she did like the way he felt inside her. But it always seemed that he was done before she really got to enjoy it. Those nights made her think of her imaginary hero, and wonder how different things would be with him; and then instantly beat herself up for having such thoughts.

∞

She suspected Jack knew about the infidelity in her heart when he got violent one afternoon. Jack took Rosie at knife point, with no warning. She felt savage hate as he took her, dry. Between the pain of friction inside her and the knife held tight enough against her throat that it left a scratch, it felt like penance for the kisses and touches she'd had with her guardian angel. While Jack laughed at the tears rolling down her face, Rosie tried to take her mind to another place and actively guarded her psychic projections so that it would spare her guardian the frustration of not being able to help her. Though her rape was terrifying and painful, at least it mercifully didn't last long.

When Jack was done, and getting dressed, she asked one question with a cautious tone to her voice. "Why?" she said not able to keep the trembling out of her voice or to keep the tears from flowing. "I'd never turned you down. You didn't need to Hold a knife to me or take me that way."

He looked at her coldly and spoke in a matter of fact way. "Never forget that I own you. You needed a reminder. All this attention to keep you safe from your nightmare had to be curbed some way. I thought this would be the kindest way to teach you. This is my world and I allow you to be in it." He got dressed and walked out without another word. The next day he was genial and even affectionate. Jack never brought the incident up again, so neither did Rosie. But, it permanently changed how she felt about Jack. Now her love was mixed with a little fear and self loathing.

∽

Every moment of Rosie's sleep time was accounted for, her friends made sure she was not left unguarded. A couple times Jack blew off their scheduled nights, but one of the others was always willing to jump in for an extra night. Rosie was tempted to try to look for her guardian angel those nights, but knew deep down that she should let him heal because he was the person she most wanted help from when the time came. Her back healed completely, and so did Frank's bruised arms, but Rosie was pretty sure her angel's wounds were more extensive since he stayed away.

During her waking hours, Rosie missed her angel more than she felt she had a right to. For the first couple of weeks after setting up her dream-guard Rosie couldn't feel her angel at all, and it worried her, but halfway through the second week she felt the faintest trace of him and was so relieved she actually cried. After that, when she focused hard she could feel a whisper of his energy or smell his scent, but nothing more than that. She wondered if he missed her as much, but then chided herself mentally for acting like he was real when she was becoming more and more convinced that her guardian could not be real.

☪

Hatter woke, with a warm afghan over him and a crackling fire in the fireplace across from him. It took a few seconds for his eyes to focus, but when they did he saw Kiri sitting next to the fire knitting. It seemed to be the default wake up scene for Hatter here.

"Feeling more rested, child?"

"Yes. Thank you. How long have I been asleep?" Hatter removed his hat and ran his fingers through his hair somewhat groggily, before pulling the blanket off himself and draping it over the arm of the chair.

"Oh, I don't know, a day or ten." She waved the question away, "So, what was so important that it was worth risking your life for it?"

"Love." Hatter stated simply with a smile. "Rosie's life is in danger, and I know you can help." Kiri nodded in gesture for him to continue. "I know you're timeless, but we aren't. You choose candidates from each generation to train, but they lose their magic or stop believing before you're done because you teach us on an immortal's timetable. For you, there's always another generation to try with, but we only have this shot to keep our magic." He hesitated a moment. "I've come to the conclusion that if you want to succeed you need to teach us on a human timetable. Or we will die waiting, each generation a failure, before we can bring magic back to the Prime Material." Hatter shifted in the chair, still feeling sore and tired, and collected his thoughts as Kiri listened patiently. "Kiri, you must have had ways to protect yourselves before you all locked yourselves safe in this world, right? Human disbelief hurt you, there must have been something to help, something I can use to help Rosie. Because she has a nasty nightmare licking its wounds and waiting to try to kill her again. I need a way to save her, or all the work you've put into her and me will be for nothing. I will give my life to save her, but once I'm gone I have no illusions that it won't kill her too. So, this is it. My plea to get you to teach me what I need now. Please, take a risk on us and teach me something that can save Rosie. It can't be when you think I'm ready. It needs to be now."

"Convincing speech, but you entering this realm without a key tells me more about how ready you are, my little pup. I suggest you practice your fighting skills, especially in that wolf form of yours. If you want to be our Rosie's knight in shining armor, you need to be able to defend her with your physical prowess. She makes a excellent sparring partner, and when asked nicely She will teach you many tricks to help in battles." Kiri paused appraising Hatter's eager agreement to her suggestions before continuing. "Rosie's first protector can teach you much, but I think I can teach you something that could really save our Rosie's life if she takes another hit from that monster of hers. I can teach you to make an amulet that will prevent damage to Rosie's physical body in the Prime Material while you fight the monster in its nightmare. It's a powerful talisman, disconnecting the damage in other worlds from effecting anyone's body who wears it. But one would not help you unless you put it on your body in the Prime Material."

"I don't have an extra body in the Prime Material."

"Whatever you say, dear." She said in a placating tone, as she stood and walked to a table filled with supplies. It held dried herbs of all kinds and gems and bottles filled with fragrant liquids. "You have much work to do before you are ready to face Rosie's fear monster, and I'm sure it is healing fast too." She gave Hatter a knowing look. "I'm guessing your partially healed wounds mean Rosie has come into her healing powers. Am I correct?"

"Yes." Hatter blushed and couldn't help but grin at the memory. "She did it accidentally at first, but once she did a little bit she could reproduce it easily. She didn't have much control to start, and I had to feed her healing back into her 'cause she was hurting herself to heal me. It was a talent I didn't know I had either."

"It's not your talent dear, it's hers. But as a shifter you can mimic others abilities as long as you have a connection to them. So, I suppose as long as you are our Rosie's protector, you will be able to heal. If you find anyone with an ability you don't have, you can learn to mimic it as long as they are with you, even without a personal connection. Lycanthropes can be very dangerous without a moral compass, it's why your kind were hunted to near extinction before the age of reason did its damage. Good thing you know right from wrong, Rosie is lucky to have such a valiant specimen in her corner. It makes you a very rare creature, almost as rare as our Rosie. But I have gotten lost on a tangent, haven't I?" Kiri picked up a piece of rose quartz and handed it to Hatter. "First I have an amulet to teach you to make. Shall we begin, dear?"

As Hatter trained in faerie, Rosie trained in her dreams, and they both longed for the other. Spring warmed toward summer, and soon school would be out. Despite Jack being a senior, he decided not to take Rosie to prom. Jack said that he'd gone stag with Nick and Frank, because his mom thought he was single. But for the week leading to the prom and the week after Rosie noticed Frank had problems looking her in the eye. She suspected something might be up until Jack soothed her into feeling that she was just being paranoid.

With the passage of time and dream training every night, Rosie was feeling tired all of the time. It had been months since she'd had a restful sleep. Rosie started to wonder if sometimes she was being watched by the monster or if the exhaustion was making her paranoid. She'd get a cold feeling and the sensation of a rock in the pit of her stomach, sure the shadows were watching her, but nothing beyond that sensation.

Jack, Nick, and Frank graduated, but didn't invite Rosie to the ceremony. It hurt Rosie's feelings that Jack excluded her, but he reminded her that it was his graduation not hers and that it was a family event. She wasn't allowed near Jack's Mom, to keep up the ruse that they'd broken up. School ended the next week, and it became tougher for Rosie to spend time with Jack. She spent most days waiting by the phone for him to call, waiting for directions on where and when to see him so that his Mom wouldn't know. It was rare that Jack called, maybe a couple times in a week, then only one of those was to set a date. She actually saw Jack more in their dreams than in person.

രു

25

When she was around Jack everything he said was so important, tho it seemed whenever a day or two passed without him she began to wonder why she was putting up with his hot and cold attitude. Was it her feelings for a man that she thought she must be making up that gave her a comparison for how someone who cared for you acted? Or was there something else? Either way, when she saw him and he turned on the charm, Rosie was willing to forgive all for the sake of her love.

Lingering in the back of her mind, she felt guilt, as if in her heart she knew she really had cheated on Jack. The idea of a dream lover lingered in the back of her mind. A man with no desire to ever hurt her, someone who would be kind but passionate. Like that ardent encounter she may have imagined the day after her virginity was taken from her. Rosie tried to convince herself that her imagination was creating this perfect specimen, because He was too good to be real. No one real could be so good that her body ached for his touch. She kept finding herself replaying the memory of his touch. She yearned so much to feel that perfect chemistry again, but perfect didn't exist in reality so he couldn't exist as a real person. He was something only a magical imagination could manufacture. So she convinced herself that she felt guilty for imagining someone else wanting to touch her that wasn't the man she pledged her loyalty to, but not for cheating.

CB

Jack played the charming boyfriend for a few days, seeing it as a game to keep Rosie on her toes. The emotional traumas always hit harder when she could not predict what was coming next. But soon enough, he was getting tired of Rosie's sickening sweetness. He wanted space from what he saw as her suffocating 'but I love you's'. So he told Rosie if she wanted to spend time with him, she would have to take the bus to the arcade in the mall and meet him, so she did. When she got there he was hanging out with his friend and a couple senior girls she didn't know. Jack did not introduce them. Instead he spent the next few hours playing video games and hanging out with 'his friends' but ignoring Rosie.

When ten pm. rolled around Jack left with Nick and the two girls in Nick's car. Jack told Rosie to take the bus home, since it was how she got there. The bus that went past the mall had stopped an hour before, so she had several blocks to get to another bus that could take her home. She was angry that they didn't give her a lift, Nick lived walking distance from her home. She felt uneasy walking to the bus stop alone in the dark, but had no other choice. It was an hour bus ride home and she didn't want to add twenty minutes walking the long way on the busy streets, so she took the quicker path down a side street and through a park. As she walked, Rosie convinced herself that Jack's good qualities outweighed these mind games. He said that he loved her and was warm and affectionate in better moods, so she convinced herself that was enough. The park was dark and quiet, making the hair on the back of Rosie's neck stand on end. She knew there was risk, but she was tired and angry at being left behind.

In the matter of a heartbeat, Rosie went from being alone to having a man pressed behind her with a knife to her throat. He had been hidden in the bushes that she'd just walked past. Her fear choked the scream in her throat, but spread out into the night. She could not see her attacker except for the grubby hand holding the knife and the sleeve of his tattered blue hoodie. His breath was rancid against her cheek and he reeked of cum and sour sweat. Rosie felt frozen with fear, the knife biting into her throat, and knowing that by the time she screamed it could all be over. The man hissed a shushing sound in her ear and spittle hit her face, he reached his empty hand towards her chest. As he groped and rubbed his reeking body against her time seemed to freeze.

೫

Hatter knew Rosie's fear instantly. Anything he had been doing lost meaning, and he was with her before the emotion hit him full on. He could see what was about to happen, but no matter how he tried to grab at the girl's assailant he could not affect any physical matter in this world. He was as helpless as if the knife was to his throat. He saw a tear well up in Rosie's soft green eyes, and felt animal rage at what this scum was about to do to his sweet flower. Hatter changed from a man to a vicious giant wolf with glowing red eyes; a form that could save the girl if only he could affect her world. For a nanosecond it seemed she could see him, and mentally called him for help, but fear blurred her sight. It was enough. Hatter made the psychic connection and jumped into Rosie's body to give her the power and speed of his wolf form.

The second ticked over and Rosie was strong enough now. She would not let this man rape her. She stomped her heel back and down connecting with her assailant's foot. Her attacker loosened his in a grip on the knife, and she kicked upward and connected a hard blow between his legs. Everything was moving so fast now, like a blur Rosie was free and running as fast as she could. With the wolf's speed she was out of the park and ten blocks away before she stopped at a well lit busy intersection with a bus stop, three past the one she intended to go to. As Rosie caught her breath the Hatter fell from her, panting and insubstantial on the ground. He had given her all his strength in a place so hostile to magic that it was hard to stay cohesive. Rosie was unaware of the sacrifice Hatter made to help her again, but she knew that something had happened, something had replaced her fear with power and the adrenalin of it still pumped through her veins. She said a silent prayer of thanks for gaining the courage to react and fight. Then she smelled roses, and she knew who had helped her. As the adrenalin wore away and the exhaustion of running ten blocks started to kick in she leaned against a lamp post and felt her neck where the knife had been pressed. She laughed bitterly to herself when she felt the smear of blood left by the blade. It was another survivors mark to match those from her back, and the other knife scratch just below this one. Things could have gone so differently, but she made it out with nothing more to show than a scratch.

Hatter receded out of Rosie's world to regain his strength. He could feel her gratitude as he slipped through the veil between worlds and knew she would be ok.

Rosie could not fully wrap her mind around what had just happened, she didn't think she could explain it. As she waited for the bus other people came to wait too, and everything seemed so normal that something clicked in her head and she knew that this was another night that she would not speak of.

ভ

That night curled up safe in her bed she let herself feel and was consumed with the thoughts of what could have happened to her. She cried silently, berating herself for taking the shortcut, and tried to forget the smell of sour sweat and cum. She had escaped, but was truly shaken. All she could do was hug herself and let the tears flow.

In Wonderland, Hatter could feel her sorrow. And despite his own weakened state, he came to her. He curled up beside her, and as Rosie hugged herself he wrapped his arms around hers.

She calmed and stopped crying, aware of the sensation of her guardian. Part of Rosie's mind was certain that the soft tickling sensation that felt so like a body pressed against her was all in her head. But her heart longed for this invisible presence to be real and true. He felt so safe and warm against her, but her eyes couldn't see anyone and when she reached behind herself there was no resistance or substance. So Rosie closed her eyes and imagined the feel of her guardian comforting her was real, willing him to be there with her.

ଔ

The Hatter was impressed. Tho she could not touch him in her waking world, especially with his essence so depleted, he could feel her awareness of him. Energy flowed between them with a deliciously sexual flavor, and it began to restore him. He inhaled, and her intoxicating scent of jasmine and honeysuckle brought his thoughts to caressing her flesh.

ଔ

She felt his breath against her neck, and it replaced the memory of the foul breath of her attacker. Rosie knew she was safe as long as her invisible guardian angel was with her. She didn't care that part of her was certain this was all in her head, she wanted him to be real so badly that she decided to treat him as real when she was alone with his imagining.

She whispered into the emptiness of the room "Thank you for helping me get away. You saved me again. You have been my guardian angel every time I really needed you. I wish I could thank you..." Rosie felt a bit silly talking to an empty room, but then felt her angel squeeze her in a gentle embrace acknowledging her words, and her breath caught in her throat.

He lightly stroked her arm and she sighed contentedly. His delicate touch was both a tickle and a strong sexual current. She leaned against him with a slight arch to her lower back, using her bottom to feel him. Rosie felt both pressure against her and a strange lack of resistance. With closed eyes she immersed herself in the light tactile nature of him, and with her focus he became a little more substantial. She inhaled his arousing sent of musk and Roses, and turned to her paramour. Rosie imagined curling against his well defined chest, and could feel muscles flex against her with the movement of his arm caressing her waist.

She felt a light touch on her cheek and a trembling finger trace her lip. She turned her face towards where she imagined his palm would be. With her eyes still closed, she slid her lip along his thumb nuzzling into the air that was his touch and lightly kissed his insubstantial hand. She could feel the shape of his hand, fingers tracing along her cheek and jaw as he cupped her face. She found his lips against hers; soft, warm, and yielding. She inhaled him again, and from that moment on she could never think of roses as anything but an enticingly masculine scent. She could feel the heat coming from his skin as they kissed again.

Rosie rolled to her back feeling his urgent kisses and weightless body above her. With building frustration, she felt his arms caress her with strength and tension in his mussels but no force to the grab. She arched her body to make contact with his and gasped when she felt him so aroused against her. She could feel his fingers tangle in her hair, and taste peppermint on his breath.

She wanted to wrap her legs around him and feel

his weight against her. Wanted to rip open his shirt, and really touch his bare skin. But when she reached for him, all she found was empty air. She could feel that he wanted her, and was frustrated that she could not have him of body only of soul. There was something almost like a spiritual worship to the energy they shared as they felt each other without true touch.

ೞ

Hatter could feel her frustration and her need. It was a need he felt as keenly as she did. Never did he want so badly. He knew it was mutual but wasn't strong enough to break through the resistance this world separated them by. He was stuck suspended between two worlds, if he pushed any further into Rosie's world injured and depleted as he currently was it might do permanent damage. And the trade of one night's passion for not being able to help Rosie next time she needed him was not a cost Hatter was willing to pay.

ೞ

As he pressed his body against her she could feel his lips and his hot breath against her neck as clearly as she could feel his delicious cravings for her. She moaned with desire, filling with need and passion; knowing that she should stop but never wanting to be anywhere but in this moment. It was an exquisite torment.

He whispered to her as he nibbled her ear lobe "I am yours, always". His voice was husky and low with passion, breathy and hungry; almost a primal growl. It took her by surprise and she jumped with a startled squeak. She felt him jump back in response. "did I hurt you?" his voice was earnest and sweet with his rich British accent.

Rosie scrambled into a sitting position, suddenly disconcerted by both the lack of solidity of her guardian angel and somehow feeling she really knew him much more intimately than she could remember. Did she really just hear her imagined lover outside of dreams? Was she truly losing it? Finally stepping the last inch into madness? Or was her angel not just vivid imagination? Was it possible he was a dream walker like her? "Hello." her voice came out timid and shaky, Rosie wasn't sure if she hoped to get a response or feared it. But there was no response. She was both relieved and saddened by the lack of response. Either she was mad, or she was cheating on Jack. She again questioned her decision to enjoy her angel. Was she cheating? Real or imagined, she could not stop longing for him.

☙

Hatter was ripped from Rosie's side. Their connection torn by Rosie's shock. She had psychically shoved him from her world with her disbelief and fear of insanity. His body hurt all over from the trauma of being flung out of Rosie's world in his already weakened state, but he felt warmed and hopeful at the same time; she had heard him on the Prime Material. No physical pain could compare to the rush of her hearing him. He felt it was only a matter of time before they could again communicate, and she could remember. He wanted so much more than stolen touches and forgotten moments. Hatter was too exhausted to move or even manifest his body, but was content to slowly reform in Wonderland knowing that the woman of his dreams was now a little more within reach.

☙

27

In the days that followed Rosie thought she felt his presence many times, but he neither spoke or touched her. Any time she felt alone or small she felt his comforting warmth or smelled the faint sent of roses and she imagined that he was watching over her. Rosie knew she was feeling him through their psychic link and he was really in another world, safe from the damaging effects of hers.

She wondered what it must have cost to give his entire being to protect her magically in a world where magic cannot survive. He was already hurt before he gave everything to keep her from being raped and cut up, she had felt it. She wondered how injured he was now, and had he sacrificed so much that he didn't even have enough energy come see her in a dream? Not that she had a night alone where she could look for him, every night was a shared dream with friends for fear of the monster attacking. Rosie missed the touch of her guardian, and the sound of his voice. Her angel was staying away so they could have the time to heal, but no matter who she was with, she felt his absence keenly. Especially with Jack, and more so when he ignored her. She busied her nights training with her friends to face the monster, but knew it was also a distraction to keep her mind off the man she knew couldn't possibly exist beyond the constructs of her mind.

She couldn't stop for a minute without feeling crushed by guilt over her secret longing for a man that was not her boyfriend. She dreaded the guilty feeling but at the same time would give the feeling up for nothing. Her guilt was tangled with the connection to her angel, and with her secret guardian was the only place that truly felt safe. Waiting to feel his touch was bitter sweet anticipation. It was like being unable to get a breath, and also feeling like it was wrong to want the air you needed to survive. Rosie wanted her angel so badly, and needed to feel his presence with her, but knew she had to wait for him to be healthy enough to return to her.

The next week was rough for Rosie. She was privately coming to terms with being jumped and narrowly escaping. Jack was pulling away again. And in her dreams, Rosie started seeing glimpses of glowing red eyes in the shadows. They were always gone before she could get a good look, and no one else saw those dark red embers or felt the ominous pressure of feeling watched. Rosie was feeling more and more like it was stalking her and watching for the right moment. Rosie was afraid of being killed by her nightmare and was responding badly to physical contact since the park, and though she didn't want to admit it, since Jack's display of ownership.

She flinched whenever anyone touched her, and didn't feel safe anywhere. She trained with her friends as she slept, seeing flashes of her nightmares glowing eyes, then spent her waking time away from her friends in private contemplation. She was coming to terms with so much, and it was exhausting.

By the end of the next week, she had decided that if she could be with her guardian angel again she would embrace the idea that he was a part of her and would never deny his touch. If she could not see him in the waking world he must be an extension of her own magical imagination, and until she had evidence otherwise she would not beat herself up over possibilities.

When she lay in her bed that night she could feel her angel's presence like many nights before, but that night she let go of her guilt and opened her senses. Rosie closed her eyes and imagined his hands traveling over her body the way she so desperately wanted. She longed to feel his solid body above her and his lips against her neck. Rosie touched herself, wishing that it was his hands and wanting him to feel how she longed for his touch. The more she imagined him pressing against her the more she felt her skin tingle, almost crackling with potential energy.

She thought of his ghostly touch leading to the feeling that he was truly there. The tingling sensation riding her skin focused where her hands were, and she hoped it was not from her touch alone. Soon she felt a tentative hand slide over her fingers. She gasped with desire, burning with the knowledge that it was truly his touch. His touch grew bolder and more confident with her reaction as he guided her fingers, but Rosie wanted his touch not hers. She moved her hands out of the way, sure that it was his hand caressing one of her most intimate spots. The movement of his fingers caught her breath in her throat, and she curled her fingers into the blanket on either side of her to keep herself from reaching for him before he was tangible. The days of growing anticipation exploded into glorious sensation, and his touch was ecstasy. With the feel of his fingers against her, Rosie's awareness of him grew. She could smell his spicy scent of musk and roses, then feel the weight of his body pressing against her like she had been imagining and longing for. Rosie felt his other hand on her, his touch becoming more and more substantial. As he traced his fingers along her skin she could feel the pressure of each individual finger against the back of her neck. She felt the strength of his hand as he raised her head up, guiding her to his warm soft moist lips.

Eyes kept closed, she kissed him with abandon. She felt his body now like it was physically there with her, she wrapped her arms around his strong solid shoulders and almost cried because this intimacy with her knight in shining armor was what she had been wanting so badly. One hand explored her body with wonderfully caressing massage while the other hand pleasured her, and his touches overwhelmed Rosie with an all consuming passion. They touched and kissed like nothing existed but their bodies; so hungry for the touch of each other's skin that nothing else mattered.

Rosie slid a hand along his spine and realized that all she could feel was flesh, no fabric got in the way of her explorations. And tho she knew she was dressed in a nightshirt and cotton panties she could feel his touch sliding along her skin like she was completely naked. With this awareness, what was already intimate suddenly became so much more.

Between his talented fingers fondling her, the feel of his smooth well muscled chest pressed and rubbing against hers, and their ever exploring kisses, Rosie began to feel the build of orgasm. It was like nothing she'd ever felt before. She threw her head back moaning quietly and writhing, feeling the weight of pleasure build deep inside her. Her invisible lover took this as his opportunity to grab and flick his curious tongue over Rosie's breast. His wet tongue and eager breath against her skin was such a sensory meal that it filled her almost as much as his quickly moving fingers. The orgasm washed over her, and she had to bite her tongue to not scream. She had never felt anything like it, this sensation was a game changer, and she wanted to play this game all the time. She rode the wave of pleasure until she was spent and panting.

Rosie lay in her bed feeling deliciously boneless, exhausted, and completely sated. The not quite weightless pressure of his body against hers lifted as he moved, but her awareness of him remained. Rosie could feel the lust coming from him like something deep and spiritual. At the same time she could feel his restraint and how hard it was to hold on to that restraint. This psychic feedback was one of the most powerful things that Rosie had ever felt. It made her want him in a base carnal way more than she had ever wanted anything, and knowing she could feel his emotions, Rosie opened her emotions wide so that he could feel her desire for him.

Rosie licked her lips slowly and heard his breath come in shaky trembling gasps; and knew that he was touching himself. She reached for him, feeling his smooth skin, and heard his breath quicken with her touch. She explored, with light fingertips trailing over his skin, and found that he was kneeling at her side. She licked her lips again, and his desire was clearly expressed with low guttural sounds. She couldn't help but smile as she reached for him with intent. Rosie's fingers twined lightly in his as they stroked his member together. He moaned with pleasure, sliding his hand out from under hers, to let her wrap her fingers around him mirroring Rosie earlier.

Rosie liked the way the skin of his shaft slid a little with her hand while being so hard just beneath the soft skin. He felt bigger than she expected as she stroked him, and he froze leaning into her touch. She felt him trembling with pleasure as he whispered "Oh God yes" in that so sexy accent of his. Though her eyes were still closed she could somehow sense the way he kneeled, almost reclined, next to her. His head was thrown back, his body arched to meet her quick hand, both hands gripping the blanket to either side of him. She continued stroking him and he made quiet noises of anticipation between lightly panting breaths. Rosie sat up, blindly facing him, being careful not to open her eyes. She slid her unoccupied hand along his stomach, appreciating his tight abs, and up to his chest. He let out a moan as she brushed over a sensitive spot before grabbing his strong shoulder to pull herself against him and hungrily find his lips. Desire rode between them like a current, and their lips connecting was like completing the same circuit their healing had.

Rosie got sensory images of her lips wrapping around him, and it keyed up her libido so much that she wasn't sure if it was his desire or hers. Her mouth watered with the thought of bringing him the pleasure he'd already given her. She moved so quickly that the feel of her mouth around his manhood caught him by surprise, "Oh God!"

His response to Rosie's attentions turned her on much more than just imagining it. She took him in deeper with each stroke, and for a split second she wondered why she wasn't gagging, but lost focus on anything but the sensation of him in her mouth and the spill of his ecstasy. She felt fingers tangling into her hair, gently but firmly holding her head so that he could thrust deeper. The confidence of his touch coupled with his psychic projection was so intoxicating that Rosie opened her eyes for a split second. She almost choked when she saw smooth pale skin instead of empty air. As surprise opened her eyes wide her vision was filled with him, and the impossibility made her freeze.

‍CB

In a heartbeat her energy went from pleasure to shock, and he felt it. With the next heartbeat he had backed up, and had dropped to his hands and knees to see what caused her alarm; bringing them face to face. Rosie saw her sexy guardian angels face, and his expression of concern washed to delight as they made eye contact.

For the first time in weeks Rosie saw his kissable lips and dreamy eyes, but she had never seen this much of him from the neck down. His strong upper body was everything she'd imagined, his skin was silky smooth and toned and she just wanted to touch every inch of his strong chest and shoulders. Rosie felt her skin burn with a blush as she looked lower and saw his manhood full and hard. She had to avert her gaze to keep from being overwhelmed. Her angel placed a hand on her cheek tenderly, and Rosie looked into his eyes. His eyes sparkled with joy and hope and deep physical need, emotions all echoed in Rosie's green eyed gaze.

As they stared deeply into each other's very souls, images of his face bruised and bleeding flashed through Rosie's mind and she knew they were some of her lost memories of him fighting her nightmare monster. The memories startled Rosie, but were soon replaced by her view of the uninjured face of the man before her now, looking even yummier than she had remembered. His deep brown eyes were searching pools of desire, his soft full lips were curled into a small but hopeful smile; just enough of a smile to see the tiniest shadow of his sweet and sexy cheek dimple. His handsome face framed by his brown wavy hair, deliciously mussed with their play, was like the cherry on top for Rosie and made him irresistible to her.

She soaked in every detail, noticing dark stubble on his lip and chin, and the moistness of his full, kiss flushed lips. She reached to touch a small faint scar on his left cheek, and watched him close his eyes and take in a trembling breath leaning in to her touch. He met her gaze again, and his dreamy brown eyes projected pure and unadulterated love.

He breathed her name, "Rose", as they leaned in to each other; lips brushing together in a delicate kiss. But Rosie needed to see him, to drink in his appearance with her eyes like she had with her hands. Rosie's head swam with too many impossibilities afraid that he would disappear if she looked away for even an instant. She was so overwhelmed that she swayed slightly.

Afraid she'd fall over, he was back on his knees in a blur of motion, helping Rosie into a more stable sitting position. All the while her angel kept intense eye contact with Rosie, like he was afraid she'd vanish too. Rosie put a steadying hand on his biceps, and the feel of his muscular arms drew her eye. She was amazed at how firm and well defined his muscles were, but how soft and smooth his skin was. His shoulders were broad and straight, his arms lean but muscular flexing slightly under her touch. His chest was smooth and hairless, his stomach trim and taught with just the suggestion of a six pack.

Rosie blushed deeply, very aware now that they sat facing each other completely naked. It was one thing to feel his bare flesh beneath her exploring hands, but another to see him nude and know that he was looking at her exposed flesh too. She instinctively looked for a blanket to cover herself with, and only then realized that they were no longer in her room but in a large dark wood four poster bed with heavy tapestry curtains. They sat on a quilted bedspread with an appliquéd rose bush taking up the space under them.

He tipped her chin up to face him again with a gentle touch. His eyes met her confusion with a knowing look, "We're in my room, in my bed." His rich accent caressed against her like his incorporeal touches, it was amazingly seductive. Just him saying the words 'my bed' in his accent was enough to turn her knees to jelly. Her blush deepened and spread.

"How?" Rosie managed to breath out the question, feeling a little faint before she remembered to inhale and start breathing again.

His smile at her sudden shyness was full of joyful pleasure, and he leaned in so close to whisper into her ear that she could feel his breath on her skin raising goose bumps. Rosie also felt the heat of his body so close, and smell the warm musk of his skin mingled with the scent of roses. "Magic of course." He answered playfully.

"Magic?" she breathed out in a trembling whisper.

"Of course." he almost rumbled in a confident whisper of his own. "Our souls and desires are so entwined that our magic pulled us together. Into each other's arms where we belong."

Rosie closed her eyes, and took another trembling breath. "I wanted you so much that I came to you without realizing I was falling asleep or knowing I was traveling?"

"A little reach, a little pull, and a little magic." He whispered seductively.

"I've missed you, and wanted to be in your arms like this so badly." Rosie whispered into his ear. "Part of me worried I'd never see you again, that I could only imagine the brush of your invisible touch and not see those amazing brown eyes or hear that sexy accent of yours." She kissed his neck just below his ear and breathed in his intoxicating scent. "And I am so sorry I sent you away, calling you a distraction the last time we talked, I was so wrong to push you away. I feel so much stronger, and safer, and happier, with you."

Her angel pulled back just enough to look Rosie sincerely in the eyes again. "I know I'm stronger with you than I ever was on my own. But you were right, you needed to find a way to protect yourself, and I think I have."

Rosie looked confused. "What do you mean?"

Her thoughts raced. 'How could he have come up with a solution beyond what I know if he's a part of my imagination'. She felt hope and dread fight within her confusion, and wondered a thought she had pondered before, 'Is he somehow really a dream walker like me and not a coping mechanism?'.

He looked at her apologetically, "I know it upset you that I knew about the Fey village and your childhood protector and mentors, but it's worse than me just knowing." He averted his gaze looking guilty. "The day you were," he paused to find the right word, "first taken by Jack," the words taken and Jack seemed to leave a bad taste in his mouth as he said them, "your connection to faerie was torn from you with your innocence. But I caught that delicate thread of a connection hoping that whoever was on the other end could help me to help you." He looked back to Rosie hoping for forgiveness. "I'm sorry I intruded on a place so sacred and special to you without your permission. I followed the thread and found your village, and met Kiri."

Rosie blinked at the name, knowing instantly who it belonged to, and also knowing that it was one of those things she had tried to remember in the waking world for years without success. "You've met Kiri?"

"Met, passed her test, and was taken on as student by Kiri and your protector." He said cautiously, quickly followed by, "Please don't be upset thinking that I stole your place. You couldn't return without the lost connection, and they agreed to train me so I could protect you outside their realm, where they never could."

"You're right," Rosie sounded stunned, "they couldn't risk leaving their world. The disbelief outside could kill them." More bits of forgotten information dribbled into Rosie's head and she continued with building realization. "It's why it was too dangerous for me to remember too much when I woke, because my own doubt in their reality could kill them. And if I couldn't remember I also couldn't lead anyone else inside. That's why Jack couldn't get in, I guess I was keeping him out, even if I didn't know I was." Rosie's angel looked a little hurt and a little angry at the mention of Jack, and she suddenly knew that he was aware of the whole of her relationship with the other man.

"Why would you want to bring his poison in there?" He seemed disgusted and genuinely confused, "That Jack hurting you was the reason I went to them for help in the first place. I wanted to protect you from his abuse, I went to find a way to keep him from hurting you so badly and so frequently that you thought you deserved it." His eyes filled with unshed tears. "Are you with him by choice?"

"I was." Rosie spoke, and realized the truth of what she'd said like a weight being lifted off her chest. "I was, but I won't be anymore. You're right, he's cruel to me and enjoys my pain." Rosie let go of her guardian angel, lost in her epiphany. "Why was that so hard for me to see? How could I believe he loved me when he treated me like a toy to be played with or discarded as he saw fit? When I return to the Prime Material, I'm breaking up with Jack. I'd rather be alone than with someone who hurts me on purpose." As Rosie's realization settled over her all her previous guilt and turmoil over Jack was just gone, replaced by a confidence she hadn't felt since before she met Jack. "I deserve better."

Her angel took her hand, getting her attention. As she looked at him Rosie could see tentative hope again in his honest smile. "I would always treat you better. You could choose to be with me." And he kissed her hand with soft lingering lips. "But, no matter how we stand, I am so glad that you've decided to end things with that monster."

Rosie let out a burst of laughter, "Jack as monster, I guess you're kinda right." Then she sobered again, "But with Jack out of the picture, I'm one person down against the real monster. Maybe more if Frank and Wendy side with Jack."

"You may be down one monster, but if the others are truly your friends they'll stand by you. If they aren't truly your friends, it's better to know before your nightmare attacks." He gave Rosie a deep meaningful look before continuing. "No matter how your friends side, I will always be there for you. Even down to my last dying breath, you will have support." Her angel's sincere words made Rosie's feelings for him so much more intense, and made her feel so secure that all she wanted to do was fall into his arms. But she resisted, so he could finish what he was saying. "Even when I'm not with you I've been spending most of my time finding a solution to help you. It's what I've been doing as we missed each other over the last few weeks, and I found something to help."

"Wait, you've been doing what?" Rosie was caught off guard, if he was doing things and learning without her, wasn't that proof that he was real? When he'd said he knew Kiri, she was focused on her returning memories, but now the thought occurred to Rosie that if he was a figment of her imagination constructed to fill her needs he wouldn't be able to go learn on his own, could he?

He kissed her hand again, patiently waiting for her full attention again before continuing in his soothing British tones. "That's what I was trying to tell you at the end of our last conversation, and what I've been doing since. The night you were attacked by the nightmare I used up my connection into faerie to keep you tethered to your body, so I had no way to return for more training. But you needed a solution so badly and their magical knowledge seemed the only way I could help. I was determined, so I forced my way back in after the last time we spoke, and spent the time since learning how to protect your body in the Prime Material against the nightmare monster." He was obviously excited to tell

Rosie what he had learned, but Rosie latched onto the statement before.

"Wait, you forced your way back in?" Rosie started to connect the phantom pain and feeling that he was being hurt that night after their last conversation.

"Yes, and I am sorry." he sounded a little ashamed. "But, like I told them, it was the only place I could think of to get help. And I was right, I can protect your body in the Prime from damage in other worlds now-"

Rosie cut him off, "But, when you forced your way back in. Did it take a long time and did it hurt a lot?"

"Yes." He seemed confused by Rosie's statement, but continued trying to explain. "I know the barrier is there for a reason, to protect the full Fey that survive there. But they were able to repair the barrier. And did you hear me? I can teach you how to protect your body because of it."

"But I felt it. It was like your flesh was burning off. I felt the echo of your pain that night." Rosie was looking at her angel with disbelief.

A look of horror spread across his face, "Oh, Rosie. I had no idea our psychic link was so strong that you would feel any of that. I'm sorry you felt any part of me breaking through the barrier. I'm so sorry I caused you pain."

"Don't apologize, you went through that to help me." Rosie started to process more of what her angel was trying to tell her, "Wait, Kiri taught you how to keep me safe from the monster? How is that possible? The monster didn't start terrorizing me until after I couldn't get back to the village..." Rosie looked into her angels eyes and for the first time had no doubts that he was real, and he wasn't a shattered piece of her psyche. He was a real dream walker like her, and for once too good to be true became simply true. Tears of joy tumbled down her cheeks, and she hugged him so suddenly that she almost knocked him over. But, instead he caught her in his strong safe arms.

"It's not an instant fix. It's an amulet that you construct in the Prime Material to protect your body. It won't get rid of the monster in your nightmares tho, just protect the body you leave behind." He clearly misunderstood the reason for Rosie's joy, and was trying to explain that the amulet wasn't the whole solution just a piece.

Rosie didn't care that her angel misunderstood the source of her joy, she was just so happy that he was real and wanted to be in this moment; in his arms. She didn't want to admit that she had thought he was too good to be true, or that after weeks of intimate longing for him she still couldn't remember learning his name. She'd had enough emotional turmoil, this moment she was filled with joy that she was completely in the right place with the right man. She wanted to hold him and feel him against her knowing that he wasn't a hallucination or bit of her detached soul. He was real, and he was her soul mate. She felt it so deeply, and for the first time she could remember she felt truly complete. They had been drawn together because they were meant to be.

"I love and hate that you've almost died and put yourself through torture to help me. And I don't know how I got so lucky that you happened to find me and think me worthy of such devotion. You can teach me how to make the amulet tomorrow. But tonight, I know I'm in safe hands and I want to enjoy our reunion." Her angel was caught off guard by her sudden shift in energy, and wasn't sure how to respond. Rosie leaned in, sliding her cheek against his, nuzzling him in an almost cat like gesture. Rosie felt the light prickle of his stubble, and inhaled his intoxicating scent before whispering into his ear. "I missed you. And I want..." She hesitated, suddenly blushing, thinking of how intimate every encounter was with him, and how much more intimate it really was knowing that he was a real man. Rosie wanted him even more now, he had been her champion, doing everything in his power to stand between her and danger not because he was a creation of her subconscious, but because he thought she was really someone worth protecting. Rosie forced herself to continue, "...to be with you..." The seriousness of being so close and so naked made it hard for her to finish telling him how much she wanted him. "...tonight, here, in your bed."

He listened to her words, breath quickening with anticipation until his need for Rosie was more than he could take. He kissed Rosie deeply, pushing her back into the bed. He looked at her hungrily and spoke in a husky voice, "You're right, the amulet can wait for tomorrow." He kissed her neck, breathing in her scent, and held her so close that he could feel her heartbeat racing as their chests pressed together.

Rosie wanted Hatter in more than just a base and physical way, but as he trailed kisses lower her physical reaction was undeniable. They touched and explored each other in a way that held nothing back. For the first time, Rosie felt no guilt or reservations about wanting to be intimate with a man. Everything finally felt right and good, she was finally free of any fog that had kept her from being with the man that completed her. She knew he had no agenda beyond wanting to be with her, and it made her want him that much more. They were in the moment, with no worries of anything outside his bed.

Soon their touches and caresses grew more forceful, with fingers kneading into flesh and mouths playfully biting as they as they licked and sucked tender places. He fondled her, building waves of pleasure that promised another orgasm. But he didn't stop with his fingers, he trailed kisses past her tummy and was soon between her thighs with his curious tongue. He licked and sucked and nibbled until she was writhing, getting harder himself feeling her euphoria infuse the scene.

Rosie lay back, focused on the gratification her hero was so vigorously giving her. Her hips writhed against his oral attentions, and in a peak of her arousal she stared up at his canopy wishing she could see him better at his exuberant work. With her thought, the beds heavy canopy was replaced with a crystal clear mirror. The sight of him stretched out before her, all compact lean muscle under smooth supple skin, feasting on her like a wolf with a fresh rabbit, tipped her over her point of no return. With a combination of his mouth and fingers he made Rosie cum again, harder and longer than the first time.

Rosie could feel that her orgasm turned her angel on almost as much as the thought of his own. A thought she wanted to fulfill for him, and that she would worked towards as soon as she could move.

He looked up along her body like a hungry predator, eyes glowing with his wolfish energy, and her body tingled under his gaze. His desire mirrored in Rosie, and she smiled impishly with renewed energy. Gesturing with a nod above them she drew his gaze to the large mirror displaying their naked forms. With his attention drawn, she quickly rolled from under her knight, flipped him on his back and kneeled between his legs. He laughed at Rosie's naughty addition to his room, loving her playful energy, and lay back with his arms behind his head to enjoy the show.

She started by returning the oral favor, picking up where she left off before the shock of seeing him derailed them earlier. She enjoyed his hardness against her tongue almost as much as he enjoyed the way her tongue explored him with every stroke. He also enjoyed the sight of Rosie on her knees before him. He reveled in her full breasts bouncing energetically with every bob of her head, and her supple bottom wiggling with the joy of her mouths play.

He was so near cumming, but wouldn't let their encounter end before he knew how it felt to penetrate her. With inhuman speed he removed his manhood from her mouth and was behind her, spreading her legs and rubbing his hardness against her wet and willing opening. Rosie was surprised for a moment before she was moaning in pleasure and rubbing against him. He carefully guided his phallus inside her, and they both nearly came with the first thrust. They built slowly, both working to restrain themselves and make their ecstasy last. But the psychic feedback was overwhelmingly erotic, and as he pulled Rosie up against him, groping her breasts and holding the side of her neck in his teeth dominantly, they both writhed against each other, fucking harder and faster until they both came screaming the others name.

Rosie hadn't known Hatter's name consciously before the moment of mutual orgasm, but as they came she knew him. Every intimate moment of known and lost memory between them all came back to Rosie in a wash of the best endorphins either had ever felt. They collapsed, bonelessly, on the bed, neither able to do more than pant for a long time.

"Wow." Was all Rosie could say as she lay in her lovers arms.

Hatter made a happy sound of agreement, squeezing Rosie gently and kissing her neck. They spooned contentedly, and as Rosie drifted off to sleep she whispered, "I love you, Hatter."

ભ

28

Rosie woke up alone in her bed, still wearing the same pajamas she started the evening in. It was still dark outside, but Rosie was too thrilled to try to sleep any more. She knew now that the naked man and his bed weren't just a really vivid dream, it was a shared dream between two dream walkers. She struggled to remember it all, but she feared it would be like most dreams, and that parts would slip away. She clung to the one part she wanted to remember the most. Her sexy angel was real and had a name, and it was Hatter; Her Hatter.

Before anything else fled her memory, she thought maybe a dream journal would be a good thing to start. Rosie scrounged around manically until she found the diary she'd gotten for a birthday a few years back but never used. It was one of those small red leather hard bound books with a strap and a cheap little brass lock. The pages were edged gold, it had a gold boarder on the cover, and slightly faded gold print declaring it a 'journal' in bold Times New Roman capital letters. She had no idea where the key had gone, but a open safety pin popped the lock with ease. On the first page she wrote one word, the word she never wanted to forget again; Hatter. With the most pressing thing done she took stock of what the nights events really meant.

She knew she had a hard thing to do and it had to be today, after last night it was clear that she needed to end things with Jack. Whatever they'd had, it seemed false and empty in the light of day and the glow of her feelings for Hatter. She was a little scared that it would go badly, Jack had a temper and could get violent when things didn't go his way. It seemed like a cop out to do it over the phone, but safer. Safer worked better for Rosie at this point.

But before she faced the music, Rosie decided to write down every detail she could remember of all her meetings with Hatter. She had forgotten for a time that Hatter saved her from the nightmare monster almost with his life, and even let Jack take credit for it before she realized it was one of Jack's lies. She knew her memory from dream walking could be taken as a price to the healing process, and she didn't want to have any more lost memories of her Hatter. Now if something made her forget, Rosie'd have her own words to remind herself.

Rosie sat at her vanity and began writing everything she could remember from their encounter last night, since it was freshest in her memory; and the memory she most wanted to retain due to sheer hotness. By the time Rosie was done writing she was feeling a little hot under the collar. Hatter made her feel things she hadn't even imagined, physically and emotionally.

Having finished her account of the night's adventure, Rosie started writing down the rest of her encounters with Hatter. She began with the earlier encounters of his smell and the feeling of safety. Then how she felt his touch, and progressed to Hatter saving her life from the nightmare monster. She'd been writing for hours and the sun had come up before she was done enough that she had to stop to grab a bowl of cereal. She looked over everything she'd written while she ate, and Rosie was more convinced than ever that rationally Hatter was too good to be true, but now she knew he was true. If she was wrong, and Hatter was some wonderful mirage she realized that she would still be better off with a make believe man that treated her with value than Jack's cruelty.

Sex with Jack had felt good, after the first time any way, but it was nothing in comparison to Hatter. With Jack sex was all about pleasing him and when he was done they were done. With Hatter, the more pleasure they gave each other the more pleasure each received. Rosie felt Hatter's lust and his love for her, where Jack had only felt like lust. It was like comparing lobster tail with drawn butter to a fish stick. Rosie had thought she'd felt so strongly about Jack, but she now saw that it was hollow. Something she felt when he was near, but it faded when he wasn't around for a while or when she thought of Hatter. It almost felt like Jack was keeping her under a spell or mind control that had to be renewed regularly, but Hatter gave Rosie the power to break the spell. Rosie tried not to think that Jack was actually casting spells on her, but he was manipulating her at the least and Rosie was relieved to be free of his control. Now she just had to tell Jack that they were done.

Rosie finished breakfast, locked the journal with

the same safety pin she used to open it, and hopped a shower. In the shower Rosie found herself taking extra time, but realized that she couldn't let her fear of Jack's anger win. As she got dressed, she half wished Hatter could be with her for support while she made the call. But she knew she didn't want Hatter to be part of this, it was something she had to do on her own.

The phone rang, and Rosie was afraid it was Jack calling before she had the nerve to deal with him. Her parents were in the kitchen having breakfast, so they grabbed the phone first. When it turned out to be Janet, Rosie was relieved.

"Oh my god Rosie! I half expected your mom to tell me you were found dead in your bed this morning instead of passing the phone to you! You had Chris and me worried sick last night!" Janet was pissed.

Rosie stammered for a moment before she could speak, she had been so focused on documenting Hatter and then how to break up with Jack that it had completely slipped her mind that she was supposed to be with Chris and Janet the night before. "I, I, I, I'm so sorry Janet. I can't believe it totally slipped my mind. I forgot I was supposed to meet up with you guys."

"How on earth could you forget that? We've had this schedule down for months now! And then when you didn't show, we tried to dream walk to you and couldn't find you! Rosie, you better have a good excuse for scaring us like that." Janet was winding herself up tighter as she yelled at Rosie.

Rosie could tell that her parents were aware of the yelling on the other end of the line, but was pretty sure that they couldn't hear what was being yelled. "Hang on a sec Janet, let me move to another room." She looked apologetically at her parents, and stepped out onto the back porch, catching the cord in the back door as she closed it behind her.

"Hang on a sec? Really? You let us think you were being chewed up by a monster and you say hang on a sec!"

"I'm sorry Janet. I had to step away from my folks. I can explain what happened last night, please just give me the chance." Rosie spoke in a hushed tone so she wasn't overheard by her parents sitting at the kitchen table.

"Ok. I'm listening." Janet had stopped yelling, but still sounded hostile.

"I was with my angel last night. Biblically." Rosie waited for Janet to react, but only heard stunned silence. "I'm not sure why you couldn't find me, except that I think I was in his dream. Maybe you need to know someone before you can walk into their mind." Rosie waited for Janet's reaction again, but continued, to fill the silence when Janet remained quiet. "I'm breaking up with Jack as soon as I get off the phone with you. Because my invisible angel came to me, and I found out he's not a figment of my imagination, and I somehow dream walked to him without realizing it, and oh my God Janet, he's real, and amazing, and I love him. His name is Hatter."

"Oh." Janet finally managed, all fire in her tone replaced by surprise.

"So, I'm really sorry I forgot we were supposed to get together. But, finding out my angel is a dream walker like us and he's done so much to protect me because he loves me not because he's a figment of my imagination, Well it's pretty huge right?" Rosie tried to keep her voice quiet, but the events of last night were life-altering.

"Hatter, huh?" Janet still sounded a bit stunned. "Strange name. But it fits that drawing you showed me of him."

"Yeah, it does." Rosie hoped Janet would say more, so she could judge whether or not she was still pissed.

"So, you found out he was real and then jumped his bones?"

"Pretty much. Only with a lot more emotional involvement."

"Wow. Ok, I guess that would be a reason to forget your guard for the night." She let out a little laugh, "I guess your Hatter was guarding you pretty close last night tho, huh."

Rosie blushed, "He was. So. Do you forgive me for scaring you?"

"I guess I do." Janet was still trying to get her head around the fact that Rosie had been so sure that he wasn't real, but now was sure he was real. "If he's real, where is he in the waking world?"

"I don't know. He might be a creature of some non Prime Material kind." Rosie sounded unsure. "I don't know, it didn't really come up. But I know he's real."

"How? If you can't call him when you wake up to check, how do you know he's real?"

"Cause he's learned things I don't know. He went to my protector and has been training with them like I did, but to protect me from the monster, and he's going to teach me how to make an amulet to protect my body from damage got in dreams. I just know, deep down, that it's not anything I was ever taught."

"That's awesome. Between his amulets and our training, I bet we can take on that nightmare monster of yours. Are you sure this amulet's legit? You sure this Hatter is for real?"

Janet had planted a seed of doubt in Rosie's mind, and tho she knew in her heart he was real she worried that her heart had been tricked before. "We made plans to see each other tonight, I could come get you and you can vet him." Rosie didn't want to share Hatter just yet, she wanted to spend every moment she had alone in his arms. But if Rosie was wrong, she wanted to know.

"Ok, but I want more feedback than just me. I think it should be all hands on deck."

"I'm about to break up with Jack, and It's not for Hatter exactly that were going to break up. I mean I think it's been past time to end things for some time now, but I'm jumping straight into a relationship with Hatter and I don't want him judged for my bad timing. I'm worried I'll lose Frank and Wendy's help when I break up with Jack, meeting Hatter might be the nail in the coffin with them."

"I think it's a risk you'll need to take Rosie, if they're your friends, really your friends they'll stand by you. And if they don't, I don't think they would have before either."

"I guess, I won't know till I talk to them about it. So, I'll see if they want to meet Hatter too. But ya know, what you just said, it's the same thing Hatter said when I told him I was worried I'd lose them."

"Then I'm liking the guy more already. I liked him for you since the first time you told me about him. You glowed when you talked about him, even when you were sure you'd made him up. And let's face it, anything is a step up from Jack. The man treated you like an object, worse, like an object he didn't much care for."

"So you forgive me for forgetting?" Rosie said apologetically.

"I guess so. But don't ever give me a heart attack like that again." Janet scolded.

"I promise. I won't get so carried away that I forget to check in when you're expecting me."

"You better not. 'Cause I'm not your mother, so don't make me act like I am." Janet's voice was like a caricature of some overprotective mom, but Rosie knew that Janet really meant every word she was saying.

"I swear, I won't." Rosie said trying not to laugh.

"And I expect you to bring this young man by tonight. You need my blessing before we put our well being in his hands."

"I promise you will see me in our dreams tonight." Rosie said stifling a giggle, but then sobered realizing that she probably worried Chris last night too. "Hey, could you call Chris and tell him I'm sorry too. If I don't deal with Jack now, I might lose my nerve."

"Sure. I'll give him a call. But you should give him an apology in person too. After you deal with your own drama."

"I will. I'll need to call Frank and Wendy too, and let them know what's up before Jack try's to turn them against me."

"Ok then, I guess I'll let you go deal with your drama. I don't envy your morning Rosie. If you need me later, give me a call."

"Thanks. And I'm so sorry I forgot last night."

"'S ok, bye." And with that Janet hung up. Leaving Rosie to deal with her issues.

ॐ

29

Rosie clicked the hook of the phone in the kitchen, hanging up on Janet and after a second released the hook. She listened to the dial tone for a moment and thought about how to do this. She hadn't called Jack at his house in a couple months because he'd said that his mom hated her, and it made Rosie hesitate. Should she call Frank or Nick and have them call Jack to broker the call? Nick was an ass who probably wouldn't pass the message, and Rosie didn't want to put Frank in the middle of their brake up. Frank had been a good friend keeping watches in Rosie's dreams, it would be a bad repayment to put him in the middle of this. So, she had to call Jack herself and deal with Jack's Mom if she was the one who answered.

She dialed Jack's number and took a steadying breath stepping out onto the porch and pulling the door shut behind her. The phone rang and Rosie almost lost her nerve, hand still on the doorknob ready to open the kitchen door and hang the receiver back on the hook. It rang a couple more times and with each ring her trepidation grew, Rosie was turning the knob when the phone was picked up.

"Hello." The voice over the phone was a cheerful female voice. It was the voice of Jack's mother, and Rosie's gut twisted at the sound of it.

"Hi, is Jack home?" Rosie was surprised that her voice didn't crack, she knew Jack would be furious and if his Mom was as opposed to Rosie as Jack had said she might just hang up the phone. It would make what Rosie needed to do much harder, but she wasn't sure what else to do.

"He sure is," her voice sounded perky and happy, Rosie thought that maybe she didn't recognize her voice. "Is that you Rosie dear? You haven't called in so long I'd thought you and Jackie might have broken up."

Rosie was floored. This happy bubbly woman didn't sound like she had forbidden Jack from seeing Rosie, she sounded glad to hear her voice. "Um, yes ma'am. I mean this is Rosie." Rosie was about to ask about Jack's claim that she demanded they break up when she missed her chance.

"Jack just walked into the room, here he is dear. It was nice to hear your voice again, you were always one of Jack's nicest girls. Bye now." Rosie heard the phone being passed off and was left confused.

"Hello?" Jacks voice sounded wary.

"Hi Jack, sorry to call you at home. It's kinda strange that your mom seems to have no issue with me calling, but that's not so important any more-"

Jack cut Rosie off with a furious whisper. "Just because she sounds pleasant doesn't mean I won't pay for it later." He took a calming breath and continued in a full volume voice. "I'm surprised to hear from you Rosie, hang on a second so I can switch to another phone so I don't interrupt my parents TV show." He set down the phone, and she heard a TV in the background for a few minutes before she heard another phone pick up. Rosie could hear a muffled, "Hang up!" Followed a few moments later by a click and the TV's sound being cut off.

Jack spoke in a hushed but angry tone. "What are you doing calling me here? I told you that I would contact you. This is not acceptable."

"Like I said, I'm sorry to call you at home. But I'm pretty confident it won't need to ever happen again." Rosie was tempted to tell him to tell him off and break up with him, but tried to remember that she recently loved Jack and wanted to be kind. "I called because we need to talk."

"Need to talk? What can be so important that it can't wait till I call you?" Jack was clearly angry.

Rosie was just so tired of Jacks superiority complex, that she decided to go with quick. "It's over Jack. I'm calling because I'm not happy and I deserve better."

"You think you deserve better? What the fuck? I've made you stronger. You should be thanking me! Where is this coming from? Who is he? Who are you fucking behind my back?" He spat his disgust at Rosie and it hurt. "I know you had help when that monster attacked you in your dreams, is that who you're fucking?"

"It's not like that Jack. It's us that doesn't work anymore, why does it matter if I'm with anyone else? You treat me like property or an accessory that you can use when it suits you and ignore the rest of the time. You've neglected me, and abused me. I'm done."

"Don't change the subject, who are you cheating on me with? Is it that knight in shining armor? Have you been fucking him all along? I mean seriously, were you even a virgin or were you already fucking him then?" Jack knew the only thing that could break his hold over Rosie was another man, and Jack was pissed that she was slut enough to cheat.

"Stop badgering me Jack. I admit that there is someone else, but I didn't do it to hurt you. When I was lonely or hurt he came to comfort me, he made me feel safe and loved in a way you didn't. I thought I imagined him, I thought I was falling in love with a piece of my imagination made manifest, but it turns out he's a dream walker like us. As soon as I knew he was real, I had to make a choice. I know that I'm in the wrong here, and this isn't fair to either of you as it stands. I loved you both, but now that I know he's real it would be wrong to keep going like it is. He's always kind to me, he protected me at great risk to himself more than once already, and would do it again. While I feel like you treat me like an inconvenience and a possession, and I deserve better. It's over between us Jack, I'm sorry."

A shocked silence stretched for long awkward moments. Jack couldn't believe that Rosie had really fallen in love while under his spell, when she should be blindly in love with him. It shouldn't be possible. "What?" Jack sounded lost and small, it was a sound Rosie never imagined she'd hear from him. "But you love me, you can't break up with me." His tone was fighting from hurt shock into righteous indignation. "You are mine. How could you be with anyone else? You shouldn't even be able to find anyone else attractive, you love me!"

"I'm sorry Jack. I did love you, but our relationship hasn't been a healthy thing for a long time. Even if there wasn't anyone else in my heart, it would be better to part ways. We just aren't a healthy fit." Tears rolled down Rosie's cheeks. She was sure that there were good times too, times when Jack was kind to her and loving, she just couldn't recall any of them right now. Rosie started the conversation strong and sure of her choice, but hearing him hurt made her momentarily doubt it. She knew how it felt to have her heart broken, did she really want to put Jack through the same pain?

"A healthy fit?" Jack's tone was mocking, but continued to fiery anger. "What the fuck are you playing at? You have begged me to stay with you! I could have walked away a dozen times, but you love me and I stayed with you, for love. You can't leave me you miserable little slut! You are mine!"

A cool resolve settled over Rosie, and she felt relief that it was finally over. Her mental shift was abrupt, it felt like a switch clicking off and she didn't need Jack any more. She spoke, and her words came out calm and unemotional, very matter of fact. "I was almost feeling bad about my choice. But you know what Jack? I don't need to take this crap from you anymore. Sorry it didn't work out. Have a nice life." As she spoke she opened the kitchen door and stepped into the room. She hung up the phone when she was done, before Jack could get in a last word.

The phone rang in seconds. Rosie knew it was Jack calling back to continue the argument, but like she'd said she was done. She lifted the receiver off the hook and hung it back up. A few seconds later the phone rang again, so she repeated the process. For the next ten minutes the phone rang every few seconds and Rosie calmly hung up the phone. Rosie decided ten minutes was long enough and was tired of Jack's drama, so when the phone rang again she picked up the receiver.

"Listen bitch, you don't hang up on me!" He was screaming and Rosie didn't even flinch at the anger that used to destroy her.

She spoke calmly and dispassionately, "If it wasn't clear enough before, I am telling you to stop calling our home or the police will be involved. Good bye Jack." Rosie hung up, and a few seconds later the phone didn't ring.

જી

30

Jack stared at the phone, livid. He had never had a girl break his control over them. Rosie had so much more tasty Fey energy, he expected to feed from her magic for many months more. He had plans to twist her will until she would do whatever he wanted, he thought he'd had her wrapped around his little finger until she started talking about that nightmare monster. Over the last few months he'd been laying the ground work with Wendy, planning to get Rosie and Wendy in bed together and make each think it was their idea. Now he thought bitterly that Rosie had taken away his fantasy of being blown by two women at once while feeding off both their magical powers.

Jack had been brooding and contemplating revenge for almost a half hour when he heard a knock at the back door. He saw Frank peeking through the door's window around the curtain cheerfully waving, and it only made him feel surlier. Jack opened the door and stood in the way of his friend entering. "What." He said gruffly.

Frank raised his hands in a passive gesture. "Whoa, dude. What's with the death stare?"

"I'm not in the mood for your bouncy perkiness today Frank. Go away." Jack spat his words at Frank.

"What the fuck?" Frank said dropping his arms and looking confused. "I thought we had plans to go hang at the arcade, something crawl up your ass and die there instead?"

"Rosie and I just broke up, and I'm not in the mood to 'come out and play' with you today." Jack managed to put anger into his air quotes, but Frank could see tears fighting to stream from his eyes.

"Hey, sorry buddy. I didn't know. But aren't you usually happy when you break up with Rosie? Don't you usually get whatever you want when you take her back? How's this different?"

"Fuck off Frank." Jack answered angrily.

"Oh, she broke up with you huh?" Frank made sure to keep his face neutral, but thought to himself 'good for her'. Jack took a swing at Frank, he dodged agilely, taking a step back from his angry friend. "I guessed right then. I thought you said no woman could resist you when you decided to have them. What happened?"

"I said fuck off Frank. And go home."

"Sorry." Frank said gingerly, and took a few steps backward starting to leave, unwilling to turn his back to an angry Jack. If they were in prison, Frank would expect Jack to shank him in the back with the murderous look on his face. Frank wasn't so sure Jack wouldn't try and beat him down, prison or not, in his current mood. So he kept an eye on his violent friend.

"The bitch fucking cheated on me. It's the only way she could have broken my hold over her."

Frank froze. "She what? And you what?"

"You heard me, dumb ass. She has to be fucking some poaching asshole." Jack swung the door open further, and stepped back into the comparative darkness of the kitchen.

Frank, knowing Jack, took this as an invitation he shouldn't refuse and stepped from the warm sunny outside morning into the somewhat colder feeling kitchen. He spoke cautiously, not wanting to provoke Jack's anger. "I'm not sure I understand what you're saying. Why are you sure she's cheating?"

Jack sat heavily in a kitchen chair, and punched the table to release some of his frustration. "I owned her. She tasted like sweet defeat, and easy prey. But then that bitch stabs me in the back before I was even close to finished munching all that potential magic out of her. When I feed off a woman, they beg me for more like I'm a drug. No way she quit me without someone touching her naughty bits to break my hold. That cunt is going to pay for walking away from me."

Frank took in what Jack had just said, and so many things about him suddenly made sense. Frank wondered how he had known Jack for so many years and not seen that he was some kind of psychic vampire. He knew that Jack was a misogynistic ass to women, and even that he enjoyed making them suffer so he could manipulate them easier when they broke. A character trait that had only been getting worse sense Jack was about fourteen, and that Frank had been having more and more issue with, especially after getting to know Rosie. But Frank had no idea Jack was literally feeding off his girlfriends. It explained why he worked his way through so many women, and why they were left such empty husks emotionally after Jack dumped them. Frank had thought the girls were just devastated by being dumped, but now realized with a sick feeling in his stomach, that there was more to it than that. It seemed like somewhere between realizing that your best friend is a repeat rapist and a serial killer. Either way, Frank didn't like what he'd just discovered, and it was the straw that broke the camel's back for their friendship. "We'll, shit."

"Exactly. Fucking bitch. Can you believe she fucking cheated on me?" It was obvious that Jack did not notice Frank having an epiphany.

"To be fair, you cheated on her a bunch of times."

"Shut the fuck up."

Frank was tired of Jack's attitude. "No. I think I've shut up long enough. I mean, I've had problems with how you treat your girlfriends for a long time. But I didn't know you were literally draining their energy too. Having one cheat on you seems like karma. The way you treat women, I'm surprised it hasn't happened before. They're people, not food." With that Frank shook his head and walked out.

Jack was momentarily stunned before the rage bubbled back to the surface. Frank had been one of his best friends since they were kids. He couldn't believe that Rosie had stolen him too. He was sure she must have used magic to gain Frank's loyalty. Jack would be sure she paid for taking from him, for cheating, and disrupting his feeding source.

☙

31

Tho Rosie was confident she'd made the right decision, and felt calm and secure with herself for the first time since meeting Jack. As she sat at the kitchen table an odd sensation settled over her. Rosie was left feeling shaken and strange, like hearing Jack's voice was trying to reassert some hold over her. She felt conflicting emotions, a small part of her wanted to call Jack back just to hear his voice and be with him again while that thought made the rest of her psyche feel ill with revulsion over that impulse. There was something really unnatural about her wanting Jack; it felt fake and forced as she explored her desires. The whole situation left a bad taste in her mouth. The more she tried to shake it off, the more the little thoughts tried to assert themselves and the more foreign she knew they were. It made her really wonder if Jack had been using magic of some kind to control her, and if that was the case she wondered if it was intentional magic or something purely subconscious. Rosie hoped it wasn't something Jack did on purpose, because that would make him a worse monster than her nightmare. If Jack was controlling people on purpose Rosie knew she would feel a need to protect other women from his predatory behavior. But not right now, now she was mentally exhausted over the whole thing and needed recovery time for herself.

Once Rosie regained her composure, she picked up the phone again. This time to call Frank. She needed to give him a heads up about the change to their nightly plans, but she also felt she owed him a explanation about why she had broken up with Jack. Rosie had become much closer to Frank over the last couple months, and really thought of him like Janet and Chris now. She would really miss his friendship if he decided he had to choose between Jack and her.

As she started to dial Frank's number, something struck Rosie and made her hang up and dial another number instead. All this time she had been wary of Wendy, thinking that she was trying to steal Jack from her. But, it was now clear that Wendy was likely being manipulated by Jack just like Rosie had been. If he had asserted some control over Wendy, she might not have had any more choice than Rosie did.

The phone rang a few times before someone picked up, and the sleepy voice on the other end made Rosie remember that it was still pretty early by summer vacation standards. "Hello?"

"Wendy? It's Rosie. Did I wake you?"

"Yep." Wendy said blearily "You know, it's like eight thirty in the morning right? I was out late last night and was planning on sleeping in today. Think I could call you back a little closer to noon?"

Rosie decided to treat the situation like yanking off a band aid, might as well get it all out there and see how Wendy responds. "Sorry I woke you. I was just calling to tell you that I've broken up with Jack, and that there's a change of plans for tonight. But if you want to talk about that later, give me a call when you get up."

"Wait, what?" suddenly Wendy sounded wide awake. "Um, I think I'm up now. What happened? He broke up with you? You sound so calm, I'm confused."

"No, I broke up with him. I realized that I deserved better than how he was treating me. He was hot and cold, like he was playing with me. And..." Rosie wasn't sure how blunt she should be, she still only had suspicions about Wendy and Jack but didn't want Wendy hurt if she was under control.

"And?" Wendy sounded concerned.

Rosie decided she could judge Wendy better if she could read her expressions. "Are you free today? Do you want to get together and talk?"

"Um, sure." It was obvious that Wendy was confused by Rosie's behavior. "How about we meet for lunch. We could grab a burger at the shack by school."

"Sounds great." Rosie said with relief, thinking that it would be good to have some time to plan what she'd say to Wendy. "How about noon?"

"Ok, noon." Wendy still sounded uncertain. "Are you sure you're ok? I mean, you're always talking about how much you love Jack. And now you're all matter of fact about the breakup."

"You know what Wendy, I'm freaking fantastic." And saying it, Rosie knew she was right. The bad aftertaste that was left in her heart and mind after breaking up with Jack was quickly dissipating, kinda like a bad dream. "He just doesn't have a hold over me anymore. And, there's more to it. We just really need to talk."

"Ok, I'll see you at noon."

"See you at noon." Rosie heard Wendy hang up, and followed suit. Part of her expected Wendy to call Jack, and worried that he would spin it in a unfavorable way. But then, Rosie knew she wasn't entirely innocent in the way things went down. She had cheated on Jack with Hatter, but she was oddly ok with that at the moment. She figured that the chips would fall where they would and she'd deal with the fall out, no reason to worry over things she couldn't control.

β

Rosie tried Frank next, but he wasn't home so she left a message and went on to her last necessary call of the day.

When she called Chris he picked up on the first ring. "Hello?"

"Hey Chris, it's Rosie."

"I know. I've been waiting." He smoothly responded. "Janet said you had a good reason to ditch us last night, but said it was not her story to tell. She also said you're done with that Jack ass who treated you like a chew toy, and I can't tell you how proud that makes me of my little sis."

"Yes, I broke up with Jack this morning. It was something I should have done months ago, but he had this hold on me that I finally managed to shake last night, so I dealt with it. He was pretty pissed, but at least it's done." Somehow it was easier to talk about her fresh breakup, than to tell Chris she's been falling in love with

Hatter for months and didn't tell Chris about him. She hesitated before saying more. "So, is that all Janet said about my good reason?" Rosie was hoping she wouldn't have to explain Hatter from scratch.

"When I asked, all she would say is 'it's true love'. Enough to get me interested, instead of pissed you ditched us. So, dish."

Rosie smiled at Janet's apt summery of her feelings with Hatter, and thought about where to start. "Remember the first time Janet and I came to see you in your dream?"

"Yea. Fun orgy, that dream." Chris chuckled.

Rosie shook off the mental image and continued. "Do you remember, when I told you about the monster, I told you someone pulled me out and saved me?"

"I do. I also remember that you seemed purposefully vague on who." Chris said sounding like he was fishing for dirt.

Rosie sighed, "Yeah, that was because I wasn't really sure at the time if he was some kind of a manifested defense mechanism that was part of me, or a real man." She smiled, seeing Hatter in her mind's eye. "I finally figured out last night, that the man that's been putting himself in harm's way for me has been real all along."

"Oh." Chris sounded a little hurt. "So, you didn't tell me about this guy because..."

"Because I thought I likely went a little mad, and was having a thing with what pretty much was an external split personality."

"Why would you have thought that?" Chris was starting to sound a little confused.

"I thought he was just too good to be true. When I was hurt or scared he comforted me, when I was in danger he was there to rescue and fight for me, he fulfilled my needs too well. I was used to the way Jack treated me, someone kind and attentive was like a dream. Plus, I haven't seen him in the waking world, I only felt him near, and heard him really briefly. He only seemed whole in dreams, so I kinda thought he was one."

"So, if you thought you were going crazy, why didn't you tell me? I would have done what I could to help."

"I didn't want help. I figured that if I was crazy, it wasn't a crazy that hurt anyone. He was a private indulgence, my guardian angel always there for me." Rosie mentally debated letting Chris know she'd had some Hatter feedback. "I told Janet about him."

"Really? You told Janet but not me." Chris sounded hurt. "I guess that's your prerogative, at least you told someone." Rosie gave him an apologetic look and he took a breath to let it go. "So, I get why you thought this guy was too good to be true. Why do you think he's real now?"

"We had a talk last night, and he knew things I never learned. While we've been training to defend ourselves from the monster, so was he. He learned how to make an amulet that should protect its wearers body from damage took in a dream."

"Really? That's fantastic. How do we make them?"

"He's offered to teach me tonight." Rosie again hesitated, she'd promised to invite the rest of her guards, but was a little afraid about everyone meeting. "Janet wants to vet him. Wants all of you to vet him, to make sure he's real and that the amulet seems on the level. I guess she's worried about my choice of men, considering Jack. I guess I can't blame her concern when this amulet could save a life or let them die from dream wounds if it fails."

"Do you think he's on the level?"

"I do. Now that I can see him for what he is, I trust him utterly. I love him, Chris. I thought I loved Jack, but he manipulated me into everything and treated me like shit. I thought I really loved Jack, but what I had with Jack feels so hollow in comparison. What I have with Hatter feels so right and true, I can feel his love for me and I really love him too. I couldn't imagine wanting to be with anyone else now that I found him."

"Hatter? Like the mad Hatter from Alice in Wonderland?"

"Sort of. He lives in a stable dream world he calls Wonderland, and he wears the exaggerated top hat that goes with most images of the mad Hatter. But he's not crazy like the guy from the story, he acts like my knight in shining armor or a guardian angel more than a crazy guy at a tea party. Hatter looks cool not goofy, he's our age, and he's way hotter than anything in a kids book."

"Hubba, hubba. Rosie, are you telling me that you got yourself a hottie with a body?"

"Oh my god Chris, you don't even know. His chest and arms are so..." Rosie imagined Hatter shirtless, and her sudden wash of desire made her squirm. "Like I said, there were reasons I thought he was too good to be true."

"Janet's right. I need to meet this Hatter of yours. If he measures up, I'll be happy to give you two my blessing."

"I thought you were my self-adopted brother, not a surrogate dad. Do we need your blessings now?"

"Damn skippy. No more Jack asses for my little sis." Chris exaggerated the word jack to make it clear who he meant, and it got a giggle out of Rosie.

"I'll come meet him tonight, but first you need to give me more details. How'd you meet? what's he look like? Aside from strong arms and nice pecs, I mean."

Rosie blushed, and took her favorite seat out on the back porch before recounting her relationship with Hatter for Chris. They talked for hours before Rosie realized it was almost time to go meet Wendy. She told Chris she'd see him tonight, and said good bye as quick as she could then high tailed it to lunch.

CR

32

Rosie was a few minutes late, she could see Wendy sitting and waiting at their favorite picnic table from half a block away. It wasn't till she was almost to the table that she saw Frank leaning against the wall chatting with Wendy. Rosie almost tripped over her own feet with the surprise, but made herself finish walking up and take a seat at the table.

"Hi Wendy," she said making sure to make eye contact, before giving Frank a nod. "Hey Frank."

"Hi Rosie." the two said, perfectly timed to give Rosie a stereo effect. Wendy had a look of apprehension, but Frank looked more serious and that left Rosie feeling more nervous herself.

"I didn't know you'd be here Frank, I was just expecting Wendy." Rosie wondered if they'd spoken to Jack, and if they had, how much they knew.

"Surprise." Frank said dryly, lacking any of his usual light hearted attitude. "I got your message after I spoke with Wendy and knew you were meeting, so this way you can kill two birds with one stone. Right."

"Yea. This does make things easier." Rosie tried to smile and relax, but she was still pretty worried that they'd side with Jack and Frank's attitude struck her as a little scary. "I broke up with Jack this morning, and I wasn't too sure where that would leave us; ya know, friend wise."

Wendy looked hurt. "Rosie, I was your friend long before you met Jack. Why would your breakup do anything to our friendship?"

"I know you've been spending lots of time with him on your own." Rosie started and then wasn't sure how to finish. "I just wasn't sure..."

"If Jack and Wendy were cheating behind your back?" Frank bluntly supplied the end of Rosie's thought.

Wendy's eyes grew large, like a deer caught in

headlights. "Rosie, I, I, I just don't know what to say."
She stammered, sounding guilty.

"Thanks Frank. I wasn't going to be that blunt,
but I have been wondering if there was something going
on between you." Rosie looked a little ashamed. "I
avoided you for a long time because I didn't know how
to deal with my suspicions. I know you spend time with
him alone, and I see how you look at him when you
think I'm not looking. I'm not angry, and it's over
between Jack and I so whatever you do is your business,
I just want to know."

Wendy glared at Frank before averting her eyes
from them both. "Jack and I have a special connection. I
feel deeply for him, but I swear on the paths between
dreams that we have never done anything more than
talk." Rosie took a deep breath and was about to speak
when Wendy cut her off. "Please let me finish, Rosie. I
wanted to be with Jack, and our talks got pretty close,
but I wouldn't touch him while you two were still dating.
I wouldn't do that to one of my best friends. Jack said
that he'd tried to break up with you dozens of times, but
he took you back because..." Wendy looked back at
Rosie, tears welling in her eyes obviously finding it hard
to finish. "I'm sorry Rosie, he told me what you tried to
do when he broke up with you."

At first Rosie was confused, she didn't know
what Wendy was suggesting. Frank was avoiding eye
contact with either women, so wasn't a help. Rosie was
trying to figure out what she meant when she
remembered some really dark moments before the first
time Hatter came to her. "Oh. How strange." She said,
feeling a little num and disconnected as she remembered
being in anguish because Jack didn't want her any more.
Rosie remembered feeling loss so deeply that she felt
like she couldn't breathe, and not wanting to live without
Jack in her life. She remembered the feelings, but
looking back now, it all seemed so strange and alien.
Rosie had tried to take her own life at least three

244

different times, and Jack had tried to help two other times.

The visual memory of Jack holding her under water in the tub till it felt like her lungs would burst took root in her mind's eye, she also remembered what he said when he finally let her up. She was barely conscious, and balls of darkness were popping in her vision from lack of oxygen. Jack had whispered in her ear that she belonged to him, and that he was the only one allowed to snuff her out. He'd said that if she tried to commit suicide without his permission again that she had better succeed or he would finish her with his own hands. A chill ran down Rosie's spine. At the time, Rosie had thought it was tough love, and that Jack was trying to teach her to be stronger to survive the pain of the real world. But now, she knew that those were Jack's words not her thoughts, she saw it for the blatant manipulation it was. She couldn't connect with how she had felt. "My God, what was wrong with me? Why did I let him manipulate me so badly that I would rather die than have him leave me."

"Fucking bastard." Frank said shaking his head. "I am so sorry I didn't stop the way he treated you Rosie. I knew he was being an ass, but I didn't want to see that my best friend was fucking evil."

"Hey!" Wendy broke in. "It's not Jack's fault that Rosie was suicidal. He worried about her mental stability, and was trying to find a way to break up with her gently, so we could be together."

"Sorry to break it to you Wendy, but Jack had no plan of breaking up with Rosie for you." Frank sighed and took a long breath before quickly blurting out the rest of his thought. "He was working on getting you to sleep with him while he was with Rosie too. And I'm sorry to both of you that I stuck by the bro code and didn't say anything to either of you."

Rosie gave Frank a nod of acceptance for his apology, but Wendy wasn't taking his statement in stride.

"Frank? Why would you say that? Jack is a good man, he would never do that. He was trying to find a way to break up with Rosie. He didn't want to hurt her." Anger was clearly rising in Wendy's voice and body language as she clenched her fists.

"I'm sorry Wendy, but Jack was lying to you. He's lied to every woman I've ever seen him with." Frank looked ashamed. "I never stopped him, because I didn't see the worst of it. I guess I didn't want to."

Wendy screamed out a primal guttural noise as she leapt across the table and took a swing at Frank. He dodged Wendy's first swing and caught her fist in his hand on the second swing. He grappled her, twisting his arm around her body to pin the furious woman against himself almost like a dance move. Wendy bucked and squirmed, screaming unintelligible curses at Frank while he held her with little effort.

"Wendy." Rosie hissed between her teeth. "Please calm down, you're drawing everyone's attention to us. Please Wendy, if you don't want someone calling the cops. Please stop trying to punch Frank. And Frank, let her go." Rosie's voice had such an air of authority that they both stopped and took a step back. "Thank you, both."

Frank and Wendy looked around self consciously. Every person in the burger shack was looking out the window at them, and they'd even gotten the attention of a few people in their cars waiting at the stop light. Wendy stood, and straightened out her clothes awkwardly.

"Why don't we take a walk to the park? And finish this conversation there. Ok?" Rosie stood and gestured for Frank and Wendy to precede her as she started to walk away from the picnic table. They followed Rosie's lead, and all walked away from the staring eyes around them. The three of them were two blocks away before anyone spoke.

"Frank? How much do you know about what

Jack does to women?" Rosie tried to ask casually, but failed.

Frank froze in his tracks, and looked at Rosie with shame. "Jack let something slip this morning. I swear, I didn't know before. I just thought he was an ass that had good luck with women. But I didn't know, not really."

"What lies are you spewing now Frank?" Wendy spun to face Frank again, fists clenched.

"Wendy, please calm down." Rosie put a hand on Wendy's shoulder trying to sooth the other woman. But Wendy flinched at Rosie's touch. Rosie remembered reacting the same way to anyone but Jack's touch only days before meeting Hatter, and realized that Jack had his psychic hooks in Wendy the same way now. Rosie exchanged a look with Frank, and it was clear he was coming to a similar conclusion.

"Why don't we take a short cut down this alley." Frank suggested, "It'll cut a bit off the walk. And how about we don't say any more till were there."

"Good idea." Rosie confirmed as they turned down the alley. Wendy kept her mouth shut, and her hands clenched stiffly at her sides, but followed the other two. A few awkwardly silent minutes later they arrived at the park. The three of them walked past the fenced in playground, and cut through the baseball field, before finally ending their walk in a clump of shade trees.

It was the most private place in the park, and it made Rosie recall coming here with Jack a few weeks back at night; and wondered if she would have agreed to him fucking her against the big tree in the middle if he hadn't been doing something to her mind. She just wasn't usually all that in to being caught, and anyone walking by would have gotten a show. Rosie pushed the thought out of her mind, and sat down in the sparse grass and dirt not by that tree. Frank and Wendy sat down too, but Wendy made sure not to sit too near Frank.

Wendy was looking rather defensive, even down

to her body language, crossing her arms in a universally hostile and self defending posture. Rosie wasn't sure how to get Wendy to a place where she would be receptive to what she had to say. "Wendy. You've known me for years, right?"

"Yes, why?" Wendy answered warily.

"In all that time, have I ever lied to you?" Rosie was careful to keep her expression and tone of voice friendly.

"No." Wendy looked from Rosie to Frank through suspiciously squinted eyes.

"Then can you keep an open mind and listen to what happened to me, remembering that I have never lied to you, and keep an open mind?"

Wendy sighed, and gave Rosie a quick smirk, uncrossing her arms. "Ok, I'm listening."

"I want to tell you both what led to me breaking up with Jack, and please don't judge me too harshly." She added quietly under her breath, but still audible to both her companions. "I've been doing enough beating myself up over the last few months for a dozen people." Rosie looked to Frank. "I suspect you know a version of what happened, being Jack's best friend for years. I also suspect that you've seen Jack's darker side, and I hope from what you said on the way over here that you might be able to back up my suspicions."

Frank nodded, "Pretty fucking likely."

Wendy and Frank listened as Rosie recounted how Jack had been toying with her and taking joy from keeping Rosie off balance, so she never knew if he was going to be charming or pin her to a bed at knife point and fuck her while he talked about how he owned her. Then she told them about the safe and comforting presence that came to her when she needed to be held. She told them about how this same energy pulled her to safety while her nightmare monster stalked and chased her. Rosie also was sure to explain her doubts and guilt over her mysterious guardian angel. She told them how

Jack had put her into a lucid dream state to find the monster, and how the monster had gotten her and would have easily killed her if not for her knight in shining armor coming to the rescue and almost getting killed himself to save Rosie.

She explained how she had started to doubt how true her feelings for Jack were when he wasn't around for a while, but every time he spoke to her again she lost her doubts and anguished over having feelings for two men, even being pretty sure that her protector was too good to be true. Until last night, when she had a big enough moment of clarity to realize both that her imagined protector was real and that Jack had been manipulating her emotional state so badly that she couldn't figure out what she really felt till she'd broken his hold on her. Breaking the hold, she was able to see that she needed to pick the type of man she wanted to be with and Hatter won easily.

Rosie told them that she planned to see Hatter tonight so that he could teach her to make a protective amulet to keep their bodies safe while they battled the monster. And finally, that she was going to introduce Hatter to Chris and Janet, and them if they wanted to meet him too.

When Rosie had finished, she looked to Wendy and Frank. Wendy looked like she was having an internal debate, but Frank looked more relieved and smiled bitterly.

"I knew he was mistreating you, just like he had all his girls before you Rosie." Frank cast his eyes to the ground. "I turned a blind eye out of loyalty to my friend. I'm sorry. But, to be honest, you lasted much longer than any of his other girls and for once I got to know one of you; and realized that you were a really nice person Rosie. I became your friend, and it became harder to watch Jack fuck with you and break you like the others. But it wasn't until today that he slipped up. He told me that he knew you cheated on him, because that would be the only way he could lose control over you. He admitted that he had been using magic to feed off you." Frank turned to Wendy, "I'm pretty sure he had you on deck as his next meal Wendy. And the way you were defending him, I'm pretty sure Jack already has you at least partially brain fucked."

Rosie breathed a sigh of relief that Frank's account backed up her own theory. Wendy didn't look so relieved, they watched her for long moments watching her internal struggle. They watched emotions play across Wendy's face, reasoning out what she felt and what Jack had told her against what Rosie and Frank were saying. No one spoke, feeling that Wendy really needed this time to work out what she would believe.

Finally Frank broke the silence, looking conversationally towards Rosie. "So, your dream walker friend is a he named Hatter?"

"Yea. You kinda already knew he was a guy, tho, didn't you?"

"I wasn't positive, but I did suspect."

Rosie cocked her head, looking at Frank quizzically. "Why didn't you say anything? I mean, Jack's been your best friend forever. Why not call me out about being with another man?"

"Turn about's fair play I guess." Frank thought for a couple seconds and continued. "He wasn't being monogamous, and he was treating you like crap, so why should you be stuck with one partner when he wasn't? I wasn't sure and I didn't want to make your life worse. You're my friend too, and you are much kinder than Jack. Take your pick, they're all valid."

"Frank, I kinda want to hug you right now. I thought you and Wendy might drop me as a friend when you heard I not only broke up with Jack, but already was in love with someone else before it was completely over with Jack."

"If what Jack said this morning is true, you probably wouldn't have broken his hold over you without this Hatter of yours. If everything you've said about him is true, then he's the guy you deserve, and I'd like to shake his hand."

"Then, you want to meet him tonight too?"

"Yep. I think Janet and Chris have the right idea, I want to meet this guy and judge for myself if he's on the up and up or out to screw you too."

"Fair enough. I did get pretty fooled by Jack." Rosie conceded with a light shrug. "But I have such a deep connection with Hatter, the sheer realness of my love for Hatter was what made me start to doubt the hollow feelings I had for Jack. I still feel love for Jack, but it's a shadow compared to what I feel for Hatter. I really hope you guys all like him like I do."

"No matter how nice this guy is, I'm not going to like him like you do. I'm not gay."

Wendy burst out laughing, drawing Rosie and Franks attention back to her. "Not gay. Good punch line."

"So, Wendy, have you processed what we said? Do you believe we're telling the truth, and that Jack has been up to no good with both of us?" Rosie was hopeful, but her stomach was still tied up in knots. With the nightmare monster probably getting close to healed, Rosie wanted as many friends around her as possible.

"I just don't know. You talk about your connection to this Hatter guy, and it reminds me of my connection with Jack. What you guys said and what Jack has been saying don't jive, but I don't think any of you would lie to me about things so serious. Maybe it's all a misunderstanding. I don't know. I'd like to get Jack's side of things, and see where we go now that you aren't an item. But I'm still your friend Rosie, and I'm still here for you when it comes to fighting your nightmare. So, I guess I'm in to meet your Hatter tonight. Those amulet thingies sounds like a good idea, we should make them and test them out before going to find your monster."

"I can't control what you do with Jack, but I'd

prefer you keep a safe distance. If you won't take my advice, will you at least promise to be careful and critical of the things he says?"

"I'll keep my eyes open. Does that make you happy?"

"It's better than nothing." Rosie shrugged, letting it go for now.

"What kind of a name is Hatter any way?" Wendy changed the subject, and as long as they didn't mention Jack, the three of them relaxed and were able to hang out and chat comfortably.

CR

33

That night, Rosie really looked forward to going to sleep for the first time in months. She couldn't wait to see her Hatter's gorgeous brown eyes, and rakishly dimpled smile again. She fell asleep thinking of his strong warm embrace, and feeling truly content and happy that she would soon be in it.

The first thing she was aware of was soft full lips chastely kissing her own, and then the comforting scent of roses and warm musk. So simple a greeting, then the brush of his fingertips as he cradled the back of her head, lightly caressing the nape of her neck, and Rosie was filled with desire for her Hatter. Rosie was only vaguely aware of standing, her focus was on the softness of Hatter's lips waiting only a breath from hers and knowing he was so close that she could feel the heat coming from his body. She leaned in to him, and hungrily found his responsive lips.

"Mmmmmm." Hatter appreciatively rumbled as he greedily wrapped his arms around Rosie, pulling their bodies into full contact as they continued to kiss. "I know it was just a day, but I missed you being here with me. I missed how brilliant it feels when you're touching me. My beautiful Rose."

"I missed your touch too Hatter. There is no place I'd rather be than here in your arms." Rosie opened her eyes, and was mesmerized by his rich brown eyes so beautifully accented by his long thick eyelashes. "I am yours, utterly and completely. Body and soul."

Hatter smiled, and it lit up his face. "I love you too." Then he kissed her again, long and deep.

It took Rosie some time until she could think straight. Hatter filled Rosie's every sense, and all she could think or manage to murmur between kisses was how much she loved him. Hatter murmured vows of love back to Rosie amongst their kisses and caressing touches.

Before they got too carried away, Rosie managed to whisper "I need to catch my breath, or I might get lost in your lips all night. Though, another night..." They exchanged a few more lingering and tender kisses before they managed to stop. Though they continued touching each other like it was a needed comfort. Rosie rested her hands against Hatter's enticingly firm chest, feeling his heart pound with barely contained desire, while he wrapped his muscular arms around her body and played his fingers lightly along the back of her waistband. She stared up into his eyes and couldn't remember ever feeling safer or more content.

"I think the green of your eyes is now my favorite color." Hatter whispered with intimate closeness, punctuating the statement with a kiss.

Rosie felt her face heating with a blush from Hatter's compliment. "Funny, I think the brown of your eyes is one of the most beautiful colors I've ever seen."

"Really?" Hatter sounded surprised."But their just brown. Boring old plain brown. Nothing so rare or interesting as your soft spring green."

"There's nothing boring about your brown. It's such a deep rich color with copper and bronze highlights, I could look at nothing else all day and be content." Rosie leaned up for another chaste kiss, but it lead to a deeper longer more sensuous kiss.

"Are you sure you wouldn't prefer something

more exotic?" He said playfully with a grin and a literal sparkle in his eye that cascaded across his irises leaving them a metallic deep amethyst purple.

Rosie giggled and shook her head. "Too raver, I like the brown."

Hatter blinked, and his eyes turned into spinning black and white spirals. "You wouldn't like to be hypnotized by my eyes?"

Rosie tried to stop giggling, but didn't quite succeed. "Na, too 'carnie.' I think your brown eyes are quite hypnotizing to me with no gimmicky help. Besides, you wouldn't want to make me dizzy would you?"

"I could think of worse things than you having to fall into my arms, but I don't have to make you dizzy for that." He said, lightly stroking the small of her back, then blinked again to change his eyes. This time his irises slowly rippled with pastel lights like they were a reflection of the aurora borealis. "How 'bout this? Would you like me with my eyes like this?"

"I love you no matter how you change your eyes. But if you want my preference, then no, they're too northern lights."

"Then this?" he asked blinking his eyes into technicolor rainbows radiating out from his pupils.

She kissed him with a small sigh, "looks like you belong in a gay pride parade," Rosie wiggled against him and Hatter reacted with an appreciative rumble and held her closer. "but I happen to know you like girls better."

Hatter shrugged, slowly blinking his eyes again. "I bet you like my eyes like this." This time when he looked down at Rosie his eyes were the preternaturally glowing golden eyes she had glimpsed when he turned into a radiant wolf and had battled her monster to save her.

Rosie instantly sobered, and reached a hand up to touch his face. These eyes weren't the silly playful things he'd been entertaining Rosie with, they were soulful animal eyes and they belonged to him as much as his dark rich brown eyes. "Those are your wolf's eyes." She breathed in a whisper, feeling tears welling in her eyes with the memory of his bravery. "When the monster almost killed us both, those are the eyes I saw when you changed to save my life. You fought my worst nightmare and were willing to die to defend me. Those eyes, they remind me how far you'll go to keep me safe." She blinked and the tears rolled down her cheeks. Rosie was so overwhelmed with raw emotion that she wasn't sure whether the tears she shed were of joy for being so lucky to have found Hatter, or so scared that something could happen to make her lose him again.

Hatter closed his eyes and nuzzled against her hand. "I will always do everything I can to keep you safe. To lose you would feel like losing the best part of me." He looked back down at Rosie, and his eyes were back to what Rosie could only see as a stunning brown.

Rosie stood on tip toe, and putting a hand on either side of his face, tipped his head so she could kiss each eyelid in turn before again kissing his soft lips tenderly. "I feel the same about you Hatter. I'm so glad you found me, and I never want to lose you again."

With a smooth motion, Hatter swept Rosie into his arms and kissed her deeply. He cradled her against him gently, but spoke in a voice that managed to be animalistic and gravelly with need but still knee meltingly British. "Shall we retire back to my bed?"

She pouted with disappointment, knowing she shouldn't say yes but really wanting to. "Oh." Her word came out as a sad whimper before she regained her voice. "I really would like that. But there are other things we really need to do tonight."

Hatter set Rosie down reluctantly. "If that's what you really want." Hatter sounded as disappointed as Rosie felt.

For the first time since falling asleep, Rosie

noticed her surroundings. They stood in a garden clearing next to Hatter's tea party set up, and Rosie couldn't help but smile when she saw the red wing backed chair he had draped himself across so seductively when she had viewed him from across realities. She liked that the place they found each other was in her Hatter's Wonderland. Looking back to her lover, Rosie noticed that he was wearing nearly the same outfit from her experiment in remote viewing. The only difference was that his leather top hat was on the table instead of on his head. He was just as enticing now standing before her offering to take her to bed as he was when he draped himself across the chair in display for her. Suddenly all she could think of doing was slowly unbuttoning his vest and shirt, removing them with caressing touches, then kissing every yummy inch of his smooth firm chest and stomach.

Hatter stepped closer and rumbled appreciatively. As he spoke, he ran his hands up Rosie's arms and across her shoulders with just enough pressure to make Rosie tingle in very private places. "Are you aware you're projecting? 'Cause if you don't want to have sex right now, you're really sending mixed messages."

"Sorry, I didn't mean to project. You just look so tasty in those clothes, and it made me think of the last time I saw you in the same outfit." She blinked slowly, holding the mental image of touching Hatter's bare flesh before she was able to get her brain back on track. "Last night you promised to show me how to make a protection amulet tonight, and I think that it's important. As much as I'd rather be in your arms, we need to do that."

Hatter whispered into Rosie's ear. "If I say that what I need to do tonight is you, couldn't we postpone being responsible one more night?"

Hatter's direct and hedonistic approach really turned Rosie on. She fought not to melt into his arms, but as Hatter nibbled her ear lobe and kissed her neck she struggled with herself not to writhe against him. Rosie had to take a slow deep breath to clear her head before she could speak. "We've already put off the amulet one night. We probably shouldn't put off you teaching me how to make it another night. The monster is probably nearly back to full strength. I've been feeling like its watching and seeing glimpses of its eyes in the shadows as its getting stronger, I'm just afraid it'll attack while we're vulnerable."

Hatter took a step back, and nodded solemnly. "You are one hundred percent right. I won't risk your safety for some really brilliant nookie. But if there's time after, I plan to strip you naked and kiss every inch of your body."

"Ok." Rosie said the word breathlessly, both blushing at his suggestion and fighting hard not to pounce on Hatter and have her way with him that moment on the thick soft grass at their feet. "If there's time, and we are alone, I would love to repeat last night's fun."

"Why wouldn't we be alone?"

Rosie averted her gaze, unable to look into Hatter's dreamy big browns. "Because that's the other thing I need to do tonight. My friends want to meet you. So I need to ask you, will you come meet them?" As Rosie made the suggestion, she was filled with worry that she was pushing things too fast. She worried that Hatter wouldn't want to meet her friends so soon, and wondered if it was a little too much like bringing a guy home to meet your parents before the first date?

Rosie looked at Hatter, afraid of what she would read on his face, but to her surprise and suspicion he was grinning ear to ear complete with knee melting dimple. "You want me to meet your world-jumping friends? You've told them about me? And they want to meet me?"

"Yes, the friends who dream walk with me. The ones who have been taking watches with me while I healed up. Is that ok? I don't want to force you to move too quickly, if you aren't ready to meet them, there's no pressure." Rosie responded, a little worried that his manic grin was a way to cover annoyance at her request.

"I'd love to meet your friends." He said with a steady and enticingly dimpled grin.

"Really? You're ok meeting them?" Rosie started to realize that Hatter's grin was sincere. She'd gotten so used to Jack's deceptive happy looking anger that it took effort to take happy at face value.

"That is what 'I'd love to meet them' usually means." Hater said taking one of Rosie's free hands and kissing it.

"I have to warn you, after Jack they're a little wary of my choice in men, and they want to vet you. Make sure you're on the level. Make sure that the amulet is on the level; so we can all wear one just in case. You're ok showing them how to make the amulet too, right?"

"Of course I'll teach them too." Hatter took a moment to make significant eye contact with Rosie. "I'm glad your friends care enough to be skeptical, and I hope I live up to their standards. They've kept you safe when I wasn't there, so I'm already inclined to like them." Hatter said, taking her other hand in his and kissing it too. He held her hands between them, closing the distance again so her hands naturally settled back against his chest. "But there is no reason to doubt Kiri's magic, they want you safe as much as I do."

Rosie felt Hatter's heart beating strong and calmly against her fingertips, and had complete faith in him. "I know, I trust you, and I trust that you've been working with my childhood protector and Kiri. The only thing that worries me about these amulets is that we can't find the right parts or put them together wrong. It's not like I can bring a note back with me to check when I wake up."

"If you are all going to use the amulets, why don't I teach you all together, that way you can compare notes when you wake up and make sure no one's forgotten any bits. I can also check your work and whisper in your ear so you can take notes to check when you wake."

"You're as smart as you are sexy." Rosie said with a grin, and was rewarded with Hatter's matching smile. "So, I guess you should come meet my friends now..." Instead of moving away, Rosie found herself gazing into Hatter's eyes with longing.

"Yes." Hatter said before leaning down for another kiss. "We should go meet them." He kissed Rosie again, and she reveled in the taste of his lips. With the press of his lips against hers, they instinctively exchanged energy. Tentatively at first, and then as they flowed into each other it filled them with desire. They kissed urgently, embracing each other with exploring hands for several minutes before coming up for air. "Sorry," he said in a husky tone, "I had to get at least some of that out of my system, so I could focus while I'm teaching you and your friends. Teaching you without thinking of throwing you down and ravaging you will be tough."

"Mmmmm." She purred happily, wondering if she could focus on what she should either. "It's still going to be hard for me to focus. When you're near me, all I can think of is this." Rosie said brushing her lips against his, stroking his chest with lightly swirling fingertips, and breathing in his scent.

"What if we don't touch? If we keep an arm span between us at all times, would that help?" Hatter said, working at calm as he filled with desire.

Rosie shook her head, "I'll get all hot and bothered just thinking about what I want to do with you."

"Yeah?" Hatter said with a roguish grin, playing his hands around the curve of her waist. "And what would you be thinking of doing with me?"

Knowing that she was projecting her thoughts to

Hatter, Rosie imagined unbuttoning his shirt as she kissed her way down his smooth chest and abs. Hatter licked his lips, and closed his eyes to better experience what his love was projecting. She imagined slowly unbuckling his belt and unbuttoning his pants while she kissed, licked and nibbled his skin just above his waistband. Hatter's breath came out in trembling gasps like he was actually experiencing Rosie's lips on his skin.

Then, before Rosie's thoughts continued further Hatter was needfully kissing her. His fingers kneading into her skin as he held her tight against him. He pulled back from the kiss panting. "If you keep going," he rumbled, "there's no way I'll be able to concentrate either." Hatter grabbed Rosie's bottom and projected his own thoughts of pulling her clothes off. "I don't think well be able to focus until we get this out of our systems, little tastes only make me hungrier for you."

Rosie rubbed against Hatter like she was in heat. "I feel like I'm starving and you're a steak dangling in front of me. So let's feed the beast now, and be sensible again after."

Hatter grunted his agreement, unable to form words around his sheer lust. He picked Rosie up with ease and swung her over onto his red wing backed chair, kissing her lips greedily as he moved her.

ଔ

Before Hatter set Rosie down, there was a split second that she felt Hatter's will push against her. She had the choice to let him alter their shared reality, or stop whatever he was doing. Though she appreciated the choice, she trusted her lover and was curious what of hers he was altering. As she landed on the chair, Rosie felt her cute cotton p.j.s transform into a black lace bra and a short little blue and green plaid skirt. She was now wearing white knee high socks and little strappy black heals. Rosie wasn't wearing a shirt over the plunging and lacy bra, but she did have a little plaid tie to match the skirt. She also noticed that she wasn't wearing any panties under the too short skirt.

As he placed her, Hatter stepped back to look at her draped across his chair welcomingly. He made an appreciative grunt looking at her exposed thighs and most of her upper body.

"You know my school doesn't do uniforms," she said coyly, "but I can appreciate the sexy school girl you've made me." Rosie looked at Hatter flirtatiously and licked her lips. "I guess that makes you the bad boy come to ravish me." Rosie grinned reaching for Hatter, and modified his clothing too.

Earlier she was thinking about slowly stripping him a button at a time, but now Rosie longed for the feel of Hatter's skin and they didn't have time for a slow undressing. She ripped his shirt and vest open, pushing them into nonexistence as she transformed his jeans into soft black leather pants and added a studded leather collar and wrist cuffs. Hatter made a surprised gasp, but seeing what Rosie had done couldn't help but grin with excitement. "Nice. Very rock'n roll."

Rosie couldn't help but fondle his well defined bare chest and arms as she pulled him close. She kissed down the front of his chest, just like she'd imagined, and she could feel Hatter's anticipation almost like a sweet taste on her lips. She breathed in the scent of his warm skin and felt herself grow moist with need. Rosie undid his belt, and easily pulled open his button fly. Her mouth watered at the sight of his fully erect member, and in a half heartbeat she was taking him into her mouth with quick lightly sucking strokes. He moaned with pleasure that Rosie could feel deliciously through their psychic bond.

Hatter ran trembling fingers through Rosie's soft red hair as he moaned and thrust into her energetic mouth. She played with him, using lightly tugging fingers below and a dexterous tongue against his shaft. He felt the electricity of their desire, and the heat of

passion flowing between them, but her feel was only part
of his feast. He really liked the sight of her as a half
dressed prep school girl pleasuring him with such joy. In
much too short a time, Hatter was near coming.

Hatter pulled back and dropped to his knees
before Rosie. He spread her legs and buried his face. It
was a move so quick and smooth that Rosie was
moaning in pleasure before she'd entirely processed that
he'd moved. She arched her back and cried out as his
tongue found a quick hard rhythm against her at the
same speed his fingers slipped inside her. She rocked her
hips with his rhythm, and as he tapped against her two
most sensitive spots she came in an explosion of joyous
sensation and sound.

Hatter wiped his wet face on the tiny pleated
skirt, and looked up at Rosie sprawled across his favorite
chair. He marveled at her beauty, and wondered if her
orgasmic afterglow would be as literal in the Prime
Material as it was here in Wonderland. She seemed to
sparkle with iridescent blue light as she lay there
bonelessly with closed eyes and a soft smile, and Hatter
was filled with love and lust for his unique Rose.

Hatter stood, and Rosie opened her eyes sleepily.
She gazed up and down the length of his body, letting
herself linger on her favorite parts. "Going somewhere?"
She asked, licking her lips as the sight of his physique
recharged her. "'Cause, after what you just did for me, I'd
love to return the favor."

"I'm not going anywhere." Hatter responded, his
voice husky with desire. He picked Rosie up like she
weighed nothing. She wrapped her arms and legs around
him as he kissed her deeply. Hatter swung her back on to
his chair, placing her kneeling with her exposed bottom
facing him, and he grabbed her hips possessively with an
animalistic grunt of anticipation that made her wet.
Rosie firmly gripped the chairs back, and invitingly set
one knee up on the armrest inviting him to slide into her.
He worked his way in slowly at first, but following

Rosie's exuberant example was soon slamming his full force against her.

They fucked like wild animals, writhing and moaning in ecstasy, coming ever closer to orgasm. Rosie reached back over her head, digging her nails into the back of Hatter's neck as he screamed with lust riding her even harder. He was on the edge of cumming, but wanted Rosie to cum with him. Hatter reached around her hip and tapped her center double as fast as his penetration. She bucked against him as she came, and the sensation of her tightening around him took Hatter too. They screamed in unison as their bodies convulsed and fluids released. They clung to each other, draped over the back of the red chair, too spent to move for minutes.

"We should probably get ourselves together and go meet up with your friends." Hatter rasped.

"Yeah, last night I really worried them when I spent the night with you and didn't check in." Rosie said, trying to convince her exhausted body to move.

Hatter gave Rosie a squeeze and got to his feet gathering some energy from the world around him. It was a trick it seemed he could only do in Wonderland, and was glad for at the moment. He buttoned up his fly and stretched out his kinked muscles a bit. When he looked over at Rosie she had rearranged herself and was sitting comfortably with her legs drawn up against her, watching him with attraction plain on her face. "Hey. None of that now. I thought we just spent the last hour getting that out of our system."

"Yeah, but tight leather pants and no shirt look really good on you. Especially when you stretch like that." Rosie made the effort to look away. "Maybe you should change back into what you were wearing before. It's still damn sexy, but not in that half naked kinda way."

Hatter laughed, and the sound further stirred things within Rosie. "You should probably get more clothes on too." Hatter said with a deep and rumbling sexy voice from inches away, obviously playing with her. When she turned to look at him he was now fully clothed. "What?" He said with mock confusion.

Rosie mock hit him on the arm, and he smoothly grabbed her hand pulling her into a tender embrace. "That is so cheating." Rosie said gazing into Hatter's eyes, and wanting nothing more than to spend the next hour in his arms too.

He grinned mischievously, "I'm cheating? Your the one pressing up against me in a sexy black bra and no panties."

Rosie made the effort, and stepped back from Hatter. She manifested jeans and a plain blue v-necked T-shirt. She kept the lacy black bra, and sock and shoe combo, but thought the plaid skirt might be a distraction for Hatter. She pulled off the tie and handed it to Hatter. "I'd like to see you in a plaid number kinda like this some time."

Hatter absently pocketed the tie. "What? Like in drag?" Hatter didn't sound too keen on the idea.

"No." Rosie smirked, "No, I meant like in a kilt. I've seen you naked, and your calves are way too sexy not to show them off sometimes."

Hatter took a relieved exhale. "Good, cause I'm not so much into guys in dresses... A kilt tho? Really?" He didn't sound like he much liked that idea either. "I didn't know American women were into kilts, I thought it was more a Scottish thing. Couldn't I just wear shorts to show off my calves for you?"

Rosie did her best sex kitten pout, "but I can't just reach under shorts to play with my new favorite toy."

Hatter laughed, "So what you're sayin' is, you just want me for my body."

"Not just your body." Rosie said emphasizing 'just'. "But I'd be lying if I said I didn't want your body too. 'Cause, yum." Rosie said sliding a hand up his chest and around his shoulder to play her fingertips into the curls at the nape of his neck.

Hatter flinched as Rosie's fingers brushed over her scratches left in his neck during sex. Rosie jumped too, feeling the wound, and turned Hatter to see the damage. The skin was red and puffy in four straight parallel lines, each ending in a bleeding crescent. She gently touched the scratches, and her fingers lined up exactly. "Oh." Rosie sounded a little in shock. "I'm so sorry."

"It's ok. I don't so much mind love marks." When Rosie still looked a little horrified with herself, Hatter shrugged his eyebrows suggestively. "Actually, I really liked it at the time, really revved my engine. Besides, you could always kiss it and make it all better. Just, for you it would really work."

Rosie laughed, "'Cause there's no chance that will distract us."

"I promise to be good if you do." His tone was now sincere, "but if you think healing me would be too much of a temptation to delay longer, we could just go. It's just a scratch, not a life threatening wound." Hatter took Rosie's hand from the scratch and kissed it. He then continued to hold her hand, almost absently stroking her fingers.

"No. I should at least try. If I get too hot and bothered I'll stop. It'll be good practice." Rosie removed her right hand from Hatter's and placed it back over the scratches. Touching Hatter did feel good to Rosie, but she was content just to be near him feeling their psychic bond. Rosie's lust was satisfied for now, but her love for Hatter was steady, true, strong, and wonderful. It was with this feeling that she pushed her healing energy along the welt marks, smoothing them out and removing the redness with a caress. The welts faded almost instantly, then she guided her energy into the scratches and it was like a tiny vibration tingled against Hatter as it knit the little bloody crescents together till there wasn't a single mark left.

"Wow." Hatter caught Rosie's attention, and she could see unshed joyful tears in his eyes. "The first time you healed me it was raw and sexual, an intense animal thing. It was awesome. But this was beautiful. I felt your love and caring, and how safe and right we feel together. When you healed me, it was like something deeper than a scratch healed. Wow, just wow. You are one magical being. I love you Rosie Cotton."

Rosie blushed, unused to such praise. "I love you too Hatter."

Hatter wiped his eyes with a chuckle. "Don't think I've ever cried happy tears before. You must think I'm a little bit of a poof."

"No." Rosie was still recovering from Hatter's ego massage, but the blush was starting to fade. "No worries about your masculinity. I was there last night and just now, plus I've seen you fight. Nothing poofie there."

Hatter kissed her hand and used a finger to tip up her face to look at him. "Hey, you ok?"

Rosie was surprised by Hatter's concern. "I'm fine, why?"

"Healing me didn't tire you? Or hurt you at all?"

"No." Rosie thought about how tired she'd been the first time she'd healed Hatter, or even when she'd healed Frank, but she was fine now. "I'm good. No problems like before. Maybe it's because I wasn't hurt too, or maybe I just had enough reserve that it's not too much."

"Or maybe healing is your real Fey talent, and as you use it you're getting stronger. Maybe you're getting better."

"Huh." Rosie thought about Hatter's idea. "I guess that's possible too." She changed the subject, "We should get going. We're keeping folks waiting." With that she turned and stepped out of Wonderland pulling Hatter behind with her.

❧

34

Rosie focused on Janet as she walked through that breath of space between dreams, and when they emerged on the other side they found themselves in a place familiar to Rosie. They were in a big meeting room in the basement of a church where Janet and Rosie had girl scouts meetings as kids. She knew it wasn't the actual meeting room, it was a dream version of it. Janet's choice of venue made Rosie smile, they'd done many group projects together sitting around the big folding table in this room.

All four of Rosie's friends were sitting at the table, it looked like they were playing cards before they walked in but now all eyes were focused on the man holding Rosie's hand. Janet had a wide excited grin that Rosie knew well, it was obvious that she approved.

Rosie cleared her throat, "Um, sorry were late. Thanks for getting together without me, hope you weren't all waiting too long."

"Only an hour." Wendy said dryly. "At least you showed, I heard you left Janet and Chris high and dry last night."

"Wendy. Stop." Janet chided Wendy before turning back to the couple. "Sorry. She doesn't always make the best first impression." Janet stood and crossed the room with her hand extended to Hatter.

"Janet, Hatter. Hatter this is my good friend Janet." Rosie started introductions as Hatter shook Janet's offered hand.

"Nice to meet you." Hatter responded a little awkwardly.

Janet looked Hatter over and nodded approval, then spoke to Rosie in an aside. "Mmmm, you are right about that accent. And He's even cuter than you described, plus a good strong handshake. Definitely not Pinocchio."

Hatter gave Rosie a concerned look and

mouthed the word 'Pinocchio?'.

Rosie shrugged slightly and blushed over Janet's frank assessment whispering back to Hatter, "you're a real boy." Then turned to Janet, "I'm glad you approve. I think." She turned back to Hatter with a mildly nervous smile. "Come meet everyone else." Rosie led Hatter to the table where she introduced the others. Hatter exchanged greetings with Frank, Wendy, and finally Chris.

Wendy and Chris's body language and quiet judging expressions made it clear that they were wary of Hatter. While Janet and Frank were almost mirror opposites, leaning in and smiling like they were really looking forward to getting to know Hatter.

Once introductions were done Hatter jumped right into teaching, and Rosie was reminded so strongly of Kiri that she could almost hear her voice through Hatter's words. "The process of making this amulet is going to take just over a full day from the blue hour before sun up to the next sun up. And that time is just to clear the crystal at the amulet's heart, the rest is about having the precise ingredients. When you all wake up, I can use my connection with Rosie to dictate the ingredients. That way she'll have an accurate list. I can't stress enough that doing things in order, with the right materials, and with the right timing are essential to how well the amulets will work."

"So, how do you know these amulets will work? Have you ever seen one in action?" This from Chris, who still looked wary.

"I've never seen one work, cause I don't have a body tied to the Prime Material like you guys do. But I was taught how to construct the amulet by a real creature of magic who has been alive for thousands of years, and she wants Rosie safe almost as much as I do." Hatter squeezed Rosie's hand, and it wasn't until then that she realized they had been holding hands since they sat down. "So, I believe they'll work."

"Um, and how exactly do we know how important Rosie's safety is to you?" This challenge came from Wendy. "How do we know this isn't just some trick from a bitter man with no physical presence on the Prime Material? Spirits and ghosts trick people all the time."

Hatter blinked in dumb confusion not sure how to respond, he hadn't expected to be challenged on why he wanted Rosie safe. Rosie jumped in, in Hatter's defense. "Hey, that is one thing I have no doubts over. Hatter has consistently put my safety first, even when it almost killed him."

"But why?" Wendy continued to prod. "You don't know us from Adam, but we need to trust that you're doing all this for Rosie? Why?"

Hatter was quick to respond. "Because I love her." He was answering Wendy, but spoke the words to Rosie with intimate eye contact. "I was drawn to her from the first moment I felt her presence across worlds, and knew we were kindred spirits. I think I've loved her almost as long."

Rosie blushed and grinned uncontrollably. She felt very exposed by Hatters public profession of love, but really enjoyed his unrestrained emotion and how easily it came. She squeezed his hand, unable to stop grinning, because Hatter loved her. "I love you too."

Wendy whispered something to Frank, and tho Rosie couldn't quite hear what she said she was sure of the message. Frank looked annoyed at Wendy before looking apologetically at the rest of the room. No one missed Wendy's aside, but only Hatter seemed to miss the gist.

Rosie felt she needed to say something, but also felt awkward. She was rescued yet again by Hatter. "Look, I know you were all probably friends with Jack. And, I know that they just broke up. But I know the pain he caused Rosie, I've been there to collect the pieces many times. I know this thing between me and Rosie seems wrong so soon, but I've been trying to rescue her from more than the nightmare monster. Hey, it'd be brilliant if you guys all wanted to make friends with me, but whether you guys like me or not isn't my goal. I came here to show you all how to make something to help keep my love safer. 'Cause if she has more backup, we have a better chance of beating the big bad. So helping you all is in my best interest because we're all on Rosie's side here, right?"

Frank spoke up. "I'm pretty sure most of us are on Rosie's side, and that means you are ok in our book." Frank glared at Wendy to make his point. "Or at least mine. Jack was a prick to Rosie, and he had her pretty well brain fucked. And it's pretty hard for me to forgive removing someone's free will. So, shit, Hatter, you gave Rosie the only tool that could break Jacks hold before he drained her of her magic and left her like a fucking husk. Love. Real love. And that means you guys were so meant to be that your love broke a nearly unbreakable spell. So, if we're all done being girls here, how about you teach us how to make this protection amulet."

Janet and Chris both nodded along to every point Frank made, and even Wendy looked a little ashamed and nodded along with the support Rosie bits.

Rosie got choked up not just by the support her friends were giving her, but that they were welcoming Hatter into the group. "Thanks, Frank. Thanks all of you. I didn't know I had such great friends before the nightmare monster started stalking me. You all stepped up, and have been amazing. I wasn't sure if I'd lose friends when I broke up with Jack, but you've all been even more awesome. Thank you."

"Hey, didn't Frank say something about stopping acting like little girls? Emo fest's over." Janet teased. "Now let's make some bad-ass jewelry."

"Fuck you, bitch." Frank offered with a grin and a nod to Janet.

"Love you too, sweet cheeks." Janet bantered

with Frank.

Rosie was pretty sure she was the only one that noticed Chris's momentary look of disappointment at their moment, and wondered just how much he really liked Janet that a taunt fight made him jealous.

"Ok, then. Hatter," Rosie segued back to the task at hand. "Want to walk us through making this protection amulet?"

"Yes." Hatter took the lead back. "The amulet basically has four parts." As he began to explain, everyone settled in to listen. "You need to get a quartz crystal that you'll clear first, and then anoint. It's the first and most complicated part. The second bit is made from sterling silver wire, pin wrapped into a pentacle. Then you'll need two amber beads for your pulse points, that's probably the easiest bit. And the last element is a little linen bag with a rosebud wrapped in the leaf of a Lilly of the valley."

Hatter paused, to see if anyone had questions, then continued. "When the amulet does its thing, it's the linen bag that takes the damage instead of your body. Like a surrogate, for when you get hurt away from your physical shell. So, if you get hurt a little, the bag will have to be replaced. If it's bad, you'll have to re-cleanse and anoint the quartz too. You may wake up with a damaged amulet, but you'll wake up."

"Ok, we get how to reset it. But how do we make it?" Wendy asked.

"Rosie will contact you with the list of supplies you'll need after you wake. You'll have to set up a quartz crystal to be cleared, but while it's in process you'll be able to make most of the rest." Hatter paused to think about where to start the detailed directions. "I'll explain how to clear the crystal first, and go from there. I'll also give you what each ingredient means as I go. Ok?" They all murmured statements of agreement, and Hatter continued. "The quartz crystal is for protection, healing, psychicism, power, and is symbolic of the spirit and intellect."

As Hatter taught them, Rosie could hear Kiri's speech patterns in Hatter's recitation, and it made Rosie feel both a little reconnected to her old protectors and made her miss the world she could no longer access. She thought maybe after they defeated the monster, Rosie and Hatter could try to return to that world together. But Rosie didn't think on it too long, she didn't want to miss what Hatter was teaching.

☘

The next morning when Rosie woke, Hatter whispered the ingredients and quantities into her mind and she wrote them down carefully. Janet and Rosie then spent all day gathering ingredients. It was a hot and muggy summer day, but the two friends had a good time hanging out and shopping. They all got together that evening, and Rosie divvied up the supplies. They agreed to set their alarms for four am. and, as directed, start clearing the crystals during the blue hour before dawn. The next day they would work on the amulets together, getting them nearly completed except the crystals. Then the day after that they would complete the amulets. On the third night they would go to sleep wearing their amulets and dream walk together. Hatter would then bring them to a nightmare not as dangerous as Rosie's, but scary enough to test both their training and the amulets. If the amulets worked, only then would they make a plan to confront Rosie's monster.

That gave Hatter and Rosie two nights to themselves. Two nights of intimate conversations, love making, and world exploration. When they weren't in Hatter's bed he showed Rosie all of his favorite places within Wonderland. When Rosie wanted to explore the hedge maze to see if she could find that stained glass window in the center, Hatter always had other places to show Her first. Rosie could see it was something that caused Hatter distress, so decided to leave it alone until they had dealt with the monster.

CR

35

The third night came, and the amulets were made to Hatter's specifications. Rosie brought her friends to meet Hatter in Wonderland, near the jabberwock's forest. They stepped between worlds and Rosie's heart leapt with joy at the sight of Hatter atop a bright pink six foot tall mushroom.

He was a striking specimen of masculinity, standing like a swashbuckling adventurer with one hand on the hilt of a large sword and the other using an old fashioned looking spy glass to scan the forest beyond. His clothing looked pirate chic, with tight dark brown leather pants and vest, a loose, but not poofy, white shirt, and leather braces that went from wrist to nearly elbow. The outfit was completed with a sword belt carrying low on one hip and a scattering of sheathed knives on his vest, bracers, and sticking out of his knee high boots. All weapons positioned for mobility and a quick draw. The sword had an intricate hilt, with a large filigreed guard that wrapped the grip. It was a dark metal rather than shiny and Rosie found herself wondering if the blade hidden by the sheath was also this dark mat metal or shiny steel. He was facing away from them, and Rosie's gaze couldn't help but notice how nice and firm his ass looked in the snug leather. The whole tableau made Rosie wish she hadn't just walked in with a crowd of people.

Hatter turned, collapsing and putting away the spyglass into a small pouch hanging from the opposite side of the sword belt. He waved at the group with a broad genuine smile, then leapt with catlike grace to the ground in front of them. He landed lightly, taking the force of his landing with bent knees before smoothly standing like he had jumped a foot, not six.

Hatter greeted Rosie with an embrace and a sexually charged but restrained kiss before acknowledging the others with a nod. He kept an arm around Rosie's waist as he spoke. "I was thinking a jabberwock fight might be a good test of the amulets and to see if your fight training is good enough. I've tracked one into a cave system a little way into the woods."

"Nice duds, dude." Frank said with obvious sarcasm before Janet elbowed him in the side. "What?" He snapped at Janet rubbing his side. "The guy is dressed like he's going to fight a dragon."

"I am." Hatter replied honestly, "The Jabberwock is Wonderland's answer to a dragon."

"I don't think any of the rest of us are complaining about the view." Janet commented suggestively to grudging nods from Wendy and Chris. Rosie tried not to smile or blush, but failed on both accounts.

"Thanks for the compliment, I think." Hatter responded feeling a little like a piece of meat, but shook it off when he saw Rosie's blush and caught her looking him over lingeringly. Hatter decided if it got him those looks from the love of his life he was ok feeling like a tasty treat. Hatter responded further. "My leathers may not fit your fashion sense, Frank, but they would give you more protection than your T-shirt and jeans combo. You might all want to manifest a little light armor as a backup to Rosie's light shields."

Chris spoke up, "Aren't we trying to test the amulets? If we protect ourselves too well, we won't know how well they work."

Rosie gave Chris a look before speaking, "We're trying to give them a little test, not tax them till they fail. We're also testing how well we fight as a team."

Hatter added, "We have home field advantage here, Wonderland is a world I can influence easily. If things get hairy I can change the circumstances and keep us all safe."

Frank laughed, "So, then you're like our professor X, and Wonderland is the danger room." This comment got a groan or chuckle from everyone but Hatter, who just nodded and moved on, seeming familiar with the cultural reference. Rosie wondered how many dream worlds included comic superheroes, and if those worlds were the inspiration for comics or the other way around.

Hatter turned his attention to the amulet hanging from Rosie's neck. "Looks like the amulets came out well." He flipped it over and really examined all the amulets' components. If not for the small linen pouch tucked behind the silver focus, it would have looked like a necklace bought at an arts and crafts festival. The short silver chain was interrupted by a round amber bead to either side of Rosie's neck, at her pulse points. It's pendant was neatly bent silver wire looking like a pentacle with a spiral overlay spinning in to the center of the star. The white linen bag rested just behind the silver wire pendant, and a clear quartz crystal hung from the pentacle, resting in Rosie's cleavage quite attractively. The crystal sparkled like it was polished, but Hatter knew that it looked so glossy from the fresh anointing oil. "Yours came out better than the first one Kiri had me make." Hatter whispered intimately to Rosie before speaking to the rest. "One of the signs that its working is that an aspect of it came with you when you traveled from your bodies." He looked around the group to be sure they all wore the protective charms, and they looked right.

"I have to say, I don't get it." Chris said crossing his arms defensively. "Why would some ancient faerie teach you how to make an amulet to protect your physical body if you aren't a human with a body? And why would they know how to make an amulet to protect half breeds like us, when they are full faeries and can't come close to the Prime Material 'cause our collective cynicism would kill their magical essence in seconds? It just doesn't add up to me."

Hatter looked hurt. "It's because Kiri and I both

love Rosie, value her as a rare and powerful soul, and want to protect her. The same reason you all are here. They know how to make these amulets from a time before the Prime Material was poison to them. You are here in loyalty to your friend, why is it so strange we would want to do the same?"

"I don't know, maybe it's because I don't know what you are. What are you Hatter? Rosie says you're Fey-born and a dream walker, like us. But that means human with a little Fey tossed in down the generations. But if you are human, why don't you have a body in the Prime Material? If you don't have a body, you aren't like us. What kind of Fey or spirit are you?"

As Chris spoke Hatter's jaw clenched and his eyes reddened with unshed tears, he didn't move from Rosie's side but she could feel all his muscles tighten with agitation. Hatter looked like he was either going to punch Chris or run away, and Rosie could feel his confusion and anger building. His breath started getting slower and more pronounced, like he was fighting for control.

Rosie took a step between Chris and Hatter. "Chris, that's enough. Back off. Hatter has proven himself to me, and I trust him. Why is it so important what he is? He's here to help. Why isn't that enough for you?"

"Come on Rosie, you trusted Jack implicitly too, and look how that turned out. He was using you as a chew toy, and made you think he loved you and you were sure you loved him too. Then this guy turns up out of nowhere to save you from Jack. And now you say you love him, and we should trust him. I just don't think we know enough about him to put our complete trust in him."

Janet stepped up to Chris, putting a hand on his arm to calm him. "Look. You and I saw what Jack did to Rosie more than most. Hatter is not the same guy. I know you think of Rosie like a little sister, but I saw how his love and protection of her made her see that what Jack made her feel was hollow. I watched her struggle with the guilt of feeling something for Hatter when she was supposed to love Jack. Now we find out Jack was emotionally and magically raping Rosie, but her falling in love with her rescuer broke that spell. No matter what kind of man he is, I'm in Hatter's corner."

Frank also took a step towards Chris. "She's right ya know. Jack told me it was a real fucking spell. He's like some kind of psychic vampire dark Fey shit head. He was my friggin friend and I didn't even suspect until he spilled about being pissed that she got away. I thought he was a player and a dog, but I didn't know he was taking people's free will and making them think..." He turned to Rosie. "If I had known you weren't making your own choices, I would have helped." He looked back at Wendy. "Like I've been trying to help you Wendy." He turned back to Chris. "All I'm trying to say is if Rosie and Hatter didn't have true feelings, Jack would still own her. So I'm willing to put faith in this stranger because I believe he wants what is safest for Rosie. I think of her like a sister too, and my gut trusts my little sister's new squeeze."

Chris held up his hands. "Ok, I give." He turned to Hatter. "Sorry dude, I get it now. I believe you have the best intentions for Rosie. And if you are someone Rosie would want to love, you wouldn't be the kind of person to wish us harm. So lead on, it's your world."

Hatter was again touched by their concern for Rosie's well being, and being included in Rosie's defense, in a way felt one of them. "Wow. I can't remember anyone ever saying such nice things about me before. Thanks. So let's suit up and go have a test run."

ℂℜ

36

Hatter had them all manifest protective clothing that they could still maneuver well in. Most of their choices looked more biker than pirate but still leaned towards neck to toe leather. Then they headed out into the forest. Hatter and Rosie were in the lead, cutely holding hands with their fingers interlaced as they walked. Janet and Chris followed behind, passing flirting looks between them but not touching so openly as Hatter and Rosie. Wendy and Frank took up the rear and more than once rolled their eyes at the snappiness in front of them.

Soon they came to the cave Hatter had tracked the Jabberwock to. Hatter quietly pointed out the signs that the Jabberwock had gone past, disturbed shrubbery, foot prints with long jagged claw marks, and scratches on rocks from it grinding its ever-growing teeth like a giant rodent. They manifested lanterns and torches before entering the cave. Hatter started to track, his eyes glowing the golden color of his wolf's, and all but Rosie were stunned by the change. Once inside, Hatter walked a few feet ahead of them, tracking the Jabberwock by scent and sight.

They followed Hatter through the twisty, turny, cave system for what felt like a long time when he told them all to stop. "I smell blood on the far side of the cavern we are about to enter. I've only smelt one animal up to this point. It's possible the Jabberwock brought some poor creature back here and toyed with it before killing it, so it's scent had left the tunnels but the blood still smells fresh." Hatter's expression showed that he didn't think that was a likely scenario. "Or something deeper in the caves came out and had a fight with the Jabberwock. I'm thinking that anything from deeper in the caves is likely to be as scary as the Jabberwock. I want to give you all the choice to leave before we go any further. Because the smell of this much fresh blood means we are likely close to danger."

They all agreed to try to quietly check out the cavern, and retreat if they found anything too dangerous. As they walked across the large cave room a disquieting shiver passed through each of them. But it was Hatter that recognized what had happened.

Hatter yelled as he ushered everyone to run back the way they'd come. "We're not in Wonderland anymore! Somehow this cave has been shifted to another world. A world where I'm not in sync with the land! I'm not in control of the world around me! We need to go back!" The group quickly turned and were retreating back the way they'd come when a wind blew coldly across the large gray cavern and a tentacle as big around as a car snaked preternaturally quickly out of the darkness blocking their retreat.

It grabbed the person closest, Wendy, and threw her across the room. She bounced off the rough cave wall with a crunching sound before dropping to the ground with a heavy thud. Wendy was grabbed so quickly that she didn't have time to manifest the white light shield to soak any of the impact, and was unconscious almost instantly. They all shined their lights on the large tentacle, but it no longer had to retreat from light, seeming to produce its own darkness, impenetrable by mundane means. The sounds of writhing wet tentacles came from each of the large cavern's dark crevices and corners.

Rosie knew right away that this was her nightmare monster, only it had grown even bigger than it had been when it caught her. She was filled with terror and panic and was screaming uncontrollably as a sharply barbed tentacle raced toward her. A shining long blade struck the tentacle, nearly severing it and making it retreat. Hatter had stood between Rosie and attack yet again. She was so terrified that all Rosie wanted was to cling to her knight, but instead she manifested a sword of her own and swung at the new tentacles that reached for her.

Chris was closest to where Wendy fell, so he quickly went to her, checking her vitals. "She's breathing! I got her!" He swung Wendy's limp unconscious frame over his shoulder.

More disembodied tentacles whipped at them from the darkness. Crevices on opposite sides of the room spewed tentacles to grab for the group as they dodged, barely escaping as they ran. Rosie was first to pull up her glowing light barrier as they ran, reminding the others to do the same as they used weapons to more actively defend themselves.

They all saw the huge bloody pile of feasting tentacles picking the bones clean of what they all assumed was the Jabberwock. Frank puked as he was splashed with gore from twenty five feet away, but continued to run and fight despite it.

As they ran deeper into the caves, they knew they were being herded, but couldn't do much about it without letting one of the endless new tentacles grab one of them. When Hatter saw a tentacle that was nearly cut through reach for him he realized that the monster must have the ability to reach through shadows like portals, and what appeared to be limitless tentacles was probably the same five to ten tentacles reaching through different shadows.

They reached a place where the rough natural cave walls gave way to man- made concrete walls. They were herded into a dim room as big as a cavern, but with many dark alcoves that might be hiding doors or the monster. As the party reached the middle of this huge gray room several loud clangs were heard around the room as doors swung shut.

For a minute the room was still and silent, with no sign of the monster. The only sound was their ragged panting breath as they circled up, backs to each other. The flashlights all started to flicker and fail so they tossed them out into the darkness, relying on the white light they each had wrapped around themselves. Chris's shield extended around Wendy's unconscious form, and with a moment to catch their breath he set her carefully in the center of the huddle and checked to make sure she was still breathing.

Janet, being the closest thing they had to a medic, went quickly to work checking Wendy's vitals. The others all kept watch, trying to keep all the shadows in view but this room was more in shadow than not.

She's still breathing." Janet confirmed in a whisper. "But she has multiple broken bones, and God knows what kind of internal bleeding. Shouldn't she have woken up? If the amulet is working, shouldn't she have woken up with the pouch all used but ok?"

Hatter crouched down to check Wendy's amulet. "The amulet looks intact," Hatter kept his voice even lower than Janet had so that no one outside their immediate circle would have any chance of overhearing his words. "Maybe there's something in this world keeping her from waking right now. But nothing I've ever heard of can keep a dreamer longer than a few hours, by morning she should wake fine."

"This is one seriously fucked up test." Frank almost spat the words, "No matter how much we trained, I don't think we could have prepared for this shit. Could your monster be everywhere at once before? Or are we dealing with a nest of these fuckers?"

"I think it's still just the one," Hatter confirmed, "but I think it's learned to use shadows as portals. This is definitely a new power it didn't have before. Something's made it more powerful."

Strange ticking sounds echoed around the perimeter of the room, like something big walking on very sharp claws. Every conscious person was immediately on their feet and searching the shadows, following the sounds that skittered in all directions.

Suddenly Janet screamed, an agonizing pained sound from the center of their huddle. Before the rest could even turn to see what had happened they all saw her light shield flicker and fail. In the moment that it took them to register what was happening to Janet, Chris let out a similar scream and his shield went too.

Hatter sliced through the air above the party and

a pencil thin tentacle was cut clean through as it was lunging for its third strike at Frank from the ceiling. While they scanned their perimeter the monster had attacked from a shadow above them. The monster screeched and the sound filled the room with its pain and rage. The cut tentacle retreated spraying greenish yellow ichor across the party. The ichor burned Janet and Chris's skin like acid where it landed, but sizzled and evaporated off the other's protective light barriers. The end of the tentacle flopped and twitched at their feet, it's tip ended in a strange sucker with a bony spike poking through the middle. Hatter thought it was strange that the monster had such a specialized appendage, obviously designed to take down their shielding.

He didn't have much time to think about the monster's adaptations, because a dozen thin tentacles snaked out towards them from all around. Each thin tentacle that snaked in toward them had the same cup and sticker at the tip, but they were coming in all at the same time so there was no way to block them all. Hatter managed to slash through the three tentacles closest to him, and Frank managed to take out two, Rosie and Chris managed to defend against a tentacle apiece, but Janet wasn't able to make contact with any. That left five attackers undefended, stabbing one into each of them. Hatter, Rosie, and Frank's shields were painfully sucked away, ripping screams from them much like it had Janet and Chris. Now that they were all defenseless the acidic spray from the severed tentacles hit them all causing painful burns. But things were worse for Janet and Chris, the tentacles that struck them wrapped around their necks and threw them across the room in opposite directions. They hit with wet pops in rapid succession and slid wetly to the ground. It wasn't something the three left standing could see, only hear, because without their shields they were left in pitch dark.

Hatter, Rosie, and Frank quickly closed ranks, backs together, and waited for the monster's next attack.

The attacks paused again. Rosie felt something brush past her face and she flinched but nothing else seemed to happen.

"Are you ok, Rosie? What happened?" Hatter whispered in Rosie's ear.

Hearing Hatter's voice beside her was a comfort even in such dire circumstances. Rosie whispered back. "I think something just brushed my cheek, but I'm ok. Can either of you see anything?"

"No, it's pitch dark." Frank hissed between his teeth. "This thing is fucking toying with us isn't it?"

"I think so." Hatter breathed. "I can't see much, but I can see a little."

Rosie saw a golden glow from the corner of her eye, and knew that Hatter's eyes had turned the glowing golden of his wolf form. "Stop." Rosie's whisper sounded near panicked, "your eyes like that make you an easy target."

The light went out before Rosie had finished. "I'm betting that the monster can see in the dark, I don't think a few seconds of glow will add to our danger. It might have helped tho, I think I saw a switch on the wall directly across from Frank."

"What do you think it is?" Frank wondered quietly.

"I don't know, but I'm hoping it's a light switch. Should we move over to it and try to turn it on?" Hatter tried to keep a light tone to his whispers, but his stress was evident.

"Sounds like a plan." Rosie whispered, fear clear in her voice.

"Ok."Frank gave a quiet agreement as Rosie spoke.

They moved as quietly and carefully as they could, making sure to keep their backs to each other. They hadn't gotten far when they heard the ticking of claws on concrete again, but also a wet slithering. Several shapes moved quickly through the darkness, and

Rosie felt it coming for her. She screamed, "Run!" To Hatter and Frank as she felt something sharp and articulated wrap her leg. "Get to the switch!"

Frank booked it to the wall, but Hatter wasn't about to let the monster take Rosie from him. He couldn't swing his sword without the risk of hitting Rosie, so he tried to put himself between Rosie and the monster. His eyes lit with feral energy, and with his wolf's eyes Hatter could see that the monster was now fully in the room with them, not just poking limbs through portals to torment and injure them.

When Hatter's eyes lit golden, so too did the monster's glowing red eyes. Rosie screamed in sheer terror as the monster's eyes brought all the fear of running from it and the fear she felt when she saw it nearly kill Hatter. The fear was like a magical intensifying of every fear she'd ever felt condensed into one sustained moment. She also felt the bone in her leg snap as the claw wrapping her calve tightened and tried to pull her to the ground. It tried to drag her, but Hatter stabbed two blades into the long armored limb. The knives kept it from pulling Rosie further, but didn't make it let go.

Frank got to the wall and fumbled blindly for any kind of switch. He thought that Rosie and Hatter had the monster's full attention as he slid his hands all over the wall. His fingers just found two old fashioned pull levers and he was grabbing them both when a barbed tentacle hooked into the back of his neck and pulled him away from the wall. Somehow it managed to miss his spine and just ripped through the side of Franks neck. Frank fell back, but gripped onto the levers pulling them down with him. The barb had ripped through tissue and veins spewing franks blood out in a spray caught in the dim emergency lights that came on as the switch made contact with a loud electrical hum. There was also a clank of bolts releasing the doors. Franks last thoughts as he lost consciousness were that he had done something heroic by getting to the switches even if he would die for it, and also that flying felt fucking wonderful even with all the pain as the same barbed tentacle stabbed him through the gut and flung him across the room and into the opposite wall.

Rosie and Hatter were aware of the emergency lights coming on, and of Frank's body being launched over head, but were busy wrestling their own bit of the huge monster. Rosie had managed to recover from the staggering fear enough to pry its claw from around her leg. Hatter ripped his knives through the carapace of that limb, trying to detach it so it would let go of her. But as they struggled against one strong limb, four more shot from the huge shadow that now stood out as unnatural against the light. Two limbs that were almost arm-like, except for the length and two extra elbows, disarmed Hatter and pinned him to the ground. The other two limbs were very serpentine tentacles that grabbed Rosie and flung her back into the middle of the room. She landed head first on the concrete, and the momentum pushed her body over her head and dropped her face down and still.

Hatter screamed for Rosie, struggling ineffectively to get free. Needing to know that she was still breathing, and wanting more than anything to get free to save his love. The monster used more appendages to hold the struggling man against the ground, keeping each limb and his torso held firmly with immense strength. Keeping his arms and legs stretched and pinned might have kept Hatter from shifting his body into another shape to escape if he had not been so determined; but as he started to shift a strange aura emanated from the monster, and held his body not only in place but form.

The monster reached out of its shadowed core with two giant spidery legs, each one ending in a serrated hook. It stabbed a hook through each shoulder of Rosie's limp face down body, and effortlessly hoisted her into the air. She hung, dangling and limp, head slumped forward, slowly dripping blood; while the monster made a slow chittering sound that seemed almost like laughter. It kept Hatter pinned painfully to the ground, unable to shift or escape but forced to watch what it was doing to Rosie. Hatter had no doubts that the monster pinned him where he did to feed off of Hatter's torment as he struggled impotently to get to the most important creature he had ever met and the woman he loved with all his heart.

The monster snaked six tentacles out slowly, winding two up Rosie's legs, two securing her arms, and a fifth snaked through her hair to hold her scalp. The sixth tentacle slid behind Rosie and wavered in the air like a charmed cobra waiting to strike. The tentacle holding the back of Rosie's head looked almost like exposed brains the way it curled and wound around her, Rosie's bright red hair tufting out of the tightly pressed creases only accentuated the illusion. It yanked her limp head up as the slender tip of the tentacle slithered down her forehead from the brain like mass. It wiggled a bit between her eyes then poked its sharp tip through her skin with a meaty tick. Hatter screamed with rage and struggled harder, watching a drop of blood glide from the wound. The droplet slid around the bridge of Rosie's nose to the corner of her eye and down her cheek, looking like a single crimson tear.

The monster seemed to be waiting for Hatter to settle before continuing its little show of tortures. It made a wet snickering sound, almost chiding Hatter when he continued to struggle. A new multi-jointed appendage with half a dozen long jagged dirty nailed fingers reached out towards Hatter, and grabbed his face to force him to look at Rosie's limp form. The nasty fingers smelled of sourness and rot scratching at his face as he struggled, but soon had Hatters face pinned in a position facing Rosie.

The monster waved the tentacle behind Rosie to

be sure Hatter was watching it before plunging it into the center of her back. Rosie screamed in inhuman agony, her body going rigid, and her eyes suddenly wide. The scream continued long after any breath could have sustained it, but it was a scream of the soul not the body. There was a crackling sound all around the room, like static jumping from wall to wall, just before Hatter felt the air stir. Winds whipped through the room at hurricane speeds all centering on Rosie's chest and the vortex that was opening into a black hole.

Through the wind Hatter could hear Rosie continuing to scream and what sounded like slurping coming from the monster. As it drank Rosie down, the monster laughed with maniacal joy, sounding disturbingly human. The winds seemed to draw faint glistening trails from the scattered broken bodies around the room into the dark vortex. Hatter felt the wind tugging at him too, but what it tugged at was his magic and soul. His energy was not as freely trailing off him as it was the others, but it took force of will the unconscious couldn't exert.

Hatter realized that he could struggle till he had no more strength and the monster would definitely kill them all, or he could calm himself and reserve his energy while he came up with a plan. It was near impossible, but he calmed his body and mind despite the ongoing scream of the woman he wanted to protect more than life itself. He turned his gaze to the monster as much as he could with his face immobilized. Through the shifting shadows that covered the monster, Hatter could make out its red glowing eyes, and there were dozens of them all clustered to face Rosie. One eye swiftly spun in Hatter's direction, like it was more floating in the darkness than attached to anything skeletal.

Hatter saw the eye rolling his way and thought quickly. Before it reached his direction, Hatter blanked his face into a look of defeat. If the creature thought he had lost the will to fight, maybe it would make a mistake he could use to his advantage. He prayed that the chance would come before Rosie was sucked dry and beyond hope. The monster snorted with satisfaction, and the little red eye looking at Hatter floated back to the cluster watching Rosie.

Hatter saw that the tentacle going into Rosie's back attached to the monster just below the eyes, and with a lurch of disgust, realized that it was really a prehensile proboscis sucking the magic and soul from Rosie and the others. If he could just find a way to cut through that long tube of a mouth he might be able to save Rosie and her friends.

The monster trembled like a druggie getting a fix, and started making noises usually reserved for extreme physical pleasure. A spiraling ball of softly glowing light was gathering in front of the vortex, it was made in part from the energies of Rosie's fallen friends, but most of the energy was pouring from Rosie herself. Faint wisps of energy trailed from the ball into the darkness in the center of the vortex, and Hatter instinctively knew if his opportunity didn't come soon he would be too late and Rosie's soul would be devoured. But in that moment his opportunity came.

With its attention so focused on its meal the monster forgot to tend its other prisoner, and the monster loosened his grip on Hatter. The nailed fingers pinning his face were no longer digging into his flesh, and the claws cutting into him no longer pressed for pain. Hatter focused his will as he quickly grabbed the claws that pinned him to the floor and twisted them painfully, they broke off just above the barbs that locked into his flesh.

The monster screeched with pain and surprise, swinging its attention to Hatter a moment too late as he rolled out from under its broken limbs. As soon as he was free of the pin whatever aura the monster had that kept him from shifting was gone, and Hatter was able to shift his hands into sharp claws of his own. Without hesitation Hatter lunged at the tenticular proboscis, forcing his magic into his claws. He made contact, and the attack sliced into the monsters feeding tentacle but was not enough to slice through it. It was enough to stop the sucking sound, and Rosie gasped in breath at the end of such a long scream. The vortex slowed, but didn't stop.

Rosie was disoriented, and about to lose cognizance again, but despite her grave injuries she saw Hatter trying to tear through a piece of the monster and had a flash of the last time she saw him tearing at this same monster. She remembered helping give Hatter the energy he needed to save them both, and instinctively pushed her power into her protector again. But this time she had a rip in her soul, and all the light gathered into the cone of the vortex traveled with the energy she pushed. It transformed Hatter with a wave of healing like the last time, turning him into a giant glowing wolf, but unlike last time her push took all of Rosie's magic combined with her friends magic. It was so much power that Hatter couldn't take it all in and some of it overflowed to attack the monster itself.

The power burned into the monster like acid, and Hatter's golden glowing wolf followed behind ripping through the monsters Proboscis. Severing the feeding tentacle caused darkness to spew from the severed appendage, almost as if the monster were a vacuum with its flow reversed. Some of the blackness splashed against the wolf, and it felt and smelled like terror, agony, disappointment, and doubt. The monster seemed to be deflating as it screamed, mirroring Rosie just moments before. As it emptied, all the monster's extra limbs desiccated and turned to powder.

Hatter spun to see Rosie falling to the ground, the vortex and everything suspending her were gone. Hatter dove for her, changing seamlessly back into a man as he caught Rosie's limp body in his arms just before she hit ground. He still glowed with her power, as his wolf form had.

Rosie saw Hatter catch her, lit from within and surrounded by a glowing nimbus, and she had one clear thought, 'I knew you were my guardian Angel' before she again passed out. And tho she spoke no words, her angel, Hatter, heard her and was filled with such love that even in the midst of the fray he couldn't help but smile.

Almost as soon as Hatter had Rosie in his arms he was pulling her away from the spewing blackness, he couldn't imagine what being hit with such negative emotions so injured would do to her. He settled her, as carefully and quickly as he could, on the floor of the far side of the room before diving back into combat with the monster.

He lunged at the now smaller flailing monster, transforming with the jump, and tore into it with teeth and claws. As he tore chunk after chunk away from the monster they all dissipated before they could hit the ground. Last time Hatter had fought the monster it was all blood and gore on both sides, but this time the monster barely tried to defend itself from Hatter's attack; like it knew it was mortally wounded. Not wanting to give the monster a chance to fake Hatter out like he had done to it, Hatter continued the attack. Hatter formed his paw into a long clawed wolf-man's hand, and plunged it into what he guessed was the monsters chest, as the rest of his body followed his arms transformation.

The monster bucked and writhed in pain as Hatter dug shoulder deep into it, feeling the gore squish between his clawed fingers. As he ripped and tore around, Hatter felt the creature's still beating heart and tore it out of its chest. The cluster of red glowing eyes all brightened in surprise for a shocked moment before the glow faded from existence with the rest of it.

Hatter looked down at his blood soaked arm and fist, still clenched tightly around the monster's heart and felt triumph. Hatter howled in victory, as a werewolf ought, before shaping his body back into his entirely human seeming. He looked down at his clenched fist, and could feel the heart continuing to beat no matter how hard he tried to crush the life out of it.

He carefully and slowly peeled back his fingers, and found the heart had turned into a glowing, pulsing, ruby-like stone. It seemed to be indestructible and he could see it beginning to regenerate as he looked at it. If Hatter didn't do something quickly the crystallized heart could grow back into a formidable monster.

He thought on how to dispose of the crystallized heart, as he went back to Rosie's side. He decided to take it to a world he'd visited before, where a mountain called Doom was filled with a volcano whose magma could destroy any magic artifact, no matter how powerful. It was an old world with tricky rules of its own, but Hatter thought it would be the best way to make sure this monster never came back for Rosie.

Hatter checked Rosie to make sure she was still breathing. She was not only breathing, but she had a strong pulse. She was still badly injured, but the worst of it did not include a hole in her chest. Hatter was grateful for that, tho her injuries were dire, she seemed stable enough to rest here while Hatter finished her nightmare monster for good. She looked like she had used up all of her, and the others, magical reserves, but that she would recover fully in time; and that heartened Hatter. He didn't want to move her too much right away, in case it made any injury worse, he would tend her properly when he got back from disposing of the last bit of her monster.

Hatter carefully adjusted her, making sure she was in as comfortable a position as possible, and kissed Rosie gently, "I need to go destroy this for you, I'll be right back." And with that Hatter stood and stepped into another world. Whatever had locked them to this world was not keeping him here any longer.

ଓ

37

Consciousness swam slowly back to Rosie.

Bodies lay scattered like driftwood on a beach. Rosie couldn't tell who the bodies in the shadows belonged to, only that they all lay as still as death. She prayed that they all had their amulets still with them here and in the waking world, or things would be very bad come morning. She tried to pull herself up from the floor, but the exertion caused her vision to pop with spots of light and dark. All Rosie could manage was to roll over and drag herself onto all fours, or at least all two-and-a-halfish, with her left wrist clearly broken and unable to carry her weight, and her right leg broken below the knee. Her shoulders also screamed with pain from their injuries, but she didn't have much choice in using her right to help prop herself.

Rosie made an effort, and unsteadily moved her head to search the dimness. She was able to identify two of the closer broken heaps as Janet and Chris. That meant Wendy and Frank were the heaps further across the room. But where was Hatter? And more frighteningly, where was the monster? It was just too still and quiet. Something felt wrong.

Just then, Rosie heard slow clapping from across the room. Jack stepped from the shadows, and glared at Rosie. He stopped clapping, "What a great show you put on for me little girl. When you wouldn't take my calls any more, I was a little hurt. Not because you didn't want me anymore, I could care less about what you want, but because you took away my food. 'Cause that's all you were ever good for. Food. You had so much tasty magic just going to waste, you and your little friends have fed me well. But there you go, breaking up with me," he laughed like a short bark, "Do you hear how ridiculous that sounds even now? You. Breaking up with me. You are so below me, what gives you the right to leave me?" He strolled over to Rosie and lifted her to her feet by the hair. She tried to scream, but after the scream her nightmare monster pulled from her she had no voice left. "What? No 'owie', at least I've managed to break you of that. I heard you, you have learned to scream well. I wonder if you have any screams left in you at all? I guess we will just have to find out." He pulled her roughly to face him with only millimeters between them, and though Rosie tried to struggle free all she managed was to make her right hand clench weakly. "Because I am going to finish what that sad little monster of yours couldn't. And no little fru-fru British ghost boy will be saving you now, because I saw him leave you for dead. Sick little pup even kissed you goodbye, he must have a thing for useless little bitches." Jack laughed at his own joke. "'Cause he's a dog and all. Get it? I bet he isn't even a man at all, just a dog that got big thoughts about humping a slightly less hairy bitch like you."

Rosie's vision swam with spots and colors that made her blink slowly, Jack shook her when her eyes started to sag and lose focus. "No you don't. No dying before you feed me one last time little Rosie. And not until you know just how badly you lost before you die." He licked the crimson tear of blood, half dried on her cheek. "Mmmm, that tastes like me winning and you about to die." He took a satisfied breath and continued. "That little monster of yours, just couldn't seem to do the job for me. Looked like he almost had you there for a bit, but your little puppy mucked that up. Your little doggie in heat isn't here now tho, he's probably off burying his bone elsewhere." Jack let out another single laugh at his own joke before returning to his villainous monologue. "But I was telling you about your oh- so-scary nightmare monster. I fed him well from the energy of your little fairy dream world, and sent him here so I could watch him tear you to shreds like you deserve for playing above your station. I was going to kill him when it was done of course. Draining it of your happy fairy worlds' defenses, your power and life force, your" he made air quotes with the hand not holding Rosie up, "friends' power, and then a little desert of its own monstery nougat center. Would have been the best feast

I'd ever had. But then instead of ripping you apart, the little shit starts hoovering you just like all the magic you wasted on that barrier protecting your bitch protector. That's ok, though, that showed me how to pull power from a person so much quicker than I ever knew possible. Just goes to show, you can even learn from a dumb animal. I wonder what I might learn from you, you are about as slow as your monster. It was thinking we'd made an alliance, just like you thought I was the love of your life. You were both so easy to manipulate and control."

From their awkwardly close positions, Jack took a moment to look Rosie in the eye. "What do you think? Should I rape you and then drain you dry, or would it be funnier to kill you and then fuck your still warm corpse?" A tear rolled down Rosie's cheek, as she struggled to make her body move and run away, but she was so depleted that her muscles couldn't respond. "It's really so hard to decide, maybe I'll do both. It's not every day a person gets a chance to play with his food so thoroughly with no chance of getting caught; in the real world they'll find you dead without a mark that can be followed back to me."

Jack threw Rosie on the floor like a discarded piece of clothing. She slid a few feet before her body hit the wall with a thud and a crack. She felt a shock of pain, and then nothing. Rosie was spent and could barely move before, but now she couldn't move at all. She hoped her own amulet was protection enough that if she did wake up, she wouldn't be paralyzed like here. She had landed with her face against someone's leg, but was too disoriented and weak to figure out who's it was. Tears streamed down her face, how had she ever thought Jack had really loved her?

"Well that is just rude. Didn't your mother teach you to look at a person when they're talking to you?" Jack kicked her over on her back so she would be staring up at him. "And haven't you been enough of a slut with

Bo-Bo the dog faced boy? Looks to me like you're trying to feel up Frank here too." He nudged the body that Rosie had slid into with a foot before he squatted in front of them both."Ya know, Frank was my friend first. And then you go and steal him out from under me. Makes me wonder if you had a bit of my talent, 'cause I can't see any reason why anyone would pick a loser like you to side with of their own free will." Jack shrugged dismissively at Frank and turned his full attention to Rosie. "Even if you have a bit of something like my talent, it would never compare to me. I could use my power to make any weak little girlie girl fall head over heels for me. Then they give me all their magic and their virginity, and then I move on to the next sweet morsel. Not to brag or anything, but I had six other sweet tasty little virgins while I was with you, and you were so in love with me that you completely missed it. They didn't have much in the way of magic, not much more than a snack each really. Not like the people you surround yourself with, it's like you inspire more tasty magic in them. It's too bad you won't be adding extra yum to my next meals, wish I could strip that talent of recognizing Fey-born and teasing up that little magic spark." He paused for a moment, smiling, like he was forming a fun new idea. "Ya know, I think I might go for some of your school friends next. You always spoke so well of me to them, and they will want to console me in my grieving for my girlfriend who died of a heart attack in her sleep. But I digress, no reason to waste too much time talking to you when you'll be dead in the next few minutes."

Jack reached out a hand to feel for Frank's pulse. "Better make sure none of your" he made air quotes again with his fingers, "friends are going to wake up and try to do anything stupid." And with that he took Frank's head in both hands and twisted it violently, it made a snap sound that Rosie knew was the sound of his spine breaking between vertebrae. She pleaded again, silently, with any deity that might be listening, that the amulets had worked and that they would all wake up safely tomorrow.

Jack made quick work of walking around the room and snapping the necks of the next two unconscious bodies, stopping at Wendy last. "You made me waste my time with this one. She's all used up now, no energy to feed off of any more. No tasty energy left from any of these four. But before you convinced her to come fight with you, and die, we were spending lots of time together. She was so sympathetic over how you just wouldn't let me go. We were putting our heads together to try to figure out a way to let you down gently. So you wouldn't try to commit suicide and would be ok with us as a couple. It would have been fun to see how that one would have played out. If this battle hadn't happened, I might have gotten a suicide out of you with her betrayal. But, you go and break up with me, and have some profound chat with her that makes her doubt me. Me! You little bitch! But hey," he reached down and snapped her neck "that's in the past."

Jack returned to Rosie's limp but conscious body, and dragged her by one foot out into the center of the room. He didn't do anything to arrange her, just left her limbs in the ungraceful dragged position. Then he was on top of Rosie, ripping her shirt open. "Interesting. The monster puts a soul sucking vortex in the middle of your chest, and there isn't a mark from it. If it doesn't leave marks, maybe I'll put the vortex in your pussy, you always did have a magic little snatch." He ripped open her leather pants with one of Hatters discarded knives, still coated in monster gore, and pulled them roughly off her body. He then looked down at her, mostly naked, with an unhappy sigh. "Sure, I'll still be able to fuck you when I'm done if I put the vortex there, but you might enjoy the attention too much and we can't have that can we?" He jumped on top of her again and leaned uncomfortably close. "'Cause I'd be opening the vortex with my mouth, and I just don't like the taste of your pussy. Your oral hygiene, on the other hand, is pretty good." Jack made eye contact again to make sure she was really listening. "You want to blow me one last time for old time's sake?" He waited for a response, but all Rosie could do was let tears spill down her cheeks. "Ya know, on second thought, just in case you get some motor control back in that jaw of yours, I'd rather not have my dream cock bit off; just in case the injury translates like your little scratches did."

Jack unbuttoned his pants with an expression of evil glee painted on his face. Rosie didn't know where Hatter was, but she was sure he hadn't abandoned her. She was afraid of what Jack would do if no one stopped him, so she mentally screamed for Hatter and had faith that Hatter would come for her like he always had.

Jack exposed himself, and he was hard, turned on by knowing he was fucking with Rosie's head. He lay on top of Rosie and rubbed against her. It wasn't like it was when she had been willing, but was similar to the time he fucked her at knife point to prove his power over her. His penis against her made her want to vomit. "I think I'll have a little taste," and he kissed her unresponsive lips "mmmm, salty from your tears, how gourmet." He spread her legs and rubbed himself against her, she hoped without penetration. With her back broken she couldn't feel what he was doing. She thought the angle would be wrong for entering her, and hoped she was right. She thought how strange it was that she could think so rationally detached and wondered if being detached from sensation made that possible, or was it that the monster had used most of her terror and now it had run out too for Jack.

"And when I'm done tasting your soul, I'll feel your nice tight pussy." He roughly grabbed the back of her head, and kissed her again. The kiss started another small vortex between them, and as Jack started to feed she felt herself slipping away, and felt her psychic wounds all reopen to fill Jacks vortex. Rosie struggled to call for Hatter, but she didn't know if there was enough of her left to call.

℘

38

Hatter finished up making sure the monster's crystalline heart was completely melted in the magma before he climbed out of the cave. He'd managed to slip in without any of this worlds nasty inhabitants noticing, and had made fairly quick work of destroying the heart.

The second he was out of the cave entrance to the volcano, he knew there was something wrong with Rosie. She was fighting to call him, to tell him that something else was going very wrong, and it felt like she was slipping away at the same time. He'd known that psychic sendings didn't work inside mount doom, one of this world's natural laws, but with her monster gone Hatter thought he had left Rosie in a safe place. He didn't stop to rebuke himself for leaving Rosie alone, as weak as she felt, he knew speed was of the essence.

Hatter went to Rosie with a step through worlds and was horrified by what he saw. The human monster Jack was on top of Rosie with his pants dangling open and Rosie with her shirt ripped open and pants across the room. Hatter was sure she was not willing this time. Furious, he created a golf club out of thin air and had struck Jack in the back of the head before he saw that Jack was draining Rosie like her monster had.

Jack was dazed by the blow, and swallowed the last bit of glowing white energy that trailed from Rosie's mouth. Hatter hit Jack two more times with the club in fast succession and he fell off Rosie; out cold.

Hatter rushed to Rosie's side, and found her skin cold to the touch, her eyes open and blankly staring. He felt for a pulse and found none. Hatter cried out in primal agony. This was so much more damage than the amulet back in Rosie's waking world could handle. It was made to keep its wearer from physical damage coming through a dream, but if her life force was completely drained the amulets magic would only make her an unscarred corpse.

He pulled Rosie into his arms, and rocked her like a child crying. But the second his skin touched her bare chest he felt the faintest tickle of something coming from him to her heart, and hope filled him. Did he carry a piece of her soul within him? When Rosie gave Hatter her heart, did a piece of her come with it? Was their love true enough that he could save her? He knew it would be tricky, but he hoped so.

Hatter placed his hand more firmly over her heart, and put his forehead to hers. He could feel a tiny flicker, like a candle who's wick is too short and the flame is sputtering just before going out. How could he stabilize her before she was gone for good? He tried kissing her, but there was no response. "Please Rose, don't go. Please." He begged her with tear filled eyes. "Rosie, please hear me and come back." He kissed her again, and felt her draw a breath so shallow he almost missed it. He felt for her heart beat and found it too, but just as faint as her breath. She wouldn't survive without a big dose of magic, and his energy reserves were dangerously low after the epic battle and a taxing trip to mount Doom, but he shared what little he had to try to stabilize her.

Hatter had given all he could without being pulled from Rosie's side, and it wasn't enough. He held Rosie's limp body, and cried for a few minutes before he heard a faint moan coming from Jack. The last thing Hatter needed was to have to fight Jack while Rosie slipped away. Then it dawned on him, he could take Jacks magic to heal Rosie. It would be a fitting punishment.

Hatter laid Rosie carefully on the floor and sat beside her. He then yanked Jack to his opposite side, striking him again in the head to be sure Jack stayed out. He put his right hand over Rosie's heart to give, and his left over Jacks chest to take. Hatter's left hand hovered over Jack without touching him, and pulled metaphysically. Hatter was loathe to touch Jack any more than necessary. The energy flow was slow without touch, but Hatter knew it would be better to be gentle with Rosie until she was stable and less fragile.

Hatter pulled energy from Jack, and the power felt tainted and slimy crawling up his arm. He used his body and will like a filter to cleanse the energy before he pushed it down his right arm and gave to Rosie. Hatter continued until Jack's reserves were empty, then rested. The cleansing process was hard work, and it had tired him further.

If Hatter stopped there, Jack could gain his magic back and be a danger within days. Hatter refused to put Rosie in jeopardy like that, he had to protect her. But even if he could protect his love without somehow disabling Jack, he would still be a danger to others. Hatter would feel responsible if Jack attacked anyone with magic again. He had to stop Jack, and the only way to do that was to strip him of his magic permanently.

Hatter wished he knew the right way to strip someone of their magic, but his training was in defense and protection not damage. If Hatter tried to take enough energy to cripple Jack, the shock might kill Rosie's evil ex. Hatter had killed one monster today with Rosie's help, but Hatter wasn't sure he wanted to deal with the consequences of killing Jack. The nightmare monster was straight forward, it attacked and fed in nightmares. But the monster Jack had been free in the Prime Material, and had almost limitless potential targets to feed from. What was worse still is that the people Jack attacked didn't know they were being attacked. Jack made his victims feel they deserved the damage and just wanted to Please him. Hatter had witnessed it with Rosie, and had no doubt she wasn't the only one. Just the idea of using people the way Jack did sickened Hatter. But he wondered if he would be just as bad as Jack if he permanently wounded the slime ball.

As Hatter sat debating his next move, he noticed that Rosie wasn't getting better. He had given Rosie enough energy that she should be waking by now. Worried, he checked her vitals, and found her pulse slowing. Hatter took her hands in his and closed his eyes to focus his other senses on Rosie. The damage Hatter could see with his eyes was nothing compared to what he felt now, it was like she was leaking energy from every wound. At this rate, Rosie's energy would be depleted in minutes and it would be fatal unless he did something.

Magic was killing the woman he loved. If she had only been oblivious to the worlds outside her own she would be safe. And then it struck Hatter, if he could bring Rosie back to the Prime Material and cauterize her wounds, for lack of a better description, she would live and be able to heal separated from magic. If he cut Rosie off from magic, Hatter didn't know if she would ever get her talents back. Without magic as a part of her, Rosie's memory of magic and everything associated with it would be gone. He realized that was why Rosie forgot much of her dream travels when she woke in her world, without magic its paradox would make remembering challenging. If it would save her life, even if he never saw her again, it would be worth it to Hatter. Rosie with a chance at a long happy life was all Hatter could hope for. He tried to push the thought of his life without Rosie out of his head, Hatter couldn't afford any doubt if he was going to save the woman he loved.

Hatter used his left fist to punch the center of Jack's chest, holding pressure there while he ripped every ounce of power out of the other man and into himself. He had to admit that Jack did have magical talent, even if he had used it to manipulate innocents, and taking all his power like this felt good. Hatter had no need for the theatrics of a pain causing vortex, if he took the time to make him hurt Hatter feared losing Rosie, so he pulled till there was nothing left but a husk. He didn't care if Jack survived, the scum had hurt Rosie repeatedly and was seconds from raping and murdering her when Hatter stopped him. Hatter privately hoped the slime would survive in a coma, trapped in his own mind alone. It was the worst torture he could imagine, and with the amount of energy Hatter had just taken in ideas of vengeance didn't just sound good, they felt good. Hatter shook off Jack's emotional baggage and centered himself within the power.

Done with Jack, Hatter turned his attentions to Rosie. Gently pressing the open palm of his right hand over her heart, he looked without his eyes to find the edges of the psychic wounds, and fed energy slowly into her while trying to hold the wounds shut by wrapping his will like a thin sheet tight around her. Hatter wished he could heal Rosie, but without her talent active he couldn't mimic her ability to heal. He couldn't knit her wounds, he could only hold them closed. "Please fight, Rose, please survive." Rosie took a deep shuttering breath, and Hatter knew she would make it as long as he finished what he started.

Hatter swept Rosie's limp body into his arms, and cradled her like a child. It took a lot of concentration and energy to hold her wounds shut and carry her into the Prime Material, but failure would mean Rosie's death and that just wasn't an option. Holding her tight to him, and extending what could only be described as a protective skin around them, Hatter stepped onto the Prime Material and into Rosie's bedroom.

ଓଃ

Rosie shivered in Hatter's arms, feeling the pain of being in her world without the protection of her body, even with his shielding. There was something surreal about holding one unconscious Rosie in his arms while looking down at the same woman asleep in her bed. Hatter could see the fine silver thread that connected body to soul, and used it as a guide to slip the one into the other. As the overlapping forms became one Hatter could see the shadows of her wounds, but nothing translated to her physical body. Part of him hoped that this would be enough to get her healing, but they continued to 'bleed' as he held psychic pressure on the wounds.

Hatter saw the amulet, with its blackened spent linen pouch, around Rosie's neck that had kept the damage from hurting her body, and with tears of his own loss he grabbed the necklace and removed it. Fresh scrapes and cuts sprang into existence all over Rosie's body, Hatter had to work fast. He pocketed the amulet, stretching both hands in the air above Rosie's core, and closed his eyes. Taking a deep breath, Hatter shook the tension from his neck and shoulders then shifted his weight between his feet grounding and centering his body. He calmed himself before he opened his extra senses to look very closely at Rosie. He could see all the ties that Rosie had to people and places she cared about, as silver filaments stretching away. Each thread that Hatter touched resonated with a unique vibration, letting him see where that strand went. As he touched the threads it felt to Hatter like he was playing a enormously complicated instrument, with some strands seeming to go together to form chords of memory and experience.

Power flowed into Hatter's thumb and forefinger, making his fingertips glow with a golden radiance. Tears silently slid down his cheeks, betraying his remorse at what he must do. With surgical accuracy Hatter carefully pinched each thread that lead to other worlds or magics. As he pinched, the glow burnt through each delicate strand cauterizing the connection of each severed thread. Each thread he severed snapped away from Rosie, whipping Hatter as it spun away, leavening his arms and hands covered in small bleeding welts. Hatter took the wounds, feeling he deserved worse for what he was taking away from Rosie.

Hatter left the thread between them for last, because cutting it would push Hatter out of the Prime

Material and away from Rosie. With one strand to go, he went to work pealing his energy compression bandage away from her. To his relief, as the magic pulled away, Rosie's physical injuries just vanished. Hatter had never been so sad and so relieved at the same time.

Rosie's breathing relaxed into the slow cadence of sleep, and he didn't know if he could sever Rosie's last link to magic, because it would take them from each other. Hatter took a moment to say goodbye properly, but knew he had to be quick. As long as she was connected, the psychic wounds slowly leaked her life away.

He sat beside Rosie and held her hand in his. He spoke in a whisper, because he didn't trust his voice not to break with the tears he shed. "I waited so long to find someone who was my true match, and you are truly the missing part of my soul. We've only had a short time together, but I guess passions that burn brightest can never burn as long." Hatter had to pause around the lump in his throat. "I hope you can hear me on some level, because I need you to remember how deeply you are and always will be loved." He leaned over Rosie and lay his head on her shoulder, needing to feel her touch one last time. "I don't know if we will ever see each other again-" Hatter felt like he was drowning in feelings of emptiness and loss as he struggled to gain composure. He was almost collected when Rosie wrapped an arm around him consolingly, causing him to lose the last bit of composure he had to heavy sobs.

ભ

Hatter clutched at Rosie, desperately sobbing. She hugged him back, making quiet shushing sounds. "It's ok Hatter, I'm all right. I'm here." She struggled to remember what happened, but everything was so hazy. She remembered that there was a lot of pain and blood, but that was it, and those memories were fading too. She was so spent that Rosie knew whatever happened must have been epic. "Hatter, what happened?"

His shoulders shook with his sobs for a few

more moments, but Hatter got control of himself and looked up into Rosie's eyes. Hatter's eyes were red and his face tear streaked. He looked so earnest and broken hearted that Rosie couldn't resist touching his cheek to wipe away the wetness with a lingering caress. He leaned into the touch, closing his eyes to really soak the moment in before he looked into her eyes again. "I'm so sorry, Rose. It was the only way to save your life. I couldn't bear it if you died. I love you too much to let you die. I ..." He tried to speak but couldn't form the words.

"I love you too Hatter. And I'm not dead, I barely hurt at all." She said consoling him, confused about what she was missing. She took his hands in hers, and brought them to her lips, kissing them. When Hatter flinched she noticed they were covered in bleeding cuts.

Hatter pulled his hands from view looking guilty, and forced himself to speak before Rosie could comment. "But to save you," he whispered hoarsely "I've taken magic from you. To protect you, I severed you from all the worlds outside of this one."

"What do you mean?" A bit of panic gripped Rosie. What was Hatter talking about, what magic? What other worlds? Something inside her head just wasn't adding up. "I don't understand."

"To save you, I had to make it so you can't understand. I took it from you, and you can't even hate me for what I've done because you'll forget. You will forget all the pain, and hurt, and trauma... but you'll also forget us. -"

"What could you have done that I would ever hate you for? And what do you mean I'll forget you? How could I forget the love of my life?" Rosie searched Hatter's face like she could find a clue in his sorrow. She felt panic rising at what Hatter was saying. It all made no sense, but utterly terrified her.

"We don't have much time, Rose, and it's a blessing that we can say goodbye at all."

"What do you mean goodbye? Please Hatter. No, not goodbye." Rosie began to feel faint and her vision swam. "I don't understand why-"

"Please Rosie, if you love me you will listen." Hatter made meaningful eye contact looking a little scared, and Rosie nodded silently. Hatter seemed to take strength from something he saw in Rosie's eyes as he began speaking again. "Please try to remember how loved you are. How much I love you. How much I want you to have a good life. Be strong, and don't let anyone ever make you feel like you are ever second best. Surround yourself with people who believe in you as much as I do. You are unique and brilliant. And I love you Rosie Cotton."

Before she could respond he kissed Rosie like it was the last kiss they would ever share. It started as a simple but hard kiss, that built into a frenzied passion of lips and tongues and bodies locked together. Rosie tasted fresh salty tears as they kissed. Then suddenly Rosie felt a sharp pain, like a tiny burn, coming from her heart; and Hatter was simply gone.

ᘒ

Rosie blinked for a moment, feeling like she had just woken from a dream. Had she been doing something? Why did she feel such loss? And why was she so tired? She looked over at the clock, it was two twenty two in the morning. Rosie thought that repeating numbers like that were pretty lucky, and that it was way too early to get up, and rolled over to go back to sleep. As she drifted off she remembered an amazing kiss, and being held by strong masculine arms. Cuddling against a man that felt so safe and so right and smelled of musk and roses. Must have been one hell of a dream she'd just woke from. Rosie thought that maybe she could finish the dream if she got back to sleep quick enough, but she knew that once a dream ended the chances of having that same dream were really unlikely.

CR39 *Twelve Years Pass, and Rosie wakes from her nap:*

When Rose woke she felt rested and content. For a moment she expected to still be in the arms of her Hatter, but then she remembered he was only a dream and it felt like a bit of a loss. Reality was just not as good as that dream. She remembered the ghostlike touches, but quickly rationalized them away, thinking she must have already been asleep.

The two dreams Rosie had with her sexy Hatter stayed with her more than most, and she read her account of it more than once in private, but time passed and she didn't have any more dreams with sexy Wonderland themes or the man taking the role of the Hatter.

CB

Weeks later Rosie had a nightmare. She found herself on the roof of a impossibly tall skyscraper, wind buffeting at her with near hurricane force and pushing her to the edge of the roof. She looked for a door or safe way down, but could see nothing through her wind whipped hair.

A strong gust pushed her over the side, and she barely got a grip on the edge as she went over. Rosie held onto the ledge with every ounce of her strength, and tried frantically to pull herself up. She glanced down and saw that she was hanging so high up that she couldn't even see the ground, only storm clouds swirling what looked like miles below her feet. The more she struggled to hold on the more her fingers slipped, numb with the cold of the wind. Rosie screamed for help, but all sounds were swallowed up by the wind. The wind flung her around like a rag doll, slamming her against the bricks so hard it knocked the breath from her lungs and made her tentative grip on the building finally slip.

Rosie fell, bouncing off the side of the building again and again, each time searing pain ripped through her with the impacts. She scrabbled to try to get finger holds while she gasped for breath. Soon the wind pushed her away from the building entirely. Rosie felt like her stomach was in her throat as she continued to plummet. The building pulled away until it was swallowed by the angry clouds she fell through. She closed her eyes, and waited for the ground to hit her and smash every bone in her body.

CB

Suddenly Rosie wasn't falling, and she wasn't smashed on the pavement either, she had been caught. She smelled roses and musk, and felt strong arms holding her. Rosie cracked an eye to look, and saw the face of her Hatter. But he wasn't the Hatter in this dream, he was a glowing angel with enormous white feathered wings. His skin was a golden nimbus and he was dressed in a loose toga-esque white and gold robe. From the moment he caught Rosie, the turbulent wind had ceased and they were floating in clear blue sky.

Rosie thought her breath was stolen more by the appearance of her sudden rescuer, than being slammed into the building while falling. He cradled Rosie in his arms and grinned, his face as lit by his smile as the radiant glow. Before she could completely process what had just happened, he kissed her deeply. She was caught off guard by the suddenness of his kiss but then melted into the raw desire of the angels soft wanting lips. They floated downward, his wings beating slowly to gracefully aid their decent, and the passionate kiss became more tender and caressing.

After such a romantic rescue she wanted to gaze upon her familiar angel. Rosie blinked, trying to see him clearly past the strangely familiar luminescent skin. without a word, he responded to her need by fading the glow till his face was only lit by his dimpled smile. Now that she could see the man more clearly she was sure it was her Hatter. She got lost in his deep brown eyes, fringed with those long dark lashes that only movie stars seem to have. There was something about his eyes that felt like home, something safe and familiar that Rosie couldn't quite put her finger on. Something she felt when she dreamt of him before, like she knew him but just couldn't quite reach the memory.

They landed on soft green grass. It looked like an open plateau on the side of a breathtaking mountain range. But despite the view around her, this angel drew her so strongly that she could only look at him. He almost reluctantly set Rosie on her feet, stealing another kiss as he carefully set her down. For a moment they were transfixed, loosely caressing each other's waists, and gazing deeply into each other's souls.

He gracefully settled his long white wings behind him, breaking the spell, and smiled a little impishly at Rosie with a definite twinkle in his eyes. "I remember you saying that you'd rather see me in this role, I guess you still do." His English accent washed over her and completed the puzzle. Between his scent, the feel of his body so close, and his voice, Rosie's memory of Hatter came back to her in a wash so strong she swooned.

Memories flooded her in a stream of image, sound, smell, and touch. It was such a sensory avalanche that for a minute all she could do was process the memories. When she came to she found herself laying on the ground cradled by a very worried looking Hatter. He was speaking but her head was so jumbled that she couldn't make sense of it.

Her head spun with questions. How could she have forgotten so much? How could she have forgotten all the ways Jack had hurt her and lied? or the nightmare monster that injured her bad enough to spill into the waking world? How could she have forgotten she had magic? She could sense other Fey and dream walk, how did she lose that without knowing she had even had it? But most of all, how could she have forgotten Hatter?

Hatter was nearly frantic, checking for any

missed physical wounds, and trying to get through to her. "- Rosie, can you hear me? Are you ok? Please be ok."

Rosie touched his cheek and looked into his eyes to get his attention. Seeing Rosie come back to her senses, a look of relief spread across Hatter's face. Rosie smiled at the man she was once so deeply in love with, and felt those emotions stir back to life. "Hatter." She relished that she could call him by name. "I'm ok. I was missing memories that I didn't know were gone, but I remember now. I heard your voice, and I remembered it all. The memories just stunned me a bit. But I remember you now, and I remember us." She kissed him with a passion built of twelve missing years, years of longing and feeling like she had a missing piece; a piece that now felt filled.

Hatter reveled in Rosie's enthusiasm, kissing her back with passions that matched hers. He had been longing for her touch for so long, it pained him physically to break from the kiss, but he needed to know if she really remembered it all. "You don't know what it means to me that you remember, but if you truly remember it all.." Hatter hesitated, unable to make eye contact with Rosie.

"I do. I remember how you first came to me as insubstantial touch and scent, and I thought I was crazy. I remember how you saved me when I was in danger, and how you," she blushed with the memory "filled other needs too."

"Then you remember how we parted?" Hatter looked back at Rosie, unshed tears glistening in his eyes. "You remember what I took from you? Don't you hate me?"

"How could I possibly hate you?" She said, staring into his very soul through the deep brown of his eyes. She touched his cheek and caught a tear as it escaped.

She leaned in to kiss his soft full lips, and inhale

his scent, but he whispered, "I disconnected you from your magic and stole your memories. I committed such an unthinkable betrayal, why don't you hate me?"

"Hatter, you saved my life. You made the only sacrifice you could to keep me alive. I remember how much it hurt you to say goodbye, I know that Jack would have killed me if you weren't there to rescue me again. My guardian angel." she said reaching up to caress a wing. "Or am I wrong?"

Hatter was so moved that he couldn't speak at first. "You aren't wrong." He whispered, "I've just hated what I did for so long, and missed you so desperately. I thought you would hate me for taking your magic from you."

"How could I hate you for saving my life? For loving me so much that you let me go to let me live? It was tragic then, but we're together now, and there are no monsters keeping us apart anymore."

Hatter's desire for Rosie overwhelmed him, and as he kissed her she responded with such need that Hatter couldn't tell where his emotions stopped and hers began. They kissed, and their bodies were drawn together like powerful magnets. Hatter effortlessly lifted Rosie off her feet, and without hesitation she gleefully wrapped her legs around him. She blushed with the sensation of him pressing against her so intimately.

Rosie came up for air, afraid she would never stop kissing Hatter if she didn't find her thoughts again soon. "When I had no name for you, I called you my sexy guardian angel." Her lips found his again, giving him a few quick but greedy kisses, like she needed to get her fix before she could continue. "You were always there to save me when I needed you, you stood between me and a messy death four times. Even when you weren't putting your life on the line to save me, I could still feel you near, giving me comfort, and making me feel loved when I felt so lost and damaged. Hatter, you saved my life in so many ways," she kissed him again,

"You taught me what it felt like to have love returned unconditionally." When she hugged Hatter, with arms and legs, her bottom brushed against his hardness. His arousal excited her, causing Rosie to blush deeper. Feeling his desire so tangibly gave her the confidence to rock against him and to whisper huskily, "You showed me what pleasure really felt like." Hatter rumbled with lust as Rosie paused to kiss him. "And the big white feathered wings are just as sexy as I always imagined."

"I'm glad you like the wings," they kissed "if you like this," kiss "we could try some other fantasies too," kiss "I like to play with my form." Kiss, kiss. They both moaned as their most sensitive parts rubbed together with a building rhythm. Hatter whispered in a sensual growl "Do you want to play?"

"Oh, God," she moaned "do you know how hot that is?" Kiss, "I wanna play with you like you're my favorite toy." They kissed, long and hard.

Hatter gave his wings a sudden pump, and they were rising into the sky. Rosie let out a short squeak of surprise as they lifted off, but ground harder and groped more feverishly as the rush of wind against her skin enhanced their passion. "You like this play?" He whispered into her ear as he nibbled her lobe lightly.

Instead of the terror she felt falling, she felt a rush of sheer joy, like flight was another part of her soul that she hadn't known was missing. It felt exhilarating to find flight with Hatter, the man who felt like another part of her soul restored. She had a fleeting wish that she could feel the warm air gliding all over her skin, and her clothes were gone.

Rosie yelped in surprise, and froze momentarily with embarrassment. The feelings of joy and freedom she was just letting in started to shut down, being replaced by a lifetimes worth of Rosie being taught she should act proper; and flying naked in the arms of a man she hadn't seen in twelve years just wasn't acceptable behavior. In that moment of doubt and shame Hatter reacted too, growling with appreciative need while running his hands greedily over her freshly exposed flesh. Rosie couldn't resist responding to his attentions. Feeling Hatter's response in more than physical caresses swung the pendulum away from her rational societal training and to Rosie's animal need. She surrendered to the pleasurable sensations of the wind on her skin and Hatter's hands sliding hungrily over her flesh.

His fingers kneaded into her bottom, pulling her so tight against him that Rosie gasped wantonly and Hatter could feel her eager wetness seep through his thin robe. She ran her hands up along his arms, feeling his muscles work as he groped her. Things deep inside Rosie tightened with anticipation and longing. Hatter ran a line of kisses down the side of Rosie's neck, eliciting eager moans. He slid Rosie's body against his, lifting her as he worked his way lower. His lips found their way from her neck lightly across her collarbone to dip lower and lick a trail to the swell of her left breast. His lips lingered over her pounding heart, making Hatter think of thrusting himself into her in time to the suggestive rhythm. Rosie cried out, feeling his desire like a phantom sensation inside her. She arched her back as Hatter's tongue continued its exploration. Their flight took a graceful curve following her movement that sent thrills though both of them.

Thinking of their safety, Hatter cleared his head just enough to push the environment. With a force of will, all solid matter that was not them fell away. Then he adjusted the gravity to make flying light work. He caressed her tender skin with his tongue as his mind busily reworked the world around them. Now he could focus fully on the sensations of touching and being touched by his long denied lover.

Rosie felt power roll off Hatter like a warm velvety cloud flowing through her, and it made her gasp. She saw the land fade away and felt almost weightless as Hatter flew in slow arches, wide spirals, and large loops.

It felt like an exquisite dance of utter trust and abandon.

Rosie's hands slid under Hatter's robe to explore his strong shoulders. Feeling the extra muscles working to control his wings, she wanted to feel the force of all his muscles working against her. She lightly traced her fingertips along his jaw, enjoying the feel of his mouth on her, before she lifted his face up to look at her, "How solid can you make the clouds?" She asked, almost breathless with want.

Hatter grinned at her request, ceasing their gliding to hover still in the air, wings slowly beating to keep them in place. "Anything my lady wants, I will provide." He said winking. Extending his right hand out into the open air he curled his fingers with tension, like he was grabbing something solid, and with flexing muscles he pulled. Moisture in the air coalesced into wispy clouds. He repeated the gesture, and the large cloud became thick. Pulling one more time, the thick cloud was drawn next to them. Rosie bit her lip with anticipation as Hatter swung her over onto the edge of the cloud, and though it was soft and wet, it held her. The clouds water beaded against her skin in cool droplets, feeling sensual combined with the warm breeze. The sensation of sitting on the cloud felt like a big fluffy springy feather bed surrounded by dense mist. Hatter restored gravity, and Rosie squirmed with desire watching Hatter so easily change the world around him.

"You manipulate my dreams like it's nothing." She said pulling him close and kissing him. "Maybe I should call you my sexy god instead of just my angel."

"We haven't been in your nightmare since I caught you and pulled you into a pocket of Wonderland. I've been manipulating this world for years. So, no." He shrugged, "Sorry, not godlike powers. Just an easy world. Remember when you manipulated the canopy of my bed into a mirror? It was easy, right."

"Doesn't make it any less sexy." Rosie said, wrapping a leg around him to pull him tight against her.

"You moved mountains for me, how many women can say their man did that for them?" She kissed him lingeringly, and could feel his desire build with each brush of her lips against his.

"Am I your man then?" he whispered intimately. "I really like the sound of that." He slid his hands over her thighs, thick with the cloud's beaded moisture, and around her hips to play at the small of her back.

"Now that I have my memory back, I seem to remember you pledging yourself to me always," Rosie said coyly. "so, then, you'd be mine." She responded playfully, clasping her hands loosely behind his neck before finishing very seriously. "Because I am very definitely yours."

"I remember. I am yours." He said misting up slightly with joy that he belonged, and was with the only person he knew that could remember that far back. Dreamers usually forgot when they woke, that Rosie really remembered him meant so much.

She curled her body around his, and leaned in to nibble his earlobe before whispering, "I'm thinking there aren't any other women that can say they made love on a cloud their man willed from thin air either." She began to kiss a trail down the side of Hatter's neck, mirroring his earlier path.

With a burst of speed and strength Hatter lifted Rosie and had her on her back in the middle of the cloud bank. He was on top of Rosie, pushing her deep into the soft cloud, and kissing her like her lips were the air he needed to live. As their flesh pressed together Rosie noticed Hatter's robe had disappeared sometime between her kissing his neck, and him diving on top of her. She reveled in the feel of his silky smooth skin. His angel wings created a canopy over them, and with the cotton candy fluff of the cloud beneath them it was like being in a very private and intimate white cocoon.

Without missing a moment of kisses, Hatter groped her soft full breast with eager hands. Rosie moaned with pleasure, enjoying his forceful touch and being kissed with such need. Her leg wrapped around Hatter's waist, and was deliciously tickled by his soft feathers from her thigh to the tips of her toes. Very aware of Hatter's hard member rubbing against her, Rosie slid her fingertips between them and lightly over his manhood. A pleasurable rumble came from Hatter's throat with her delicate touch, that grew into a moan as she played.

They intimately whispered to each other, but soon touches and suggestion weren't enough for Rosie. She guided him and Hatter thrust inside her, unable to restrain his fervor. His wings spread, stretching to their full and impressive span as he arched his body to pound into her with a hard fast rhythm that made her scream with abandon. Hatter felt better to Rosie than he had at the tea party before she remembered, and even better than he had all those years ago. Hatter's raw psychic power had grown, and so had his experience in hitting all the right places to make her squirm with ecstasy. Hatter felt the same about how amazing Rosie felt moving against him and gripping him inside her.

He was close to cumming, but wanted so badly for this wonderful encounter to last. With every bit of restraint he could muster, Hatter pulled out. With a pump of his wings he swiftly drew his body back, lifted her hips, and brought her to his mouth.

She was so much wetter than the dew of the cloud glistening over the rest of her body. She tasted like lust and desire and sex, and it was a flavor Hatter relished tasting. He licked her in hard eager strokes, and the orgasm that had been building inside her tore free with a gush of wetness and sensation. She screamed as her orgasm flowed over her, peaking in wave after wave of pleasure, each wave cresting higher and higher as Hatter continued. Rosie's vision exploded in washes of color to go with the waves of ecstasy. Every muscle in her body contracted with the height of this rolling orgasm until she had no more strength and was left feeling boneless and spent. Hatter paused, enjoying an echo of what Rosie had felt through their strengthening psychic bond. The world settled and stilled into a velvety afterglow, the cloud's soft moisture caressed her skin and it seemed to enhance the scenes soft focus.

Rosie gazed down the length of her body to see Hatter's face still nestled between her thighs, grinning up at her. Hatter's large feathered wings swept to either side and curved forward making him look majestic, while his eyes twinkled with mischief. It struck Rosie that in this tableau Hatter seemed to embody both an angel and a devil. Then almost like he knew what she was thinking, he raised an eyebrow and ducked back between her legs to lick a long hard stroke. She cried out as his tongue glided over her, her raw nerves jolted electricity through her body like orgasmic aftershocks.

"Mercy." Rosie gasped, breathless.

Hatter untangled himself from her and flopped onto the springy cloud next to Rosie, smiling gleefully. He wrapped an arm around Rosie's waist and pulled himself closer to snuggle against her. He laid his head on her chest gently, and lay a soft wing over her like a blanket. "Your heart's pounding, did I tire you out to much?" Hatter said playfully.

Rosie snuggled against Hatter's warm embrace, "I think I'll recover."

"Soon?" Hatter said hopefully, making Rosie laugh. Which oddly refreshed some of Rosie's spent energy. "Because if you fall asleep now, and disappear from my world, I will be left very disappointed that I didn't get to..." He paused to search for the right word, "finish."

"Well, I wouldn't want you to not," Rosie gave the word the same pause Hatter had, "finish. Especially when I just got to" pause "finish, so spectacularly." Rosie said, smiling contentedly and stretching languidly as she settled her arms behind her head.

Hatter lifted his head to look up at Rosie, eyes twinkling with joy. "spectacularly you say?"

"So spectacularly." Rosie confirmed, and leaned forward to kiss Hatter tenderly. He tasted like sex, and that revved her up just a little bit more, helping to restore her energy.

"I am just thrilled that you like my work, I really did put my best effort into it." Hatter continued the playful banter, propping himself up on one arm.

Rosie bit her lip, watching a drop of the clouds condensing water slide across Hatter's bare chest. "I hope that doesn't mean you've used up your best effort, and now all that's left will be kinda half-assed." She teased.

Hatter laughed and responded in a mock serious tone. "Well, you do have a lovely ass, but," He continued with a more seductive note. "it's not your ass I want to do..." He lifted his wing, and looked over Rosie's naked body lewdly. "Yes, I still have a lot of effort in me." He rocked against Rosie's side and she could feel his hardness. "I think I have enough effort to give you at least two more," he paused for effect, leaning in tantalizingly close, and almost kissed her with the word "finishes."

Rosie kissed Hatter deeply. "I think, you will definitely be finishing soon."

"Not too soon I hope, I like to enjoy the journey before I finish." He said trailing his fingertips along the curve of her side.

Rosie propped herself up into a lounging position, mirroring him, and looked Hatter's body over just as lewdly as he just had. "I like," she paused for emphasis, "long," she licked her lips "journeys."

Hatter's grin broadened, as he made a mock shock expression "Why, Rosie Cotton, are you making a pass at me?" Rosie nodded biting her lip not to laugh. "That is fantastic!" Hatter said bouncing up excitedly, his wings almost pulling him aloft, before he settled standing ankle deep in cloud.

Hatter smiled knowingly, and reached up into the air with a little flourish. He pantomimed pinching something between two fingers and pulling it back just a little bit. "Round two." He said releasing his fingers to the sound of a loud brass bell ding. It brought to mind one of those bells you'd see in an old time boxing ring. Rosie laughed, delighted at his theatrics. She loved it when Hatter manipulated reality, and found it was especially true when it was something fun like this.

Before the echo of the bell had quieted, Rosie's attention was already being drawn to the form of her Hatter standing naked before her. The white feathered wings were bold but soft window dressing to his delicious body. Hatter was a prime example of masculinity, with broad strong shoulders and a well defined muscular chest tapering to slim hips and strong legs. She knew his skin was silky smooth to the touch, and with water beading all over him, it made Rosie want to lick every dewy inch.

Rosie stalked towards Hatter on her hands and knees. "Mmm," she rumbled "you look good enough to eat." She licked along the front of his thigh in a long stroke, drinking the sweet clean water droplets. Her tongues path ended at the front of his hip, tantalizingly close to his phallus. She heard Hatter's breath quicken on her slow exploration. His response thrilled her, encouraging her to lightly flick the tip of his manhood with her tongue playfully before she licked a matching line up his other thigh. By the time she was to his hip Hatter was trembling expectantly, lightly touching Rosie's head to steady himself.

Hatter dropped to his knees, grabbing Rosie's face in both hands before kissing her hungrily. Rosie reluctantly pulled back, sitting in front of Hatter she gave him a quizzical look. "You give very well, but it seems like you have an aversion to receiving that you didn't used to have."

Hatter's eyes widened, "receiving? I enjoy receiving very much."

"So, why, when I am about to..." Rosie paused not sure how to word it without sounding trampy, and then suddenly felt kinda trampy for always jumping into bed with Hatter. Rosie averted her gaze, taking critical stock of her situation. Hatter and her had started as something innately physical, and every time she saw Hatter, she just wanted to strip him down and play with his amazing body. He was like a drug, and she just wanted to lick him. She wasn't a love sick teenager any more, she was a love sick adult. And adults didn't jump into bed like this. She hadn't seen Hatter for twelve years, twelve years that she didn't even remember him. Rosie knew she had changed in the last twelve years, Hatter must have too. Aside from their overwhelming physical attraction and a history of Hatter being her knight in shining armor, she didn't know anything about him. But she still offered herself to him naked on a cloud. She suddenly felt very exposed, and very trampy. What if she was just an easy lay? She crossed her arms to cover her breasts, and willed bits of the cloud to fluff into a covering fog that obscured her lower half. Shouldn't she be getting to know him before offering to bed him? When she was a teenager she'd had sex with him as soon as she knew he was real, and after twelve years apart had sex with him again before she even remembered who he was. As soon as she remembered him it was sex again, but they'd never even met in the flesh, only dreams and astrally.

Hatter felt Rosie's sudden shift. "Wait, what did I say. I don't understand what could have happened in your head just now, I thought everything was going so wonderfully. I'm sorry Rose, please don't pull away from me." He reached out a hand to Rosie. "Please tell me what I did wrong, and I will never do that thing again." Hatter sounded close to panic, and it snapped Rosie out of her critical introspection, but she still couldn't make eye contact with Hatter.

"I was just thinking, this isn't the way a responsible adult acts. I haven't seen you in twelve years, and I throw myself at you like I'm still a hormonally ravaged teenager. This just isn't how I act. I'm cautious and think things through, I plan and follow social guidelines like 'you don't strip off your clothes and try to molest anyone until at least the third date.'" The fog rose higher and tightened around Rosie, covering her nakedness entirely with soft whiteness.

"Rose. Please." He touched Rosie's chin and turned her face so she would have to look at him. Tears streamed down his cheeks. "Please don't pull away from me."

Rosie was surprised to see tears in Hatter's eyes, she was so busy self demeaning that she'd hurt the man that she knew completed her. "I am so sorry." She said taking his hand from her chin and kissing his palm before placing it over her heart and holding it there with both of her hands. "I was thinking about myself, I didn't mean to hurt you. I jumped into a physical thing with you before I even knew your name, I don't do that. It's so out of character for me. I feel like a slut. When you dodged what I was about to," she hesitated, "when I was going to," She started to get hung up on wording again but managed "pleasure you." Rosie took a deep breath before continuing. "It made me realize I was acting so trampy, offering to," Rosie made a frustrated gesture with her hands unable to say the act in her current prim state of mind. "And then how bad must I be that you would avoid?- "

"No." Hatter stopped her before she could say more. "I wasn't trying to dodge you Rosie. I would never describe you as anything but the woman I would do anything to be with. I wasn't turning down your advances, you being so forward is sexy as hell. You just turn me on so much that I need to touch you," Hatter caressed her skin, feeling the pounding of her heart. "and to kiss you," he leaned in and stole a chaste kiss from his love. "Because I have been starving for your touch for twelve years. I love you Rosie, and I have loved you since the first day I saw you. So distraught and vulnerable and alone, like me." Rosie opened her mouth to speak but Hatter gave her a pleading look that quieted her. "I loved you, but couldn't see or smell or touch you. I couldn't even know if you were having a good life. I thought after twelve years I would never see you again, never be able to touch you. Never find anyone who felt so right, and so balanced me. With you anything is possible; alone, I've just been so lonely. Then you came back to me, and touched me, and gave me hope I could be with you again. I crave you when you aren't with me, and I crave you even more when you are. I just can't believe you're here with me again. I was in purgatory without you, if I can't keep my hands off you long enough for you to," he smiled "pleasure me, it's not because I don't want you to, or because I think anything less of you for wanting to touch me too, it's because I need to kiss you, often and thoroughly, and know you are truly here with me. Because I love you so much that if I don't kiss you, I feel my heart will explode."

Rosie tackled Hatter like a lovesick teenager. She flung her arms around him, kissing him like it was the most important thing in the world. They kissed each other for long sensual minutes, but without any clothes on soon their embraces became full contact explorations again. Rosie felt Hatter's hardness pressed against her, so smooth and rigid. So inviting that this time she didn't start with any teasing foreplay. Rosie grabbed Hatter and bent down to lick him like a lollipop.

The clouds moisture and their play had left Hatter tasting of clean water. Rosie enjoyed exploring the texture of him and the taste of his skin. Hatter moaned as Rosie took his shaft into her mouth. Rosie's worries were pushed out of her mind by the pleasure of feeling Hatter's reactions to her attentions. Hatter thrust into her mouth, reveling in the sensations, grunting and moaning with pleasure. The more he enjoyed himself the more Rosie's enthusiasm grew, creating an ever building psychic feedback loop. He especially loved the way her tongue stroked him almost independently of her bobbing head. Wave after wave of pleasure rolled over him until he was at the brink of coming.

"Oh gods, Rosie. I'm going to cum! Ungh!" With his exclamation her energy heightened and speed increased. "I want to be inside you, but you're so amazing I won't- Oh gods!" Hatter howled a deep primal scream of ecstatic release as he came. Semen hit the back of Rosie's throat in a powerful gush of salty hot liquid. He was so deep that the only option was to swallow it down, but as she swallowed she sucked lightly and was rewarded with a deeper release as Hatter screamed his joy to the universe and spilled a second wash of cum down her throat before collapsing into the clouds' soft fluff bonelessly. Rosie gave him a couple more teasing licks, making Hatter twitch involuntarily as he panted for breath.

Rosie crawled next to Hatter, and snuggled into the crook of his arm. She had felt his psychic overflow while his pleasure built, sending exciting thrills through her body, and as he came it washed over her too like an exquisite echo. Now he was spent, and she found herself as happily tired as she was when she came. There was something about sharing a bit of Hatter's orgasmic energy that felt intimate and right and good. She wrapped her arms around him, as she rested her head on his shoulder and twined a leg over and around his. She thought of his words just before she tackled him, and smiled happily. "I love you too." She whispered intimately, and a deep contented peace washed over them both as Hatter lightly hugged her to him. They lay together in a wash of calm peaceful love for a long time, happy just to be together.

Hatter nodded off briefly, and awoke with a

start, afraid that Rosie would be gone again. But she still lay in his arms, coiled against his body sleeping soundly. Secure that she was there with him, he drifted back off to sleep, wrapping his wings over them like a blanket.

As he lost consciousness Hatter felt Rosie's warm body snuggle against him. She murmured in a sleepy voice almost too quiet to hear, "round three after a nap." And he drifted off smiling.

ᥴᏅ

40

Hatter woke feeling content and whole. He lay there, eyes closed, and reveled in the awareness of his lover. He enjoyed the weight of Rosie draped across him and breathed in her scent; it felt like home. As her silky soft skin pressed against him, it made Hatter's skin tinge. It felt to him like wherever they touched, his skin was so happy it was dancing on the cellular level.

Hatter loved that she still had the same rich smell of jasmine and honeysuckle. After twelve years he had almost forgotten the scent of her, but now he breathed her in and knew it, felt it, this was the mouth watering scent of his Rose. Hatter felt himself harden with the awareness of her. Beyond Rosie he felt warm, dry, and covered. Hatter no longer felt the extra muscles it took to move his wings or their bulk, so he assumed the wings faded as they slept.

Hatter opened his eyes, took in his new surroundings, and wondered if it was his or Rosie's subconscious that had created them. They were nestled in a large four-poster bed, dark wood and carved much like his, but there was no canopy above except leafy green tree boughs arching overhead. The curtains were white and sheer, but hid detail, so all he could see was the silhouettes of a lush Forrest surrounding them. It struck him that with the opacity of the curtains, from outside, watching two people make love would look like silhouettes being drawn by a sensual artist.

Hatter looked closer to him and enjoyed the

coppery shine of the light playing on Rosie's hair. It had darkened to a richer auburn, but the fire of her teenaged color still sparkled in the light. Hatter thought that the richer color suited Rosie more now. He could see her alabaster shoulders, and arms, but the rest of her was covered with a blanket.

They were covered by a thick comforter, it was jewel toned red woven brocade with tone on tone roses that had little dragonflies and butterflies flittering between them. The sheets were white and crisp and clean, and the bed and pillows were as soft as the clouds had been. A warm summer breeze blew across them, caressing their exposed skin, and making the bed's curtains dance elegantly.

Rosie stirred with the breeze, making the tiniest of sounds as she snuggled closer. Her movement sped his pulse and sent delicious waves of pleasure down his spine. His manhood brushed against her hip, and Rosie woke with a pleasant rumble, "Mmmm." She stretched languidly, and her skin slid against his. They both reacted with eager hands gliding over flesh.

Rosie turned her head to look at Hatter with her penetrating sensuous green eyes. "Morning," she purred, happily writhing under his touch. "I'm so glad that we're still together. I thought I'd wake up in my bed alone, and have to go back to sleep to be..." she blushed and bit her lip before sliding an eager hand over his engorged member, "with you again."

Hatter moved into her touch, pulling her body against his with one arm. He slid his other hand along her supple shoulder to cup the back of her head and lean in to kiss Rosie deeply before responding verbally. "I was just thinking that it's really brilliant that you're still with me too. It's..." he made a deep rumbling sound of appreciation as the movement of Rosie's hand stroking him also made her bosom brush rhythmically against his chest, "amazing that you're as eager as I am," he took a steadying breath, enjoying her touch, "to make up for lost time."

Rosie sat up and the blankets slid off of them, exposing both their naked bodies. Rosie licked her lips looking slowly over his broad and well developed chest, along his sleek abdomen, and lower. "We have so much lost time to make up for."

While Rosie was memorizing Hatter's physique, he was drinking in her appearance too. Her body had filled out in all the right places. She was beautiful before, but now she was radiantly beautiful. Her skin was like porcelain. She had more curve to her hips, and her breasts had gotten fuller and more inviting. She had a wonderful soft hourglass shape, and he wanted to run his hands over every wonderful curve. She leaned towards him, licking her lips again, and it was more than he could take.

He pounced, flipping her onto her back and covering her with his body. She yelped in surprise as her back hit the bed, but had no desire to protest further because he was kissing her deeply. Hatter pulled back enough to speak in a low needful growl as they rubbed together. "This is not, and never will be, me avoiding your advances. You are more talented with your mouth and tongue than anything I have ever experienced, witnessed, or even imagined. And I can't wait for you to taste me, but I also can't imagine another minute passing without touching and tasting you." Rosie grinned, arching an eyebrow suggestively as she bit her lip. It let Hatter know that she had gotten past her insecurities of the night before.

He tasted her neck with slow sensual strokes before intimately whispering, "I want you. Let me dominate you till you cum so hard you can't see straight." Hatter rubbed against her like a sleek predator, "Let me pleasure you. Lay back and enjoy every touch. Let me take the reins. Then, after I have sated you so completely that you couldn't imagine coming harder, I'll be yours to command."

Rosie squirmed with anticipation, feeling his words like touches. "I'm yours to play with." She said breathlessly. She bit her lip, barely restraining her desire to roll on top of him and ride him like a bronco, she could wait her turn. She lay back, relaxing into the soft bed, and looked at Hatter with smoldering desire.

Hatter's own anticipation rumbled from him in bass notes of desire and lust looking at Rosie waiting so invitingly. He kissed her soft red lips lingeringly as he trailed fingertips from her waist between her thighs. Her breath caught as a fingertip tickled her most sensitive spot before sliding inside her.

She reached for him, but he grabbed her wrist firmly, "ah ah ah," he playfully chided her, "no cheating. I want to be able to focus on what I'm doing to you. Immerse yourself in sensation and pleasure." He moved her arm above her head and pinned it there, to Rosie's obvious delight. "Wait for your turn, please, and I promise to deny you nothing in my power to give." He drew her other arm over her head, pinning both wrists firmly with one large masculine hand.

She pouted coyly, "Sorry, I couldn't help myself. You just felt so good that I had to touch you." Her pout slid into a grin as he continued to touch her. "You can't blame me that you're irresistible." She panted with need.

"Then I suppose we will have to take measures to make sure you don't cheat." He whispered, nibbling on her ear lobe and licking her neck. Reaching towards the bed frame, Hatter tugged at reality. Then he picked up one of the long deep crimson silk scarves that now trailed from each bedpost. He bound Rosie's wrist just tight enough to hold her in place, and kissed her again before binding her other wrist. "I could feel how much you enjoyed a little light bondage when you were playing my March Hare." Rosie nodded enthusiastically, as Hatter kissed his way down her body, pausing at her full breasts to fondle and lick before continuing.

He stopped, playfully winking before bouncing

to the foot of the bed, and Rosie reacted with surprised giggles. Hatter knelt and secured Rosie's ankles much like he had her wrists, then enjoyed the view for a lingering moment. He thought how exquisite it was viewing her naked, bound, aroused, and trusting him to do anything he wanted. Hatter felt like a kid in a candy store, almost too excited to know where to start.

His gaze slid over her exposed flesh, enjoying every curve, and as he came to her face he saw that she was looking at him with a similar joyous lust. Rosie made eye contact, then slowly licked her lips as her eyes wandered down the length of his body. When Hatter chuckled at her display, she spoke in seductive tones, "You have me body and soul, one hundred percent at your mercy. But until you bring my attention elsewhere, I'm going to be thinking about how much I like the way your pleasure tastes, and what I can do to get that taste in my mouth."

"Then I'll have to bring your attention elsewhere, won't I?" Hatter almost growled as he settled between her legs. Then, sliding his hands under her bottom, he kissed each creamy thigh tantalizingly close to her pleasure center. She could feel his breath tickle her, but he didn't touch her where she wanted him to; not yet. He adjusted his grip to her hips, kneading into her with a pressure that made Rosie moan.

Hatter took one long slow lick, making Rosie cry out, finishing with a quick wiggle of the tip of his tongue. As she reacted to his dexterous tongue, he stopped, eliciting a frustrated whimper from Rosie. But soon he was sliding his flesh against hers, kissing a slow meandering path up her body. He rubbed himself against her leg while nuzzling the tender flesh of her breasts. She gasped and moaned as he suckled her, then added the sensation of sliding one of his hands teasingly between her legs. Rosie writhed as his nimble fingers pleasured her.

He alternated between hard sucks and licks as

his fingers stroked inside her, being sure with every thrust his thumb grazed her clit. He curled his fingers to hit just the right spot inside her, knowing she would cum quickly. Rosie's cries grew louder, and Hatter could feel her building to orgasm, but just as he was sure she was near the tipping point he sprung back at almost preternatural speed and buried his face between Rosie's thighs.

The light breeze caressed her moist breasts, building on the layers of pleasure Hatter's tongue was bringing her lower. Rosie screamed as she came, her body rolling through waves of ecstasy. He continued to lick and sucked hard and with excitement, loving the taste of her orgasm on his tongue as much as the feel of her pleasure echoed in his mind. He didn't stop until Rosie's orgasm started to fade, but then moved inhumanly fast, pulling his body into position.

Hatter thrust his hard length into Rosie, feeling how wet and tight she was post-orgasm, and had to struggle to control himself as he felt her grip him deep inside her. His beast within howled with joyous lust.

Rosie cried out with Hatter's unexpected penetration, his hard shaft stimulating freshly sensitive nerves. Following his first thrust she felt his primal howl tear silently from deep within, and he started to fuck her with a ferocious energy and speed. His animalistic enthusiasm flat out did it for Rosie, and soon a second orgasm rocked through her. Tight contractions hugged his manhood and psychic waves of pleasure rolled over him, the sensation nearly took Hatter too but he had other plans.

When he felt Rosie's second orgasm ebb he reluctantly pulled out. His beast within screamed to ride her till climax, but Hatter's conscious mind had better control and knew if he wanted this to last he needed to pace himself. He looked down at Rosie, breasts rising and falling in panting exhalations as she recovered. He thought how beautiful she was disheveled and radiant with afterglow.

Hatter stood, holding onto one of the bedposts at the foot of the bed, as Rosie gazed up at him with contented love. "Do you trust me?" He asked looking her over lustily.

"With every fiber of my being." She said, and Hatter could feel her complete trust.

Hatter smiled and theatrically made a flipping gesture with his right hand. The four ribbony scarves animated, flowing off their bedposts like they were caught in a current. Rosie watched with eager curiosity, and waited to follow Hatter's lead. The top two twined across to twist and bind Rosie's wrists together above her head. The bottom two scarves slid along each of Rosie's legs, winding up to wrap each leg like a silky corkscrew. Rosie clearly enjoyed the silk scarves caressing her skin as Hatter guided their paths with subtle finger gestures. Kneeling next to Rosie, he brought her bound arms down, hands nestled between her breasts. Rosie gave Hatter a quizzical look, but he just smiled impishly. He caressed her face lovingly and kissed her tenderly before running a hand slowly and seductively down the side of her body. Hatter reached to her far leg and slid a firm hand from ankle to knee, enjoying the feel of her flesh and the soft silk of the scarves. He grabbed the sheer ribbon as a handle, and pulled her onto her side. Rosie realized that it was more comfortable with her arms down where she could brace against the bed than they would have been above her head, and smiled at Hatter's forethought.

Hatter straddled her free leg and pulled her other leg against his stomach and side. Rosie quickly forgot about her arms, watching Hatter grab himself with intent and guide his shaft inside her with sure strokes. Rosie reacted enthusiastically as he gripped her knee to his chest, and pounded her deeply. They both screamed their pleasure out into the forest as they hit another fast hard rhythm. Hatter liked the angle, and the new places he hit inside Rosie. He also liked the way her bottom leg caressed his balls with each stroke. He felt orgasm coming, but he wasn't ready yet, he still had more plans for their romp.

As she deliciously brushed against him, he decided to turn his focus to doing the same for her. Hatter slid his thumb over Rosie's clit, rolling it with small circular motions in rhythm to his penetrations. She cried out, redoubling her enthusiasm as she crashed into him. Rosie came for the third time, even harder than the first two. Hatter managed to hold off, but only just barely. He had to pull out as her muscles tightened in orgasmic bliss.

Hatter again brought his face down to her cleft, licking greedily as she came. He loved feeling her writhe against his face. Her cries to the heavens increased, as Hatter lapped against her soft pliable skin.

Feeling her psychic echo was almost like coming without ejaculation. Hatter knew he was on the finest edge of coming himself, and didn't want to come without Rosie wrapped around him. Hatter smoothly flipped Rosie onto her belly, putting her weight on her bound forearms, and the silk scarves rubbed between Rosie's breasts deliciously. Hatter kneeled behind her and lifted her against him like an x-rated wheel barrow game. He plunged back into her wetness, almost coming as Rosie collided wantonly back against Hatter. Rosie continued to cum even harder as Hatter hit a place so deep inside her that it felt like it pierced through the core of her. Hatter came with such force that she felt hot liquid pumping into her like a high pressure jet. They came together, and it spread from a physical orgasm to meld with their metaphysical energies. They came in light and color and sound and sensation, like the finally of a fireworks show that felt as good as it looked.

Hatter and Rosie collapsed in a heap of happy, completely satisfied, boneless exhaustion. Both enjoyed their cosmically connected afterglow, psychically wide open to each other and all the worlds that stretched out from this one. They both felt a profound sense of contentment and joy as they got comfy, spooning together.

ॐ

41

"Wow," Rosie exhaled. "You definitely won." She looked at her bound hands, wiggling her fingers just slightly, and the scarves unwound themselves. Looking at her own fingers, she thought of the way Hatter had moved his thumb in the midst of their play. Smiling to herself she commented, "And I now have no doubts you could pat your head and rub your belly at the same time. I'll have to remember how well you can multitask."

Hatter wrapped his strong arms around Rosie and felt like he held the most precious jewel in the universe. "I love you Rosie Cotton."

Rosie took a deep and satisfied breath, snuggling against her Hatter and really enjoying the safety of his strong warm arms. "I love you too, Hatter." She paused in thought, "Is Hatter your first name, or your last name? Or is it a nickname, because you live in Wonderland?" Rosie had thought she was making light get to know you conversation, but instead he didn't answer for a long time and she felt Hatter's muscles tense as he started to pull away.

She looked behind her, and saw Hatter in deep thought. She was relieved he didn't look angry, but this look of total introspection was almost as disconcerting. His face cleared as he realized she had turned to look at him, and as he met Rosie's eyes his face flooded with love. He shrugged, "I don't know, I've been Hatter as long as I can remember. It might have been a nickname, but that memory is so vague and was so long before I met you. I'm sorry, Hatter is the only name I have to offer."

"I'm sorry, I didn't know I was bringing up such a serious topic. We were having such a nice morning, I don't want it to end yet." Rosie wiggled against Hatter, thinking that they could cuddle for a while, but could feel him growing hard with the smallest rubbing against her flesh. "Really?" Rosie felt surprised and aroused that he could be so attracted to her that he could be able again so soon after coming. "You haven't even had a chance to get soft, and your getting hard again." She rubbed rhythmically against Hatter, "would you be up for my turn then?"

His voice was low and husky with desire. "Oh, I'm up for it." Hatter kissed the back of Rosie's neck, and his hands slid over her breasts, grabbing them with urgency.

"Either you are like eighteen in the waking world, or you've taken magical Viagra. 'Cause I don't think this level of amour could possibly be normal." Rosie turned her body to face Hatter, propping herself up on one arm.

Hatter's hand settled at the curve of her waist as he thought over his response. He smiled puckishly, absently trailing his fingertips in little circles and figure eights. "You surely know I'm well past eighteen, or I would have been six when I first met you. And I have some ideas what magical Viagra might be from a few disturbing dreams I've walked through, but I need no pills. All I'm sure of is that my amour for you is epic, why wouldn't my desire match?" Hatter looked deeply into her soft green eyes. "My body and soul have longed for you for twelve long years. No pleasure I could find could compare to the feel of your naked body against mine. I can't promise to be this persistent every time we make love, but I am currently still reveling in being with you again," he kissed Rosie rubbing sensually against her, "and again."

Rosie pushed Hatter onto his back, straddling him, and kissed him deeply. "God, I love the way you talk." She again sounded eager and full of energy. He smiled at her dominance as she rubbed against him.

"That accent of yours, and the words you use. You say all the right things." Hatter opened his mouth to respond, but Rosie put a finger over his lips to silence him. "But it's so much more than words, everything about you turns me on. You kiss," Rosie kissed Hatter before continuing, "amazing. And your body," she added a slow exaggerated hip roll into her rhythm against him, "Mmmmm, I could just lick every inch of you. And those deep brown bedroom eyes," she bit her lip, "and your soft eager lips," she kissed him again, "can't have the kissing without those lips," another kiss, "but you keep going, beyond all that," she kissed across his broad shoulders, taking a playful light bite at his neck.

"Oh, my Rose-" Hatter began eagerly, but again Rosie silenced him with a finger. She covered his chest with kisses and licks.

"I'm transfixed by your handsome face." Rosie kissed his chin, cheeks, eyebrows, and nose before again kissing his yearning and responsive lips. She sat up, gesturing at their surroundings. "Then you play with the fabric of reality around us, setting such hot scenes for us to play in. You use magic to manipulate things, even your form." Rosie rubbed against Hatter as her voice rumbled with desire. "Those angel wings were so hot, I can't wait to see your next fantasy. You're just so damn sexy." She sighed, "And that you want me as badly as I want you," she grabbed his erect member, stroking him, "god, I just want to fuck you till you can't see straight. And we have this connection I didn't even know was possible, I feel this shadow of what you're feeling, and it's just beyond words. I can feel how much you enjoy me Touching you, and rubbing against you." Rosie took more liberties with Hatter, kissing him and writhing against his bare flesh. "You seem to be everything that I want. Ya know, for a long time I thought you were just too good to be true, I couldn't believe you were really real." She played her fingers through his hair, before kissing him tenderly. "Oh Hatter," she sighed, rubbing against him with animated hips, "at this moment, I love you so deeply and want you so much it's almost painful."

Hatter's eyes misted with joy over Rosie's proclamations. "I'm thrilled you know I'm real now. I suspected you were struggling with Jack's mind control, but I didn't know he'd messed you up so bad that you couldn't tell I was real. Never doubt that I'm real, and want you more with every passing second. You know that I am yours." Hatter said sincerely, "Forever." Tangling his fingers in her hair, he pulled her in for a deep exploring kiss. He was moved, but also really turned on. "You can have me whenever you want me." And he pulled her into more groping and kissing. They pressed against each other needfully, their earlier exhaustion long swallowed by desire.

"Hey," Rosie said in mock shock, pulling away from Hatter. "No cheating." She playfully chided him. "It's my turn now. And you offered that I could do whatever I wanted to you." She pointed playfully at his chest, trailing her fingertip over the swell of his smooth pecks.

"Yes, mistress." He rumbled, keeping intense eye contact.

She blushed for a second before forcing herself to relax and enjoy the moment. Rosie purred, "I kinda like that. Mistress. We'll have to remember that one." She kissed Hatter quickly, and leaned in to whisper in his ear. "I can feel how much you like it when I suck your cock, I think I'll start my turn there." She kissed her way down his body, settling between his legs before kissing his member playfully. He moaned, as she ran her tongue over his member and took him in deeply. This time he did taste of her, and Rosie cleaned him off with long full strokes, until all she tasted was his skin. He writhed with her touch, thrusting his cock deep into the back of her mouth. Hatter gripped the sheets to either side of himself to keep from grabbing Rosie and fucking her again. She felt so good wrapped around him that it was hard to be passive under her touch.

She played with him, lightly massaging the sensitive orbs inside his pouch as she worked his shaft in and out of her mouth. She played with the tip of his hard cock, loving to swirl her tongue over and around the most sensitive part of his manhood. His lustful enjoyment poured from him, and feeling the raw emotion made Rosie enjoy her play even more.

When she tasted a bit of salty cum at the tip of him, and he thrust deep into her mouth crying out, she knew he was about to release a lot more than a few drops. She stopped, looking at his unfocused eyes. "I wanted to ride you like a bucking bronco, but it seems this foreplay has gotten you too close."

Hatter laughed, responding breathlessly, "Your idea of foreplay is better than most people's getting to..." he paused for emphasis, smiling "finish."

Rosie flicked the tip of Hatter's cock with her tongue, causing it to bob a little as it stood at attention, and Hatter moaned reaching for Rosie. "Ah ah ah, It's my turn to enjoy you." Rosie playfully smacked his hand and cleared her throat to get his attention. "No cheating. I want you to do only what I tell you to do."

"Yes Mistress." he said with raw lust as he put his hands up in surrender. He stretched, crossing his arms behind his head as he relaxed, waiting to see what Rosie wanted. His penis stood at attention, and Rosie couldn't help but take a few more delicious strokes.

"If I ride your cock right now, will you cum sooner than you'd like?"

"If you rode me right now, I would probably be coming in seconds." Hatter confirmed with a husky growl, "But if you let me lick you a little first, I could recover enough to fuck you for a nice long time."

"Do you really enjoy pleasuring me," she paused to get the word to come out of her mouth, "orally, that much?" Rosie blushed, not accustomed to such open talk during sex.

"More, because I can feel how much you enjoy it too." he said licking his lips. "If you want me to stay passive, you can sit on my face." Hatter projected a little psychic preview, he imagined licking and exploring her opening with his tongue.

Rosie moaned, and arced her back just subtly. The motion was enough to draw Hatter's attention to her pert nipples, and he mentally caressed her creamy, smooth, tender, breasts. Rosie had to grab the sheets to stay steady. She looked into Hatter's eyes with an unfocused blissful expression before she fought to get back some control. "That is definitely cheating."

"It's not my fault you're so irresistible." he said teasingly. Rosie gave a full body blush, having trouble playing the dominant under Hatter's intense attentions. "You're still holding back. Why?"

"It's hard to overcome twenty-eight years of being told to be a good girl." She said averting her eyes.

"There's no doubt about how good you are, you are brilliantly good." Hatter projected his lust towards her, but resisted touching her, it was her turn. "But you're a good woman now, not a girl."

Rosie's eyes dilated with arousal as their gaze locked. "You really want me to let go? And take what I want?"

"Yes please." his voice rumbled from a deep primal place within him. Rosie saw his arm muscles straining, like he was fighting against himself to grab her, and the way they flexed made her desire for him burn.

His member still stood hard and ready, and it made Rosie's mouth water. She sucked him energetically, soaking in the sensation and desire that rolled from Hatter. She felt him coming near to orgasm and paused to take a long appraising look over his entire deliciously masculine body. She slid her hands across his smooth and well muscled chest, kneading into the muscles with groping fingers and the slight prick of her fingernails.

Hatter gasped as her nails pressed into him, and she watched as she saw the tension in his arms strain against his will to touch her. He bit his lip and she felt psychic caresses across her breasts and between her legs.

"No cheating." she gasped, but wanted more than the ghostly touch he was offering her.

He smiled in mock innocence, but his eyes were full of desire. Rosie resisted her life's programming and straddled him in a sixty nine. Before she could get her mouth wrapped around him he was grabbing her by the hips to pull her against his face. He tasted her in hard quick strokes that tore moans from her. She enjoyed his enthusiasm as she felt that delicious pleasure build within her. He slipped his tongue inside her, and she cried out as he flipped his tongue back and forth with a dexterity she didn't know tongues could have. As she rode his face, he licked her clit and penetrated her with his tongue in several passes back and forth. She was almost about to cum when she caught sight of him, hard and ready, and remembered her intent to blow him while he ate her.

She dove on him hungrily, filling her mouth with him as he thrust his tongue inside her. Hatter let out a rumbling moan in mid lick, and she felt it vibrate through her. It felt so good that she couldn't help but react, taking him deep and fast. The feeling of Hatter's talented tongue combined with his hard cock filling her mouth was almost more than she could take without the echo of his pleasure, but with their psychic bond it was Rosie's new favorite position. They fed into each other's pleasures like a steadily increasing feedback until they were both at the edge of orgasmic bliss.

Rosie continued to plunge Hatter's shaft into her mouth, loving the feel of his hard but yielding flesh, when she felt him struggling for restraint. She realized that he was fighting not to cum, and that pushed her over the edge into orgasm for the fourth time since waking in Hatters arms. Hatter continued to hold her against his face, pushing his nose inside her as he lapped at her clit. She let out a muffled screamed, with his cock still filling her mouth. She came so hard that she couldn't keep moving over him, but he thrust into her mouth heightening all the sensations ripping through her body.

Coming, with him hard in her mouth, made her want him even more, made her want to feel him inside her body not just in her mouth. Taking a page from Hatter's play book, she moved faster than would be humanly possible in the waking world, and was off his face and in a reverse cowgirl in under a heartbeat. They both cried out as she slid over Hatter's member. He fucked Rosie with manic energy and she felt like she was riding a very naughty mechanical bull. As she rode him his scrotum bumped against her causing waves of delicious sensation, and she was building already to a fifth orgasm. But this time she wanted to climax gazing into Hatter's eyes.

Hatter felt so amazing inside her that it was hard to stop for any amount of time, especially feeling that they were both so close to coming. Rosie slowed her pace, making Hatter moan with need, and dismounted her bronco reluctantly but with sensual slowness. She turned, and he was already sitting up, reaching for her with desire written all over his face.

With a palm planted firmly on his chest, Rosie pushed Hatter back against the bed. "Did I say you could get up?"

Hatter replied with an appreciative growl, "No, mistress. But please mistress, I need to fuck you now." Hatter's voice was raw with desire. "Please don't stop."

Rosie kissed him deeply as she straddled him and sheathed him with herself. She began to ride him with slow full strokes. "I had no intention of stopping, I just wanted to look into your eyes when we come together."

Hatter thrust deep and hard, changing Rosie's slow pace to a joyously fast pounding rhythm. Rosie reveled in this new pace, sitting up and riding him as fast as they both wanted. She grabbed his hands, and pulled them to her breasts. Hatter eagerly groped her, using her full breasts like grips to brace her body and pound deeper into her. Rosie cried out, feeling something both beyond and part of her orgasm growing within her. She rode him faster yet, feeling his manhood hit all the right places within her while the friction against her clit from riding so rough was bringing her that way too. She dragged her hands along his arms, leaving red scratch marks that made Hatter release a primal growl of ecstatic lust. She grasped his biceps, giving her the leverage to grind harder into him too.

Rosie arched her back, feeling their orgasms ripping through them both at the same time. She felt Hatter's seed release in a hot jet of fluid deep inside her, but as Hatter's cum pounded into Rosie she felt something rip inside her. It was like a deeper hymen had just been broken, but not in a wash of pain like her first time, this time she felt pain and pleasure mixed so closely that the pain felt good. The tearing sensation traveled up her spine and exploded through her shoulder blades. Rosie was flung forward onto Hatter's chest as large cobalt blue membranous wings tore from her back. She screamed in agony and utter ecstasy, feeling the wings tear through muscle and skin to free themselves as she climaxed.

Rosie and Hatter lay there panting, covered in Rosie's blood and gore; in shock but also strangely in afterglow. Awkward moments passed before either of them could find words. "What was that?" Rosie rasped, afraid to turn her head and look.

"I think you just got your wings." Hatter said clearly in awe.

"My, my what?" Rosie stammered in disbelief.

"Your faerie wings, love. You've just gotten your faerie wings. And they are so beautiful." Hatter was unable to tear his eyes from the shimmering deep blue wings that had just unfurled out of the back of the love of his life. They were wet with Rosie's blood, giving them a purplish hue, and they were still pretty shriveled like a butterflies wings fresh out of chrysalis, but Hatter could see how magnificent they would be when dry.

The afterglow started to ebb from Hatter, and it struck him that these wings had just torn out of Rosie's back in a spray of blood and gore. He wrapped his arms carefully around Rosie, afraid he would feel her back ruined beneath the wings. "Are you in pain? Is there-" he stopped mid sentence, feeling Rosie's back whole and unblemished beneath her wings.

Hatter felt Rosie's pulse speed, her heart pounding against his chest. "Why?" She sounded frightened, "There was a lot of pain, well pain-pleasure, kinda. Is it awful? Am I all torn up, but not feeling it from the shock? Will I be-" Rosie babbled in fear.

He kissed her and in the beat it took her to refocus, Hatter answered."Your back is fine and whole. Not a scratch on it." He ran his hands over the smooth flesh of Rosie's back beneath the wings with wonder, her skin was even dry beneath the wings.

"So, I'm all normal back there?" Rosie said with caution.

"Aside from the faerie wings." Hatter confirmed with a smile.

"Yes, aside from those." Rosie said dryly.

"Then yes, you're brilliant." Hatter said hugging Rosie to him.

Rosie turned her head to look over her shoulder. Her wet wings were a deep iridescent blue folded across her back like a moth. They trailed behind her, long enough to cover most of Hatter's legs. As she realized she wasn't injured, Rosie felt the need to stretch her wet wrinkled wings. She experimentally tried to move them, half expecting that they wouldn't move, but they twitched and fluttered just slightly.

Hatter let out an abrupt but stifled laugh. "Please

stop, that tickles." He squirmed under her, trying not to laugh; bringing Rosie's attention back to the feeling of his member still inside her. Her muscles contracted around him almost involuntarily, eliciting a happy rumble from Hatter.

Rosie turned back to look Hatter in the eyes, trying to lift her wings just enough to not brush against Hatter's legs. "Sorry, I've never had to worry about wing clearance before." Rosie was so overwhelmed with what this meant, that she was having trouble processing everything. "This is all so surreal." She said in a daze, then something occurred to Rosie that scared her. "Is this going to happen every time I cum now?"

"I don't think so. We may be different kinds of Fey-born, but I'd be surprised if it's that different from how I transform. Something really similar happened to me the first time I shifted into my wolf form, but only the first time. Each time I shifted it got easier, and now I can do it with just a little force of will, no mess or pain."

Rosie let out a relieved breath that she didn't realize she had been holding, causing her wings to dip slightly to trail against Hatter. "Oh, thank you."

"Hey!" Hatter playfully bounced his hips under Rosie, bumping his softening manhood inside her, "I said quit that please, it tickles."

"Sorry. I need to get used to having wings." Rosie lifted her wings, to avoid tickling him, as she climbed off Hatter. Rosie noticed that the wings made her move somewhat gracefully, helping her balance. She kneeled beside him, sitting on her heels to give her wings a little more room. "I was worried that it would be like this every time I came from now on." She motioned to the blood and meat staining the white sheets and the white curtains. "I feel a lot better about dousing my boyfriend with blood and gore knowing its probably..." She balanced what she'd just said in her mind for a moment. "No, no I still feel really bad about that, sorry by the way, but I'm pretty happy I'm not likely to do it again."

Hatter rolled onto his side, facing Rosie, and beamed at her. "What?" She asked with confusion over his joyful reaction. "Do you like the gore?" She asked warily.

He grinned, almost looking a little high, "No, not anything to do with the gore." Hatter tapped a finger absently on the bed, and all the mess sprayed everywhere lifted off in little bubbling sparkles, dissipating and popping into nothing. Rosie was delighted by the sparkly show, but Hatter wasn't paying any attention to his own manipulation, he kept grinning at Rosie and continued as soon as he had her attention back. "You just called me your boyfriend," he took her hands in his, "and I really liked it."

A similar expression spread across Rosie's face. "My boyfriend, I guess I did say that." Her wings unfurled a bit with her joy, starting to smooth into giant but delicate looking dragonfly wings. The sensation of her rumpled wings beginning to straighten out gave Rosie a chill that ran down her spine, but also felt hot as she felt blood and energy flowing out to plump the veins. She spoke as her wings stretched, beginning to look almost like stained glass. "You've been my sexy guardian angel, my hero, my Hatter, and just recently my man. I guess 'my boyfriend' does imply something a little more formal. We've got time now, and we're starting to feel a little more, domestic I guess. I mean, no monsters to fight, no narcissistic energy vampire mind controlling boyfriends or exes to save me from... no romantic relationship in my waking world to complicate things." She looked into Hatter's eyes significantly as she said the last bit. "How about you?"

"No, nothing to complicate things here. Most dreamers I meet don't remember me for long, and a lot of the others you meet... Well they aren't usually looking for a relationship. No one in the twelve years since you've been gone have even come close to you, no one else is you Rose. You were the one that got away." Hatter took a slightly giddy breath. "So, can I call you my girlfriend?" he asked, bringing her hands to his lips and kissing them.

Rosie beamed back at Hatter, "Calling me your girlfriend does sound kinda nice. Does this mean we're exclusive?" She asked nervously.

"Is that what you want?" Hatter looked serious but hopeful.

"If it's what you want." Rosie countered cautiously, trying not to sound too eager.

Hatter smiled again, and looked deep into Rosie's eyes. "I do." His words were sweet and sincere, and made Rosie want to jump up and down like a giddy schoolgirl.

Rosie smiled so hard that it made her cheeks hurt. "So, it's official then. I guess we're a couple." Hatter sat up and pulled Rosie into an embrace, kissing her tenderly but thoroughly before Rosie continued. "God, I feel like a sappy teenager in love. Reunited star crossed lovers, just in the beginning of our new relationship..." she kissed him back, and with their lips a breath apart whispered intimately, "fucking like bunnies."

Hatter kissed Rosie lustily, pulling her tight against him. "I really liked your sexy March Hare coming to see me at my tea party, it was the best reunion I could have imagined."

"Yeah, that was pretty hot." She said winding her arms around his shoulders. "Oddly, with all that crumminess, the thing that sticks in my head now is you caressing that tramp stamp bunny tail tattoo. Almost makes me want to go get one in the waking world."

"Mnh." Hatter grunted appreciatively. "I wouldn't mind that, it was hot sexy. But it was only so sexy because it was part of you; like your wings are now. They're pretty damn hot too. And your lips," he kissed her solidly. "they're sexy enough to write songs about."

As they continued to kiss and cuddle. Rosie realized she had instinctively tucked her wings in close behind her, and nicely out of the way, almost like they were limbs she'd always had. She glanced at them, noticing they were no longer wet and wrinkled, they had filled out and were almost dry. She remembered the thrill of flight from the day before, and it made so much sense now. "Would you teach me how to fly?" Rosie looked up through the open canopy and back to Hatter with a blush. "I was thinking, if these wings are functional and I get the hang of flight... it's kinda an aphrodisiac."

Hatter easily picked up Rosie, pulling her into his lap so that she was again straddling him. Rosie wrapped her legs around Hatter's waist, and he kneaded his fingertips into her hips while he spoke. "Then I'd say a flight lesion is definitely on my to do list."

Rosie whispered intimately, "I like being on your to do list." before hungrily kissing Hatter.

Hatter smiled, and looked at Rosie with desire. "You've been on my to do list all morning, but I'm definitely not done yet."

Rosie laughed, blushing slightly. "Oh, I've been done quite nicely." She broke eye contact coyly, "and I wouldn't mind being done a time or two more before we leave this bed."

Hatter made a happy rumble, kissing the side of her neck and across the top of her shoulder. Hatter's teeth brushed Rosie's shoulder with a light bite, and a shiver ran through her that danced out to the tips of her wings. He playfully kissed and nibbled his way back up the side of her neck, watching her wings tremble with every contact. "Those wings of yours are a pretty big tell," he said with a smile, "they flutter every time my lips touch your skin." Hatter kissed Rosie's neck tenderly, and again her wings reacted. "It makes me think of a puppy thumping it's foot when you rub its belly just right."

Rosie blushed, and her wings gave another quick blast of movement, this time making a momentary low buzz. "I guess I am a little like an excitable puppy. I think these wings of mine are going to take a little while to master. I guess they vibrate a little when I'm in a heightened state." Rosie's expression slipped from embarrassment to slightly blanched worry and her wings oscillated steadily speeding till the movement was making a low note. "Do you think they'll always do that?"

Hatter felt her worry growing towards a small panic attack, and smiled as he thought of a way to distract her. "If you want, I'd be happy to get you to a-" his smile took a suggestive little corner up tilt, "heightened state for a nice long while so we can see if the vibration is a new tell or just you getting used to wings."

Rosie nodded, and looked more worried as her fears fed the twitch and they continued to vibrate the air audibly. Hatter placed his hands to either side of her face, and gave her his best bedroom eyes as he leaned in for a slow and sensual kiss. At first her wings sped with her heart beat. The sound her wings were making raised in pitch with her pulse, and made Hatter think of an ethereal musical instrument. As he continued to kiss her, he enveloped her with his desire to give her a warm and safe place to be with him.

Rosie became more aware of Hatter's spicy scent of roses and musk, and melted into his kisses. She felt so safe and warm and loved that a few long tender moments passed before Hatter leaned back just enough to look her in the eye. He smiled at her, and she dreamily smiled back feeling like a smitten kitten. Then she realized that her wings were as relaxed and calm as she felt in Hatter's arms.

"Better?"

"You have a talent for making everything all better, don't you?" She said sliding her arms around the back of his neck.

"I do try." He smiled sweetly but confidently.

Rosie enjoyed the warm contentment Hatter shared with her. It reminded her of how she had experienced Hatter before she ever saw his face. When she was scared, she felt his comfort like this. But this was so much better now because she could see him and feel him with more traditional senses at the same time he opened himself to her psychically.

Her trip down memory lane shook another memory free too. "I think I remember something Kiri once taught me about a faerie's wings."

"Who?" Hatter asked like he knew it was a name he should know, but just couldn't place it.

"Kiri. From the Fey world I went to as a child."

Hatter still looked a little lost, and dropped his hands to rest at Rosie's hips. "Um. I have trouble remembering too far back. Was she a friend?"

"You trained with her too. She taught you how to make those protection amulets."

"Oh, yeah, right. I got you now. *That* Kiri. I remember now; she made me prove my intentions with you were good. Then she taught me so I could help you where they couldn't go." Hatter was making a good connection, but it was obvious to Rosie that he was clearly fuzzy about the details of his memory.

"How is it that you can remember things I said twelve years ago, or even that we've been apart for twelve years, but have trouble remembering spending time with full faeries being trained in magic?"

Hatter shrugged, "You're worth remembering." Hatter's accent seemed to get stronger the more serious he was. "I have gladly released other memories to hold on to details of the love of my life." He kissed her. "To remember the taste of your lips, I would forget my own name."

It struck Rosie that he may have done just that, she was pretty sure that he wasn't born with the lone name of Hatter. It also brought curiosity to her mind about who Hatter really was and where he came from, it was a mystery that Rosie suspected Hatter wouldn't know how to solve any more than her.

"What was it you remembered your faerie friend saying about wings?" Hatter said bringing her attention back to their conversation.

"Oh, right." Rosie said, focusing on the memory. "I vaguely remember her teaching me that, before the age of reason, some Fey-born could manifest full Fey abilities when they came into their wings. But it hadn't happened since magic left the Prime Material." Rosie racked her brain to see the memory clearer. "I remember there was something about the number five causing release or five releases, and that another Fey-born of equal power needed to be involved." She struggled to remember more. "And there was something about sharing energy with a shifter." She blurted out the recollection with a little excitement. "But she always talked around things more than about things. Do you think we accidentally performed a magical rite to get me my wings?"

"Well, let's take a look at the bits you remember. We have shared a good amount of energy since we woke up this morning, and I am a shifter. We are Fey-born of similar powers, and you did cum five times in fairly quick succession." Hatter couldn't help but smile as he thought things through. "I'd say an orgasm is a pretty good release. So, Yeah, I think you might be the first Fey-born noble in centuries to get your wings. And likely first to get your full Fey abilities."

The thought settled in, and Rosie was almost speechless, "Wow." Rosie felt a little intimidated at the thought that she had, with Hatter, just done something that no one had done since before magic had retreated from her world. She also wondered how no one had stumbled upon this before, maybe the form of the release was lost information, or maybe they'd discovered a whole new way to express the release.

"I always knew you were something unique and

wonderful." Hatter said hugging her.

The close hug made them both very aware that they were sitting together completely naked, and just how good it felt to be touching. Rosie felt Hatter's manhood filling and hardening against her. She slowly rocked against him, happy to be sitting in his lap.

"I'm thinking that you are just as unique and wonderful as me, if not more unique and amazing." Rosie said kissing Hatter, and could feel their love almost as a tangible thing. "I am so grateful to whatever part of the universe that led us to find each other again. If my wings are a mark of the ability to gain full Fey talents, I would have never gotten them without you, you really do complete me."

"At your service, m'lady." Hatter said with a small knightly bow to his head, but followed the gentlemanly nod with a rakish smile and a gleam in his eye. "And thinking of servicing, I wonder if anything more would happen if we got to ten?"

"Ten?" Rosie purred with interest. "That's a pretty impressive goal," she rocked her hips rhythmically against him, "aren't you worried we'd exhaust ourselves too much and be raw and achy tomorrow?"

"Well," Hatter rumbled as he stroked the small of her back and over her suggestively moving ass, "sleep will fix the exhaustion, and I'm lucky enough that my girlfriend is a talented healer that can fix any sore muscles and friction burns we end up with."

"I don't know if I have enough reserve to make it to ten, but maybe we can get you to five." Rosie rolled against Hatter, and as her erect nipples pressed against his firm chest he let out a deep animal rumbling of pleasure that made her tighten and moisten with want. "That'd be a goal I would enjoy trying to meet. I'd love to see how many times we can," Rosie accentuated the next word with slow sensual lips "release, before we collapse."

ଓଃ

42

Again they woke together, contented and happy to be with each other and hungering for more physical releases. They were consumed with desire, exploring new positions and locations. They alternated between slow and sensual tender love making and hard fast animal-lust-filled fucking. They played till their bodies couldn't move and then they slept. When they woke they indulged their flesh several more times before needing to sleep again.

Between romps they ventured into the forest around them and confirmed they were still in Wonderland. But with Wonderland's mutable nature it was a new place since Hatter had been in this part last, so they explored the terrain as they explored each other's bodies. They found a waterfall and a pool to play in, as well as a cave with smooth walls, perfect for fucking against, behind the falls. They did more than make love, but it seemed that every long intimate talk became physical and so did their flight lessons.

Together their carnal appetite was insatiable and wonderful. They knew their needs were way beyond what was normal for either of them, but with Rosie's healing touch neither of them got sore for long and, they both agreed, they did have over a decade of lost time to make up for. Days and nights began to blur into a hedonistic romp through Wonderland with pauses for sleep to recharge so they could fuck more. Eventually they made their way back to the tea party and into the castle where Hatter kept his bedroom. His bed brought back memories of their first time, and soon they were making new memories in his canopied bed and on his dresser.

ᑕᗷ

When they next woke, still together, Rosie realized that they had been rutting with each other for days without thought of Rosie's body left in the Prime Material plane. "I think our bacchanal needs to end."

Hatter pouted playfully, "But, you would make Bacchus so sad. We have been very good nymphs, what would the god of revelry do without our carnal offerings?" The way Hatter spoke of myth in his accent almost drew Rosie back into their feast of flesh.

"I'm sure the rest of the world could pick up a little of our slack." Rosie said moving just out of Hatter's reach. "And, by the way, it's really hot you know what a bacchanal is." She commented before starting to explain her worry. "But something occurred to me, we can't just keep having sex forever." She stepped further from Hatter.

Hatter watched Rosie move away from him, and was mesmerized by her nude supple form moving across the room. "Ooh, are we playing a chase game this morning? If I catch you, does the big bad wolf get to eat you?" He rumbled provocatively, and rolled into a position on all fours, his muscles tense and looking ready to pounce.

A whimper of frustration escaped Rosie's lips, nothing sounded better at that moment than being ravished by Hatter. "You're a hard man to turn down." She manifested clothes by swiping her hands quickly down her torso. Rosie went with jeans and a girl cut light blue backless t-shirt that complimented her dark blue wings nicely; covering but still flattering.

"Yes, I am a hard man." Hatter gave Rosie his sexiest dimpled grin, lifting an eyebrow suggestively. "Was there something you said after hard?"

Rosie stifled a giggle as she struggled to be serious and to not let her eyes linger on Hatter's excellent physique poised in a moment of such delicious physical tension. With his muscles flexed, and his erect phallus peeking from the shadow under his fit body, he looked really yummy. "Please put some clothes on, it's har- " Rosie caught herself, and decided to use a less erotically charged word, "difficult to talk to you seriously when you're being so..." Rosie paused to find the right word.

"Tasty?" Hatter supplied, jumping up gracefully and swaggering towards Rosie. "Sexy? Irresistible?" He wrapped his arms loosely around her waist and bit his lip with a playful grin.

"Frustrating." Rosie put her hands firmly against his chest between them to keep Hatter from pulling her too close and distracting her. She tried not to smile, and widened her eyes in mock anger. "Distracting, infuriating," she teased.

Hatter pulled Rosie against him, and she realized that her hands on his well muscled chest were not keeping them apart and were almost as distracting as his strong arms snugly around her. "Nope, the word you are looking for is tempting." Hatter subtly wet his lips and grinned down at Rosie.

Rosie gave a little. "Ok, I'll give you tempting. I am tempted." Rosie said in a breathy sigh, and kissed Hatter greedily.

After a satisfying kiss, Hatter leaned back without letting go of Rosie. "Wait, are you saying I'm not tasty?" He over dramatically feigned hurt. "Or irresistible?"

"You know you are. Do you really need to fish for compliments? Haven't I proven how much I like the taste of you over the last few days?" Rosie lightly stroked Hatter's chest with absent little circles as she tried to focus on anything beyond the feel of her lover pressed against her. "You are the sexiest man I've ever met." Rosie bit her lip and closed her eyes to try to clear her head, but instead found Hatter's lips pressed firmly against hers and almost forgot what she was trying to talk to Hatter about. She kissed him back, filling her senses with the warm touch of his skin and his intoxicating scent. She felt his heartbeat speed against her fingertips and it reminded her of her body waiting in the Prime Material.

Rosie stepped back shaking her head, freeing herself from the arms and attentions she craved so desperately. "Hatter, the way I crave you is overpowering. I want you so badly, my body aches for you when I'm not touching you. Seeing you stand there naked," Rosie averted her gaze before watching the play of his muscles made her forget everything except the salty sweet taste of his skin. "But we have been enjoying each other for days, and I only feel like I need you more. I love you Hatter, but were acting more like addicts than people in an adult relationship."

Hearing Rosie, Hatter sobered. He manifested clothing with the twitch of his middle finger; dark blue jeans and a black t-shirt with a colorful Japanese anime style werewolf on it howling at the moon. He stepped up to Rosie also wearing his concern on his face, and put a hand on her arm. "I'm sorry. I guess we've both been acting like happy addicts. I just can't get enough of you, and I really enjoy being with you so frequently. But if something is bothering you, I'm here for you." Rosie looked up at Hatter and was as relieved to see him clothed, as she was disappointed to lose her favorite view. She made eye contact as Hatter continued to speak. "I'm not just a fun ride." He said smiling, thinking of the last several days. "What's up, my love?"

"Time in Wonderland, does it move at the same rate as the Prime Material?"

"I don't know, time in the worlds is pretty subjective." Hatter started to catch on to Rosie's logic.

"We've been together for days, and I'm thinking that my body might be in trouble without food or drink for who knows how long."

"Oh." Hatter sounded pensive and worried. "I think time's been moving at about the same speed as in the Prime Material. With you here, it's likely to keep rhythm with your clock and spending almost all your life so far in the Prime Material..." Hatter tried to stay calm, but his eyes held the edge of panic. "I'm sorry Rose. I swore that I would do anything to keep you safe, but in our hedonism I was so consumed with the pleasures of your flesh that..." Hatter couldn't bring himself to say that her body might have died while her spirit was away.

Tears of panic welled in Rosie's eyes. "How many days have we been together? Is it possible I'm already dead?"

"I don't know. I've never known someone like you to stay out of their native world so long. Dreamers from your plane usually don't stay more than a few hours." Hatter paused in frustration hanging his head, "Or maybe I have, and I can't remember. I'm so sorry Rosie. Yours is the only memory I've been able to hold onto so long. But, I'd think that we'd feel it if your body expired."

"I need to wake up. I just don't want to lose you. What if I can't find you next time I fall asleep? It was months between last time and this time, and twelve years before that." Rosie felt panic over both leaving and staying.

"But, you have to go." Hatter's voice sounded urgent, but as he took Rosie's hand and made eye contact she could see the fear and uncertainty in his eyes. "I swore I would always protect you. Now I swear that if there is still life in my body, I will always find you. As long as we are psychically connected, I will feel my way to you." Hatter squeezed the hand he held while he put his free hand tenderly on Rosie's cheek. "I don't know how long your spirit can survive separated from your body, don't pass up a lifetime of possibilities between us for a little more gratification now."

"You're right." Rosie took a deep breath, catching the scent of roses and musk, and felt so safe here with the man she loved. "I have to wake up now, and see to my body. Will you come see me tonight when I dream?"

Hatter smiled, "Wild Bandersnatches couldn't keep me away."

"I love you Hatter."

"I love you too, my sweet Rose." He kissed

Rosie gently at first, but as he cradled her face with both hands their desire transformed their kiss something much less chaste. They finished their goodbye kiss and lingered a moment longer; their foreheads resting together and their eyes closed to feel each other better with less concrete senses.

As Rosie made the effort to wake and felt herself reluctantly leaving Wonderland she heard Hatter quietly in her mind. "Wake safely, my love."

ℭ

43

Rosie struggled to wake, but it was hard to get her body to respond, like it had to remember how to be part of her again. With effort she started to feel her body, but it felt odd and heavier than she remembered. She could hear a monitor quietly beeping with her heartbeat and smelled sterile antiseptic, so she knew she was in a hospital well before she was able to convince her eyes to open.

Her eyes were bleary and took some time to focus, but she knew it was daytime outside by the blinding light that filled the room. She lifted an arm to shade her eyes and hit herself with the iv coming from the back of her hand in her clumsy attempt.

She heard movement, but couldn't quite make out who belonged to the blurry shape. "You want me to close the shade?" The voice was female and sounded familiar but Rosie couldn't quite place it.

"Yes please." Rosie croaked from an unused and dry throat.

She heard curtains closing with loud metal rollers. "Sounds like you need some water too." The familiar voice continued as the room darkened. Rosie heard the woman call directions to someone out of the room, but Rosie wasn't able to process what was said just yet.

"How long?" Rosie rasped trying to clear her head and straining to focus on the face coming closer.

The sound of metal chair legs scraping against linoleum flooring told Rosie that the woman was pulling up a chair. "About a week as far as we can tell." Rosie finally made sense of who was speaking as the woman sat next to her bed and her vision focused. "But, we aren't exactly sure how long you were out before you were found. You've been here for five days." The face that came into focus belonged to Janet.

Rosie blinked at her old friend, thinking that it was all way to coincidental that she finds Hatter and now the doctor at her bedside happens to be Janet, a woman she hadn't seen in almost as long as Hatter. "Janet? Wow, I haven't seen you in years."

"I guess that answers if you memory's been affected, at least partially." Janet poured Rosie a glass of water from a dull yellow plastic pitcher, and handed her the matching plastic cup. As Rosie took a sip and cleared her throat Janet grabbed a clipboard and flipped a few pages. Clicking her ball point pen, Janet looked at her old friend with a relieved smile and asked. "What's the last thing you remember. Any idea what knocked you out? Like did you hit your head before bed or anything?"

Rosie debated telling Janet that the last thing she remembered was kissing Hatter before waking up, but thought better in case Janet had the same missing memories she'd had, and sent her to the psych ward. "Um, I remember going to bed like any other night. No head trauma that I remember."

"Yeah, I didn't think so. We couldn't find any signs of trauma, but then we also have no idea why you fell into a coma. It's a mystery." She said shrugging. "We were hoping if you woke up you could shed some light on why. But sometimes in medicine, we just don't know why a thing happens." Janet looked through Rosie's records for a moment then spoke again. "I am a doc in this hospital, but I'm here as a friend right now. The attending will be in a while to examine you and ask you more questions."

"Thanks Janet." Rosie was thoughtful for a moment before asking what was really on her mind. "So, what exactly happened while I was asleep?" Rosie asked, "I'm curious who got me to the hospital."

"I guess I started the ball rolling." Janet began, setting down the clip board she'd been making notes on. "You usually share lots of funny quotes and pictures on Facebook, and I noticed that I hadn't seen one in a couple days. So I checked your wall and noticed there was no activity. I saw that it didn't follow your pattern for at least the last couple years." Janet looked a little uncomfortable. "I know, sounds kinda stalkerie, but that was it. I just had a feeling something wasn't right. When I looked up your number to call and check on you, I got no answer. So, I decided to stop by your work. And they said you were off for the last two days, but hadn't come in that day with no call. They said that it wasn't like the responsible Ms. Cotton they were used to either. So we got the cops involved, and in no time your super was letting some nice officers into your apartment." Janet took a breath and shrugged. "We found you in your bed with no sign of foul play or reason we couldn't wake you. You were really dehydrated, so we figured you'd been out for a while. I had you brought here where I could keep an eye on you, and that's pretty much it. We've had you on an IV to keep you hydrated, and if you didn't wake up soon we'd have had to put you on a feeding tube." Janet seemed to need to change the subject. "On the up side, I think you've lost like fifteen pounds."

"Really?" Rosie asked, looking under the hospital blanket at herself. She had lost weight. Her body didn't look exactly like it did in her dreams with Hatter but Rosie suddenly realized that the body Hatter had been nearly worshiping for days wasn't an exact match to Rosie's reality. In her dreams, Rosie was usually a more perfect version of herself, toned and firm where Rosie's waking form was a little squishier and saggier. But with the coma, she had lost a bit of the squish. Rosie decided to start working out more regularly, to try and match what Hatter saw in their dreams to what he might see if he came to her insubstantially like he had when they were teenagers. "Seems like the coma did me a favor." Rosie commented looking back to Janet.

"I guess, but I wouldn't recommend it as a diet plan." Janet shifted in her chair and put the clipboard down, looking seriously at Rosie. "I'm really glad you woke up Rosie, and I'm sorry we drifted apart. The only way I've known anything about you over the last few years is through passive social media. We've been living in the same city, and we never even bothered to get together for a meal or to see a movie. I didn't even know you were living alone."

"Is this the 'no one came to see me while I've been in a coma' pity party?" Rosie sounded tired. "I've been fine by myself. I enjoy my job, and I have lots of time to read."

"Some of your work friends came to see you, so no, that's not where I was going. But, Rosie, if I hadn't thought to check on you as a random fluke, you might be dead in bed at home until the smell made someone notice." Janet said looking uncomfortable. "It's not like we were close any more, what if I hadn't noticed a lack of posts."

"They would have missed me at work, and librarians are smart enough to follow through. I'm grateful you realized something was wrong and found me, but don't feel an obligation to reconnect with me because I was in a coma."

"But that's the thing. For some reason, I started to wonder about you when I hadn't thought about you for years. And then I find you in an unexplained coma. It just seems weirdly coincidental, don't you think? I think I'd like to start hanging out again."

"So long as it's not out of a feeling of

responsibility," Rosie started, "I'd like to hang out again too. I have missed you."

Another doctor knocked at the door to check Rosie out, and Janet excused herself promising to stop back later.

A long interview and several medical tests later, Rosie was cleared to be released from the hospital. When Janet offered to give Rosie a ride home she accepted. Rosie wasn't sure how much of their past dream walking Janet remembered, but she hoped the drive home would present a way to broach the subject without sounding crazy.

It was evening when Rosie was wheeled to the front door. She felt silly sitting in a wheelchair when her legs were working fine and not two hours earlier they were having her run on a treadmill to see if the stress would put her back into a coma; but hospital policy was you go to the door in a wheelchair, so she was being wheeled out.

Rosie saw Janet pull up in her green hybrid and got up to meet her. Rosie had a strange feeling of déjà vu getting into Janet's car and pulling away from the hospital. Janet's car was different, and they'd never left a hospital before, but it was familiar and comfortable to be driving off with Janet. It somehow felt like no time had passed since they were close in high school, and they could pick up where they had left off.

Rosie broke the silence first, "I always thought it was a shame that we lost touch."

"Me too."

"I don't even remember if there was a reason we stopped hanging out." Rosie said trying to find a way to judge if Janet remembered them all being beaten soundly by a monster.

"I guess different classes in high school, then going to different colleges." Janet said with a shrug as she navigated her way through the traffic around the hospital. "Your weird unexplained coma feels kinda like fate pushing us back together, tho. Don't you think?"

"Yea. Even down to you being in the room when I woke up. Lots of coincidences." Rosie tried to feel out the situation a little more. "But, what if the coma had an explanation."

"What do you mean?" Janet said somewhat distractedly as she worked her way out onto the busy street. "Did you think of something you forgot during your interview?"

"No. But..." Rosie trailed off, not sure how to broach the subject without the chance of Janet turning the car around and checking her back into the hospital on a much more secure wing.

"But?" Janet prompted, starting to sound interested.

"Maybe this is one of those things best discussed over a quiet drink." Rosie said, losing her nerve.

"Ok. I'm in."

"What? Now?" Rosie felt a small ball of panic growing in the pit of her stomach. "I was thinking like next week some time."

"Why wait?" Janet suggested. "I'm off tomorrow, and you have doctors orders to take it easy a few days, so you won't be working tomorrow. And after sleeping for a week, I bet you aren't really tired."

"True. But I kinda have a date tonight." Rosie confessed.

"A pre-coma date?" Janet asked a sounding a little surprised.

"Not exactly." Rosie stalled.

"You made a date today? In the hospital?"

"Yes and no." Rosie hesitated and then finished the thought. "In that order."

Janet stopped at a red light. She gave Rosie a look that let her know she was waiting for clarification. When Rosie shrugged and made an apologetic face Janet prompted. "So, you made a date with someone today, but not in the hospital."

"Yes." Rosie answered, wanting to tell Janet everything about Hatter like she had when they were teenagers, but afraid Janet wouldn't believe her. Luckily, the light turned green giving Rosie more time to think.

"God, you are still one frustrating chickie. If you don't want to hang out, you don't need to make up a date. No skin off my back." Janet sighed as she watched the road.

"No. I swear, Janet, it's not that I don't want to hang out. I really do have a date tonight. But, it's not till later, so maybe we should talk over a glass of something. I do really want to talk, you might be the only person I know who could get what's going on, but not while you're driving."

"Ooookaaay. You are about as clear as mud." Janet shook her head and they drove in silence for several awkward minutes. Janet broke the silence as they got closer to Rosie's apartment. "You got booze at your place? Or do we need to stop?"

"We should probably stop." Rosie said with some relief that the silence was done. "I'll buy."

"Works for me." Janet said pulling up to a liqueur store.

೧೩

A short time later they sat in Rosie's living room with a bottle of Jameson's and two newly emptied glasses on the coffee table between them. "Ok, I'm not driving now. Why would the cause of your coma be explainable, and who's this mysterious date with?"

Rosie took a deep breath and contemplated pouring a couple fingers more of the Jameson's into her glass. "I'll answer your questions, but I need to know what you remember from the spring and summer after sophomore year first."

"What does that have to do with anything? Rosie, should I be taking you back to the hospital? You are really saying some odd disjointed things. Maybe we should check you for a stroke."

"Janet, I'm not having a stroke. I'm just being cautious. Please trust me, it's relevant. Now, what do you remember from that spring and summer twelve years ago?"

Janet squinted her eyes and twisted her mouth up in an expression of thoughtfulness. She looked more like she was thinking of if Rosie was having a stroke than trying to remember the time they spent dream walking together. "How about I just grab a few instruments from my car's trunk and check you out. If your pupils are fine and your blood pressure are fine I'll worry less."

"If you really need to, you can look at my pupils and whatever else will convince you I'm not having some other symptoms to go with the coma." Janet smiled at Rosie's permission and, grabbing her keys out of her purse, jogged out Rosie's front door.

Rosie sighed and poured herself more Irish whiskey while Janet ran to her car. As she waited, Rosie sipped her drink enjoying its oakiness and its clean burn going down. She thought about how she wanted to explain everything to Janet, but Rosie was sure Janet would have said something if she remembered. Rosie thought that maybe she needed something to trigger Janet's memory.

Having a few days to process her missing memories, she recalled the old leather bound journal with its crappy lock and her sketch pad both full of Hatter and monster memories. She'd kept them with a few other memories from her younger years in a box that she hadn't even looked in since high school. She knew that she had them and it never occurred to her to go through her old stuff, but at the same time she never even thought about tossing the box. Rosie thought it was strange, but no stranger than having your magic stripped from you so that you couldn't remember ever being magical. But if magic worked on belief, it made sense that without it you couldn't see what you no longer believed in. It was what made the Fey go into hiding and forsake the Prime Material.

Rosie tried to remember where the box with her journal and sketch pad would be. She had narrowed it down to the back of her bedroom closet or the front hall closet when Janet came back in. Janet had a blood pressure cuff sticking out of the side pocket of the bag slung over her shoulder, stethoscope around her neck, and a pen light in her hand.

Janet scooted Rosie from the center of the overstuffed love seat with a wave and sat next to her. She clicked the pen light on to look into Rosie's eyes. Janet reached up with one hand to open Rosie's eye lid wider as she swept the pen light past, but the moment Janet touched Rosie's skin her eyes widened in sudden shock.

Janet launched herself back, tripping over the arm of the love seat in her scramble to move away from Rosie as quickly as possible, but couldn't seem to take her eyes off her estranged friend. "What the fuck?! Rosie, you have transparent ghost fairy wings or something!" Janet landed awkwardly on the floor and froze in disbelief, all color drained from her face. "Why do you have big blue ghostly fairy wings?"

"You can see them?" Rosie was almost as surprised as Janet, but not nearly as thrown. "I thought they'd only be around in dream worlds."

"Wait, but, why?" Janet was staring at the wings she could see gracefully spreading from her old friends back, and knew that they were impossible. "How?"

Now that Janet had seen Rosie's wings, Rosie could feel the faint shadow of them attached to her back, and ruffled them slightly just because it felt good to move them. "So, this may sound crazy... but since you can see my wings I'm thinking it'll maybe not sound quite so crazy. While my body was in the coma over the last week or so I was awake in a dream realm;

Wonderland. Reunited with the long lost love of my life, earning my faerie wings." Rosie smiled and blushed slightly with the memory.

Janet managed to settle herself cross legged on the floor and was regaining her faculties, but still hadn't taken her eyes off Rosie's wings. They went insubstantially into the couch, like there wasn't a couch there to keep them from moving freely, but moved so naturally as Rosie shifted her body slightly to face Janet better.

Janet processed Rosie's words slowly. "The love of your life? I really hope you're not talking about that abusive ass you dated in high school. What was his name," Janet wondered out loud before remembering. "Jack. You don't mean Jack, right?"

"God no. Turns out I was more his prey than his girlfriend. I'm talking about the man who saved me from my nightmare monster and the Jack monster. You may not remember this, but back when we were in high school you were the first person I told about my sexy guardian angel, my Hatter. I forgot him for twelve years because of the injuries in the battle the night we all were going to test these protection amulets we made. I think we all forgot. But Hatter and I found each other again, and he helped my memory return."

"Hatter? That name sounds familiar. Why do I remember thinking that it was a strange choice of character to emulate..." Then, much like it had with Rosie, Janet's memories that had been repressed washed over her.

Rosie saw Janet's eyes flutter as she swooned and fell towards the floor. In a heartbeat Rosie had leapt over the coffee table and slid across the floor to catch Janet before her head hit the hardwood. She gently cradled Janet's convulsing frame, and settled her head on a pillow Rosie placed in her lap. Rosie was surprised at her own speed, sure that a week ago she would have never caught Janet before she hit the ground.

Rosie watched Janet ride the seizure until her body settled and her eyes relaxed and took on an unfocused look. She knew that this was how she looked to Hatter when she had gotten her memories back, and understood his worry. Rosie, having experienced the same traumatic barrage of memories, knew that Janet would be fine.

Rosie stroked Janet's hair soothingly until she had regained herself enough to focus on Rosie's face. "Feeling better now?"

"Um, I think my brain just got fucked hard by a stream of missing memories." Janet blinked slowly, "That was a trip and a half. How did I lose like half a year's memories without realizing it?" Janet sat back up, a little unsteadily.

"At least you didn't forget the love of your life. I'd been going through life not knowing why no man ever felt right, and feeling like a part of me was missing but never being able to figure out why." Rosie sighed, then stood and tossed the pillow from her lap back over onto the sofa. "I thought it was chemical depression, but it turns out my subconscious was longing for Hatter and not letting my conscious mind in on it."

Rosie offered Janet a hand up, which she took and got unsteadily to her feet. "I don't know. I may not have lost memories of the love of my life, but I'm thinking Chris might be the one that got away. We were in some serious flirting before that monster of yours tossed me across the room." Janet moved over to the sofa and sat down. "This is a lot to process. Did your memories returning knock you on your ass too?"

"Yup." Rosie confirmed, walking around the coffee table to sit back on the love seat. "Scared the shit out of Hatter." Rosie couldn't help but smile at the memory of him staring down at her with such worry and then such relief when he realized she was ok.

"Smitten." Janet said with a friendly teasing tone. "You were smitten in high school, and you're just as bad now."

"Well, we haven't been together since high school." Rosie blushed when she thought of all the ways they were together over the last few days. "And it was pretty easy to pick up right where we left off."

Janet laughed, "I bet. So, he still the love machine he was in high school?" Rosie's deepening blush was all the answer Janet needed. "You little slut." She said with approval obvious in her voice. "Good for you. I'm glad you didn't get in your own way. I can recall many times, when we were kids, that you over thought a thing and missed out because of it." Janet leaned in to pour whiskey into the two empty glasses. "So, how was it?"

"Mind blowing." Rosie said with a sigh taking the glass Janet handed her.

Janet leaned back and took a sip of her own drink, "Bet your mind wasn't the only thing getting blown if you and your sexy angel were alone together for days."

Rosie almost choked on her drink with Janet's implication. "Janet," She said in a mock chiding tone, "a lady doesn't kiss and tell."

"Good thing we both know that no woman is a lady when dishing with friends." Janet said dryly with a raised eyebrow.

"Ok, yah." Rosie admitted, "My mind wasn't the only thing blown." She settled back into the love seats pillows, and relaxed. "God, Janet. Sex with Hatter is..." Rosie waived her empty hand making a couple groping gestures while she searched for words to describe the way she felt with Hatter. "I can't even describe it. We have this psychic connection, and we can feel what the other is feeling. And we can kinda push energy in a way that's like being able to touch inside. And god," Rosie grunted just thinking about touching Hatter. "does he ever know how to use that tongue of his. And the things he can do with his hands, dexterous doesn't even begin to cover it. And oh my freaking lord, can he fuck." Rosie made eye contact with Janet, "I'm telling you, you would not believe how hot his body is. And he's all about giving pleasure, not just getting like you'd expect in someone as hot as him. I'm telling you, Hatter is the most gorgeous person I've ever known, inside and out."

"Sound like you are one lucky girl." Janet said with a smirk.

"Sorry, I didn't mean to brag. I'm just so happy." Rosie was smiling so hard her cheeks ached.

" 'S ok. You're a woman in love. A certain amount of obsession is expected." Janet said with a wink. "But, not to pull you away from your mental masturbation, now that I have my memories of dream walking back why did we lose them? And what happened after I was k.o.'d?"

"Well, the amulets did their jobs. Our bodies were untouched by damage. But the monster must have had a way to keep us from waking when we went unconscious, and then it drained all the magic from the room it could. Apparently, the way our psyches deal with the loss of our magic is by stuffing the memory of what we lost so deep we can't access it." Rosie took a sip of whiskey and savored the taste for a moment before continuing. "That's how you lost your Fey magic, the monster took it. The monster took out everyone but Hatter, and it kept him pinned so he had to watch. I was in and out, and I was hurt bad and being drained. I don't need to relive the details, but Hatter managed to get free and with what little help I could add he took out the monster." Rosie took another sip, and tried not to remember too vividly. "The kicker was, when Hatter thought it was all over and I was safe he left to make sure the monster couldn't ever return; not knowing that the monster had gained a master." A tear rolled down Rosie's cheek, saying what happened out loud was harder than she thought.

She was trying to tell the story from a detached

place, but the memory was hard to leave in the past. She felt Janet's hand on her shoulder before Rosie realized she'd come to sit next to her. Rosie smiled at Janet, but the smile didn't reach her eyes.

"Sorry. It's oddly fresh, it may have happened twelve years ago, but I just got the memories back a few days ago."

Janet squeezed Rosie's shoulder, "No, I'm sorry. If it's too hard, you don't have to tell me."

"You were there, you should know." Rosie took a deep calming breath. "When Hatter left, Jack came out of his hiding place. He told me that he'd been feeding the monster power, making it stronger to take me out. He was pissed Hatter took away his show, so he threw me against the wall and broke my back. Then he walked around the room and snapped each of your necks to make sure you wouldn't wake up and try to stop him, then he..." Rosie took a shaking breath. "Anyway, Hatter got back and saved me, but the cost of saving me was to disconnect me from magic so I forgot everything too." Rosie took another breath and relaxed a little. "So, that's pretty much it."

"Wow. I thought Jack was an abusive ass, but... he didn't know about our amulets did he?"

"He didn't seem to, no."

"So his intent was to actually kill us in our sleep?"

"Yup. That is what he said."

"Well, fuck."

"He tried that while I was helpless too. It seemed to be part of his evil monologue along with the 'I'm killing all your friends' bit." Rosie sighed and downed the rest of her drink. "So, bad shit went down twelve years ago, and now it seems we've healed enough to get our Feyness back."

Janet and Rosie sipped their drinks quietly for a moment before Janet spoke up again. "The thing I don't get is the wings. You never had wings before, not even in lucid dreams where we could do whatever we wanted."

"They kinda surprised me too when they happened. But then I remembered a bit from that training I could never remember before." Janet gave Rosie a look of confusion so Rosie continued. "The world I used to go to with the nameless ageless woman who protected me."

"Oh yea. It's what gave us the idea to try dream walking back when we were kids. What did She tell you?"

"About the last Fey-born to get their wings hundreds of years ago. If we did it right, then I should be coming into my full Fey abilities. I'm betting you being able to see my wings is part of that."

"That's frickin' cool. I bet you're right." Janet paused and looked at Rosie suspiciously. "You said we, what needed a we?"

"Well," Rosie blush resurfaced. "It takes a noble Fey-born, a shifter Fey-born of the same power, and five..." Rosie bit her lip and averted her gaze, having trouble getting the word out. "Five releases in quick succession."

"What kind of releases?" Janet asked knowingly.

"I'm pretty sure you know the kind of releases." Rosie said hip bumping Janet's leg next to her.

"So, you and Hatter spent the last week fucking like bunnies, and now you have your wings. God I love the way Fey magic works."

"And my date tonight is going to sleep and seeing Hatter in my dreams."

"You are insatiable." Janet said patting Rosie on the knee before standing and stretching. "Are you sure you'll wake up tomorrow morning?"

"I hope so, but I won't know till I try." Rosie shrugged. "It's not like I have much choice, I have to sleep. Might as well enjoy the company of my beau while I'm there." She finished, smiling.

"I could stay over, make sure you wake up tomorrow." Janet offered.

"You sure?" Rosie said, sounding a little surprised.

"Like I said, I don't have work tomorrow, so why not."

Rosie was touched by Janet's offer. "I'd like that. Thanks. But it's still pretty early in the evening, you want to order some take out and watch a movie or something?"

Janet smiled sincerely, "I'd like that."

ॐ

44

Rosie found herself standing in a large white room. The first thing she noticed was a long swath of translucent white fabric in the middle of the room. It stretched from a circle on the high ceiling, draping in a graceful arc to pile in a large oval on the white tile floor. The floor was the little white antique hexagonal ceramic tiles that always made Rosie think of a time when beautiful craftsmanship was the standard. She smiled because that tile was always what she imagined in her dream bathroom. The curtain seemed to be hiding something rather large, but she couldn't see exactly what because of the sunlight streaming in from behind her. Turning, she could see where the light was coming from. A large window filled one wall of the room from practically floor to ceiling. It had drapes that matched those that made up the feature in the center of the room. They were just transparent enough to let in lots of light but opaque enough to block anyone's view from outside. Continuing to look around she noticed the ceiling was trimmed with ornate crown moldings the same white as the rest of the room. Rosie took a step as she was turning back to the draped area in the center of the room and noticed a bit of color through the edge of the curtain. Walking around the drape, Rosie saw a dark wood dressing table against the far wall. It had a small seat, an almost bare table, and a large mirror. On the table was a folded card. The vanity's mirror faced back to the fabric swathed center of the room and showed what was inside through a split in the drapes. Inside she could see a large claw foot tub with bare copper piping up to an impressive shower.

Rosie stepped up to the vanity and picked up the paper. Unfolding it she read the message printed in bold black letters, 'Long hot slow shower'. She looked back at the curtained tub and read the card again, 'Long hot slow shower'. The suggestion sounded pretty good to Rosie.

She pulled the curtain open just enough to step into its circle. The drape enclosed the tub but still left room enough for it to feel open once inside. In fact it seemed like there was more room inside the enclosure than it looked like from the outside.

Rosie looked at the shower and there were two heads. One shower head was a big square rain shower that was fairly high above the tub, the other a smaller removable head with a hose hooked to the pipe leading up to the big head.

Rosie looked down at the tub and noticed that it didn't have a drain. Peeking beneath the tub, she saw a drain in the floor, but none in the tub itself. Rosie couldn't help but wonder how the tub was drained once full, but didn't dwell too long on it. When she saw the drain in the floor Rosie also noticed a basket with a big fluffy towel, a large sponge, and a few small bottles of soap. One bottle had a tag reading 'lather me'. Something about the card put her in mind of the 'eat me' and 'drink me' messages in Alice in Wonderland.

Rosie reached for the hem of her shirt, intending to pull it over her head, but suddenly realized she was already naked. She thought she had been wearing clothing, but now that she thought about it she really wasn't sure. Maybe she had been naked all along. She sat on the edge of the tub and turned on the faucet's porcelain handles. The water rushed out the spigot, it was hot but not scalding. Happy with the temperature, Rosie flipped the lever to turn on the shower.

The shower hissed to life, pouring water in a sheet of large heavy droplets, just like a good summer rain. The big shower head covered a large area of the tub, while the smaller shower head remained off. Rosie swung her legs over the edge and stepped into the tub. The water felt good on her skin, almost like human touch. She stepped into the center of the downpour and let the water flood over her face and hair. Rosie liked to get wet everywhere before soaping, and the water felt so wonderful that she just stood under the spray for long lingering minutes. She enjoyed the feeling of the water running through her hair, down her back, over her ass, and trickling over the backs of her thighs and calves. The tub was slowly filling as she stood under the spray enjoying the perfect temperature and water pressure. Rosie ran her fingers through her hair taking out the excess water. She arched her back to let the spray glide over the front of her body the way it had across her back. The water felt better than any shower she ever remembered taking, and Rosie loved the feeling of water on her skin in most circumstances. She turned to face the spray and luxuriated in the feel of the water pounding on her face, every drop somehow feeling like a kiss. Where the hot water ran down her skin it felt like a caress.

She opened her mouth and filled it with water to rinse like she usually did. The first mouthful she swished and spit, but taking in a second mouthful she noticed something different. It felt like the water was moving around her mouth of its own accord, like a strange deep liquid kiss. She spit, thinking that the sensation must have been her imagination and a trick of the water pressure. Shaking off the odd thought, Rosie turned her attention back to the water cascading down the front of her body. Where it hit her nipples it felt like tongues licking in hard quick strokes. As Rosie's body reacted to the delicious sensations she thought 'this hot shower is about more than temperature'.

She leaned out of the tub and picked up the

sponge and the bottle with the tag. Her movement shifted where the water was focused. The water caressed across her lower back, around her bottom, and somehow defied gravity running up to tickle lightly between her legs. She gasped, grabbing the edge of the tub, and spread her legs a little almost involuntarily in reaction to the sensation. The water flowed more intensely and intimately exploring her nether region with obvious intent.

Rosie's thought that this was not just water was suddenly clear in her mind with no doubt that it was in her imagination. She froze, her muscles all tightening with the tension they get just before the flight instinct kicks in, and she was about to bolt when she smelled the intoxicating scent of musk and Roses. The fragrance washed over her with the hot water and she relaxed into the pounding droplets, enjoying the touch that could only be her lover. The water lapped hard at her clit, making her moan and her knees go weak.

"I won't be able to lather like you want, if you are so..." She fumbled for the right word as the water slid over her skin making it hard to think. "...distracting." The intensity and gravity defying nature of the water stopped abruptly. "Oh, so you do want me all soapy." Rosie stood, with a coy smile, and got the sponge wet. Stepping out of the shower spray she poured a bit of the body wash on to the sponge and inhaled it's fragrance. The soap smelled much like Hatter with the primary scent being roses, but it also had notes of jasmine and hibiscus with a hint of sweet cherry blossom like the soap and lotion she used when she was a teenager. She wondered if the smell of cherries made Hatter think of her the way musk and roses made her think of him. Rosie worked the large soft sponge into a good lather with her hands before stepping back under the softly pounding water. It was less obvious than before, but the water still softly caressed her skin as it passed over her body. Rosie wondered if she would ever be able to shower again without imagining it as Hatters touch.

She began to soap her body in slow sensual gliding strokes, aware that she was giving Hatter a good show. The suds slid down her skin, and as some slipped over her breasts and across her nipples Rosie felt delicate licking as bubbles popped. Continuing their way down, some of the suds cupped and fondled her breasts as other bubbles caressed over her lower back and lightly fondled her bottom. As the water and soap slid over her body, Rosie felt like she was being touched by dozens of delicate silky hands. It was like being in a solo orgy, and it became difficult to stand in the wash of sensation.

With the tub almost full, Rosie turned off the shower and slid her body down into the water. The soap seemed almost reluctant to part from her skin as she relaxed into the soothing hot liquid. Rosie dipped the sponge in the water and squeezed it over herself a few times trickling water against her skin to wash away the rest of the soap. The water seemed to react to her slow sponge bath, rolling against her body in little eddies.

Lying in the hot tub, she could feel water currants caressing her skin and exploring every inch, fondling her all at once in an undulating rippling rhythm of soft and firm touches. The pleasure was overwhelming. Then one sensation exploded to the forefront, making the rest feel like a pleasant background to this new intensity. It felt like a focused and forceful jet of water pounded against her clit, caressed & flowed over her labia while pounding in a larger jet inside her. Rosie climaxed in seconds, unabashedly screaming out her pleasure. But the water didn't stop and the orgasm continued to build to another height. The water flowing in and out of her twisted and writhed while the stream pounded into her clit with circular motions that tugged and almost nibbled. Rosie's body was one raw nerve being pushed to higher and higher peaks of joyous noise. Then, when she just couldn't take any more, the water took one last simultaneous thrust over every sensitive place. Her orgasm peaked anew before her last had even began to ebb. She came harder than she had ever imagined possible. Her sight was explosions of color, sound, touch, and smell. The sensations were all overwhelming as she felt the fabrics of multiverses all connecting and flowing through her orgasm.

When she came back to her senses, the tub was dry and she lay in Hatter's arms. Both of them so spent they could barely move. Hatter quietly chuckled in her ear, almost panting "I've been wanting to try that with you for years."

ભ

45

Life was stabilizing for Rosie now. She'd been out of the hospital for a week and had even gone back to work at the library for the last couple days. She was spending time getting to know Janet again, and felt just as close to her now as they were when they were kids. Most nights she saw Hatter as she slept, and had made sure to wake so she didn't leave her body in the lurch again.

Rosie was able to spot Fey-born from a distance now, much better than she could at the height of her talent twelve years ago. Then, she had to get to know a person to feel if they were Fey-born, and it took time to figure out what kind of Fey was most dominant in them. Now, she knew who had Fey heritage and how strong it was within them as soon as they were close enough to see, and she could see what flavor of Fey they were just by looking closely. Rosie figured one in about twenty people had some Fey in them at most common places, like train stops and stores; but at the library it was more like one in ten, and of the Fey-born at the library more felt stronger. Rosie started to think of the strength of Fey in a person as shining brighter or dimmer, though she didn't see it visually as light, it felt like shining to Rosie.

Rosie's first day back at the library, she found that she had to be careful with touch. While checking out a book for a Fey-born, that radioed satyr to Rosie's special sense, she accidentally touched his hand. He saw her ethereal wings and freaked out, screaming and knocking over a book rack in his surprise. Rosie managed to convince her coworkers that he was someone she knew and a harmless college kid whose friends 'must have slipped him 'shrooms as a joke', but that he was a good kid and she should take him someplace private to ride it out. It was harder to calm the satyr down enough for a private word of explanation, especially because he hadn't known he was Fey-born before seeing Rosie's wings. The guy left disturbed, but with a whole new world opened to him. Rosie was sure she'd see him again, but was a little worried she wouldn't know how to do anything for the guy if he needed any kind of Fey help. She started wearing leather gloves after that, telling her coworkers that she'd contracted a skin infection in the hospital and the best treatment was to keep her hands covered. Rosie was sure most people didn't believe the infection line, but they were too polite to challenge her about why she was wearing gloves. She had been much more careful to avoid accidental skin contact after the first day back at work.

Now, it was her first relaxed Saturday completely to herself since waking from the coma. No doctors, not even Janet. No other Fey-born walking down the street around her that she had to be sure not to bump into. It was just her and her thoughts, and her apartment seemed so lonely now. Rosie used to be content to keep to herself and hide in the comfort of her solitude. But that was before she remembered, before she knew why she felt different, and most of all before Hatter was back in her life. She wished Hatter could be with her in more than just dreams. She wanted to take him to her favorite places and introduce him to the people in her waking life that were important to her. She wanted to snuggle on her couch and watch TV with him. She wanted to wake up in his arms without having to worry about throwing her body back into a coma.

Rosie reminded herself that she may not have him in the waking world, but life was so much better since she remembered Hatter. Better since she realized he was what had been missing from her life. She was in love, and felt complete. No more pining for something she couldn't quite put her finger on. When Hatter wasn't with her she knew who it was she was longing for now.

Rosie spent the morning doing mundane tasks, but her thoughts were anything but. She did her laundry and cleaned her place as she thought about how normal and un-magical the waking world was. There were Fey-born around most corners but they went through life not knowing their heritage or magical potential. In her dreams she had tangible wings visible to all, could heal people, and had a shape shifter boyfriend that was the love of her life. Rosie preferred her dreams.

Hatter could share his world with her, but Rosie couldn't share her world with Hatter and that saddened her. Rosie felt that if Hatter were here with her, in the waking world, that maybe there could be real magic here like in their dreams.

Thinking of Hatter made her miss him, even though she'd just seen him a half a day ago. 'Ah, new love.' She thought to herself. Knowing that when love was new, lovers usually couldn't get enough of each other. It was a meme in more books than she could remember reading. Despite the fact that Hatter was a creature of the dream worlds, it gave her comfort that love still worked the same no matter what world you came from.

Rosie dwelt on the thought of Hatter being a creature of the dream worlds. He'd said that he was Fey-born, meaning human with a mix of Fey heritage. He also had said that he had no body in the Prime Material, implying that he didn't belong to her world. Rosie kept wondering, how could he be Fey-born if humans came from the Prime Material? The way she understood it, Fey-born with the right talent could dream walk, going into other worlds using a form of astral projection. But there was always a body in the Prime Material. Rosie had dallied in Wonderland with Hatter for so long that her body here had started to fail, and if she hadn't woken up when she did she would have been on a feeding tube in days. Rosie pondered if Hatter might have a body somewhere in a deep coma for more than twelve years. What if he'd been in the dream worlds so long that he couldn't find his way back to his body, and had forgotten that it ever existed. She knew that he had forgotten a lot from when they were together as teenagers. She knew his memories were limited and he held onto memories of her by letting go of other memories. Rosie postulated that he'd need a physical brain to store more memories.

If he were a full blooded Fey, like the ones who hid in their own pocket world, he should be able to remember more wouldn't he? The Fey Rosie knew from childhood lived for thousands of years and remembered things personally that were lost to humanity. But as a Fey-born he would need to have a body, and if he forgot about that body it would probably leave him much like he was. Rosie decided to see what Hatter thought of her theory.

As Rosie cleaned, she cranked her favorite play list and danced around her apartment feeling happy and free at the thought of finding Hatter's body and waking it. Rosie might be the mild mannered librarian at work, but in the privacy of her home she was all rock. She thought of taking Hatter dancing, and had a hard time imagining it unless the image was of them alone dancing and clothing became optional. It struck Rosie that she didn't know what kind of music Hatter liked. She hoped that he would have similar tastes to hers, his usual attire did seem pretty rock 'n roll, so she had hope.

One of Rosie's favorite songs came on. It was a

song that got Rosie hot and bothered before her reunion with Hatter über revved up her sex drive, but now it was ten times sexier. Rosie remembered how Hatter had come to her in the Prime Material all those years ago, through insubstantial touches, before they really connected in dreams. In dreams she could see and feel Hatter, in the Prime Material it had been a struggle to feel more than his presence. But as Rosie passed a mirror and saw her wings, she wondered how much that had changed with her enhanced Fey abilities.

∞

Rosie finished up her chores as quickly as she could and got ready for a little test. Spending a few hours cleaning had left Rosie feeling sweaty and dirty, and after Hatter's long hot shower a few days ago she thought she'd like to try her test under some steamy wetness. Rosie set her speakers so the music filled the bathroom nicely. First she got thoroughly clean so she could enjoy the music and the water for fun not function. Once clean, she stepped out to queue up the play list she usually listened to when she was feeling especially randy, and slipped back into the shower.

With the start of the first song she stepped back under the hot water and psychically projected her show to Hatter. She smelled his intoxicating scent of musk and roses almost as soon as she started to dance under the pour of water. The water pounded hot against her skin with the heavy back beat of the song, and it felt deliciously primal deep in her core. She danced with the powerful slow rhythm of the drums, swinging her hips in slow undulations that moved up her body and ended in arms sweeping up through her hair. The water clung to her skin as it flowed down along gracefully swaying arms to slowly rolling shoulders and glided down the curves of her body. As the music gained momentum she sped her hip swings, rolling and popping her hips with the savage beat of the music. All the while mouthing the sexually explicit lyrics. Rosie projected the thought that 'sometimes belly dancing moves can be applied well to this flavor of fuck me music', and felt psychic agreement from her insubstantial lover.

Rosie ran her hands through her wet hair as she danced, then ran them slowly across her chest as her breasts heaved with her fluid movements. Rosie could feel Hatter's desire arrive ahead of his faint gliding touch wrapping around the curve of her waist, and pulling his invisible form tight against her back. Rosie rolled her body against the intangible feel and heat of Hatter standing behind her. She could feel his hard smoothness rub against her bottom, his manhood tickling the cleft where cheeks met back. Rosie moaned with his touch but continued to whisper the lyrics of the erotic music.

Hatter was deliciously overwhelmed with sensory input. Rosie projected mental images of them enacting the lyrics of the song to the beat of its music, as she danced like a water nymph in the hot spray of her shower, writhing against his astral body like she would if he were fully here in the Prime Material. He heard the lyrics of the song playing, but felt Rosie singing them to him. She placed a foot on the edge of her tub, opening herself to him physically as the lyrics begged him to feel her from the inside.

Hatter dropped to his knees before sliding invisibly under Rosie's dancing form. Rosie knew that Hatter had let go of her, but didn't know where he'd moved to till she felt his very dexterous tongue gliding between her nether lips. She cried out, feeling his tongue and the press of his face against her like he was there much more than intangibly. Her enticing dance forgotten, Rosie gripped the tiled wall to steady herself as the physical pleasure of him sucking her clit between periods of hard long licks washed over her with the water and music. She felt him grab her hips so he could really push against her hard, and it pushed her toward coming. He slid his tongue off her clit to tongue fuck her in hard quick thrusts while the tip of his nose tickled frustratingly close to her clit.

Rosie moaned, "Oh god Hatter, I'm so fucking close." And grabbed his head as she rocked against his jackhammer of a tongue, feeling him solidly between her legs. She tangled her fingers in his thick wavy hair, moaning in lust filled ecstasy as she pulled his head a little forward and adjusted the roll of her hips to get his tongue to slip up and down her, riding against her clit on each eager upswing. He used his tongue to taste her sweet honey pot while other senses tasted her building orgasm. He eagerly pleasured her orally as he slipped a hand between her thighs and inserted two fingers inside her, pumping it to the beat of the music. Rosie's receptors were filled with Hatter eating her to the music and thud of water against her back and ass. Rosie came so hard that her knees gave but Hatter held her weight.

Rosie felt Hatter slide out from under her as she regained her footing, but before she caught her breath he was touching her again. She felt his hands sliding up the back of her thighs, and the warm press of his lips against her bottom before he stood. She felt the heat of him standing behind her before his fingertips dug into her flesh groping her ass and grabbing her hips to pull her against him with a needful grunt. Hatter's fingertips trailed up her back and massaged into her shoulders as she felt his lips press against the side of her neck. She arched her back, pushing her ass against Hatter's impossibly solid feeling body.

She heard Hatter's growl of appreciation as she rubbed against him. Hatter gripped Rosie's shoulders to brace against her as they slipped against each other in the slick wetness of the shower. Rosie could feel Hatter's fingertips pressing into her skin, but couldn't even see a shadow of his physical presence. Once that would have freaked her out, but she had learned so much since then, and didn't need her eyes to confirm the touch of her lover now.

Rosie closed her eyes and concentrated on

Hatter's touch. Rosie was quickly recovering her energy as it matched her desire for Hatter. Rosie tilted her hips and again opened herself to Hatter physically and psychically. Instantly she knew that he could feel her desire in his echoed lust. His hands moved quickly, one to roughly caress her hip, the other to guide his manhood inside her. He felt deliciously thick and hard as he pushed inside her. At first he had to push hard because she was so tight from coming, but as soon as he was in, her natural lubrication made for a nice easy slide that begged for a slow build. So did the rhythm of the next song that began as he reached deep inside her.

Rosie moaned with each stroke and joyously pushed back to meet him. The angle of Hatter's penetration hit wonderful places deep inside her, and she couldn't help but squeeze his hard manhood as he slid into her so slowly and with such control. Hatter took his time building speed, loving her wetness and how she grabbed him from inside, her moans complimenting the slow sensual pace of the song.

With every stroke Hatter felt more solid crashing into Rosie, but so did Rosie's wings trembling with pleasure between them. Rosie pushed her palms against the cool tile wall, bracing her body so that Hatter could thrust deeper.

As he grabbed Rosie's hips, Hatter couldn't help but feel the bottom edges of her wings brushing his forearms. Hatter thought about how Rosie's wings looked like delicate dark blue cellophane stained glass, but they had proven to be strong and flexible. He could see that her wings were connected much like arms, with strong small almost shoulder like joints directly over Rosie's shoulder blades. It gave Hatter a naughty idea that truly excited him.

Hatter slowed his pace, sliding his hands up Rosie's sides behind her lovely wings. Fingertips caressingly lingering on the sides of Rosie's breasts before grabbing her shoulders forcefully with a hard fast thrust inside her to match. Rosie cried out, writhing joyously. Hatter rotated his arms like he was curling weights and grabbed the top edges of her wings close to the joint. Hatter pulled Rosie tight against him with a masculine grunt of satisfaction.

The tug against her wings and his chest firmly pressed against her back and wings heightened Rosie's pleasure and made her squirm to fuck Hatter faster. He inhaled her scent, so strong at the crook of her neck, and gave in to a beastly want. He bit her neck hard enough to feel her flesh against his teeth, but not hard enough to draw blood. His thrusting hips showed none of the restraint of his mouth, and pounded into Rosie hard and fast.

Rosie cried out to the heavens, building quickly to another orgasm. She felt Hatter building with her, and it heightened her pleasure to the tipping point as they both rode the wave of ecstasy to orgasm. As Rosie came her wings curled back around Hatter's biceps and crossed his back so that the tip of each wing cupped his tight ass. The caress of Rosie's wings made Hatter cum even harder, and he threw his head back in a guttural scream to avoid biting down too hard into her tender flesh.

Their orgasmic releases used so much energy that neither of them could hold Hatter's form solid in the Prime Material any longer, and his touch dissipated to the whisper of an idea in the afterglow before fading entirely from Rosie's tactile senses. Rosie slid down to her knees and sat in the tub with the water pounding on her back while the next song from her play list offered to take a ride with her through her world. Rosie thought to herself that the ride they'd just taken through her world was something she bet no other person in living memory could have taken. She felt Hatter's strong, safe presence around her, and was happy and content in the euphoria of their afterglow.

A thought struck Rosie and she laughed out loud. "Boy," she said wryly, "the lengths some men will go to avoid snuggling after sex." Rosie could feel Hatter's amusement and his wish to be holding her now. "I love you too Hatter. But I want my snuggles tonight after more play in my dreams." Rosie couldn't help but smile.

Hatter was spent. It took a lot of energy to express himself in Rosie's world, even tho Rosie had used a lot of her power too, to make him solid, Hatter had still used more than he could recover from quickly .

He whispered in Rosie's mind before retreating out of the Prime Material to rest. "I do love you, my delicious Rose." He thought in her mind, still tasting her skin and her sweet nether nectar on his tongue. "I'll have to go rest up so we can play tonight. I promise to set you a sensual scene with some brilliant sex and satisfying cuddles after."

Rosie felt the faintest brush of sensation against her lips and knew it was a goodbye kiss as Hatter's presence faded. She felt like the luckiest woman in the world to have been reunited with Hatter. Her life had changed so much in the last couple weeks, and she really liked the direction it was taking.

◌

46

After a relaxing amount of recovery time, Rosie cleaned up and got dressed. Following her successful test of their increased talents, Rosie was more determined to find a more concrete way to be with Hatter in the waking world. Today, Rosie finally had time to retrieve her box of high school memorabilia from the back corner of her closet. She hadn't opened the box since before she left for college, but now understood why she kept it anyway. She knew the box held her journal and sketchbook, and felt deep down that the books held the key to finding Hatter. A closet dig later, Rosie sat the old beat up box on her coffee table and opened the old packing tape with a pen that happened to be close at hand. Despite it having been sealed, the contents of the box smelled dusty. Inside she found many treasures from her past, but the treasures she wanted were her little red leather bound journal and her old sketch pad. She set everything else aside, and pulled them out.

First she flipped through the drawings, and had to linger on the ones of a hot teenaged Hatter. She noted that he was broader in the shoulders now, and looked somehow more finished in the face. She decided that he was hot then, but drop dead gorgeous now. She was sure she would love Hatter no matter how he looked, but was pretty happy that he looked the way he did. Flipping back and forth she found a chunk of six pages that would have been from the year she met Hatter.

She paged back through her sketches and stopped at the first one. A drawing of the stained glass window in the center of the hedge maze. She was sure, if he had a body in the waking world, it was definitely a clue. The drawing of the window looked like a family shield, but it wasn't one she could remember seeing outside of the hedge maze. Her colored pencil drawing had a dark blue shield with three golden yellow tied bundles of wheat, two at the top and one centered at the bottom. The three wheat sheaves were separated by an upside down v of the same golden yellow. There was a scrolling blue ribbon above the shield with a note in the margin of the sheet that there had been writing on the ribbon. Probably a family motto in Latin, she thought that it would be a common arrangement for a coat of arms like this. Above that was a knights helmet, and above that a small stag in the same golden yellow. Rosie was sure if she looked online she could find what family the shield belonged to.

The next page was a sketch of a dark room seen through the window, she hadn't remembered this image until she saw it, and now it seemed to confirm her suspicion that it was showing the room where Hatter's body was. It was a posh bedroom with a bed much like the one she knew Hatter still slept in, in Wonderland, and an IV and monitoring equipment that trailed tubes behind the beds heavy red curtains. The sketch of the room didn't give her any real clues to where he was geographically, but it somehow made her happy that it looked like he was well cared for in a home setting instead of a impersonal hospital.

The third sketch showed a landscape, Rosie assumed it was the view from the room in the previous sketch. There was a meadow with cows and softly rolling hills fading into a wooded area. This told Rosie he was likely in the country, but not a whole lot more. As far as she knew England was full of rolling hills.

The next page held a sketch of one of her nightmare monster's claw-like hands. The two pages after that were drawings of Hatter. The first one was just his mouth and eyes, she'd managed to capture his playful smile and remembered being proud of that. The second was his bare upper body. She remembered that at the time she'd drawn it, she hadn't seen Hatter without his shirt on, but in hind sight she had definitely gotten it right. It made her wonder how much her expectation of Hatter colored his appearance. He was psychically linked to Rosie and had really good control of his shifting abilities, it wouldn't be too hard for Hatter to adjust his appearance to her desires. She thought that Hatter might have even made subconscious alterations to his appearance because of their connection. Then she dismissed the thought as being a little too narcissistic.

The first three pages were much more helpful than the next three, but the last two were really fun for Rosie to look at. She put down her sketch book, and pulled out her tablet. She did a web search for English coats of arms, and then searched for wheat sheaves on the British heraldry site the search led her to. A few minutes later she was looking at a coat of arms that matched the stained glass from the hedge maze, and the name it went with totally floored Rosie. It was the shield for Hatton.

Rosie was sure the name being so close to Hatter was no coincidence. Her suspicion that Hatter could have been a nickname seemed almost definite, especially with Hatter's admitted memory issues. Rosie continued her research into the name and found that the family came from Cheshire county. Rosie laughed out loud to herself when she wondered how many other Alice in Wonderland references would to go along with this search. Suddenly the books seemed so plausible; and if it was, at least one of Hatter's ancestors were likely part of a little girls dream walking experience.

As Rosie read more, the next probable link to Hatter wasn't a reference to Wonderland, but his Fey-born gift. According to a wiki on Cheshire England, in 1069 the earl of Chester was nicknamed Lupis or 'the wolf'. Rosie would bet that this Earl was an ancestor of Hatter's, and that his nickname must have been referring to their shape shifting heritage. Rosie played in her mind with the name she'd found, Mr. Hatton from Cheshire county England. It had a true ring to it, and she hoped her instincts were right.

Rosie was excited by the hope of waking her love and being able to share their lives together, for real, not just in dreams. It felt like things were really coming together for Rosie. Just a few pages of a sketch book and Rosie had a probable surname and possible location for Hatter. She wondered if there were any other important bits of info her subconscious had her tuck away in this box. Rosie rummaged in the box for any other clues that might help her find Hatter's body.

She didn't find anything to help find his body, but she did find a small box full of something that would probably help his body once she found him. In the little box were all the supplies to make the protection amulets that had saved her and her friends' lives all those years ago. Rosie remembered that part of the amulet's magic was to bring the spirit back to the body unscathed, and

Rosie couldn't imagine a better use for that than to wake Hatter from a very long sleep. The Fey that trained Rosie, and hid the information from her conscious mind, were always telling Rosie that she would remember when the time was right. Hatter had trained with the same Fey after Rosie could no longer get to them, teaching him to make those amulets. She had an inkling that part of Kiri's reason to teach Hatter how to make this amulet was to help wake him 'when the time was right'.

Rosie grabbed her journal and popped the little brass lock before flipping excitedly through the pages to find her notes on amulet construction. She skimmed through the content until she was almost at her last entry, and there it was, detailed instructions complete with measurements and illustrations. Rosie set down the journal and weighted the pages open like she would a cook book. She laid out the contents of the small box of supplies, and was happy to find she had enough to make more than one amulet. When they'd all made their amulets together they made extra crystals and pouches since they were the parts that would need to be replaced if they took damage. Too bad they'd all taken too much damage to remember about protection amulets back then. Or, Rosie thought, maybe it was her current good fortune that the supplies were available now.

Rosie knew what she was going to spend the rest of the day doing. She was going to make two amulets, one for her and one for Hatter's body when she found it. Rosie grabbed a pen and a piece of paper, then went through the ingredients carefully to see what she'd need to replace. She knew she'd at the least need to make new anointing oil, and she'd have to stop at a florist for the rosebuds and the lily-of-the-valley leaves.

She thought about trying to find if there were any matching coma victims with the last name Hatton, but the thought struck her that maybe she better talk to Hatter first. Find out if Hatton was a name that sparked any memories. It was possible he was a true creature of the dream worlds, and all she'd found online was coincidence. If she got her hopes up too much that he did have a body in the Prime Material, and he turned out to be a being of the dream worlds, it would be harder to accept that she would never be able to really touch him in her waking world. So she was caught between hope and caution, and decided she would talk to Hatter about it that night. An extra amulet, just in case, seemed to be a good idea either way. If Hatter had no body to put it on, she'd give it to Janet.

Rosie noted what she'd need, and ran out for supplies. Rosie really hoped that Hatter was a Fey-born, and that she could reunite him with his body. He had been her guardian angel so many times, she really wanted to save him this time. It would be nice to feel like a little bit of a hero to the man that had repeatedly given everything to be her hero.

☙

That night Hatter made good on his promise of more brilliant sex. He played a very sexy wolf-man drawn to the scent of Rosie in bed. Rosie enjoyed his selective shape changing, especially his long dexterous tongue, so much that she almost lost track of talking to Hatter. After screaming mutual orgasms they lay in the bed Hatter's imagination had created for their play and cuddled bonelessly.

"Thanks" Hatter breathed sleepily with a satisfied grin. Rosie wiggled tighter against him, and in response Hatter wrapped his arms more securely around her. Feeling the warmth of her skin so near his lips, he kissed the nape of her neck; gently eliciting a soft happy sigh from his lover.

Now that Hatters wolf-man fantasy had played out so deliciously, Rosie decided to try to broach the subject of her hopes about Hatter having a body somewhere in a coma. "I've been thinking about seeing you when I'm awake."

"Yeah," he said wistfully, "I wish that we could," Hatter sighed sounding drowsy and content, "but I can't fully manifest myself in the Prime Material. Partial manifestation is even tough to maintain long."

"But what if we could really be together in the waking world?"

"That would be brilliant. But Rose, I'm sleepy now. Can we talk about this after some rest? You really tired me out earlier today, and just now." As they spooned, Rosie could feel Hatter sleepily grinning, even without seeing his face. "Not that I'm complaining, just really tired."

"I guess so." Rosie sighed and snuggled into Hatter's strong arms. Soon they both drifted off into a restful sleep within their shared dream, contently tangled in each other's arms.

☙

47

Rosie woke with a start and an odd sensation of loss. She looked at the clock and saw it was still the middle of the night. She wasn't usually the type to wake up less than half way through the night, especially when she was with Hatter. A strange fear crawled up her spine and she instinctively reached for Hatter through their connection. That was when she realized what was missing, she couldn't feel Hatter. She tried harder to reach him but it was like she was flailing some psychic arm into the darkness and found nothing there. In panic she pushed even harder, and felt something weak and tentative. It was like a whisper in her mind, a confusion of lust and desire mixed with love and longing. It was the barest brush of a disoriented Hatter, then his presence faded.

Rosie panicked, something had just gone very wrong and she didn't understand what it was. This wasn't the most conducive emotion for falling asleep, but she needed to get to Wonderland and find out what happened; and to find where Hatter was. She lay back in her bed and fought to calm her body, taking deep slow breaths and trying to will her pulse to slow. It wasn't working. While dream walking she could close her eyes and wake with a force of will, falling asleep from a panicked state was very different. She was so terrified that something awful had happened to Hatter that she couldn't possibly suppress her distress and fall back asleep.

She thought to herself, 'desperate times call for desperate measures' and decided to hold her breath till she passed out and hoped she would dream once unconscious. It was fast thinking, and Rosie felt that speed mattered. She also hoped her rash choice wouldn't be a mistake, but if Hatter was in distress Rosie would go through anything to save him.

As she held her breath she realized it was much harder to not breathe than she'd known, but her need to find Hatter was stronger than the urge to breathe. Her lungs burned and her head began to pound as she struggled not to take gulps of air. It seemed to be taking forever, and her lungs felt like they were going to explode. But, after what felt like an impossibly long time, her head started to swim and black spots exploded in her vision. Then she was out cold, but her body involuntarily gasped in air and started breathing.

೦౩

Rosie opened her eyes, and found herself sitting in Hatter's big red wing backed chair. His tea party scene spread in front of her, but no sign of him. Her head was still killing her from holding her breath, but she forced herself to stand on wobbly legs. Rosie took a couple deep breaths and tried to clear her head so she could orient herself.

Right away, Rosie headed for the hedge maze. She remembered where it was from their recent week together, and ran to find it. From the outside, the hedge maze was just like it had been when she found her way to the middle as a teenager. But a gusting wind kicked up as she stepped inside the labyrinth, tossing loose twigs and straw through the air and often into Rosie. She continued further into the maze, feeling sure she would find something significant in the middle of the maze. She kept following one side of the hedge and only turned left, knowing that it would eventually get her to the center.

As Rosie moved towards the stained glass window the winds grew more intense, almost blowing her off her feet more than once. The debris also got bigger, twigs ripped from the bushes stinging her face and arms, leaving little bloody scratches. It felt like she was walking into a tornado, and she just knew that the center of the maze was the eye of the storm.

She pushed through, using the sturdier limbs of the maze to not only help her forward but to keep her from being flung out of the maze. Then, as things in dreams often do, the things being flung at her changed. The wind itself took on colors, making it harder to see where she was going. She was nearly blinded by bright reds, vivid greens, garish yellows, and thick dark blues and purples, that all shoved and spun her like the wind was trying to disorient her intentionally. Then something small flashed white in her vision and sliced into her cheek painfully.

In Rosie's frantic need to find Hatter she had only one drive, to get to the window, but the pain of the deep scratch reminded her that she needed to protect herself too. She manifested a white light shield a heartbeat before another flash of white struck her in the arm, this time it bounced off harmlessly. She continued to inch in towards the center of the maze, and the white bits of debris started coming more frequently. One of the white things hit her shield and was trapped against her for a second by the colored winds and Rosie realized what was hitting her were playing cards. If she weren't fighting to save Hatter the cliché would have made her laugh.

As she turned a corner the cards flying at her grew larger and the edges glinted in the light like metal, she was also pretty sure that the faces were baring their teeth at her menacingly, but despite the sharper edges they couldn't break through Rosie's shield. She pushed onward and despite losing her footing a couple times she slowly continued towards the center.

Around another turn a new type of debris flew at her mixed with the Chinese throwing star like cards. Now large cut flowers pelted her too, but they weren't like flowers from her waking world, the center of each flower was a round mouth with rows of shark like pointy teeth. Rosie kept her focus up for her shield, but the little mouths locked onto the white light itself and began to drain it, kind of like bright colorful pretty leaches. Rosie put more energy into her shield, but knew that if she didn't get to the eye of this storm soon the flowers would drain it away and she'd have to rely on her new amulet to save her.

Despite the deterrents being thrown at her, Rosie couldn't give up. She redoubled her efforts to move forward, and a few challenging minutes later she could see the clearing in the center of the maze. Through the color tornado it was hard to make much out, but one thing was clear, nothing in the clearing was moving.

Rosie pushed into the eye of the storm and with a good amount of effort pulled all the leach flowers off her. Her nearly depleted shield flickered and failed with the last flower being disengaged. Rosie was exhausted and sore, but she'd made it. As Rosie caught her breath, the tornado outside vanished in a wisp of colored light and glinting metal edged cards.

She looked at the clearing and saw the stained glass window with the Hatton coat of arms just like it had been the last time she was here except for one thing. Rosie noticed something in the well manicured grass below the impossibly hanging window. She moved to it and looked more closely. It was the amulet she'd worn all those years ago. It was burnt out, the linen bag was a charred mess, the amber and quartz were cracked and blackened as well, even the silver star was a little melted to itself.

Rosie reflexively touched the new amulet she wore around her neck, and saw that it was still intact. She wondered if she woke without healing all the little scrapes and bruises, would the amulets linen bag be spent like this one. She was sure the rest of it would be intact, the damage from this mazes defenses were nothing in comparison to what the nightmare monster and Jack had done to her.

She stood and looked around the clearing, hoping that she would find Hatter curled up in a shadow like she had last time. But Rosie was the only person standing in the center of the maze. She looked back at the window and knew it was early morning where the window looked. She saw the rolling meadows and old trees, but it was the other side of the window that interested her more.

♋

Looking through, she saw the room with the four poster canopy bed, but it wasn't as still as it had been last time. Two people in lab coats were working solemnly over the bed, blocking her view even though the curtains were open. A petite young woman, with an uncanny resemblance to Hatter, stood off to the side leaning against a tall dark haired man who stroked her arm comfortingly as tears rolled down her cheeks. But Rosie gave the couple no more notice, she needed to know what was happening to Hatter.

Rosie was sure that Hatter was in the bed beyond the doctors, they were doing something and it frustrated Rosie that she couldn't see what it was. Then it struck her, Rosie was in Wonderland looking out onto the real world, why not see if she could crawl through the window like Alice had the looking glass in the story. She tested her theory by putting a hand to the glass, and as she'd hoped, her fingers pushed through. Rosie quickly crawled through the stained glass window without a scratch. It was like moving through a very thin, but very firm layer of jello.

When she got to the other side no one reacted to her, so she guessed she was as invisible to them as Hatter was when he came to her in her waking world. Her skin burned like she'd spent too much time in the sun, and Rosie guessed that it was what Hatter felt every time he had come to her waking world. She smelled Hatter's scent clearly, knowing that some of the smell came from the bouquet of roses sitting on a nearby table, but not all of it.

The crying woman shivered as Rosie stood and started towards the bed. Being in the same room, it was clear to Rosie that the woman was a shifter like Hatter, and the man was some woodsy kind of Fey-born. The woman alertly looked around the room and sniffed the air, not seeing Rosie but aware of something. She looked to the tall man who smiled reassuringly and brushed a lock of hair out of her eyes before wrapping the small woman in his arms. Though she was sure he couldn't actually see her, Rosie felt it as the man looked through her with a wary expression. Rosie's mind quickly filed that information away for later. Under other circumstances Rosie would have been interested in trying to communicate with them, but now all that mattered to her was Hatter.

The medical professionals were slowly pulling something with a long tube out of him, Rosie guessed it was a feeding tube. She rushed to his side, moving through the doctors like she was a ghost, and grabbed his hand in a panic, but her fingers whiffed through Hatter's hand too. Rosie looked down at Hatter through tear blurred eyes and tried to hold his hand again, this time she moved more slowly and deliberately willing her hand to be solid for him.

This time she felt his skin, but his hands were

cool to the touch and boney, so different from his seeming in their dreams. Rosie could feel his presence faintly, but it was a fragile and tentative thing. She willed Hatter to feel her and know she was here with him, and was rewarded with the slightest momentary squeeze from his hand.

"Hey, did you just see that?" One of the doctors commented, sounding puzzled. He had a British accent, similar to Hatter's. "It looked like his hand just flexed a little."

"Probably just a muscle twitch, I wouldn't read too much into it." The other doctor commented quietly. "We don't want to get anyone's hopes up. Her grandmother was convinced that he'd be waking up, now that she's gone there's no need to drag this on longer."

The young woman stepped away from her companion's embrace and came closer to the bed. "Don't worry. Our grandmother lived in hope for the last fifteen years, taking every minute incident as a sign of him waking soon. I know that the body has responses not driven by will, and I'd rather let him move on than keep his body alive for a one in a billion chance." The woman's accent was like the doctors, but there was a quality to her voice beyond accent that tugged at Rosie's heart. Her voice was so like Hatter's, if it had been an octave lower it would have been almost indistinguishable.

"Of course, my apologies miss." Responded the first doctor. "I think we're done here. The feeding tube and oxygen mask have been removed, and so has the IV. He's breathing shallowly on his own, but I don't expect that to last too long. Would you like a few minutes alone with him before he passes?"

Rosie was filled with a heightened sense of panic. "No! He's still in there! Put him back on life support!" She screamed, but no one heard her. Rosie turned to the love of her life slipping away. "Hatter, please hold on. I'll figure this out. Don't die on me.

Please. I love you. And I need you to hold on for me."
Still no one responded to Rosie's insubstantial pleas.

The tall man was looking in Rosie's direction but
said nothing if he could in any way sense her. Hatter's
relative shivered as Rosie pleaded, but gave no other
sign that she was aware of Rosie. "Yes, I think I would
like a few moments with him."

Rosie turned to the woman as the doctors left the
room taking armfuls of medical equipment with them.
"Can you hear me? Please hear me. Don't let him die!"
Rosie pushed as hard as she could and tried to grab the
woman's arm.

The woman that looked so like Hatter shivered
again. "I guess death is bound to give anyone the heebie-
jeebies." She said quietly, reaching for her friend's hand,
and taking obvious comfort in the touch. He kissed her
hand and gave her a sad smile before following the
doctors out of the room.

As the room emptied Rosie really looked at
Hatter, and saw a very different physical version of the
man of her dreams. He was thin and paler, with a sunken
chest. Rosie was shocked at how atrophied his muscles
were. She looked at him, and appearance didn't matter,
she loved him desperately and would do whatever it took
to save her soul mate. Now that she'd found him again
she wasn't sure she could live without him.

When the woman was alone she turned to Hatter.
"I wish you could have been around to know the person I
grew up into, I'm not the same annoying little brat
anymore."

"Please Hatter, hold on for me. I will find a way
to get to you and let them know you are still in there."
Rosie bent to kiss Hatter carefully, and knew that she
didn't have much time, he was fading away as she
brushed against his soft lips. They were still Hatter's lips,
but his spirit was starting to let go. "I will find you." She
confirmed as she let go of his hand and ran for the
stained glass window. She heard the woman speaking to

Hatter as she pushed her way through the glass and back into Wonderland. "I know I should get the cousins to say their goodbyes, but I just need a little more time-"

Rosie fell onto the soft lawn as she tumbled through the window. She stumbled, getting untangled as she started to run out of the hedge maze, before she realized that she could just wake up.

☙

48

Rosie woke in a panic with a pounding headache. Hatter was gone, and she didn't have nearly enough time to find him and make sure he would be safe. She reached for her tablet sitting on her bed side table, she shook with anxiety as she impatiently turned it on. It's clock told her that it was four am., not more than a half an hour since the last time she woke up.

As a librarian, Rosie was at an advantage, research was in her wheelhouse. Fast accurate Internet searches were second nature to her. She jumped online and started by searching for news articles about people in long term comas in the British isles. In minutes she was sure she found him, but wished she hadn't as she read the article she'd found.

Rosie found a story, dated the day before, about a rural noble woman who had passed recently. The woman's name was Mary Hatton, and Rosie's stomach knotted, finding the name belonging to the stained glass crest in Wonderland. The article stated that the woman left her estate to her granddaughter Sarah, but that she was also survived by her grandson, Wolfric, who had been in a coma for the past fifteen years. Rosie thought, 'Wolfric Hatton has to be my Hatter.'

Digging a little more, Rosie found that Wolfric Hatton had been in a vegetative state for over fifteen years, and despite the agreement of several private doctors that he would likely never wake, the family was keeping him alive at the grandmother's insistence. With her passing, the family had decided to remove the twenty eight year old from life support. The article ended with the information that the family planned to pull the plug before the funeral so that extended family could say goodbye to both family members.

According to the story the funeral was happening the next day, but the article was dated yesterday. Rosie felt panic as she did the math for time zones, England was six hours ahead, and realized that Hatter's disappearance correlated to the morning of the funeral. Of all the stories she'd found, this one seemed to hold too many coincidences to not be her Hatter. She felt he was the right coma patient, and was too frightened of loosing Hatter to doubt her gut.

Rosie worked frantically to find a contact number for Sarah Hatton of Cheshire England, and soon found one. She dialed the number before she had thought about what she would say to the woman that was likely Hatter's sister.

"Hello?" The voice of the woman who answered sounded like she could be the woman in the room through the window in Wonderland.

"Hi, is this Sarah Hatton?" Rosie asked nervously.

"Speaking." Sarah replied warily.

"Hi." Rosie repeated her greeting nervously then froze for a moment, afraid of spooking this complete stranger and not being able to help Hatter. But with time already run out, she didn't have time to do anything but be direct. "I don't know how to say this, but please, please, reconnect the life support on your brother."

"I don't know who this is, or what you're playing at, but you're sick calling me about Wolfric." Sarah sounded pissed, in the American way not the British. "My brother has been in a coma and unresponsive for over half his life. If this is some religious plea, I don't think god would want him to be kept alive when he's not going to wake up." Rosie heard the click and abrupt silence of being hung up on.

"Hello? Hello? Are you there?" Rosie repeated hoping that Sarah hadn't hung up. When she got no answer, Rosie flipped off her phone, gave it a second to disconnect, and redialed the number. It rang several times before she heard it pick up. "Hello. Please, don't hang up. I have information about your brother, please. I think I can wake him up."

A few silent seconds passed as Rosie listened to the person on the other end breathing thickly like she was silently crying, or angry, or both. "Who are you? And what do you know about my brother?" The anger had sunk back to skepticism.

"My name is Rosie, and I'm a friend of your brother. I know you just took him off life support, but I know his spirit is still very much alive. Or was very recently. Please, please turn the machines back on. You need to get him breathing and oxygen to his brain before it's too late." She pleaded, not caring how crazy she sounded and whispered quietly to herself "Please, Hatter, hold on. Don't die."

"Look, whoever you are, Wolfric didn't have any American friends I ever heard of. And even if you were his friend when he was a kid, I haven't heard anything about an American trying to contact him in all the years since the accident. So I doubt you're a friend, now sod off, lunatic." And the phone clicked dead.

Rosie dialed the number again, but this time it picked up more quickly. "Please. Please. Don't hang up. This isn't a prank, or a religious thing. I swear. Just please revive him. Please!" Rosie was trying to hold it together, but she had started to cry uncontrollably and it was audible in her voice.

The voice that answered Rosie sounded shaken. "Just before I hung up a second ago, at the end of you talking, what did you whisper?"

Rosie hesitated, afraid of making things worse, but tried to explain herself. "I guess I was talking to your brother. I know he's there with you, but," Rosie sighed heavily, "I was begging him to hold on."

"But, what did you call him?" Sarah asked, sounding extremely cautious.

"Hatter. I called him Hatter." Rosie said, wiping her eyes, and hoping.

"His school friends called him that." Sarah said almost numbly, then took a shaky breath, and continued with steel in her tone. "If this is a con, so help me."

"No. Please. This is no con. Please put him back on life support, before it's too late."

"Why? What do you know that a hoard of doctors and specialists don't?"

"I know he can wake up. I know, if you keep him alive, he can wake up. I can wake him up." Rosie believed what she said, and Sarah could hear her conviction. "Please. Get him back on life support, and give me enough time to take the first flight out. I'll reimburse you for all the medical expenses of reviving him and keeping him alive till I get there if I'm wrong. But I know I can do it. I can't lose him again."

"You aren't shittin' me, are you?" Sarah was starting to hope the crazy American was being earnest. "Why do you think you can wake Wolfric?"

"It'll take a long time to explain, and we don't have time for long. so, I'll be the first to admit that it might sound crazy. But I swear, your brother and I have a connection and I just know that I can wake him. Please. I only found him just now, please don't let me be too late. Hatter saved my life more than once, help me return the favor. He's been lost in dreams, but I know I can guide him back to his body." Rosie waned to crawl out of her skin as she waited for another click or for Sarah to respond.

A moment later Sarah responded in a slow cautious voice. "Our grandmother said that. Every time the doctors said the chances of him waking were impossible, she'd say he was just lost on his dreams and he'd find his way home if we gave him the time..." Sarah was clearly spooked, but she took a steadying breath and found a bit of back bone. "The doctors are still here. Call back in an hour, and I'll tell you if we got him stable."

"Thank you." Rosie exhaled with relief, and felt like she could breathe for the first time since she was jarred into wakefulness at the loss of Hatters connection.

ଔ

The phone clicked, and Rosie waited impatiently. She sat in front of the nearest clock, waiting for the hour to pass. She sat very still for what felt like a long time, and hoped with every cell in her body that Hatter wasn't dead for good. She prayed that the doctor would be able to get him stable because she didn't know how she could live without him now. She hoped that fate wouldn't be so cruel; to bring them back together only to take him away. Her heart would break for good if he died before she ever got to look into his dreamy brown eyes while they were both awake. She hoped her life was more of a romantic comedy than a drama. Rosie thought to herself, 'as long as my life is like a rom-com Hatter will live. Please life, be a rom-com just this once.'

Rosie couldn't take the clock watching any more, it had been ten minutes since she hung up with Hatter's sister, but felt like a lifetime to not know if Hatter was alive or dead. She had to do something or she'd break down and be no good to anyone. So she decided to spend the rest of the hour packing a bag and finding tickets to England online.

She packed a couple changes of clothes in a carry on, then panicked when she couldn't find her passport right away. After tearing her bedroom apart, she finally found it and packed it in her carry on along with the amulet for Hatter and a couple books for the flight. She hesitated before ordering the tickets, but figured that she needed to go see her Hatter now, no matter what the outcome. Either they would be reunited, or she would be attending his funeral. She bought herself a one way ticket to Liverpool's John Lennon Airport as tears streamed down her cheeks. Based on the article about Hatter's grandmother, Rosie was pretty sure that Liverpool was the closest city she could get to by plane, then reserved a car at the airport to take her the rest of the way.

Rosie had held it together as best she could, but the thought of seeing Hatter's body lifeless was too much for Rosie, and she crumpled to the floor sobbing. It only reminded her of all the times Hatter was there for her when she was distraught, and she longed to feel his calm and safe presence now, but found nothing but an empty ache.

She cried until her tears ran dry, and numbly got up off the floor. Rosie went back to her computer and sent an email to her boss letting her know that she would be taking another week off, connected to her recent coma and her recovery. She left it vague, but firm. She was sorry for the late notice, but it was a matter that could not wait.

Rosie looked at the clock again and wondered how time could go so slow when she needed it to go a little faster. She still had ten minutes to go, so Rosie sent an email to Janet. The email said that she'd found Hatter but that his coma had been going on for fifteen years, and that she hoped she wasn't too late to save him because his family had just taken him off life support before she got threw. She added that she would call to update her tomorrow after her plane landed in England.

Rosie watched the last couple minutes tick by, phone in hand, before she could punch Sarah's number back into her phone. She called with a minute left to go because she just couldn't wait any longer. She needed to know if they had managed to get Hatter stable again, or if they were too late. She hit send and impatiently waited as the phone rang.

"Hello." Sarah's voice sounded hopeful and Rosie was able to breathe again.

"So, then it worked? Is Hatter stable?" Rosie blurted out with hope in her voice too.

"The doctor said we changed our minds just in time. They've been stabilizing him for the better part of the last hour, but he's mostly back to where he was before they took him off life support."

"Mostly?" Rosie asked with a tremor of fear clear in her voice.

"They didn't put the feeding tube back in." Sarah hesitated, "I told them a specialist had contacted me from America, and that she wanted to try an alternative therapy that had a chance of waking him. I really hope you can do it, or I am likely to sue you for emotional trauma, like you Americans tend to."

Rosie let the threat of a lawsuit slide off her back. "Oh, thank god. I don't know what I would have done if they weren't able to get him stable." She took a couple deep breaths and sent gratitude to whatever powers that be that had kept Hatter alive.

"So," Sarah began, again sounding wary. "Now that Wolfric is stable, I think I deserve a little more of an explanation. How exactly do you know my brother and why do you think you can wake him?"

Now that her panic was ebbing Rosie was suddenly unsure how exactly to explain how or why. Then she thought of the woman crying at Hatter's bedside and knew how to start. "This will be hard to believe, but if you keep an open mind it will all make sense."

Sarah cleared her throat, "Ok, open mind." Rosie just wished Sarah sounded as open as her words said.

Rosie spoke slowly and cautiously, "When the doctors were taking Hatter off life support, you felt something in the room. And you smelled something. Then the doctors mentioned a hand twitch. Right?"

"How?" Sarah sounded on edge, but took a breath and continued. "Right, open mind. Yes, I remember all that, it happened an hour and a half ago.

Are you some kind of psychic?"

"Um," Rosie wasn't sure how to answer Sarah's question, but did her best. "Sort of. But not like the kind you'd find with a crystal ball." She took another breath and continued. "I was there. Astrally, I think."

"Excuse me?" Sara said in disbelief. "You think you were there?"

"No, I know I was there. I'm just not sure if astral projection is the right term for how I got there."

"I'm not sure I'm following." Sarah seemed to be less convinced of Rosie's sanity than moments ago.

"What I'm trying to tell you is that your grandmother was right." Rosie thought there was no way to explain the next bit without sounding mad, so she went for it. "Hatter was lost in his dreams. He's been living and traveling through people's dreams since before I met him twelve years ago."

"But Wolfric was already in a coma for three years, twelve years ago." Sarah stressed his given name, and Rosie wondered if Hatter was a nickname she didn't like.

"That's what I'm trying to explain. Your brother found me when he was," Rosie paused not sure which term to use, "we'll, I had been calling it dream walking, but Hatter, sorry Wolfric, called it traveling the worlds. He taught me about how to find stable worlds and how to skip through people's dreams. He had been traveling the worlds for years when I met him, and he'd forgotten he even had a body in the waking world by then. It was only recently that I figured out he might have a body here, when I slipped into a coma myself. Is this making any sense or do I sound like I'm bat shit crazy?"

"You are sounding like you're off your rocker." Sarah confirmed, "But, you did know pretty specific details about when we were taking Wolfric off of life support. So, I'm still listening." She didn't sound convinced, but she wasn't hanging up on Rosie either.

"I'm sorry, I know it sounds crazy, but I swear

it's the truth. Your brother and I are dream walkers, and we were together when we were teenagers. We got separated when he saved my life twelve years ago, and we just found each other again a couple weeks ago."

"And you realized he might be in a coma when you were in a coma?" Sara asked still a little unclear.

"More like when I woke from the coma. When we found each other again, we lost track of time while we were," Rosie hoped her blush was not evident over the phone, "getting to know each other again."

"So, what I'm supposed to believe is that you lost track of time while you were shagging my brother in a dream and then woke up from a coma." Sarah's tone was cynical and sounded dry in a way exaggerated by the British accent.

"Yup. Pretty much." Rosie said uncomfortably. "When I woke up in the hospital and found out I'd been in a coma for a week, I started putting the pieces together about your brother. When you stay in dreams too long you start to forget things, and I was pretty sure he had just forgotten that he once had a body. Yesterday I put some clues together from when we were teenagers. I figured out he was a Hatton from the stained glass window with the coat of arms that's in his room, cause it's in Wonderland too. The one in Wonderland is a portal to his room, and I went through it to find him when he went missing. That's when I saw you crying and him being taken off life support by those two doctors. When they noticed his hand twitch, it was him responding to me trying to hold his hand. I tried to touch your arm too, because you seemed to be at least a little aware of something in the room. But I couldn't communicate with you there, so I woke up and did some frantic research online till I found a number for you. And here we are." Rosie took a breath and waited for Sarah to respond.

A few long moments later Sarah responded. "I'm still not sure you aren't trying to con me somehow, but I'm not sure how, so I guess I'll believe you for now. Do you want money for coming and trying to wake him?"

"No." Rosie was a little hurt by the accusation, but understood how crazy her story sounded and would probably react similarly in Sarah's shoes. "Of course I don't want any money. I want to wake up your brother so he can remember who he is the way he helped me to remember what I lost over the last twelve years. Hatter literally saved my life more than once, I just want to return the favor." Rosie was tempted to tell Sarah that she loved Hatter, but thought that it might be too much too soon.

"So, what do you want then?" Sarah asked, still wary.

"Just let me come and try to wake him. I got a plane ticket while I was waiting to call you back, I should be there tomorrow. Just keep him stable till I get there, and let me try to wake him."

"Why do you think you can wake Wolfric when no one else has been able to?"

"Because we have a connection. We have this psychic link, and we can feel each other through it. If anyone can wake Hatter, it's me." Rosie spoke with more confidence than she felt, she just knew she had to do anything she could to try to help him. "So, do I have your permission to come?"

"I suppose so." Sarah said sounding unsure. "But anything hinky and you are out of here."

"Of course. I won't do anything without your permission until Ha- Wolfric wakes up." Rosie mentally chided herself and tried to remember to use Hatter's real first name. "So, I need to hop on the bus and get to the airport real soon, so can I text you my contact info and have you text me back directions from the airport? I have a car rental lined up so you don't have to do anything else."

"Ok." Sarah seemed to still be looking for Rosie's con angle, but not seeing one yet decided to see where this strange woman was going.

"Ok, then. I guess I'll see you tomorrow. I know this all sounds crazy, so, thanks for giving me the benefit of the doubt."

"It sounds bloody mad, but it also sounds a lot like what our grandmother said for the last fifteen years. I really hope you're right. I've been mourning the loss of my brother and my parents since I was ten, it would be nice to get one of them back."

"Whatever put Wolfric in a coma took your parents too? I'm sorry, I didn't know."

"It was a car accident. Drunk driver. Killed both our parents, and left my big brother in a persistent vegetative state. If I wasn't visiting my grandmother at the time I might be gone now too." Sarah said wistfully. "But that's all in the past, and now I suppose you have a plane to catch."

"I do. Thank you for giving me a chance to help your brother."

"Bye then." and with that, Sarah hung up.

Rosie texted Sarah her phone number, email, and flight info just in case then grabbed her stuff and headed out the door. As she waited for the bus in the dark of night Rosie received directions from the airport to the Hatton estate.

Rosie wondered if she was nuts to fly off to the UK with no notice, to a country she'd never been to. Rosie hadn't ever left her own continent, let alone flying on a red eye to Europe for more than she'd ever spent on a trip before. The only place she'd ever been to outside the US was Canada, and it didn't really feel like a foreign country to Rosie, she hoped flying to England wouldn't be a mistake. But as Rosie was at the height of worrying about her choice to just pick up and go she thought of seeing Hatter in the flesh, and being able to hold his physical hand or kiss his real lips, and suddenly she had no doubts. She just wanted to get to Hatter.

୧

O'Hare airport was pretty empty when she got there, so check-in and getting through security went smoothly. She was able to grab a breakfast sandwich at a kiosk just before the plane boarded, and then she read while the plane waited for the better part of an hour on the Tarmac. Once they were in the sky Rosie's nerves returned, she couldn't believe that she was really being so impulsive. It was so out of character for Rosie Cotton, quiet librarian. Maybe Rosie Cotton, Fey-born dream walker, was more spontaneous.

By the fourth hour of the flight, Rosie had spun herself up and calmed herself down at least a dozen times in her head. She was distressed that even though the doctors had stabilized him hours ago she still couldn't feel him through their psychic link. Rosie couldn't feel any kind of link between them and was terrified that his soul had already moved on before they stabilized the body. She had felt him very faintly when she went through the stained glass, so maybe he was just too weak to make contact.

Starting to feel how little sleep she'd gotten that night, Rosie nodded off to strange dreams. She traveled from world to world looking for Hatter, and each time she thought she saw him he would vanish. Eventually she found herself in a pitch black and featureless place, but there was a faint scent of roses and musk so she stayed in the nothingness hoping to feel Hatter's touch. She reached for Hatter psychically, but the more she reached for him, the more the presence eluded her.

Rosie realized that searching for Hatter wasn't the way to find him and decided to change her tack. She sat down in the darkness and centered herself, psychically broadcasting her position like a homing beacon. She made her being luminous on every mental wavelength she could imagine, and as she did she also sent out her love for Hatter.

Her body took on the luminosity she was projecting, a soft pale blue glow built slowly but steadily until she had lit an area around her the size of a small room. The light emanated from her heart and spread out through her limbs, making her large dragonfly like cobalt blue wings sparkle like cut glass in sunshine. She also realized that she was now wearing a softly draping gown made of what looked like opaque light.

Rosie looked around herself in the empty dark expanse, and she saw something glowing very faintly ahead of her. At first she thought it was something reflecting her light, but as her eyes focused she realized that the glow was golden not blue. She could see two small glowing circles of golden light, and in that instant she knew what she was seeing.

Hatter's wolf eyes looked at her from a distance. She got the feeling that he was not fully connected, but a primal part of him was there with her. She was afraid if she tried to go to him she would spook him, so she patiently waited.

The golden lights crept slowly closer and she could feel his curiosity connecting with her psychic broadcast. He edged around Rosie's aura, and though he stayed just out of the light, she could smell him. When Rosie smelled Hatter it was usually the roses she smelled most with an undertone of musk. But now his rich earthy musky scent dominated the sweet smell of roses. There was something so primal and masculine about this scent. Between his scent and the energy that came from him like heat, he felt like a feral animal. Rosie realized what she was witnessing was an aspect of Hatter, and she didn't want to spook the animal side of her love. He may not have been whole, but it felt good to connect with any part of Hatter. She could feel that his spirit was injured and longed to make it whole.

Hatter inched closer, and Rosie could see that he was himself physically but he was moving crouched on all fours more like an animal. A lot of Hatter's body was hidden in shadow, but what Rosie could see wasn't wasted like his body in England, but broad and strong like he had been in all their other encounters. He moved cautiously closer, but flinched and backed up when Rosie's light touched him. Rosie slowly pulled in her glow, and Hatter followed until he was inches away and there was almost no light.

"Eyes, like mine." Hatter whispered very quietly, projecting what he was seeing and feeling. First Rosie felt love so pure that it almost made her cry, then she saw herself like looking into a mirrored window with Hatter on the other side of the glass. They were overlaid so that their eyes lined up, and Rosie's eyes glowed with blue light to match his gold lit eyes; then the double image faded. He looked into her eyes and smiled in wonderment, whispering, "Heart, like mine." He leaned closer and sniffed her, so close that Rosie could feel the heat rolling off his skin.

She wanted to touch him, and to hold him close to her. But Rosie could feel that if she moved he wouldn't react like a man but a wild animal, and she didn't want to scare him away. "Hatter." Rosie whispered his name soothingly, but he flinched and backed up, muscles tight and poised to either pounce or flee. Rosie could feel his confusion, but wasn't sure why he was projecting that emotion. Rosie thought maybe he wasn't connecting with his name, so she tried another name. "Wolfric?"

Hearing that name he jumped back several feet into the darkness. She couldn't quite see him moving, but she could feel him stalking through the darkness as he circled Rosie once before stopping back in front of her. She tried again, speaking in a calming whisper. "Let me help you, you're hurt. I love you too much to leave you so damaged."

"Love, like mine." Came the whisper from Hatter sitting in The darkness. Then there was quiet for a time before Rosie heard Hatter again. He spoke in a regular volume, that sounded obscenely loud and jarring compared to their whispers. He sounded so much more like himself, but the sound came from a different direction than his whispers. "My Rose. I am whole in your love, but I am broken with my body." And then he was gone.

Rosie woke with a start. The captain was speaking, telling them that the plane was beginning its decent into John Lennon airport. Rosie felt frustration, she was so close to reconnecting with Hatter and then he slipped away again. She thought it odd that he had used the words 'I am broken with my body' not that his body was broken or he was broken. She wondered if what he meant was that his spirit couldn't get back to his body, but figured that she'd have a better judge soon enough when she saw him in person.

She went through security, got her passport stamped, and then headed straight to the rental car desks. Her phone flashed an out of network message so she didn't call, but she was able to pull up the directions Sarah had sent her. She picked up her car and was on her way to Hatter as soon as she could manage it. Driving on the opposite side of the road was a challenge, especially in her current state of heightened anxiety, but she managed it. She wondered if it would be easier after she got some rest and wasn't so tired. She realized that she felt more tired than she did before sleeping on the plane, and now she supposed that she'd have jet lag too. She wondered if she should have booked a hotel room, but between the plane ticket and rental car she was pretty sure her credit card was near maxed. She could deal with that after she saw Hatter.

Rosie figured if things went well she probably wouldn't need a hotel, Hatter's bed was big enough for them both. If things didn't go well... Rosie didn't want to think about that too much.

She tried to enjoy the beautiful country side she was driving through, but all Rosie could think of was Hatter laying in his bed looking so small and weak. Her hero needed saving, and she really hoped her new full Fey abilities would be enough.

☙

50

Rosie hadn't realized what a country estate meant until she turned onto the estates private drive, and it took another couple minutes before she could even see the house. When she cleared the trees that arched over the narrow road she was floored at the houses imposing size, but was also struck by how familiar the building looked. It took her a few moments to realize that it was the same castle that bordered Hatter's tea party in Wonderland. It seemed fitting to Rosie that the same castle held Hatter's bedroom in both realities.

Rosie parked the rental car and found she was too nervous to get out right away, so she sat there for a few minutes trying to gather herself. She sat, staring up at the impressive building, and it struck her that Hatter was a landed noble. He wasn't just her Hatter any more, he was Wolfric Hatton and she was worried she wasn't in his league now. She had no title or money, and felt like an uncouth American. Rosie worried that she might make some big social faux pas and not even know she was making one. Her worries were making her feel very small and insignificant in the shadow of Hatter's family home.

Suddenly there was a knock on her driver's side window, and Rosie jumped letting out an unladylike squeak of surprise. Hatter's sister stood outside the car. Rosie had been so preoccupied with her insecurities that she hadn't noticed Sarah walking up.

Rosie opened her door and tried to stand before she realized she was still wearing her seat belt. She awkwardly untangled from the restraint and stumbled as she got out. "Sorry."

"What for?" Sarah asked looking amused at Rosie's gangly car exit.

"I was getting my nerve up to get out of the car.

I didn't even see you coming, and now-" Rosie stopped herself before she rambled on too much. She was sure that she wasn't making the best first impression. "Sorry, I'm a little nervous suddenly. I seem to have this problem that the more I want to make a good impression, the more I end up looking ridiculous." Rosie stopped speaking and took a deep breath before trying to start over. "Hi. I'm Rosie Cotton. We spoke on the phone earlier." She extended her hand to Sarah and half expected Hatter's sister not to shake it.

"Hi. Sarah Hatton. Pleased to make your acquaintance." She said with proper etiquette shaking Rosie's hand firmly. Sarah noticed the leather gloves Rosie was wearing, on a warm summer day, with mildly suspicious eyes. "You've had a long trip, and I'm sure you're jet lagged. Why don't you come in and get yourself together."

"I'd like to see Hatter as soon as possible, if that's ok." Rosie requested sounding much smaller and unsure than she wanted to.

"Sure. I sent all the family and most of the staff home so you could do..." Sarah paused looking at Rosie with uncertainty, "whatever it is that you need to do to wake Wolfric. If you're up to it, we can see him now."

"Please." Rosie tried not to sound too eager as she grabbed her carryon bag from the car. Rosie noted just how much Sarah looked like a petite version of her brother. Sarah was short, even compared to Rosie who was almost never the tallest person in any room. The strong angularity of Hatter was replaced with soft feminine curves, but they both had the same rich brown wavy hair, the same smooth clear skin, the same full lips, the same rich dark brown eyes, and the same wolfish energy. Rosie wondered how much Sarah knew about her heritage.

The same tall dark haired man from Hatter's room watched Rosie from the shadow of a tree as she followed Sarah towards the castle of a house. She already knew that he was Fey-born, and he looked like he belonged to the tree more than the big manor house but from the look on his face there was clear loyalty to Sarah. She was sure that if things didn't go right, this man would be at Sarah's side and it gave her added incentive to somehow wake her true love. The man nodded to Sarah but didn't speak or move from his place. Rosie tried not to let her panic surrounding waking Hatter show.

೮ဒ

Rosie was even more impressed with the inside of the house than its imposing exterior. She had never been in a real life castle before, and she couldn't help but stare at its polished dark wood accents, posh antique furniture, and beautiful paintings on every wall. Rosie would have liked to look at things more closely but Sarah didn't stop, so Rosie continued to follow her as they ascended the grand staircase to the second floor.

They walked across a wide hall and into a familiar room, it was Hatter's room. Rosie froze in the doorway, taking it in. She recognized the stained glass window across from the door, the one she'd come through less than twenty four hours ago. Hatter's bed drapes were closed, and a large bouquet of roses sat on a table near the bed, filling the room with their sweet smell.

Sarah walked over to Hatter's bed and pulled the drape open. As soon as Rosie laid eyes on Hatter nothing else mattered to her. She walked over to him, clearly saddened by how frail he looked. Seeing him hooked to heart monitor leads, an I.V. line, and oxygen to help him breathe blurred Rosie's vision with unshed tears. Every fiber of Rosie wanted to crawl into Hatter's bed and just hold him, but she was sure that wasn't an appropriate thing to do. She took a deep breath and blinked back her tears before turning to Sarah.

Rosie dug into her bag and pulled out the amulet for Hatter. She held the necklace up to show Sarah. "This is an amulet that Wolfric taught me how to make twelve years ago. I made it for him after I began to suspect he had a body to come back to. It's designed to protect its wearer from carrying damage from a dream to their bodies, but it is also meant to help the spirit find its way home. Can I put it on him?"

"It won't hurt him will it?"

Rosie pulled the twin of the amulet out from her shirt. "I'm wearing one exactly like it. It won't hurt him at all." She tucked her amulet back in and held the other out to Sarah. "If it would make you more comfortable, you could put it on him."

Sarah took the amulet and turned it over in her hands to examine it. "What's in the little pouch?"

"A rosebud wrapped in a lily of the valley leaf. The rosebud symbolizes Hatter's heart and soul, and the leaf represents its protection." Rosie left out the anointing oil with her blood in it, and simplified the symbolism because she didn't really know Sarah yet or what would freak her out.

Sarah sniffed the bag and smiled. "I've always been fond of roses," she gave a little side nod to the large vase of roses, "it's a family thing."

Rosie smiled too, "That doesn't surprise me at all. I always knew when Hatter, sorry I mean Wolfric, was nearby because the scent of roses always preceded him."

Sarah examined the amulet a little closer, and then eyed Rosie appraisingly before handing it back to her. "You can put it on him."

Rosie took the amulet back from Sarah. "Thank you." Rosie's words were sincere. She sat carefully on the edge of Hatter's bed, and leaned over him catching his scent. Until she got closer it was hard to separate his scent from the roses nearby because the musk element was so faint. It made Rosie think about her dream on the plane and how faint the roses seemed then. She knew she needed to make him whole, and soon.

Rosie touched Hatter's sunken cheek and tears welled in her eyes, he just looked so frail and helpless laying there unconscious, so different than the strong guardian angel who was always there for her.

"You did know him, didn't you." Sarah said, standing nearby. "I don't know how, but I can see how you look at him, and you love him don't you?"

"I do." Rosie replied thickly, trying to be strong and not cry. "I love him more than anyone or anything I've ever known. I don't know what I'd do without him." Rosie unclasped the amulets silver chain and placed it carefully around his neck. She reclasped the chain and adjusted the amber beads to settle over his necks pulse points, saddened by how faint Hatter's pulse was. She then made sure the linen pouch and silver charm sat three fingers below the divot between his collar bones. Then settled the quartz crystal, and couldn't help but let her fingers linger over his heart chakra. Rosie wished that she had thought to remove her gloves before, so she could feel Hatter's soft skin, but felt awkward removing her gloves now and touching him with Sarah standing over them watching so closely.

"So, that will wake Wolfric up?" Sarah asked, sounding both restrained and hopeful.

Rosie looked at Hatter, hoping that she would see some sign of him waking, but saw no change. "I hoped it would help him find his way home." She said, taking Hatter's hand and willing him to wake. "I think he's more lost now than he had been. I had a glimpse of him in a dream on the flight over, and he was damaged."

"So, what's the next step? You said you could wake him." Rosie wasn't sure if it was fear or anger that tinged Sarah's words.

"I'm not sure. I thought between the amulet and me being here physically he would find his way." Rosie felt helpless, and wished she could just have some time alone with Hatter.

"So do something else." The desperation in

Sarah's voice was clear, but so was her strength. "Take off those gloves. It's obvious that you are wearing them to keep from touching people, your touch must do something. Touch Wolfric. Now isn't the time to be prim."

Rosie turned to look at Sarah. "Ya know, you're right." She realized that Hatter's life was much more important than any discomfort, and decided to follow her instincts no matter the consequence. "Please, back up and give me some room."

Sarah backed up to the doorway quickly and without another word as Rosie rolled her shoulders and shook out any remaining tension from her body. Rosie removed her gloves and tossed them to the floor. She picked up one of Hatter's hands and held it to her lips while centering herself, and opened herself to Hatter. She felt the faintest glimmer of his presence, it was weak but definitely there. She moved her right hand and slid it inside his shirt so she could press her palm over his heart. Taking a deep breath Rosie pushed some energy into him, the way she would heal when dream walking.

Hatter's chest was thin, and Rosie could feel is breastbone beneath her touch. At first she thought it wasn't working and began to feel silly for believing she could do anything in the waking world that she could do in dreams, but just as her doubt was creeping in she heard Sarah gasp behind her.

"What the fuck?" Sarah exclaimed in shock. "You have wings? You're a bloody fairy!"

Sarah's reaction was all Rosie needed to bolster her confidence. If Sarah could see her wings without even touching her, Rosie knew she had the power to heal Hatter. She pushed her energy into her love, and felt the magic flowing. Hatter's chest suddenly rose as he took a deep breath and Rosie could feel his heart beating stronger but he still didn't wake. "Come on, you can do it." She whispered encouragingly, and focused on her energy coursing through his body, repairing withered muscle and strengthening all his vital organs. "Don't wait twelve years and then let a little thing like your body take you away. Just let me know you can still hear me and I will find a way to pull you back." She spread up into his brain and found damage, so many electrical pathways that just couldn't conduct any more. "Please Hatter, you promised me. You said you'd always find me. I'm here, find me."

Rosie was feeling a little woozy and her breath was becoming a little labored from expending so much energy to heal Hatter's body. She was trying to find a way to give a little more when she felt a hand on her shoulder.

ೞ

Sarah stepped up to Rosie, somehow aware that she was using her own life force to heal Wolfric. She didn't know how Rosie was fixing her brother, but knew that she needed more. She saw that Rosie had deliberately used her left hand, and put the same hand on the near stranger's shoulder. Sarah made sure to give the impossible translucent wings plenty of room, and thought about giving Rosie whatever she needed to help her big brother. "Take what you need to help Wolfric." She felt a strange pulling sensation from her hand, through her arm, and into the core of her body. It felt tired and draining and exhilarating all at the same time.

ೞ

Rosie siphoned energy from Sarah, through herself, and into Hatter. She closed her eyes tightly and focused on her ability, feeling the energy she guided traveling along dead pathways within his mind and bringing them back to a conductive state. A few minutes later Rosie smelled Hatter's musk slowly rising, and she knew that his spirit was trying to come back together and mend itself.

Rosie opened her eyes and looked at Hatter's slightly less sunken cheeks getting a almost healthy blush to them. She looked over her shoulder to Sarah, who was looking exhausted. Sarah had a sheen of sweat on her face, and eyes that glowed with almost the same shade of golden light as Hatter. "Thank you. You gave enough energy to help me finish fixing Hatter's body." Rosie gave Sarah her best gracious smile. "But you have probably given a bit more than is healthy in one shot. So, as the most experienced magic user conscious in this room, I advise you to go sit down and drink lots of water."

"But he hasn't woken up yet. He looks healthier, but a healthy body with no mind isn't Wolfric. I can give more. I'm healthy. If a little more will wake him, take it."

"Sarah, his body and brain are healthy again, and that is largely thanks to you." As she spoke Rosie realized that she knew what she needed to do next. "But waking him is something I need to do alone." A faint blush started to rise in Rosie's cheeks.

"Why?" Sarah said with innocent confusion.

Rosie averted her eyes, "Because it takes a slightly intimate exchange of energy."

Sarah quickly snatched her hand away from Rosie's shoulder. "Oh." She said in realization. "Oh, eww. That's my brother, and you are right I don't need to be part of that." She crossed the room on slightly wobbly legs to a chair and sat down heavily.

"I'm not planning on molesting your brother in front of you." Rosie said, a little icked out. "It's just going to take a 'sleeping beauty' to wake him." Rosie looked back at Hatter's still face.

Sarah laughed quietly to herself, "Of course, a fairy would wake her prince with true loves kiss."

Rosie thought that she couldn't have thought of a better way to say it herself, as she leaned over Hatter and gently removed the oxygen. Touching Hatter's cheek tenderly with her right hand, Rosie stole a tender and chaste kiss. The energy flowed through their lips just like it had all those years ago, completing the circuit.

As their lips touched and the energy flowed between them, Hatter kissed Rosie back. He responded so quickly that Rosie thought it was just a reflex, until he reached both hands up to hold her face. Hatter sat up, kissing Rosie with a dozen joyously happy little kisses before the kiss deepened. The beeps from Hatter's heart monitor sped and Rosie felt giddy sharing the wash of memory and emotion that filled Hatter as his spirit knit back together. She was encouraged, knowing that he must be very mentally strong to deal with the wash of memory without swooning like she had.

"Oh." Sarah exclaimed from across the room. It was the kind of elongated 'oh' that was usually paired with kitten videos. "I know it's with my brother, but that's the most romantic thing I've ever seen in my life."

Hatter broke the kiss and sighed, "Sarah. Of course you would be here." He looked to his sister with an amused smile and shook his head. "I have missed you, sister, but... I have some private thanks to give to the love of my life for saving me. Think we can catch up in an hour?" he glanced back at Rosie and gave her one of his mischievously charming and completely suggestive smiles, "or two." He looked back at his sister, "I promise, later we will talk, and we can discuss the miracle that just happened and how magic is real, but right now..." He gave Sarah a very serious look, "I love you to death sis, but please get out."

Sarah laughed and put her hands up in surrender. "Ok, I'm going. I'm gonna have a snack, and a drink, and take a nap. I had no idea magic would be so draining. Come find me when you two are done doing things I don't want to know about." She started to leave but paused at the doorway, leaning back in for a moment, "I'm so happy you're awake Wolf, I've really missed you. And I love that my big brother is kicking me out of his room so he can be with a girl. I never thought we'd get to do this kind of normal sibling stuff. And Miss Cotton, thank you for not giving up on Wolf." And with that she left, closing the door firmly behind her.

Hatter turned his full attention back to Rosie. He

raised an eyebrow and rumbled with a deep resonance. "My Rose." He kissed her tenderly, "Your love was like a deep thrumming homing signal pulling me to you. I'm finally whole, with all my memories and with you. Thank you for saving me and being my sexy guardian angel this time."

Rosie melted under his gaze, but one question tugged at her, "So, I have to ask. Wolfric? Really? With your bonded animal? How did that Happen?"

Hatter shrugged, "It's an old family name, traditional for the first born male air. I always thought it was so old fashioned, that's why I liked being called Hatter. But since learning about my gifts, it makes perfect sense. I'm betting the shifting is a family gift as old as the name." He leaned in so close that Rosie could feel the heat of his skin, then whispered so that his lips brushed against hers with each syllable. "I wouldn't mind you calling me Wolf if I get to pounce on you and act like one." He wrapped his arms around Rosie's waist to pull her closer, but paused and leaned back, looking at his thin arms. "My god, look at me. All that training for all those years and I'm a ninety-eight pound weakling when I finally wake up."

Rosie used a fingertip on Hatter's chin to bring his gaze back to her. "You are perfect to me, however you look physically. I love you, not just your rockin' dream bod." She kissed him deeply, loving the velvety softness of his lips and the responsiveness of his body as he pulled her against his slight frame. Rosie leaned back with a wicked grin, "Besides, since my wings came in, it seems that I can do things in the waking world that I learned to do in dreams. So, between you being a shifter and me being able to heal, I'm betting that your well earned physique will be back in no time."

They held each other, staring into each other's eyes. "I love you Rosie Cotton." Hatter whispered as he leaned in to kiss her.

"I love you too, Wolfric Hatton." She said,

glowing quite literally with joy, and pulled him close in a passionate embrace. As they kissed, Rosie remembered his strong broad shoulders and felt the prickle of their shared healing energy. Hatter's muscles filled and the skin grew taught and supple under Rosie's touch. They both smiled, knowing that before they left Hatter's bed he would be the Hatter of their dreams again. Magic had returned to the Prime Material and their waking world would never be the same.

The End...

About the Author: R. R. Surbier

I'm an author who believes that character development often happens in intimate and intense moments, and that's one reason my writing tends to skew erotic. When characters fall in love, it only seems right to follow the journey without pulling punches. I want my readers to fully experience the private moments of my characters, especially when writing in a setting where intimacy advances plot. Plus, what healthy adult doesn't enjoy a good sex scene?

My personal life is not my writing, I want to take my readers to intimate places in my books but as a introvert I prefer to keep myself much more private. I want to share my writing with the world, not my mundane info, so my author bio is more about my writing than me.

The setting of the Wonder series, a world with hidden descendants of long departed faeries and other magical beings, has been in my imagination most of my life. It wasn't until I dreamt of an encounter between Rosie and Hatter that the idea for the Wonder series, and the plot of the first book, gave me the inspiration to share Fey-born with the world. I hope my worlds will inspire my readers imaginations (the place where real magic springs from), and it will replace a little banality with Wonder.

Www.facetsofwonder.com

Acknowledgments:

Thank you to all my friends and family who encouraged me to write Madness and Wonder, in person and on social media. More specifically, thank you to Joshua for giving me the time and resources to be able to write and get this book into print. Thanks to my best friend, Kyber Bree Keefe, for many hours spent helping me fine tune and being a great sounding board. Thanks to Benjamin for being a sounding board for broader world building ideas. Thanks also, to my first test readers, Lynn Actaboski and Stephanie Lundeen, for great feedback and giving me the confidence to publish. And finally thanks to Patrick O'Connor for finding the typos computers can't see.

www.ingramcontent.com/pod-product-compliance
Lightning Source LLC
Chambersburg PA
CBHW030540260626

47157CB00006B/2120